Syrie's Strength

Book Two
in the Series of Four

Dena Smallwood

Reecer Creek Publishing
Ellensburg, Washington

ISBN: 978-0-9660761-7-2

DEDICATION

For my Michael. Thank you for helping me find the security and serenity to allow me to find my voice.

ACKNOWLEDGMENTS

Syrie's Strength is a work of fiction. Syrie, Jedidiah, Noah, and the other main characters are fictional; any resemblance of them to actual persons – in the present or past – is purely coincidental. Some historical characters are based on established accounts of their lives.

.

CHAPTER ONE

Noah Hickman, a tall, muscular man, long, blonde hair caught in a tail by a rawhide thong, straightened from his panning when he heard his stallion nicker. He saw riders approaching the spot along Deer Creek where he was working. It wasn't usual to see anyone this far off the main road into Mormon Basin, so he put down his pan and moved towards his Hawken rifle where it leaned against a cottonwood tree.

"Hello, the camp," the taller of the two riders called out. "Can we come in?"

"What is your business?" Noah asked as he cradled his rifle in his arms. His voice was deep and strong belying his 60 years.

"We saw your smoke. We are lost and wondering if you could point us towards Mormon Basin?" The riders continued to approach slowly until they were within 20 yards of Noah.

"That's close enough."

"We mean you no harm," said the shorter rider.

When Noah looked closer, he discovered the smaller rider was a woman, riding astride, dressed in men's trousers and a plain shirtwaist. Noah relaxed a little.

"We are simply looking for directions," she said.

"Mormon Basin is a large place. You are in part of it now."

"Oh," the man replied. "Well, I guess we should have asked where the diggings are. Is this your claim? How are you doing here?"

"West." Was all Noah said as he pointed with his Hawken.

As Noah turned his head toward the direction he was pointing, his eyes briefly left the two riders. As his gaze shifted, the woman, drew a pistol and aimed at Noah's head. When he turned back, the woman fired, striking Noah below his left eye.

Noah's body crumpled to the ground.

"Now why did you have to shoot him?" asked the man.

"How could you not see the size of him and that gun! That bullet would have gone right through you and me. And didn't you see the pack saddle over by the mule? Look at the bags on it. If that is all gold, we have ourselves a rich claim. This is far enough from the diggings that no one is going to know he was even here."

The two dismounted and approached the mule and the sawbuck pack saddle. As they did so, Noah's stallion moved to put himself between Noah's body and the two people.

"Hey, that is some horse. Did you ever see color like that?" asked the woman as she admired the chocolate brown horse with a blanket of white and brown spots across his hindquarters. "Well, he will have no more use for him. I'm going to catch him and take him with us."
As she approached the horse, the stallion's nostrils flared and he stretched his great neck out to bite the woman.

2

"That bastard horse is crazy."

The woman tried again to approach the horse and this time the stallion whirled and lashed out with both hind feet, narrowly missing the woman who stepped nimbly aside. This time the woman drew her pistol and aimed it at the horse.

"Now, just leave him be," said the man. "You have killed enough for one day. We have other things to do here. Just leave the crazy horse alone."

The woman holstered her pistol and joined her partner who was going through the panniers.

"Clothes, some flour and such. Ammunition. Wow! .50 caliber. You were right about that gun. Ah! Here we go!" the man exclaimed as he lifted two small, heavy leather pouches. "If this all came from this claim, we are going to be very rich indeed!"

They gathered up the gold, each one taking a sack and putting them in their saddle bags.

"Let's take this to Baker City and get it assayed. We'll wait a few weeks and then we can re-file on this "abandoned" claim. We're going to be rich, sweetheart!" the man said as he kissed the woman. They remounted and turned their horses away from Noah's claim.

CHAPTER TWO

For the second time in her life, Syrie was washing the body of a husband in preparation for his burial. It was a beautiful spring day in 1868 and the first wildflowers were starting to bloom.

She remembered being a young bride washing the body of her first husband in the waters of the Snake River at Three Island Crossing. The river had snatched her love, her future and the father of her unborn child. She remembered the other women of the wagon train helping her bathe and dress Jedidiah before they buried him in a crude grave covered with planks on the hillside above the river that had killed him. It was the last clear memory she had until she had awakened in this room, this home she had shared with a good man for 23 years, a man who now lay on planks on her kitchen table.

She moved mechanically from table to hearth to warm the water she needed to bathe his body. She and her friend and helper, Painted Pony, lifted buckets of water, time and again to the large kettle. There were hired hands outside who would have helped them as well as her youngest son,

Michael, but this was something the women wanted to do. What Syrie felt she had to do herself. The very last thing she would do for the man she loved.

As she worked, she smiled as she remembered how different physically her two husbands had been. Jedidiah, small, wiry and endlessly amused at life. Noah, large, strong, and determined to bend the world to fit his will. But both had loved her and loved the children she bore them – or would have loved them in Jedidiah's case. And Noah had loved, protected and guided her two daughters who were not of his blood, as well as the four children they made together. Both men were tender and attentive and had made her the center of their lives.

Now she worked washing the dried blood from Noah's body. Her eldest daughter, Lucreta, would probably arrive tomorrow. Her second son, Benjamin, had ridden to fetch Lucreta and her husband, Noah Crow, from their homestead at Plano Creek. He would tell them the news and escort them back to the family home. Syrie didn't want her other daughters, Theresa and Abagail, to see their father bloodied like this. Better they remember him as being full of life.

The bullet which had killed him had left his body intact but had shattered his skull. She thought it would have to be a shot to his head to take the breath of life from him. He had been stabbed and shot before and his body had the scars to prove it. A shot to his body probably would have only incensed him. It had apparently been a small caliber bullet that had entered his face below his left eye. So., he had been facing the man who had murdered him. He had faced death just as he had faced everything else in his life. And he had probably been shot from a distance, as no man she knew of could have bested him in a fight, even with Noah being past his 60th birthday.

As she washed the dried blood from his long hair and beard, sh0e marveled at how little grey there was in it, as her own brown locks were now liberally streaked with grey. His body was nearly as muscular as it had been when they had first married, though it had thickened some. Hard labor all of his life, had kept his body fit and strong with no fat to slow him down. It had been a big, powerful body, but also capable of so much tenderness.

She still remembered how he had held their second daughter, Theresa, when she had been but a baby with her tiny head cradled in his enormous hand and her tiny toes not even reaching the crook of his elbow. How he had tenderly lifted each of their other children to bathe them after their births, then gently laid them in the cradle he had fashioned for his unborn child so many years ago. Even though there had been women to help with each of the births, it had been Noah who had first touched their children, raised them up and then gave them their first baths. Spotted Fox, the Cayuse women who had helped with the birth of their first son, Daniel, had not been surprised at Noah's tenderness toward his new son. The later women, including Painted Pony for the last two births, who had attended her, had tried to usher Noah out of the bedroom for the births. He had stood his ground and wouldn't leave her side. Four times he had been there for the birth of their children. When their daughter, Abigail, had been born, he had cried. Syrie wasn't sure if it was because she had at long last had another girl or the fact they had decided to name her Abigail after his late mother.

After the women had bathed Noah's body, washed and trimmed his hair and beard, they carefully dried him. Painted Pony started scrubbing the bloody water from the floor as Syrie went into the bedroom he had built for her. For them.

Before their marriage, he had enlarged the cabin he had originally built, to include a separate room for just the two of them. At the time of their marriage, Lucreta had been a young girl and Theresa had been less than a year old. Noah had a sense of privacy about him which demanded solitude for him and Syrie when they consummated their marriage. In preparation for the marriage, they had moved the big bed from the main cabin to the bedroom and had moved Lucreta's small bed into the loft. Theresa's crib they had left by the hearth in the main cabin where Syrie would hear her if she cried. Syrie had moved into the bedroom before their marriage, but Noah had insisted on sleeping in the lean-to until the marriage.

Their first marriage had been in the Cayuse tradition. Their second marriage - the white man's marriage he had called it – had taken place in Oregon City the following summer. Syrie had told him she already felt married, but he had wanted the legality of the white man's way to protect her for the future.

She opened their trunk to get the clothes she had decided to use for his burial. She had chosen to bury him in the ceremonial buckskins of his adopted people, the Cayuse. Their friend, Spotted Fox and her mother, Snow Goose, had made the tunic, breeches and moccasins for their wedding. The buckskin suit was beautifully beaded and dyed and Syrie knew there were hundreds of hours involved in the making of it. She caressed it tenderly as the memories swam in her brain. So many friends. So long ago. As she lifted the buckskins out of the trunk, she saw her own ceremonial clothes folded neatly beneath, also made by the two Cayuse women. She remembered the day Spotted Fox had made her the gift of the beautiful doeskin suit.

Spotted Fox had seen Syrie was puzzled by the gift and said, "I had thought you might want to wear it if you marry

Noah." Such a beautiful and wise woman who had known even before Syrie had admitted it to herself that Syrie loved Noah Hickman.

She hoped to be buried in her white doeskin dress. Syrie dashed the tears from her eyes. She must remember to talk to Lucreta and Theresa about that.

She closed the trunk and returned to the kitchen and the women dressed Noah. After Noah was ready for burial, she opened the door in the front of her house and spoke to the men assembled outside.

"He's ready to be carried into the parlor," she told them. "They brought sawhorses from the barn and you can leave him on the planks. It will probably take four of you to move him."

Four of the cowboys who worked for her and Noah, now just for her she realized, moved slowly past her into the kitchen. Her youngest son, Michael, and her youngest daughter, Abigail, moved to either side of her and put their arms around her as she stood in the doorway. She hugged them back and kissed each of them.

"It will be okay. We'll get through this as a family."

Her second daughter, Theresa, stood a little ways off. Theresa was the picture of her birth father, short and slim, with Jedidiah's elfin face and turned up nose, her gray eyes bright with unshed tears. As usual, she was dressed in buckskin breeches, boots and a flannel shirt. Syrie knew she had been out checking cows and had probably just arrived back at the ranch house from her own place on the homestead she was proving up. Theresa crossed to her mother and siblings and reached out to touch Syrie's face. "How, Ma? How are we going to get through this?"

Syrie could see the tracks previous tears had made down her cheeks and knew how hard it was for her tough daughter to let anyone see her mourn.

"I don't know. I just know we will. When I left New Hampshire, my father said to me, 'You are an Adams and you are sturdy enough to handle anything that life gives you.' Well you are all half Adams and we will handle this."

As a unit, they all turned when the men gently picked up Noah's body on the planks and moved it through the wide opening between the kitchen and the parlor and on into the parlor. Syrie didn't know how they had come to the arrangement, but she knew one of the men would stand beside Noah's body all through the rest of this day and the coming night until the burial tomorrow. Just as she knew someone had likely already started digging the grave up by the cairns which had been placed for Noah's first wife and unborn child.

Syrie hugged all her children in turn.

"Now, we have a lot to do. The chores don't stop for anything. You all know what has to be done. Do the best you can, but don't do anything you don't have to do today. You have to take time to remember your father."

As Syrie stepped outside she noticed the first harbingers of spring. The aspen Noah had planted in the middle of the compound bore a slight haze of green on their branches, the ice was all gone from the stream and she could see the increased flow from the snow melt. Soon it would flow with the spring flood in earnest. She must remember to have someone hook the team to the spring house and move it above the flood stage of the creek. She also knew it would only be a few days until she and Painted Pony could begin planting the garden. She had saved the seeds from last year's garden and her sister, Sarah, had sent her more flower seeds for Christmas. Syrie was anxious to get those planted as well.

That was another thing which was so different about Noah's death, she thought. When Jedidiah had died Syrie had no idea what the future held and she had no family close, nor had she a home. Thanks to Noah, she now had all those things and that made it possible for her to go forward. She knew she would mourn Noah, but she also knew she would survive and she would see to it that her family did as well.

As she and Painted Pony stepped outside with the empty water buckets to go to the stream below the house, Syrie glanced back to the cairns and saw Noah's friend, George Rogers, digging the grave. Like her washing and dressing Noah, she knew George was performing one last service for his friend.

CHAPTER THREE

Lucreta surprised her mother by riding in alone, arriving shortly before dark. Syrie stepped out of the kitchen door to greet her, wrapping a shawl around her shoulders against the chill.

"Where are Benjamin and Young Noah and the children?" Syrie asked.

"Benjamin's horse was played out and so was he. He must have run the horse nearly the entire way to our place. He will come on later with Noah and the children in the buckboard. I just had to be here with you. Where is he?" Lucreta asked as she stepped down from her horse.

"He is laid out in the parlor. One of the men is with him."

Lucreta tied her own spent horse to one of the posts on the front porch and went in the front door of the parlor removing her coat and scarf as she went. She knew one of the hands would come and get the horse, cool him out, rub him down and put him in the big barn.

She stood next to the body of her father in silence for a few minutes. There were candles placed around the body and she could see that, except for the wound in his face, he looked exactly as he had the last time she had seen him.

"Who did this?" she asked her mother.

Syrie studied her daughter thoughtfully. Though Lucreta was just over a decade younger than Syrie, now she looked older than Syrie herself, the grief and the hard ride etching sharp lines through the dust and deep into her face. Her blonde hair was windblown from her frantic ride, wisps of hair escaping from her waist-long braid. Her cornflower-blue eyes were bloodshot and grief-stricken.

"We don't know," Syrie sighed as she reached for this woman who had started as a daughter and was now a friend and confidant.

She held her close and Lucreta rested her head on Syrie's shoulder.

"There may have been a robbery. I don't know exactly what he took with him when he went to the claim. He had been there several days and he probably would have had some gold panned. When George found him there was only the gold in the pan. Nothing else seemed to be gone, though George said the panniers had been gone through. Otherwise, he couldn't tell if anything had been taken.

"George dug the grave up by the cairns. I'm not going to question him for now. Tomorrow after Young Noah and Benjamin arrive, after we have the burial, we will have a family meeting and George can tell us what he knows and what he thinks happened. I don't want George to have to tell it twice. George is a remarkable tracker. I'm sure he at least knows how many.

"You know your dad. It would have taken more than one unless he was ambushed."

Lucreta stepped back and swiped at her face.

"I must look a mess," she said.

"You look like a woman who has suffered a great loss and there is no harm in that showing."

"It is so different and yet so very much the same as when Jedidiah died, isn't it?"

Syrie couldn't respond for the lump in her throat and the threat of more tears. She just nodded and looked at Noah's body.

"How many more, Ma?" Lucreta implored as she thought of her birth mother and father, her younger brother, and her second father. "How many more will we have to bury?"

"I don't know. I just don't know. Sometimes I wonder why the Lord asks so much of us.

"Come on, honey. Let's go into the kitchen and we'll have some tea. You can get cleaned up a little. I'll loan you one of my nightgowns and you can sleep in Theresa's bed. I think she is going to spend the night at her cabin up on her claim. If not two of you girls can double up.

The two women, arms entwined around each other's waists, stepped through to the crowded kitchen. In preparation for the viewing of Noah's body, the big dining room table and most of the chairs had been moved from the parlor into the kitchen. Those along with the old kitchen table and benches Noah had built years before, made for tight quarters. As they entered, Theresa and Abigail, went to their sister and hugged her. Michael stood by George Rogers and they both were drinking coffee near the hearth. A large coffee pot sat at the edge of the coals even though there was a new wood cook stove nearby.

At 16, Michael was still trying to find his bearings as a man. He was going to be tall like his father and was already taller than George. Michael had dark brown hair and dark eyes like his mother. He had a precise, logical, analytical mind with a calm exterior. His calmness was something Syrie always marveled at because both she and Noah were fiery people. Michael had been the child who sat back and watched everyone around him, saying little and remembering everything.

Lucreta reached a hand out to him, even as she was hugging her sisters and he set down his cup and crossed to the three of them.

"Michael, are you okay?" she asked as she took his hand.

"I'm doing okay, I guess, Sis." He responded. "I'm just not sure what I'm supposed to do next. I always followed Pa's lead and now I'm just lost."

"I know. I know. He always tried to take such good care of all six of us. He left a big hole in our lives, didn't he?"

"I don't know how to go on." Michael said.

Lucreta gently unwound herself from her siblings and went to George as he stood staring into his coffee cup.

"Uncle George?"

"How's my best girl?" George tried teasing her as he had since he had first begun wintering in the Burnt River Canyon 15 years ago. "How are those babies of yours?"

Lucreta looked at this man who had become an integral part of their family over the years. The dark brown hair and beard were now completely grey and she could see the grief in his eyes. George had known their father longer than any of them. Longer even than their mother. And he had been the one who had discovered Noah's body.

"Are you okay, Uncle George?"

"No. No, my girl, I'm not. I'm kind of like Michael. I can't figure out a world where Noah Hickman isn't a part of it, with his big laugh, his big heart. I'm having trouble navigating."

"When I got back here from Baker City three days ago," he paused and smiled rather ruefully. "This is the very last thing I thought I would be doing."

As Syrie stood watching George, she suddenly felt very selfish. She had been so wrapped up in her own grief, she had failed to see how deeply others were affected. She had never really thought about how Noah had impacted those around him who weren't family. She had always just accepted that he was an impact. It was enough.

Syrie busied herself. She felt she had to keep moving. Had to keep doing. She had Painted Pony make coffee as she checked her supplies so she knew what she would make for tomorrow for the dinner after the burial. She had no idea how many people would have been notified. She had only sent for Lucreta. Their little world was a lot more populated than it had been 20 years ago when she had arrived in the Burnt River Canyon. She knew word could seemingly fly on the winds, so she wouldn't be surprised if a couple dozen people showed up tomorrow.

Lucreta watched her mother fly from one thing to the next and she knew immediately what Syrie was doing. She was doing the same thing she had done when Jedidiah had died. She was keeping her body busy so her mind didn't have time to think. Syrie would bear watching, Lucreta thought. She couldn't let her mother go down the path she had walked after Jedidiah had been killed.

"Ma," she said, "is there any hot water? I think I'd like to clean up a little."

"Sure, honey. Let me pour some in a pitcher for you. You can use my bedroom if you want."

Lucreta took the hot water but didn't go into her mother's bedroom. Couldn't go into her mother and father's bedroom. She poured the hot water into a kitchen bowl and wiped the dust from her face and hands at the hearth. She loosened her hair and was starting to re-braid it when Syrie stopped her.

"Here, let me."

Syrie got her own brush from her dressing table and sat Lucreta down in one of the kitchen chairs. She calmed as she brushed Lucreta's hair, which nearly reached the floor from where Lucreta sat, and carefully re-braided it.

Syrie found it restful to do a chore she hadn't done since her girls were little. She hadn't braided Lucreta's hair since Syrie had attended the birth of Lucreta's last child, little Arthur.

After she had finished, she stood back, gathered herself and said, "It's going to be a long day tomorrow. We will have lots to do with the burying and all. It is long past dark and we need to find our beds. Theresa, are you staying here or going to your cabin?"

"I should probably go on to the cabin."

"You know you are welcome here. This is still your home."

"I know, Ma, but I have stock to tend. I'll be back for breakfast." Theresa kissed and hugged her mom. Then she patted her leg and her two border collies got up from their places near the fire and followed her out the door. She went out to find her horse and her way home.

Painted Pony banked the fires and retired to her little cabin. She would be up before everyone else tomorrow. All the others went to find their beds, though there would be little enough sleep in the house that night.

The next day dawned cloudy with bouts of scattered showers and a brisk spring wind.
Syrie had risen early from her sleepless bed and started fires in both the big fireplace and in the new wood cook stove Noah had installed. She wasn't surprised when Painted Pony showed up a few minutes before sunrise.

Painted Pony was peeling potatoes and slicing bacon from a large slab of pork and Syrie was making biscuits when Abigail and Lucreta walked through the parlor from the girls' bedroom.

"I had to walk by Pa." Abigail said. "Ma, it is so strange to see him so still. He was never still."

"I know. I'm sorry. It probably won't seem real for a long time."

"One of the hands is in there with him. Not saying a word. Just standing there with him."

"It is an old custom, to not leave the dead alone. I need to take in some coffee. And the candles probably need to be replaced."

"Yes, most of them have gone out or nearly so. I can get the candles and take them in." Abigail stopped partway through the door way.

"Ma, can I ask you a question?"

"Sure, honey," said Syrie as she paused from forming biscuits. "Anything you want. You know that."

"Why, Ma? When there are so many worthless people in this world. People who don't do a bit of good for anybody else, why take Pa? It isn't right." She didn't wait for an answer, just continued into the parlor with the candles.

As Abigail was taking the candles into the parlor, Syrie poured a half cup of coffee for her and filled it the rest of the way up with milk, adding two spoons of sugar. Then she poured coffee for herself and Lucreta. Abigail came back into the kitchen and sat at the table with the glimmer of tears in her eyes.

"Here's your coffee. I'm going to take some into the parlor."

"Coffee? Do I smell coffee?" George said as he descended the ladder from the loft.

"Good morning, George. Pour yourself a cup. We're making breakfast now. Abigail when you have your coffee, could you please go get the eggs?

"Michael?" Syrie called up to the loft. "Time to get up. Cows' going to need to be milked and the coffee's ready."

"Yes, Ma."

Syrie smiled. Michael never grumbled about chores.

Syrie and Lucreta stepped outside to go to the spring house to get butter for breakfast and watched as the cowboys rode out to check on stock and move them to fresh pastures. Everyone started their usual chores, milking the cows, gathering eggs, feeding chickens, cows, horses, goats, sheep and pigs. It would be hard to see any change from any other day on the Rafter S ranch.

"Lucreta do you remember when Davey Johnson built this spring house? How proud he was of it?"

"Sure. And it has held up really well. Have you heard from Davey and Laura?"

"We got a letter from them last winter. Their oldest is getting married. Will be married by this time. Looking forward to being grandparents."

"It is hard for me to picture them as grandparents." Lucreta shook her head. "I still see them as they were when they pulled out of here all those years ago."

"Well, look at you," Syrie said. "Not only all grown up and married, but a mother of five. I'm sure they are having the same problem picturing you that way as well. It is a shame we will likely never get to see them again."

"Maybe someday when the travel across the mountains isn't so hard. It has been really wonderful to be able to write to folks on the west side of the mountains, though."

"Yes. Yes, it has been wonderful. I always looked forward to Mattie's letters when she was still alive," said Syrie. "You know, Vesta still writes from time to time."

The women interrupted their talk as they returned to the house and the task of getting breakfast ready. The three women easily fell back into the rhythm they had established when Lucreta was still living at home. They moved about the kitchen, not in unison, but never getting in each other's way and everything they did complimented what the other did. They set out biscuits, gravy, bacon, ham, fried potatoes, homemade jams, butter, soft cheese, eggs and lots of coffee and cold milk.

"You know, Theresa and I could never seem to work together in the kitchen like you and I do. I wonder why that is?"

Lucreta snorted, "Well probably because she took off after Pa every chance she got. That girl never wanted to spend one extra minute in the house that she didn't have to."

"Look who's talking about spending time outside!" Syrie laughed. "I seem to remember another young girl who followed their Pa around. I can still see the two of you, the tow-head and the tiny, curly brunette, trying to keep up with Noah's long legs. When Theresa would get tired, you'd pick her up, put her on your back and on you would go."

"Good memories. Speaking of daughters, where is Abigail?" asked Lucreta.

"Since you are here to help me with breakfast, I asked her to start on the beds and sweeping out the house. I think she's sitting in the parlor with Noah, though. Leave her be. She is having a hard time with this. She is very angry."

Lucreta nodded understanding then stepped outside onto the porch and rang the bell to call everyone into breakfast. It took time for everyone to get in, fill their plates, eat and go back out again. There was no grace said as this meal was eaten in shifts as everyone finished their morning chores. Grace was saved for the evening meal when everyone was at the table at the same time. Syrie, Painted Pony and Lucreta stayed busy cooking up more eggs and meat as the platters were emptied. Abigail didn't come to the table.

True to her word, Theresa showed up just before the last of the breakfast was gone. She took off her hat and coat, hung them on a peg in the wall of the kitchen and poured herself a cup of coffee. She didn't set down at the table, just made herself a sandwich of ham and a biscuit and sat by the hearth with her border collies.

"Ma, can the boys have a biscuit?" she asked.

"Of course, they can," Syrie cooed. "And maybe a wee bit of bacon as well."

Both of the dogs knew the sound of that voice and became immediately attentive, sitting up, ears perked, heads cocked, looking at Syrie.

Syrie tossed each of them a half slice of bacon, followed by half a biscuit each. They ate every crumb and returned to their attentive posture.

Lucreta laughed.

"I swear if those two aren't biggest beggars we have raised yet. Who were their parents? I don't remember," said Syrie.

"These two are full brothers. They are out of the last bitch Mr. Gregor sent to us and the old male we had. Shamus. They are his last sons."

"Oh yes, I remember now. Shamus threw some good pups. Hopefully these two will be good sires as well."

Syrie took down two tin plates, had Painted Pony scoop the last of the fried eggs onto them and added a splash of milk to each. The dogs waited patiently at attention, until she stepped back and signaled them to eat.

"Maybe I will buy one of the next batch of pups you have Lucreta. I've always enjoyed the Gregor dogs so much. It will be a welcome companion for me with your Pa gone."

Lucreta had to swallow before she could speak.

"Sure, Ma. You will have pick of the litter next time. I'll let you know when we have another batch on the ground and weaned. And you won't be paying us for it."

CHAPTER FOUR

The buckboard carrying Benjamin, Young Noah and the five children rolled into the home place mid-afternoon. A few of the neighbors had arrived as well, though there had been little time to get the word out to many of the far-flung homesteads or mining claims. Syrie had changed her clothes and was wearing a grey woolen dress. Everyone else was cleaned up and wearing clean clothes, but no one was wearing fancy clothes. Theresa was wearing a dress belonging to Syrie because she hadn't made a new one for herself in a long time. Even the cowboys had freshened up and had polished their boots and belts.

"As soon as you've had a chance to wash the dust off and get a bite to eat, we'll go up to the grave," Syrie said. "Abigail, Theresa, will you please go down to the spring house and help Painted Pony bring up some cheese, milk and buttermilk. There is cold beef and bread in the house on the table."

She hugged Benjamin and Young Noah and tousled the hair of each of her grandchildren before giving them a hug as well. She watched as the girls ran toward the house, the eldest, Mae, helping her little brother up the path.

Lucreta walked up to her husband and hugged him, then she buried her face in his chest and wept. He held her gently for a moment before looking over her head at Syrie.

"What happened? Do you know? All Benjamin could tell us was Noah had been shot and was dead."

"We will have a family meeting after the burying and we will all find out what George can tell us. We don't have many answers yet."

Syrie hugged Benjamin again. "Thank you for making that ride. I know you probably half killed yourself and your horse to get there as quickly as you could."

"I hated to leave you Ma, but I knew it had to be done. And I'm the oldest one here until Daniel comes home, so it fell to me."

As they walked across the compound back to the house, she put her arm around Benjamin's waist. So like his dad, she thought. Tall and blonde with that incredible temper. Just coming into his strength at 19. He would be a formidable man, just as his father had been. He was talking about apprenticing as a blacksmith. A trade his father had done as a young man. She hated to lose him to the ranch, but she knew her children were only hers for a little while.

As there were no men of the cloth within a day's ride of the ranch, there would be no preacher presiding over Noah's burial. Which, Syrie and his children agreed, would probably have pleased Noah. Noah had been a deeply spiritual man, but not a religious one. Syrie didn't know if he had ever been inside a church in his entire life. It was never a conversation they had. He had been respectful of the man on the wagon train coming west who had been a minister but had always stood apart or even rode out if there were religious services being held.

As the oldest male present, George Rogers agreed to say a few words and read a passage from the Bible Syrie had chosen, Psalm 23:4. After George had read the psalm, which had also passed as the opening prayer, he began to speak.

"I think I knew Noah longer than anyone else here. I knew him when both of us were fur trappers and wagon train guides. I could tell you stories about Noah, but this probably isn't the proper place for a lot of them. I will tell you he was the bravest, the most honest, the orneriest man I ever knew. And I don't think he feared to "walk through the valley of the shadow of death" this time because he walked through it so many times before. I will also tell you he was the most stubborn son of a bitch to ever walk that valley.

"I know Syrie and his family will miss him and mourn him and so will I."

George stepped back from the grave, grabbed a shovel and threw a shovel of dirt onto the coffin the ranch hands had made. Then he handed the shovel to Syrie, who did the same. The shovel was passed to each member of the family in turn, finally held out to Abigail by Michael.

"Here, Abby, it's your turn."

Abigail looked at her brother in astonishment.

"I am not going to bury my Pa until I see his killer buried."

Dry eyed, she left the grave and strode back to the house.

Michael stood a minute looking lost until the foreman, Horace stepped up and took the shovel from Michael.

"You all go on back to the house. The boys and I will finish filling in the grave."

"Thank you, Horace," Syrie said as she gave him a smile and a pat on the arm.

After a meal prepared by Syrie's family and augmented by food brought by her neighbors, Syrie stood on the porch and thanked each person who had come to Noah's funeral. After the last person had departed, Syrie went into her bedroom and shut the door.

No one said anything. They all knew Syrie had been up for two days straight and they assumed she had simply run out of steam. Lucreta wondered if her mom would come out of the room again or if she would retreat into her own mind as she had done so many years ago.

A few minutes later, Syrie reappeared, having changed out of the grey wool dress and back into her normal calico with her customary shawl around her shoulders.

Everyone settled around the big dining room in the parlor. Lucreta and Young Noah held the youngest children on their laps while the older children played quietly in the corner watched over by Painted Pony. Theresa and Abigail brought in the coffee pot and tin cups. Syrie took Noah's chair at the head of the table instead of her usual spot at the foot of the table closest to the kitchen. No one failed to notice the shift. She was now in charge of this family.

"If everyone is ready, we can start preparing for our future. We need to decide what each one of us is going to do about the ranch and the claim near Mormon Basin.

"Regarding the claim. It is my wish that we not discuss plans for it at this time. The gold has lain in that creek for a long time and I don't think it will be going anywhere anytime soon.

"This ranch isn't huge, but it is large enough to be a lot of work. We have a good crew and we raise a good product in our horses and cattle. We bring in extra money selling produce, pork and other things to the mines in Rye Valley and Mormon Basin. I can run this ranch alone, but Noah and I built this ranch as a gift to our children. All of our children," she said as she scanned the faces around the table, "and it was always our dream for you to not only run this ranch, but to expand it as well.

"Lucreta, you and Young Noah have made a fine start on your own ranch and we were very proud of what you have accomplished in a short amount of time. It is my wish we continue with the partnership we have established in the breeding and selling of horses. Having two locations to house the brood stock has been beneficial.

"Theresa, you are establishing your ranch next to ours and, again, your father and I had always planned your place would be an extension of the main ranch just as Lucreta and Young Noah's ranch is. Another place to raise and separate brood stock.

"Of course, each of you adult children are free to make your own determination about your land. We just gave you the seeds. You are the ones who will work the land and decide the direction you want your ranches to take.

"Daniel is at Harvard and I will send for him. He will probably be establishing himself as an attorney at some point. That doesn't preclude him from being a rancher, but, again, it will be his decision.

"Benjamin, I know you are coming to a point in your life where you have to decide if you want to stay here on the ranch or if you want to walk another road. I know of your interest in the blacksmithing trade. Your father was proud that you would seek out the trade he had done as a young man. I am going to ask you stay here until we have re-established order on the ranch. After that, I will support you in whatever you decide to do. If you want to homestead, I will see to it that your fees are paid. If you want to apprentice to a blacksmith, either locally or elsewhere, I will pay for your apprenticeship.

"Michael and Abigail. You are too young yet to establish your own homesteads, but when you are old enough, I will pay for those as well. If either one of you want to attend college or apprentice in a trade, I will support you in that as well.

"I will be keeping this ranch. It has been my home for nearly 25 years and my wish is to be buried next to your Pa when my time comes. I can, along with this crew, run this ranch. Your Pa and I discussed every aspect of this ranch before any decision was made. So, my decision is to continue what he and I started."

She turned her attention to George.

"George, if you are able, can you tell us what you found at Noah's claim, what you suspect and what you know about Noah's killers."

George Rogers thanked Theresa for the coffee refill and cleared his throat.

"As you know, when I arrived here three, no four, days ago, Syrie told me Noah was working his claim. So, I decided to go up and see him. I changed horses and rode on up to the claim. When I got there it was nearly dark and I didn't see Noah at first." George paused and swallowed several times.

"What I did notice was Noah's horse and he was blowing and kind of lunging at me. That got me to looking around for Noah because that wasn't like this horse, especially towards me. I have been around that horse since Noah delivered him and he has never shown me any kind of aggression.

"So I stepped down off my horse and approached him," George paused for a second. "That's when I saw Noah's body. The horse was protecting Noah. He was standing right over top of him. It took me a good long while to get up to the horse where he could see me real good and smell me. Then he let me pet him and lead him away from Noah's body.

"I could see he was dead and had probably had been dead for a while. I can tell you he didn't suffer. From the wound, I would bet he was dead before he hit the ground."

Syrie looked over at Abigail who was sitting stone still and barely breathing. Theresa was also silent, with her head lowered, petting one of her dogs. Lucreta had put her head on Young Noah's shoulder and was crying softly.

"I'm sorry to have to say it like that, but it is what I found.

"Noah's body was cold so I knew he had been killed some hours before. I started casting around for sign while I still had some light. It was clear what had killed him. The stallion hadn't moved much. Had only moved from where he had been standing near the trees to where Noah fell. The mule was picketed, so there were no extra tracks from her.

"I found two sets of boot tracks, first around the sawbuck and panniers. One large and one small. That tells me white men. One heavy and tall and one short and skinny. In fact, the smaller ones were so tiny and faint, I thought it might be a child or a woman, but no child or woman would be part of a murder. The panniers had been opened and searched, but I don't know what Noah took with him so I don't know what was missing. His Hawken was there right beside his body, extra ammunition, a little food, some clothes. The only gold I found was what was in the pan lying in the creek.

"I followed the tracks back to about 20 yards from Noah's body, where I found prints from shod horses. Again, white men. I back trailed them until I came to the main road going up into the Basin. That's where I lost them among all the other horse prints and wagon ruts. Then I went back to Noah's camp. I laid Noah's body out and covered him with a blanket, took care of the horse and mule and made my bed for the night. At first light, I went

27

back over the area again and I didn't find any other sign, so I packed up and came back here.

"So what I know is this. Two white men. One pretty good sized and one short and skinny. Probably shot him from their horses about 20 yards from where he was standing. That tells me whoever made the shot was a better than average marksman. I think Noah had bagged up gold because you told me," he nodded at Syrie, "he had been gone about a week. I think they stole that. I also think they will be back to the claim to try to work it. Maybe even try to claim it in their name. I think we have one stone cold killer and one thief or we have two men who are both killers and thieves."

Everyone sat in silence for a bit and Young Noah broke the silence.

"So what are our options? Is there any way to bring those men to justice?"

Syrie studied her son-in-law as he asked the question. He looked so much like his mother, her friend Spotted Fox. He had a masculine version of her face, her height and even her grace when he moved. She knew him to be a brave man who had inherited his father's warrior heart. And she knew his rage at the white man and injustice lay just beneath the surface. She hoped for her daughter's sake he had it firmly under control.

"I'm at a loss to figure out how," said George. "We don't have any witnesses and any form of law is a long way from here."

"Well I know where justice can be found," said Young Noah. "I'm going to Umatilla and get my father, Ten Crows."

"No, Noah" pleaded Lucreta. "You can't. You know they won't let you off the reservation once you step foot there. You'll be kept in a cage there for being an outlaw."

"Noah Hickman is the only man I ever admired as much as my own father," Young Noah said hotly. "That is why I carry his name along with my father's. He is why I carry the white man's name of Noah Crow instead of my real name, Spotted Buffalo. I will avenge his death."

"No, Noah. You can't. I can't raise our children alone. I can't lose you as well as Pa. Let's see if we can find another way around this. I want to see my father's killers brought to justice just as badly as you do. But, please! There has to be another way."

Benjamin was the next to speak.

"I understand your anger and I agree our father's death must be avenged, but we have to know who is responsible. I also agree your father, Ten Crows, must be informed of his death. He is, was, our father's best friend and he will want to be here. I will ride to Umatilla and make arrangements to get your father off the reservation for a time. I don't know how I'll do it, but I'll do it."

"I may be able to help with that," said George Rogers. "I have some experience dealing with Indian agents. I dealt with them for my wife before she passed and for some of her family after she passed. I will go with you."

"It is clear we are not going to be able to find out who killed Noah yet," Syrie held up her hand when Noah and Abigail began to speak. "I said 'yet.' I have to believe we will find a way to do that. I refuse to believe Noah's life can be taken and no one pay the price for it.

"I know of another old friend of Noah's who lives on the west side of Oregon state. His name is Joseph Meek and he used to be the U.S. Marshal for the Oregon Territory. Like George, he and Noah trapped and guided together for a time. I will write to Meek and beg for his help. If he can't come himself, perhaps he can find someone who will be willing to help us."

George nodded his head.

"Meek is a political animal, but he is a true friend. He will come if he can."

"Syrie, after I go to Umatilla with Benjamin, I have to go back to my farm in Oregon City and get my crop in, but I will return as soon as I can. I will hand deliver your letter to Meek and I will add my voice to yours to get him to come here. I will be back in the fall after my crops are harvested."

"Thank you, George. You were always a good friend to Noah and this family. I appreciate everything you have done over the last few days."

George stood and addressed the group. "I will seek my bed in the loft as I want to get an early start. I'll be ready when you are, Benjamin. I will say goodnight and leave you to conduct the rest of your family business."

George left and Lucreta took the opportunity to put her children in Syrie's bed as they were nodding off one by one. Little Albert had fallen fast asleep in Painted Pony's lap in the rocking chair. Then Lucreta re-joined the group.

"I will also be sending a letter to Daniel. I will be asking him to cut short his education and come home. The family needs him here. Perhaps this is why he chose to be a lawyer. We will need his education and his wits to find out who killed your pa.

"So, this is what we are going to do. We are going to continue to run this ranch. We are going to continue to breed cattle and horses. This is how we are going to do it.

"Theresa, you spent the most time with your pa out with the cows. I want you to be the cattle boss. Horace will support you in this. He is a good man with a lot of good common sense and he is a good foreman. If any of the other hands have problems taking orders from a woman, I want you to fire them. They do not want me to get involved with that process because I will take a horse whip to them. If any of them come to you boys complaining, I want to know about it immediately. You both know your sister is the most capable person to handle this job and I expect you to support her.

"Benjamin, you know the horses better than anyone else. I want you to take care of the breeding program and the horse sales. You decide which horses are going to be sold and you will deliver them to the drop off point. You and I need to have a discussion about introducing some draft blood into our herds for possible use in the mining operations. Let's find out what those people need.

"Michael, I want you to handle the sheep and the pigs and getting those products to market. You may need to look over the accounts so you know what the market prices are and where to take the product.

"With the mines in Mormon Basin and Rye Valley growing, we have a market closer to home for beef, pork and lamb. Let's take advantage of that. Michael we also need to continue with your schooling.

"I want all three of you to work together and with me to make sure we are ready for next winter. That we have all the hay we need, that the fences are in good repair and that the winter pasture rotation is in place."

If any of her family was surprised at the depth of knowledge Syrie had about the ranch's operation, they wisely kept it to themselves. Lucreta breathed a silent sigh of relief that her mom was going to be okay.

"Lucreta and Noah, you have your own place to manage and your beautiful children to raise. I will call upon you from time to time and, of course, we will continue to work together on the breeding programs and the round ups. I am asking you especially, Noah, to put aside your grief and your anger and be patient until we find out if the law will be able to take care of this. If it can't," she shrugged her shoulders. "Then we will see to finding our own justice as a family.

"Abigail, I need you to help me with the accounts and keeping this compound running. We have people to feed and clothe. This compound is the lynch pin to this ranch. We will also be continuing your school work. Another reason I need you close to the compound.

"Anyone have any questions?"

"What about the claim? Are we going to let those killers just take it?" asked Abigail.

"No, I don't intend to let anyone just "take" what your father worked for. Not the ranch. Not the claim. None of it."

"But I think it is too dangerous right now for any of us to go back there. George brought the stallion, the mule and your father's things back with him when he brought your father's body to us. There is nothing there now that ties the claim back to us, so the killers probably think he was a lone miner. It will be safer for us if they continue to think so."

Abigail shoved back from the table so hard she nearly knocked her chair over. "I don't care what is safe. I want my pa's killers to hang!" She stormed out of the room and into her bedroom, slamming the door behind her.

Syrie paused for a moment, the grief and hurt bright in her eyes as she gazed at the closed door. She took one deep breath and continued.

"I will consult with Meek and with Daniel when he arrives and we will come up with a plan to guard our rights to the claim. You should know my name is on the claim as well as your pa's. It will not become an abandoned claim."

Benjamin cleared his throat.

"Ma what about money? Do we have money to buy supplies when we go to Fort Boise or Baker City next? Do we have money for leather and harness, horseshoes and nails? All that stuff?"

Syrie smiled at your son's practical question.

"I think you are all old enough to know about this now. I will ask that what I am about to show you go no further than the walls of this house."

Saying that, Syrie took a lamp from the table and led them into her bedroom and opened one of her trunks. Carefully laying aside her white doeskin outfit and other articles of clothing, she removed a board that covered the bottom of the trunk completely, effectively creating a false bottom to the trunk. When she removed the board and set it aside, she motioned everyone to come closer.

What they saw had them all holding their breath for a heartbeat, then all exhaling at once.

The entire bottom of the trunk up to a depth of six to eight inches was covered with closely packed leather bags.

"Is that gold?" asked Theresa.

"Yes, that is gold. I don't remember how many bags are in here. We have spent some over the years. This paid for Daniel's schooling. It paid for the ranch's homestead fees and Lucreta's and yours, Theresa. It will pay for Benjamin's apprenticeship if he chooses to do one. It also paid for lawyers for the Cayuse who were tried for murder after the Whitman incident, though it did no good.

"Some of this belonged to your father before I married him. Lucreta, do you remember the heavy trunks that were in the loft when we moved Davey and Laura into it? Part of this gold was in those trunks. Gold wasn't discovered in Mormon Basin recently. Your pa found it there 25 years ago. He just didn't tell anyone. There was no territorial government to file a claim with and there were no other white people here then. He didn't file on his claim until those two guys went around yelling about finding gold."

"So, yes, Benjamin. There is money for supplies and all the rest we need. We have tried to keep this in reserve and just live off the profits from the ranch and we have pretty well succeeded in doing so. But the money is ours and we can spend it, wisely, as we need it.

"Your father and I talked long and hard about whether or not to spend this gold. About raising you to work hard and know the value in that or raising you with wealth and privilege. We chose the former and looking at you here today, I know we chose wisely."

She carefully fitted the board back into the bottom of the trunk and layered the clothes back in as well.

"Please don't tell Abigail just yet. She is raw emotionally and she is the youngest. I don't know how it will sit with her. Let's all go back into the parlor."

They all sat around the table. Again Syrie asked if anyone had any more questions.

"Ma, I think it's time we went to bed. The babies are just plum worn out. It was a long trip for them in the buckboard today. I want to get them onto pallets and I am about exhausted as well."

"Of course, honey, you are right. How about if we make pallets in my bedroom for them and you and Noah can sleep in there tonight as well? There are extra quilts in one of the trunks. I'll sleep in my rocking chair like I did when you all were little."

"No, Ma. I'm going back to my place tonight," said Theresa. "You know, stock to tend to. You take my bed. Abigail has probably already cried herself to sleep anyway."

"Yes, you are probably right. My old bones might not be able to sleep in a rocker anymore any ways. I'll wish you all a good night." Syrie arose, cautiously opened the door to the girls' bedroom and disappeared inside, closing the door softly behind herself.

Michael and Benjamin made their goodnights and went up to the loft. Theresa and her dogs faded into the night and Lucreta and Noah retired to Syrie's bedroom.

As she did most nights, Painted Pony banked the fires and went out to her own little cabin.

Lucreta and Noah gathered up quilts from another of Syrie's trunks and made pallets for the children, moved the sleeping children onto them and then they laid down on Syrie's bed, still fully clothed.

"Noah, can you put your anger aside for a time?"

"I don't know. I haven't been this angry since my mother, sister and brother died from the white man's disease."

"I know how you hate most white people and God knows you have reason to hate. But this time you will not be helping your family, you'll be hurting them. If you kill the wrong men, the white men will hang you and all the gold in that trunk won't save you. They will remember you are an Indian and there will be no mercy in them. You have passed as a white man for more than 10 years now. Can you wait a little while longer to get your revenge?"

"I will try. I need to talk to my father. Hopefully Benjamin and George will be able to bring him to us."

Lucreta put her head on her husband's shoulder and after a long while, he realized she slept. He laid awake for a few minutes longer, then he adjusted her head so it was more comfortable for his shoulder and he too succumbed to sleep.

CHAPTER FIVE

It took Benjamin and George just over a month to return to the Rafter S with Ten Crows, along with Young Noah, Lucreta, and the children, who they had picked up along the way from the reservation. As Lucreta handed down the little ones from the carriage, the older children took charge of them and ran for the house to their grandmother. Soon Syrie was surrounded on the porch by giggling little girls and a very solemn little boy. She shooed the children into the parlor and stepped off the porch to greet Ten Crows.

Syrie was dismayed to see how the decade of captivity had aged him. His hair was nearly all grey now and he was stooped, no longer the erect and proud warrior she had last seen in 1856 when he left for the reservation. She knew he was of an age with her Noah, but he looked much older. Living the white man's life was obviously aging him before his time.

She held out both hands to him. When he had dismounted from his horse, he took her hands and she realized he had lost much of the strength in his hands. She wondered how long it had been since he had used a lance or a bow. It broke her heart to know this brave warrior had been stripped of his culture and his self-respect because he could no longer defend his people.

"Ten Crows, how wonderful to see you old friend."

"Syrie. The sight of you brings pleasure to these old eyes." The years had not erased the slight British intonation to Ten Crows' way of speaking English. "It is wonderful to have our family all here and together again," he said as he looked around the compound.

"This is where it all started, isn't it?" he remarked.

"Yes. It is. Do you remember the first time we saw each other?"

"Of course I do. How could I forget the tiny white woman holding a rifle nearly as tall as she. And the brave little slip of a girl standing next to you with an equally long rifle. You both showed such courage that day."

"We were prepared to do what we had to do to protect the others inside the cabin. I am certainly glad you came in peace," Syrie laughed. "We were both shaking so hard, I'm not sure we could have hit anything if we had fired those rifles."

"I'm not sure I ever faced a fiercer or a more determined warrior in battle than you," Ten Crows smiled as he said it. "And I know I do not want to ever find out what it would be like to have you as an enemy. Noah told me one time that you were the only person in this world that he feared. He said he never wanted to make you mad because he might find himself without his scalp one morning."

"I will admit I have a bit of a temper," Syrie laughed. "Come in the house. Painted Pony will be fixing coffee for everyone. I know you will want to see her."

They stepped up onto the porch and Ten Crows stopped and looked at the house.

"I remember when Noah built this place. I thought he was crazy to work so hard on a place he would leave for half the year. You have made it larger. And you have built a bigger barn. You will have to tell me what all these other buildings are for that you have built."

"Yes, we added on to the house as the children came. We have plenty of room for everyone. We'll have to double up in some beds while everyone is here, but we'll make it work. We can move the boys to the bunk house. We can take a tour after you have some refreshments. Do you want to visit Noah's grave?"

"Yes, I would like to do that first. I need talk to him there for a little while."

"You go ahead. I'll see to the refreshments."

Everyone else was gathered in the kitchen having coffee, or milk, and cake, when Ten Crows came back from Noah's grave. Painted Pony's eyes sparkled with excitement when she saw him. She approached him and held out her hands, speaking in their native Cayuse tongue. Syrie had never learned the language though Noah had been fluent in speaking it. It was obviously a joy for the two people to hold a conversation in their native tongue, something Painted Pony hadn't had a chance to do since Noah's death. They talked for a minute, then Painted Pony pointed to the table and went to get coffee for him. Syrie served him cake and the grandchildren gathered around their grandparents trying for more cake.

Syrie asked George if they had any trouble getting a pass for Ten Crows.

"Not a lot. Just as we suspected, the Indian Agent was a snob and a pencil pusher," said George. "He's just like every other Indian Agent I have ever dealt with. Your name, and Noah's, went a long way toward getting Ten Crows a pass, and the gold you sent along didn't hurt anything."

"I'm just glad we had it to send with you. I had a suspicion it wouldn't hurt to grease a few palms in the process."

"Well, he is most certainly getting his greased," said Benjamin with derision as he stirred his coffee. "It is plain as day the only reason he is there is to feather his own nest. He doesn't give a damn about the welfare of the Cayuse or the Walla Walla or the Umatilla."

Syrie looked over at Ten Crows and saw his head was bowed. She could see that the way his people were treated was painful to him. He still felt he was responsible. He was still their leader in spirit.

"Ten Crows, how long has it been since you have had any real say in what happens to your people?"
He raised his head and stared at her.

"I don't remember, Syrie. I really don't remember. The white men take more and more of our land. We fight almost daily to get what we were promised. I fear it is a losing battle. They want us to farm, but there are never enough tools or seeds. There is little rain and no game. We can still fish, but we can't travel outside the reservation to trade our dried salmon."

When Painted Pony heard this about the plight of her people, her hand flew to mouth as she stifled a sob, then she ran out the back door of the kitchen and went to her own cabin.

Ten Crows continued turning and looking at Young Noah, "I am so glad you were able to escape the reservation. Noah was right to counsel you to hide your true nature. Our people are done, my son. But you can continue and you can thrive and raise your family in peace by being white."

"But it is a lie!" Young Noah exploded as he erupted from the chair, startling the children. He stopped when he realized he was scaring the little ones. He ushered them into the parlor calming them as they went. Then he came back and took his place again at the table.

"I am Spotted Buffalo. I am a Cayuse. Son of the great warrior Ten Crows. It is my mother's breast those miners are ripping and tearing with their picks and shovels. It is our land being fenced and sold."

Ten Crows nodded his head.

"You are correct, of course," he said and paused a moment before continuing, looking into his son's eyes.

"I knew before you were born that the end of our people was coming. I learned that when I went away to the North to study. That is why your mother and I sent all you children to Syrie to study and learn the white man's knowledge and his ways. We tried to fight them after Whitman died and we lost. Did I know it would be as bad on the reservation as it is? No. Do I regret not fighting on. No, because too many of our women and children had already died.

"When your grandmother, your mother, your brother and your sister died, so did my heart. What happens to me now doesn't matter. I try to help the others as much as I can, but I have no heart and no power now.

"All I have is you, Lucreta, and your children. You must continue to live your "lie." Love your wife and raise those children. They are my future as well as yours. Someday, maybe they will be able to honor the part of them that is Cayuse."

Young Noah hung his head and stayed silent for a long moment. Then he brought his eyes to meet those of his father.

"Is this the path you want me to follow? To be a white man and turn away from the Cayuse?

"It is my wish as your father that you do whatever you need to do to protect yourself and your family. That includes not being Cayuse."

"As your son, I will honor your wishes, my father."

Syrie didn't realize she had been holding her breath, until she exhaled. She realized she had been terrified Ten Crows and his son would decide on death and revenge. She knew Ten Crows was still a respected leader among his people and if the decision had gone another way, many would have died on both sides.

"From this day forward, I will no longer be Spotted Buffalo, son of Ten Crows. I will be Noah Crow, white man," he said to the group. He squeezed his wife's hand and turned his face to his father.

"But there is still the question of avenging your friend, Noah Hickman," said Young Noah.

"George Rogers and I have spoken about this on the way to your ranch and we discussed different plans about how to proceed. Syrie, I understand it is your wish to call on another old friend of Noah's to help and also to ask your oldest, Daniel, to come home," said Ten Crows.

"Yes. I want to give the law a chance to work. I am still reserving the right to take matters into my own hands if justice can't be served any other way."

"If you cannot get justice with the white man's way, then I will leave the reservation again and I will find justice for Noah in my own way. George tells me it was definitely two white men, and they might be miners and still in the area. They took gold from Noah. It is enough for me to start.

"But for now, George agrees with your plan. He tells me there is little sign to point to the exact people who are the killers. I trust George's ability to track and read sign. If he says there is no sign, I believe him. However, I want to do something else to find the killers. I want to do a sweat lodge ceremony and try to summon a vision. It may work and it may not. The visions are never guaranteed. I need the sweat lodge to purify myself before I seek the vision.

"I would like to go back to your ranch, my son, and spend more time with you, Lucreta and the children. I want to get to know the children. I can build the sweat lodge there. Syrie, I will let you know if I learn anything from the vision quest."

"For now, I would like to spend the rest of today with my family, both white and red. Then ride back to the Rafter L tomorrow. I want to see the horse herds here. And a special favor. Can I see the horse that protected Noah? I think I may learn something from him."

"Of course. Benjamin, will you see to it that Ten Crows has everything he needs? Thank you, son."

The group got up from the table and the men left the house and headed for the barn to saddle the horses.

"Oh, Ma, it breaks my heart to hear what he has gone through and how he looks," said Lucreta. "He was such a great warrior. He owned vast herds of horses. Now he is a weak old man. I wish my children could know him as he used to be."

She stood up from the table, gathering dishes as she went and putting them in the wash basin.

"I need to see to my children. I think their father frightened them," she said as she went into the parlor.
As Syrie was washing up the dishes, Painted Pony came back into the kitchen. It was obvious she had been crying. Syrie dried her hands and went to her, wrapping the grieving woman in a hug.

"I didn't know it was that bad. I didn't know," Painted Pony said. "Those are my people. My cousins, aunts and uncles. Part of me wants to go with him back to the reservation to be among my own kind, but I know I wouldn't be happy there. I might not even survive. Why did the white man have to come at all?"

"I don't know, Painted Pony. I always thought we could all live here together. Then the Whitmans died, and everything changed. Now there is too much hate on both sides.

"I'm glad you came to us when the rest went to the reservation. You have been such a good friend and I couldn't have run this ranch and raised my children without you."

"You and Noah gave me a good life. One better than I would have had with anyone else. And you protected me when I needed it. I will never forget that."

The two women hugged again and finished clearing the table to prepare for the evening meal. Lucreta joined them after the children were settled and the three women soon fell back into the old routines they had developed when Lucreta was still at home.

Benjamin and George saddled two fresh horses and led them out to the stand of aspen in the middle of the compound where Ten Crows and Young Noah waited, quietly talking.

"Here you are. These two are fresh and should carry you without trouble as far as you want to go today," said Benjamin as he handed the reins to the two men. "When you come back, just tie them to the hitching rail in front of the barn and one of the hands will put them away. Noah, I think you know where the horse pasture is?"

"Yes, it is downstream near where our old camp used to be."

"Yep. Ten Crows you'll have no trouble picking out Pa's horse. Flashiest stallion in the bunch."

The two men mounted and Benjamin noted even though Ten Crows was bent, when he got into the saddle on the Nez Perce mare, his back seemed to straighten and he seemed more his old self than he had before. They took off at an easy walk through the compound to keep the dust down and didn't kick up into a canter until they were on the opposite side of the creek.

The two rode in companionable silence as they made their way downstream. This country was like an old friend to Ten Crows. His people had been camping in the meadow they were riding through as long as he could remember, at least once a year. The urge to keep riding was so strong it was almost as if someone were shoving him forward; forward to the Wallowa Mountains, forward to the great Snake River, forward over the great mountains beyond which the buffalo hunts had taken place. But he knew he would never ride those trails again.

The meadow had been abandoned as a Cayuse camp so long ago, there were no longer any signs of human habitation. No teepee poles, no drying racks, nothing that spoke of the time his people had been here. He wasn't sure if it was better to have left no trace upon the earth as his people did or to leave markers and monuments behind as the white people did.

They pulled up their horses at the fence line of the horse pasture. Young Noah let out a whistle and several of the horses lifted their heads and nickered.

"You'll probably see a few old friends here. We swap the horses between the two ranches for breeding. I think some of the ones you gave Lucreta and I for our wedding are in this group. Of course they have some age on them and are not good producers anymore, but we keep them for the memories."

"Can we ride out among them?" asked Ten Crows.

"Sure. I'll get the gate."

Young Noah side-stepped his mount to the gate, reached down and pulled the rope catch over the post and side stepped the horse against the gate to open it. After Ten Crows had ridden into the pasture, he repeated the procedure in reverse, again fastening the gate.

"That's a neat trick," his father noted.

"Yes, it is something a vaquero who spent a couple of years here, taught us. Saves a lot of leg work and mounting and dismounting when you are moving cattle between pastures or pens. We train all the ranch horses to do it and some of the ones we sell as cow ponies as well. We don't bother with it for those who are going to be riding horses."

They rode slowly through the horse herd, Ten Crows stopping occasionally to ask his son about the breeding of a particular horse. When they spotted Noah's stallion, Ten Crows got off his horse and slowly approached the animal on foot. When he was about a yard away, he sank down to the ground in a cross-legged position and waited for the horse to approach him. He kept his head down and did not make eye contact. The stallion eyed him curiously for a full minute, then he reached his nose out to get a good smell of the man. Cautiously the horse approached, taking a step, stopping, sniffing, then taking another step. Finally, the stallion stretched out his neck and put his nose directly on Ten Crows' head and took a hard inhale. Then he pulled his head back and waited. Ten Crows quietly and slowly extended his hand towards the horse. The stallion made no move. Then Ten Crows laid his hand on the horse's face and held it there, not stroking, just letting his hand lie there as long as the horse would accept it. Ten Crows raised his head and looked directly into the horse's eyes. After a long minute, he rose gracefully to his feet from his cross-legged position and turned to mount his own horse.

"That is a war horse," he told Young Noah. "A true warrior's heart beats inside this animal. I am not surprised he protected his rider and friend. I wouldn't be a bit surprised if he had bitten or kicked the people who killed Noah.

"I must talk to Syrie about him. She must not let anyone else ride this horse. He must never be forced to accept another rider. He must never be sold away. Another may ride him, but it will be on the horse's terms. Not on the human's.

"I am tired, my son. Let's go back to the ranch house." Supper that night was a festive affair. Syrie and Painted Pony had killed two young roosters and there was fried chicken, beef steak, potatoes fried with onions, corn mush, fresh biscuits and dried apple pie for dessert with sweet, thick, yellow cream on top. There was talk and laughter until the sunset shone through the windows of the parlor.

"Syrie, I thank you for your hospitality, but I need to be getting back across the mountains on to my farm," George stood up from the table. "It will soon be time to start planting there. I will be back again after harvest. If you have anything special you need, send me a letter and I will get it for you. We are getting more and more goods and people all the time.

"If it is okay with you, I'll wrap up some beef steak and biscuits for my breakfast. I'll sleep in the bunkhouse tonight, so I don't disturb you when I leave tomorrow. Good night, all."

George went out the door to a chorus of good nights, be safe, travel well and God speed.

"Syrie, I would be pleased if you would show me where I can lie down for the night."

"I had planned on you sleeping in one of the boys' beds in the loft."

"I appreciate that, but I have never learned how to sleep in a white man's bed. Not even after spending all those years at the boarding school in the queen's country to the north."

Spotted Pony said, "I have a buffalo robe in my cabin. You can sleep on it in front of the fire in my cabin if you would be more comfortable."

"That would be very nice. Thank you. I'll come with you when you say good night. Right now, I think I'll take my coffee out to the porch and have a smoke."

Syrie grabbed a shawl and followed Ten Crows outside.

"I wanted to thank you for what you said to Spotted Buffalo today. I didn't want to see any more blood shed by this family and I know how close his anger lies to his heart. As always, you are wise and protect your people."

"My words were spoken by my own truth. My heart lies empty and cold within me. The only spark left is Spotted Buffalo and his children. If I lose them, all is lost.

"I won't see the time when it will happen, but someday, those children will be proud to be Cayuse. It will be up to him to protect them and maybe their children until that time comes."

"I will do all I can to protect them as well. They are my grand babies as well as yours. And I know you are as proud of them as I am. The youngest, little Albert, is already so smart and so sweet."

"I'm sure you will do all you can to protect them. And I am proud of them, and I do love all of them. It is so hard for me not being able to see them whenever I want. It is just too dangerous for Spotted Buffalo to come to the reservation. Maybe when they are older, things will change."

He paused and smoked for a bit before he spoke again.

"Syrie, I need to speak to you about the horse the Noah was riding the day he was killed."

"Ten Crows, do you know the story of his breeding? Did Noah ever tell you?"

"No, I was already on the reservation when that stallion was foaled."

"That stallion was not the result of a random pasture breeding. Noah took great care with the selection of the dam and sire. He went to Idaho to the camp of the Nimi-pu people in Lapwai. He was riding his old stallion and he took along our best mare. A beautiful leopard with black spots. He asked for the right to breed his stallion to the best of their mares. In exchange he would leave his best mare with them to breed to their best stallion. He came home with a solid black mare with a black and white blanket. She was the mother to that stallion. When the stallion was weaned, Noah went back to Idaho and retrieved our mare and returned theirs. He was told the mare he came home with was the mother to their best stallion and had thrown nothing but fine, strong, intelligent foals. I can believe that after seeing the stallion we got from her."

"That confirms what I felt today."

"What did you learn?"

"The heart of a warrior lies within the horse. He is a true war horse. I am going to ask that you never sell him, that no one else ever rides him. Someday one will come along who is worthy of the horse and the horse will allow that one person to ride him. You will know when that someone comes. It may be a man or it may be a woman. But you will know."

"I will do as you ask. He will not be sold."

"Maybe someday he can become a sire to a new crop of horses for the Cayuse people."

"I'm sure Noah would be very proud, if that is what happens."

"I also need to speak to you about revenge," said Ten Crows as he turned and looked directly at her. "There will be a reckoning for Noah. I am agreeing to hold until you find out if the white man's justice will work for Noah. But, I have no faith in the white man's justice.

"If the white man's justice fails, I will not. It does not matter to me if I kill one who did not kill Noah. It does not matter to me if I kill more than one. Do you understand what I am saying?"

"Yes. But will your reckoning include Spotted Buffalo?"

"No. It will not. If I am successful, no one will know it was me. But I think you will know when a certain group of people die. You will know it was me."

"I understand and I accept what you will have to do. No one will find out from me we had this conversation.

"I'm going to leave you to your smoking. I'll see you in the morning."

Ten Crows sat in silence, smoking and thinking about what was and what might yet be.

CHAPTER SIX

Daniel Noah Hickman, eldest son and Harvard student, sat in his rooms in Cambridge, Massachusetts and read his mother's letter for the third time.

His father was dead. Murdered his mother's letter had said. Yet that was impossible. His father was indestructible. Noah Hickman was the largest, strongest, most alive person Daniel had ever known. It was impossible that he was dead and buried and had been for the weeks it took his mother's letter to reach him.

Impossible. Just impossible.

Daniel rose from his desk and paced his small rooms. He remembered the last time he had seen his father. It has been five years ago when his father had put him on a stage somewhere in Idaho Territory to start his journey to the east.

They had ridden east and south from their ranch in eastern Oregon and Daniel was soon lost in the unfamiliar terrain, but his father knew exactly where he was going. It had been a pleasant trip with no trouble from the local tribes or other travelers. They had camped out every night and Noah always made sure their camp was well sheltered and, Daniel had later realized, easily defendable. Daniel had never had this time alone with his father. Having six children and a ranch to run had left Noah little time for individual time with his children.

"Have you been this way before, Pa?" asked Daniel one night.

"Yes, several times," was Noah's reply. "Going both east and west. Sometimes alone, sometimes with other trappers and sometimes guiding for wagon trains. This is the trail your mother came to Oregon over."

"Has it changed?"

"There's a lot more people now and I'm not sure that is all for the good. In some ways it is nice to be able to get supplies and to be able to pay for a ferry instead of having to swim horses across the rivers. But the game is all gone. The tribes are scattered or locked up on reservations. I miss the wild. But I suppose I am partly to blame for the number of people here since I guided wagon trains.

"I met your ma on the last train I guided. Your mother's first husband was killed along the trail while trying to cross one of the rivers."

"Did that happen a lot? People drowning, I mean," asked Daniel.

"I don't know what you mean by a lot, but I personally lost my first wife and child and buried two others who died in river crossings. I suppose if you measure the number of lives lost against the number of people who made it safely across, it wouldn't seem like much. But if you ask those who lost loved ones, it was a pretty stiff price to pay."

"I didn't know you had another wife and Ma had another husband. I always thought you two had been married forever."

Noah laughed his enormous, booming laugh.

"Son, there's a lot you don't know about your ma and me and a lot you will never know. Some things you may be told when you are older.

"Yes, I was married before to a Cayuse woman. She was carrying our child when she died. Your mother's husband was killed while she was carrying your sister Theresa. But now Theresa is mine, just as Lucreta is mine and as all of you are mine. There is no difference in my eyes."

Daniel thought now how true that had been. His father had loved all of them equally. Noah had been a stern father and Daniel had earned his wrath more than once, but he had never been cruel and had never withheld his affection from any of his children. Daniel had to smile as he remembered his father had been the biggest kid of any of them at birthday parties and other celebrations.

Daniel remembered the last words his father had spoken to him as he settled him on the stagecoach.

"Your ma and I have raised you to know the value of hard work. I expect you to work just as hard at your schooling in the East. You won't have to work outside of school. Your ma and I have seen to that. But we expect honest effort from you in your studies. You will miss home. That is to be expected. But you are my son and you will stay until the job is done. You will stay until you have your diploma. Be safe and be careful. Write to us often."

As there were people all around, Noah shook Daniel's hand, but Daniel could see he wanted to embrace him. He wished now he had taken the initiative and hugged his pa despite the people standing there.

And now he was dead.

"Come home with all possible speed. Your family needs you. Come home."

The school year was nearly over. He was so close to graduation. Only a couple more weeks. "All possible speed" the letter had said. His mother never said anything she didn't mean. If she said he was needed at home now, then now it must be.

Daniel grabbed his greatcoat and donned his cap, as it was raining again. Spring was fickle in New England. He walked briskly along the cobblestoned streets until he came to a house he knew well, the home of his mentor and professor, Dr. Angus MacLeod. He stood stamping his feet against the chill and damp after he rang the bell.

The door was answered by Dr. MacLeod's housekeeper, who showed Daniel into the front parlor. He stood near the fire warming his hands, wondering why he hadn't thought to grab his gloves.

Dr. MacLeod soon joined him.

"Daniel. What brings you out on this blustery day?"

Daniel just handed him the letter when he found he couldn't trust himself to speak the words, 'My father's dead.'

Dr. MacLeod adjusted his glasses to the end of his nose and started to read the letter. He lifted his brows and glanced over his lenses at Daniel when he had finished.

"I'm assuming you are here because you intend to honor your mother's request?"

"Yes. I am going home as soon as I can book passage on a train to the west. It will probably take me several weeks to get there. I have no idea how far the railroad has pushed to the west and I will probably have to make part of the journey by stagecoach or horseback. When I left the ranch, I came most of the way to the east on horseback and stage. It was still pretty rugged to get to our ranch five years ago and I don't know how much things have changed."

"Yes, you will have a long journey. No doubt of that. But what of your studies? You are nearly through reading for the law. If you leave now, you will not get your law degree and your diploma."

"I am aware of that. I have worked these past five years to get my diploma, but my family has to come first. It is only with the support of my parents that I was able to come to Harvard in the first place."

"Yes, yes, I know," sighed Dr. MacLeod. "And knowing the man you have become, I would have expected nothing less than you doing your duty despite any personal cost to yourself.

"Can you delay a week?"

"Possibly, but why?"

"Let me talk to President Hill and see if we can find a way you can meet your obligations and still get your diploma. I will get word to you as soon as I have an answer."

"Thank you, Dr. MacLeod. I am in your debt."

"Nonsense. You are a good lad and you deserve that diploma. And my condolences on the loss of your father."

Dr. MacLeod shook Daniel's hand, laid a gentle hand on his shoulder then escorted him to the door.

"Do you have sufficient funds to make the journey?" he asked as an afterthought.

"Yes, my mother included a bank draft with the letter. I will be going to the bank as soon as I leave here."

"Good, good. One less thing to worry about. I will send word as soon as I can. I know you are anxious to begin your journey."

"I still can't believe it. You would have had to have known my father to understand, but it is just impossible for him to be dead.

"Good day, Dr. MacLeod and thank you again," he said as he walked out the door.

True to his word, Daniel received a note by courier from Dr. MacLeod the afternoon of the following day.

"Dear Daniel, I have had a very productive meeting with President Hill. He has reviewed your grades, your extra-curricular activities and notes from your professors. To say he was impressed would be understating it. He agrees with me it would not be just for you to come so close and miss your diploma simply because you are doing your duty.

Therefore, he has agreed, if you take the final exam for my class and succeed, thus showing your mastery of the material, he will sign your diploma. He has also agreed to waive his customary fee in light of the untimely death of your father. You may make arrangements with a calligrapher of your choice to ink the diploma and it will be forwarded on to your ranch in Oregon at a later date.
Dr. Angus MacLeod

P. S. You may take the final exam in my office commencing on Monday next. Please expect to take one full day in this endeavor."

Monday next was three days away! Three days to read and memorize the course work for the rest of the school year. Daniel could have wept. Three days to cover the reading and review the material.

Suddenly he could hear his mother's voice in his mind, "You are an Adams and you are sturdy enough to handle anything that life gives you." Well, he might be only half Adams, but he was also half Hickman and that made him even tougher. He would read. He would remember and he would pass the exam.

Before he started studying, he went to the train depot and booked passage for Wyoming with a stateroom car and dining car service for the following Tuesday. He would have his bags packed and be ready to leave as soon as the exam was over. Pass or fail, he was going home next Tuesday. He stopped at a local market and gathered what food he thought he would need for the next three days then returned to his rooms.

He laid out his books examining them carefully. He decided against re-reading Blackstone's Commentaries as he had read it three time already over the course of his studies. He instead would work on Chitty's Pleadings, Greenleaf's Evidence and Story's Equity. He would read them all once and then he would skim all four books on Sunday. He took off his tie and his vest and got to work.

Daniel slept on the train for most of Tuesday and part of Wednesday, rousing occasionally to have a meal delivered from the dining car. On the Wednesday following his exams, he forewent a delivered meal and instead he sat in the dining car and looked at the passing scenery. They were apparently in the Midwest, for all he saw were fields, few trees and no mountains. He had made a sort of bath in his stateroom car and had managed a shave and had gotten his hair mostly clean. He realized his dark brown hair had gotten rather long while he had been at school. He also could see the circles under his dark brown eyes, a sign of the lack of sleep he had experienced over the past week. Hopefully a few more hours of sleep and he would look like himself again. He suddenly thought, will they know me?

He wondered how much everyone else in the family had changed in the five years he had been gone. Probably Abigail would have changed the most. She had been a little girl of seven when he left and now she was nearing her teenage years. Suddenly he was more homesick than he had been at any time since the first month he had spent at college.

He wanted to be home again.

It had been exciting seeing the big cities of the East, meeting his mother's family, studying at a prestigious college and later at the university. He hadn't been home during school breaks, not only because of the expense of going home, but also because of the time required. The extended Adams family had made him welcome in their homes in New Hampshire and he had been able to meet his grandmother, Theresa, before her death in his second year at Harvard. She had told him how much he looked like his mother. It seemed to really please her to be able to meet one of Syrie's children. Of course Grandmother Adams knew all of the children's names and when they had been born, but because the ranch in Oregon was so remote, she had never seen what they looked like. He got to meet his cousins and there were a lot of them. He never had managed to remember what child belonged to which of Syrie's brothers and sisters. But he had liked and enjoyed them all and had spent happy summers in their company.

The visit he had enjoyed the most had been when he met the seafaring portion of the Adams family. He had met Aunt Sarah Adams Skimmerhorn and Uncle Stephenson Skimmerhorn. Uncle Stephenson was a ship's master based out of Portsmouth. His Uncle Jackson Adams was retired from the sea, now owning a small fleet of ships. Over a dinner at Uncle Jackson's house he had been fascinated by their tales of the sea; the unusual places they had been, the customs of the various peoples around the world, the danger and the hardships. His Aunt Rebecca Adams kept a fine house for herself and her husband and displayed many of the oddities that Jackson had brought back from his overseas journeys. He had kept up a regular correspondence with his uncles and had returned to their homes on several of his school holidays, even after his grandmother had passed away. It had also led to an increased interest on his part in the specialty of maritime law.

He knew his father's people lived in Kentucky, but as Grandmother Hickman had died shortly after he was born, he had not made the trip to the south. Additionally, that family also lived in a rather remote part of Kentucky and his father had not been sure if any of his brothers and sisters still lived in the same area. Now he was a little sorry he hadn't made the effort. It had always seemed like there would be time later.

He watched the prairie fly past the windows of the train and he remembered his mother talking about how long it had taken them to go west with the wagons. His own trip to the East had been much quicker because he had traveled most by stagecoach. If transportation kept changing and they got the transcontinental railroad built, it actually might be possible for his mother to go back to New Hampshire and see her family again.

His train ticket would take him as far as Wyoming covering the nearly 2,000 miles in four days. The ticket master had advised him he wasn't sure exactly where in Wyoming as they were laying more track every day. When Daniel told the ticket master he was going home to his family ranch in Rye Valley, Oregon, the ticket master had been very confused. He had assumed Daniel was going to Oregon City or the new town of Portland. When Daniel mentioned Baker City, Oregon, the ticket master did find it in his book, but said it was impossible to get there.

That made Daniel laugh and he told the man to just get him a ticket on a train as far west as the train would go and left it at that. Daniel would figure it out from there. He was confident he could find a stage or a horse at whatever the last town in Wyoming was and continue on his way home.

When the train arrived at Cheyenne Wyoming, Daniel took the opportunity to talk to the station master during the time the train was taking on water and fuel. The station master told him the tracks had been laid nearly to Laramie, but he wasn't sure how far beyond that. As the ticket master in Cambridge had told him, they were laying new track every day and the trains were carrying people right behind the track layers.

Not wishing to risk having to wait for more tracks to be laid or not being able to find an outfit in whatever the last town was on the route, Daniel opted to leave the train in Cheyenne. He could probably put together an outfit to get himself to Oregon without too much trouble. There seemed to be a good number of stores and livery stables available for a frontier town. Daniel asked the conductor to see that his bags were delivered to the hotel closest to the station and then he went exploring.

Cheyenne was a well laid out city with a spacious grid of streets. The main thoroughfare of Cheyenne seemed to be mainly characterized by the number of saloons and brothels lining the streets. The citizens seemed to be mostly rough looking men, and Daniel was suddenly very aware of how he looked. A small statured man with thoroughly Eastern attire. He didn't even own a gun. The only weapon he had was his walking stick which was pretty useless in any kind of a fight. Once he had made a circuit of the noisy and congested main street, he went back to the hotel to register and secure his belongings.

Upon returning to the lobby, he asked the desk clerk where he might find a clothing store, a reputable livery stable and a place to purchase a firearm.

The desk clerk, looking him up and down, said, "What kind of clothing are you looking to purchase?"

"I am going to be riding to Oregon from here," Daniel replied. "I need more suitable clothing for the journey." Daniel realized he must look like a real greenhorn, but he didn't realize that in his five years in Cambridge, he had acquired a definite Eastern accent.

"Well, son," said the clerk, "I'm going to figure you don't know nothing about putting together an outfit. So, if you will wait until morning, I will go with you and see that you get fitted out proper."

Daniel started to open his mouth to protest that he did indeed know how to put together a proper outfit, but Cheyenne was a strange city and he had been away from the West for a long time. So instead, he smiled and said, "Thank you. I'll see you after breakfast. Say 8:00?"

Daniel was drinking his after-breakfast coffee when the clerk came into the dining room of the hotel.
"Are you ready?"

"Yes. Just let me get my hat," Daniel said as he reached for his bowler.

"First thing we got to do is get you a proper hat," the clerk said laughing as Daniel settled the bowler over his long hair. "And a haircut."

"I didn't get your name last night," Daniel said. "You have an advantage as you know my name from the register."

"Just call me Joe," said the clerk.

As promised, Joe took Daniel on a tour of the town's stores, remarking on the ones they didn't go into as to what shady deals the shop owners were likely to pull on unsuspecting greenhorns. They only went into one store, a general store and Daniel could see they would likely have nearly everything he would need. He estimated he would be on the trail for eight or maybe ten weeks. Some of the time he would be able to find stage stops and inns just as he had when he headed east, but he would also have to do some rough camping as well.

After Daniel had purchased clothes and boots, a pistol with a holster, a rifle with scabbard and ammunition for both, he concentrated on food stuffs and gear to cook over an open fire. Joe made a few suggestions and Daniel happily allowed him to guide him in some of his purchases.

After they finished the purchases, they left instructions for the bundles to be delivered to Daniel's hotel room. Then they walked to the outskirts of town to the livery stable. It wasn't the biggest, but Joe assured Daniel it was the most reputable.

"Any horse or mule you buy from here, will be exactly as advertised. He don't make no shady deals," Joe said.

Daniel was surprised to see that the livery was owned and run by a black man. Daniel had seen many black people in the East, but he was surprised to see one this far west. The man was also a blacksmith and was working at his forge when the two approached him.

"Daniel, this is Cletus Beauregard. Late of Louisiana. Cletus, meet Daniel Hickman, late of Harvard College."

"Pleased to meet you Mr. Hickman."

"I am pleased to meet you, Mr. Beauregard," Daniel said as he extended his hand to shake the blacksmith's hand.

"Mr. Joe," said the blacksmith. "How have you been? I'll bet business is good at your hotel, with the railroad and all now."

"Can't complain," said Joe.

Daniel filed this information away. So Joe was not only the clerk, he was apparently also the owner of the hotel.

"What are you working on there, Cletus?" asked Joe.

"The missus wants a new knife for the kitchen, so I am making one for her."

"Can I see that?" asked Daniel.

"Sure. It is nearly done. Just a little more shaping," Cletus explained the process needed to make the knife up to that point. "Then I just need to take it to the Arkansas stone and put an edge on it," Cletus said as he cooled the metal then handed Daniel a 10-inch blade. "It needs to be polished as well."

"That is beautiful," observed Daniel. "What are you going to use for a handle?"

"I have a piece of oak around here somewhere. I think it will work real nice for a handle. I need to shape it yet so it is comfortable for her little hands. My missus is a tiny little thing."

Daniel laughed as he handed the knife blade back.

"There must be something about big men and little women. My pa was about your size and my ma's no bigger than a minute."

Daniel was still staring at the knife blade.

"Mr. Beauregard, how much would you charge for something like that?"

"Please, call me Cletus. I don't rightly know. I've only ever made them for friends and family. I'd have to study on it and figure out how much time I have spent making it. Never really thought about selling my knives."

"I think you should consider it. This is as beautiful a knife as I have ever seen."

"Cletus," Joe joined in the conversation, "this young man is bound for Oregon. Says he needs an outfit. Can you help him out?"

"Certainly. Young mister, do you know what you want in a horse? Or do you want a mule?"

"I want one of each. A good, sure-footed riding horse and a pack mule that I can ride if the need arises."

"Okay, well come on out back and we'll see what we have in the corrals. Will you be needing saddles as well?"

"Yes, I have nothing. I don't need fancy, just serviceable and ones that will stand up to a long journey."

"I understand. I think I have a couple that will do you real nice," said Cletus as he led them through the stables and out to the corrals in the back.

"Take a look and tell me if you see anything you like, young mister."

"Please, call me Daniel. I am just a student trying to get home. I'm nobody's mister."

This earned a smile from Cletus who replied, "Long habit, son, long habit."

Daniel walked around the corrals, carefully studying the stock. He had only been 16 when he had left the ranch, but he had been taught early by his father what constituted a sound horse or mule. For no particular reason, he went to look at the mules first. He chose a short, stocky, brown john mule with a kind eye and no bells cut into his tail. He had no need for anything other than a pack mule. If he had to ride it, then he would just cross that bridge when he came to it. He wasn't a novice at training stock.

He next started studying the horses. He immediately rejected those that were very tall and lanky and appeared to be some or all Thoroughbred blood. He also reluctantly rejected a fine looking bay that Cletus identified as a Tennesse Walker, because he wasn't sure how it would handle the narrow, rough mountain trails, though he knew it would be a joy to ride in the prairie.

He spotted a smallish, gruella gelding standing somewhat alone in one corner of the corral. The little horse was about 14.2 hands, deep through the chest with his legs set square under his body. He had small feet and powerful hindquarters. Daniel went around the fence line to do a closer inspection of the little horse and was gratified by what he saw.

"This one?" he asked Cletus. "How much?"

"Well, you do have a good eye for a mountain horse", observed Cletus. "That's a Rafter S horse. Kind of rare to get one for sale in these parts. Most folks don't want to part with them. This one is only available because his owner didn't draw quick enough in a fight over a saloon girl."

"I know the Rafter S horses," said Daniel. "The Rafter S is my family ranch."

"Well then you will know where to look for the brand. It's right there on his near shoulder."

Daniel didn't have to climb over the corral fence. He already knew he would find the Rafter S brand. "How much?"

"Well, the horse has been here about a week at a buck a day. Plus you said you'll be needing a saddle, a saw buck, some blankets, saddle bags, panniers, probably some hobbles. Anything else?"

"I don't think so. I already bought lash rope, manty, grain, and a lead line over at the general store."

"Okay, then how does $150 sound for the whole outfit?"

"$125 sounds better."

"Ok," laughed Cletus. "$125 it is."

"That's fine then. If you will have them fed and saddled for me around 7:00 tomorrow morning, I'll bring my gear from the hotel and start loading up.

"Thanks again, Cletus. It has been a pleasure doing business with you," said Daniel as he shook Cletus' large, horny hand. "You know your hands remind me of my father's. He was a blacksmith in his youth, and he had hands as large and strong as yours."

Daniel turned quickly away as his voice threatened to break.

"Until tomorrow."

Joe followed Daniel as they made their way back to the hotel. "You didn't tell me your family owned the Rafter S," said Joe.

"I have been away for five years and I am honestly amazed our little horses have made it all the way out here. When I left, nobody outside the Oregon and Idaho Territories had ever heard of our ranch and our Cayuse horses. Pa and Ma must have done real well with their breeding program."

"Yes, they have. Say, how come you let me think you were a greenhorn and didn't know about the West?"

"Because I don't. I have been away a very long time and all I have known since I was 16 is the East Coast and Cambridge. Things have changed a lot. I knew Cheyenne would be a rough town to do business in as soon as I stepped off the train, so I am very grateful for your help."

"More than happy to help. How about I buy you a drink for your last night in town and then we'll go on back to the hotel and have some supper. I'm sure you want to get a good night's sleep before you start out tomorrow."

Daniel was up with the sun, ordered coffee sent up to his room, then started sorting and packing his things. He was glad he had elected to have his books held in Cambridge until he could find out what was happening at home. If he stayed in Oregon, he would have them shipped. He had left them with a friend of Dr. MacLeod's who was also the calligrapher he had chosen to ink his diploma, so he knew they were in good hands.

Daniel debated what to do with his Eastern clothes. He knew he wouldn't need them on the journey or at the ranch, but they were still serviceable. and he might need them later. He rolled them tightly to be put in the bottom of one of the panniers. If nothing else, they would provide protection for anything delicate he might pack later. His bowler hat he sat aside. He thought Joe might like to have it as a gift. He packed a spare set of trousers, a shirt and a coat to be put in the other pannier, trying to balance the weight. He had dressed in heavy trousers with a wide leather belt, a light shirt, a bandana and a wide brimmed hat. He put on the holster and slid the pistol home. He would take some time along the trail to familiarize himself with both weapons. He hadn't fired any firearm since he had left home and he knew he needed the practice.

He rang for the bellboy and together they packed all the bundles downstairs.

"Joe, I'm leaving now. I wanted to thank you again for all your help."

"Aren't you going to have some breakfast?" asked Joe.

"I really need to be going, it's nearly 7:00 already."

"Hold on a sec. Let me ask cook if she can pack you some biscuits and ham or such." Joe disappeared into the rear of the building.

Daniel got the attention of the bell boy and said, "Do you think you could help me carry this to Cletus' livery at the end of the street? I'll have a two-bit piece for you if you can."

"Sure, mister. For two bits I'll carry all of it myself," said the young bell boy.

Joe re-appeared in a few minutes with a bundle wrapped in a bandana.

"Here you go, Daniel. Cook fixed you some grub for the trail."

"Please thank her for me. I really enjoyed the meals I had here.

"Do I owe you anything more for this?"

"No, your bill was all settled last night. You don't owe me a penny more."

"Joe, I'd like you to have this. To remember me by." Daniel handed Joe the bowler hat. "Perhaps if I get back this way again, I can buy you a drink and dinner."

"I'd really like that. I'll walk you down to the livery. Looks like you have a might of stuff to carry."

The bell boy started to protest, thinking he wouldn't get his two bits, but Daniel assured him a deal was a deal and they all went down the street to the livery.

With Cletus' help, Daniel soon had his panniers and saddle bags packed and ready to go. Both men checked the knots and the ropes one last time, then Daniel swung into the saddle and slid the rifle home in its scabbard.

"Feels good to be on a horse again," he remarked. "Hope it still feels good after the first 20 miles."

Cletus stepped to Daniel's side and gave him the knife that Daniel had seen him working on, as well as a fine leather sheath.

"This is for you. I want to thank you for taking an interest in my knives. No one has ever said anything about them before. You may have just given me a new product to add to my income."

Daniel pulled the blade from the sheath. Cletus had ground the edge to razor sharpness and had polished the metal until it gleamed. He had carved and sanded the oak handle into a beautiful shape and Daniel noticed his Rafter S brand had been burned into the wood. Cletus had also etched Daniel's initials into the blade where it met the handle.

"I don't know what to say, Cletus. I will be very honored to carry this. It is a beautiful blade. Thank you very much. But, is this going to get you in trouble with your wife?"

"Oh no. She doesn't know I had this knife nearly done. I'll make her another one."

Daniel carefully placed the knife in his saddle bag. "Thank you both for everything. I'll look you up if I get back to Cheyenne," he waved to them as he set off down the street at an easy pace pointed towards the west and home.

CHAPTER SEVEN

Dottie and Billy Lattimer spent their stolen gold wisely and quietly. They went to Baker City after the murder to trade in Noah's gold dust for coin and script. Then they purchased a gold pan, a small tent, cots, blankets, and other necessities to set up their new identities as miners. They also bought new clothes, a new suit of work clothes for Billy and two plain dresses for Dottie. Then they bought a buckboard and a four-up team at the livery. The rest of the money they deposited at the bank.

They returned to Mormon Basin and set up their little camp beside an unoccupied site alongside one of the creeks. They panned a little and found a little color, but it was the people they were really interested in – discovering who was desperate, who was a real miner and could be bet upon as probably finding gold, who was gullible and who was a waste of their time and talents.

To any serious prospector, it was obvious Billy Lattimer was no miner. The tall, red-headed man had soft hands and had a way of talking that spoke of wealth and class. People didn't fail to notice he actually spent little time digging or panning, but mostly spent his time talking to people. He could be found most days at what passed for the local saloon, often buying drinks.

Dottie was a dark-eyed, beauty with a soft Southern drawl. Her dusky skin could have been a product of any number of racial mixings, but she never spoke of or claimed any family other than Billy. She did speak quietly to the few women who were living in the gold field, but mostly she kept to herself. She walked frequently around the diggings and often quite a ways out. She had a quick way about her that told people she missed nothing.

One day, the owner of the local tent saloon was killed in a shootout with one of the customers over the quality of the whiskey, or rather the lack thereof. Since the saloon owner had no known relatives, Dottie and Billy quietly took over the running of the business and began pouring drinks. They erected a frame front for the tent and built a floor which was raised a foot or so above the ground so the mud was no longer a problem. Next, they imported women to work in the little tents out in back of the saloon. Because the men outnumbered the women three to one in the gold fields, they made a tidy profit. They gradually expanded their holdings in Mormon Basin, building a bath house and later a frame structure that they would run as a boarding house, while they lived on the main floor. They hired the wives of two of the miners to cook and clean for them. They were model citizens, promoting peace and justice and they gave generously if anyone was in need in their community.

Billy was jovial and always glad to meet everyone. He was the perfect bartender and boarding house host. Dottie was the silent enforcer of the pair and soundly pistol-whipped a man who refused to pay his tab at the bar. She also ran the girls in the tents and wasn't afraid to discipline any john who got too rough with any of the girls. This was not out of a sense of human friendship and caring, but because the johns were damaging her merchandise. Of course, her enforcing was done in the dark or behind the scenes. No man who had been on the receiving end of her "enforcement" would ever tell anyone he had been beaten by a woman. To all outside eyes, she was the perfect, quiet, dutiful wife of a successful businessman. She seemed shy and unassuming, not joining any of the get-togethers with the other women. Billy reinforced this by telling everyone, "She's happy just being a wife and keeping a home for me. Never has caused me a minute's trouble."

Between the two of them, they ran a profitable business empire and were always looking to expand.

Word soon got around the mining camp that Billy was willing to buy claims for any who were moving on to other strikes. He also would lend money against proven claims. The word that didn't get around was what happened when the money couldn't be paid back at twenty percent interest. Some of the people who borrowed money from the Lattimers seemed to experience a lot of bad luck, from falls to accidents at their claim sites to the loss of their tools and equipment.

Another money maker they used was one they had used successfully in many other small settlements along the frontier. Choosing only single men with a proven claim, Dottie would pay the miner a late night visit. She would turn her soft, chocolate-brown eyes on him and tell him that she needed a real man in her life. She would loosen the top of her dress, letting it open until her breasts were showing. As soon as the miner put his hands on her, Billy would be at the door with a pistol in his hand. If he didn't have gold on hand, the miner would suddenly decide to sell out and try his luck somewhere else and he always "sold" to the Lattimers. People in the Basin didn't seem alarmed because miners were always looking for the next big strike somewhere over the next mountain.

The Lattimers soon held a respectable number of claims in Mormon Basin. They hired outside workers to actually do the work of the claims while maintaining the façade that the men working the claims owned them. The Lattimers didn't get their hands dirty and they pocketed the profits. Because of the large amount of cash they accumulated, Dottie and Billy formed business alliances with the bank in Baker City and with several of the larger merchants there as well. For the first time in their lives, they were respected members of the community and wealthy as well.

This pattern of grift, extortion and blackmail went on for most of the summer, until one of the miners refused to be blackmailed.

The miner was one of the more prosperous miners in the area and he had built a small cabin on his claim. Dottie visited him late one night and the miner was certainly enjoying the attention, his eyes alight and fastened on her breasts, but he was slow to act and touch her. In fact, Dottie had to undo her dress completely to the waist, and was thinking about undoing her chemise before the miner grabbed her and threw her onto his cot. He threw her so hard that Dottie's head swam. Billy was making his way through the door as the miner was undoing his pants and Dottie was afraid for her safety for the first time.

The miner was furious when Billy came into the cabin.

"Get the hell out of here! Your woman tells me she needs a real man in her life and I am going to show her - and you - what a real man can do for a woman."

"That's my wife. You get your hands off her!"

The miner continued to undo his trousers and was focused solely on Dottie.

"I'll kill you where you stand," said Billy.

"Bull! You don't have the spine to shoot an unarmed man in the back. Now get out of here unless you want to watch me take your woman. Unless that is how you get your fun."

The man's pants were down around the top of his boots now and he was fumbling with the buttons to his union suit.

Dottie had regained her senses and realized the man was serious in his threat to take her whether Billy was in the room or not. She reached her hand down under her skirt to the small derringer she kept in her garter.

For the first time, the miner realized where the real danger lay. As calmly as if she was killing a spider, Dottie aimed the derringer at the center of the man's chest and pulled the double triggers. The miner put his hands to the gaping wound in his chest, then fell forward across Dottie, covering her chemise in blood and trapping her beneath his bulk.

"Get him the hell off of me!" she shouted as she squirmed to get free. "Move your ass, goddammit!"

Billy quickly holstered his pistol and ran the few steps to the cot. The miner had been a large man and it was all Billy could do to move his body turning it over so the dead miner was facing the ceiling. Dottie wriggled free and stood beside the bed putting her clothes back together.

"Now what are we going to do? We've never killed one of the men before," Billy said looking at the body. "They are going to hang us for murder!"

"No they aren't. Use your head. He was going to rape me and you saved me by shooting him. Come on, we've got to be quick. Those gunshots will bring people.

"Hit me," she said. "Right across the face."

"I can't do that!"

"Hit me! Do you want to hang?"

Billy took a tepid swipe at her face.

"Make a fist and hit me!"

Billy took a deep breath and did as she demanded, instinctively stepping back after he did so. The blow rocked Dottie back a few steps, split her lip, bloodied her nose and brought tears to her eyes, but she quickly recovered and let the tears and the blood flow.

"Good. Now we have to get him positioned. It has to look like you shot him, not me. It's a good thing most of my clothes were off or I would have too much blood on me to explain. Now it just looks like the blood came from my face."

Dottie helped Billy drag the man's body off the bed and onto the floor. Then she ripped the bodice of her dress nearly to her waist as they heard steps on the front porch of the cabin. Dottie was as good an actress as any Billy had ever seen on the stage and she immediately turned on the tears and buried her face in Billy's chest.

The miner who lived closest stood in the doorway, obviously roused from sleep by the shot.

"What the hell happened here?" he demanded.

Dottie lifted her tear stained and bloody face from Billy's chest and said, "He asked me to help him home from the saloon because he wasn't feeling well. Billy said he would be right along, so I agreed to help him. He seemed pretty sick and he said he had a fever. As soon as we got into the cabin, he attacked me. I'm so thankful for my husband. If he hadn't come as quickly as he did, I'm afraid," her breath hitched dramatically, "I'm afraid of what this animal would have done to me."

Fresh tears flowed as she sobbed into Billy's chest again.

Billy cleared his throat and spoke haltingly and with great emotion.

"I never would have expected such a thing from him. I had no choice but to kill him. I had to save my wife from him. I never thought anyone would try to take advantage of Dottie's kindness."

"I'm sure you had no choice," agreed the miner. "Let's get your poor wife home."

Soon the little cabin and the porch was so crowded with people that Billy and Dottie had to maneuver their way through to reach the door. One of the women, firmly, yet gently took Dottie in hand and said, "Come on dear, let's get you home and get you cleaned up and into your bed." The woman covered Dottie's ruined dress with her own shawl, ignoring the blood.

Dottie looked frantically at Billy to rescue her from the well-meaning woman, but the others only saw shock and dismay on her face. They made the assumption it was from the shock of being attacked and seeing a man killed in front of her.

"Now Mr. Lattimer, let's get you back to your saloon. I'm sure you can use a drink to settle your nerves. Some of the fellows will take care of him and get him ready for burying, though a Christian burial doesn't seem quite proper."

Billy allowed himself to be led back to his own saloon and managed to keep the relief from his face and voice. He concentrated on setting his face into lines of sorrow when all he wanted to do was jump for joy at not being hanged. Thank God for Dottie's quick thinking.

Dottie was having a harder time maintaining her façade. She had to allow the women of the camp, thank heavens there weren't many of them, to help her wash herself, change out of her blood stained clothes and into a flannel night gown. One she had never worn, though they didn't need to know that. They solicitously made her tea and watched her closely to see that she drank it. She managed to shed a few more tears and shake when she held her teacup, but inside she was seething with rage that all of these women were clucking and fussing over her. God, she wished she were a man, because she knew Billy was drinking at the saloon, being congratulated at his heroics in saving his poor little wife.

Feigning extreme exhaustion, she managed to get to her bedroom and closed the door. Then she waited quietly hoping they would think she fell asleep. Once the door creaked and she quickly closed her eyes as the light from the other room fell across her. The door quietly closed and she could hear the women leaving. She waited another few minutes and cautiously crossed the room to the door and listened closely. Silence.

"Yes!" she thought as she went out into the adjoining parlor. She didn't dare light a lamp, because someone might see she wasn't asleep. Billy still wasn't home and she crossed carefully to a cabinet and was reaching for the door when she heard boots on the front porch. Damn!

She quickly ran back to her bedroom and closed the door. Billy was ushered into the parlor by a group of men. She could see he was well into his cups. Bastard.

"You sure you boys don't want to stay a while?"

"No. No. Thank you anyway. We wouldn't want to wake the missus after the time she had tonight. It is late and we all have to be up early in the morning."

More good byes followed and she heard the front door close and the sound of boots on the porch again. Finally!

When she entered the parlor, she found Billy sprawled out on the settee, his head nodding on his chest.

"Wake up you idiot. You're drunk. I certainly hope you didn't run your big mouth about what really happened tonight."

Billy raised his head and tried to focus on Dottie.

"No. I didn't say anything," he protested.

As his vision stabilized he gaped at Dottie. "You are wearing a nightgown!" he exclaimed.

"I had to play the part of a poor little woman who has been through an ordeal. I could hardly tell those fool women I sleep naked, now could I?

"Get your clothes off and get into bed." she ordered as she lit a lamp and again crossed the room to the cabinet. "I need a drink."

She poured herself three fingers of a fine, imported brandy and knocked back most of it in one swallow. "I really needed that," she said as she sat in a rocker near the parlor fireplace and sipped at the rest of the brandy. "That was too close for comfort tonight."

Billy was still sprawled on the settee and he managed to straighten a bit as she spoke.

"Maybe we should stop running that game," Billy said.

"You're drunk," she reiterated. "And in no shape to make any kind of plans. And I need to get drunk. I told you, go to bed. I need to think."

Obediently Billy got up from the settee, swayed, regained his balance and lurched toward the bedroom door. Dottie continued to sip her brandy and think.

Still playing the victim of an attack, she didn't join the boarders for breakfast as she usually did. She had Billy tell the cook to prepare a tray for both of them and to bring it to their quarters. He was to tell her that Mrs. Lattimer was still too shaken to get up from her bed. He was to say he was going to stay with his wife for a bit before he went to the saloon for the day, still playing the part of the worried husband.

Though his head was splitting with a hangover, Billy did as instructed and brought back a breakfast tray for two and a pot of coffee. He laced his cup of coffee liberally with good whiskey and nearly sighed as it hit him. As he was too hung over to have an appetite and ate only a piece of toast, Dottie gladly polished off the tray that was supposed to be for two people. When she was full, she indicated Billy should take the tray away from the bed where she was sitting. She didn't want to take any chances with anyone seeing her as anything but a distressed woman today, and maybe for a few more days beyond that. The more time the community focused on her and her plight, the less likely they were to be inquisitive about what had really happened. She needed them to think of her as a victim and the miner as an animal. Once he was buried and the cabin cleaned of all evidence, she would relax a little.

"Okay, we need a new plan," she said to Billy as they drank another cup of coffee. "You were right to think about stopping that game. We got lucky last night and we may not get lucky again. So we will need to think of another way to get more gold."

"We're doing really well with the girls, the saloon and the mining claims," noted Billy. "I think we could go 100 percent real business and do just fine."

"I don't want to do 'just fine'. I want to have enough money so we can go back to New Orleans and live like we always should have been able to. I want a house overlooking the river and I want servants, a fine carriage and jewels. I want it all."

"Okay, Dottie. Whatever you want. How much more money do you want us to get."

"I think $50,000 would set us up for the rest of our lives."

"$50,000! That's a lot of money! Even if we sold everything we've got here, we couldn't get that much," exclaimed Billy.

"I know that! It's why I think we need to expand. We need more businesses. We need more claims. I've been thinking about the claim we saw when we first came into the Basin. On my walks, I've been watching it. I watched it for a long time after the horse, the mule and the miner's body disappeared and no one has been back to work it and no one has re-marked it. Now I think is the time for us to take over that claim."

"Do you think it is rich?" asked Billy.

"We took nearly $3,000 from that big miner. That is more than most of our claims make in two weeks. Unless he had been there for a month, and it didn't look like he had, it could be our richest claim yet."

"Okay. I can see that. What other businesses are you thinking about?"

"I want to build a house for the girls. It is easier to watch them that way and I can control who comes in. I think they are giving it away too much of the time. I know a woman I can send for who can act as madam.

"I also want to start a dry goods store. We can start a freight company and import our own goods into the Basin. If we control the flow of goods people need and the freight to get them in and out, we can control nearly everything about this place, with the businesses we already have.

"We need to make a trip to Baker City and file on that claim. You can tell people you are very concerned about my health after the attack and you are taking me to see the doctor. Really play it up about how sick I am, how I am not eating, how I am shaking all the time."

"Not eating!" he snorted. "Nothing interferes with your appetite!"

"No one needs to know that. You can sneak me food and make sure the liquor cabinet is well stocked. I am going to have to stay in this bed, so you had better take good care of me," she threatened.

Billy rose and went to the bed, kissing Dottie on the forehead.

"Don't I always? I'd better get to the saloon. I'll pass the word around about how poorly you are and see if I can earn you more pity. I'll be back in a couple of hours."

"Oh and make sure to tell any do-gooder women you see that I am just too fragile for visitors. If they must, they can send soup or some such stuff. But keep them away from me. I can't hold my temper around them."

"Sure, Dottie, whatever you want."

CHAPTER EIGHT

As summer crept into fall, Syrie wondered when Daniel had left Cambridge. She never had any doubt he would respond to her request. She also knew any letter from him would likely arrive after he did, if he had left right away from Cambridge. She also knew how many troubles could befall a traveler on that long journey. She had buried friends along the route.

She kept herself busy with the running of the ranch, getting ready for winter, schooling for Abigail, and to a lesser extent for Michael, and a score of other things. She had sent Michael into Baker City with the letter for Daniel and a request for a bank draft the day after Noah's funeral. She had also sent a letter for the sheriff, the assay office and another for the Lands Office clerk who oversaw the filings of the mining claims. In the letter she notified them of Noah's murder and she told them she would be assuming control of the claim. She instructed Michael to privately ask the clerk for his help in watching for anyone who might make inquiries into the claim. Mr. Brainard was asked to get as much information as he could and relay it to Lucreta and Young Noah at Plano Creek. They would then get word to her.

The nights were the worst. That is when the doubts crept into Syrie's mind. Would they ever find out who had murdered Noah? Would she be able to find a way to channel Abigail's grief into something healthy? Would Daniel make it back okay?

And God, how she missed Noah sleeping in that big bed! She even missed his snoring and him stealing all the covers.

But mostly she worried about staying in the present where her family needed her. Her friend, Mattie, had told her what had happened to her after Jedidiah had been killed at Three Island Crossing. How she had crept into herself and had become like a life-size doll that would keep doing repetitive chores, but otherwise was not present. How she wouldn't eat and would barely sleep. Syrie found herself drawn to that place again. That peaceful, quiet, cotton-filled world, where nothing hurt. The first days after Noah's death, it had been her children who had kept her from that world. They needed her to point the way forward. To be strong enough to keep the ranch going. To love them even though her love had been taken from her by a bullet.

She decided to ride every day. Riding had always been a joy to her and Noah had seen to it that she always had good, solid mounts from the first filly he had trained for her. They had often ridden together over their ranch and the range they controlled. It was their own personal time and Syrie missed the conversations and the camaraderie. It brought tears to her eyes to remember the good times. As she always had, Syrie now found solace in horses. Found solace in their calmness and their understanding. As she had hoped, as the days went by, she found herself less and less attracted to the dark places in her mind.

She might never be fully free of it, but for now, she could resist it. For now, it was one day at a time and her children and her duties kept her moving forward. For now it was one day at a time as she forced herself to eat and to go to her bed, to shut down her mind and to rest.

About a fortnight after Noah's murder, James W. Virtue, the sheriff, had ridden out to the ranch from Baker City. It was a long two-day ride and the sheriff looked tired and dusty when he pulled up at the house in the evening.

"Mrs. Hickman," he said. "I apologize for not getting out here sooner. Sometimes things in Baker City are quiet and sometimes they aren't," Sheriff Virtue said in his thick Irish accent. "These past days have been the 'not quiet' kind.

"I was really sorry to learn about your husband. Mr. Hickman was well liked and well respected in Baker City. He will be missed as a leader of our community."

"Thank you, Sheriff Virtue. Won't you come in? We will be sitting down to supper in a little while. Can I get you a cup of coffee in the meantime?"

"That would be most welcome, ma'am."

"Abigail, would you take the sheriff's horse down to the barn and have the men tend to it? Thank you. And come straight back as we need to get supper on.

"Sheriff Virtue, would you be our guest for the night? I would hate to think about you setting out again for the return trip to Baker City. It is not safe after dark with the Paiute raiding right now."

"I would appreciate it. And I'm sure my horse would as well. But I'm not actually heading back to Baker City. There has been a murder up in Rye Valley and I have been called up there. The townspeople have the suspect in custody and I am going to transport him back to Baker City for trial. But, I would be very happy to take you up on your offer," the sheriff dusted his hat against his chaps and stepped up onto the porch.

"Is there some where I can wash up? I'm a bit dusty from the ride."

"I'll have Painted Pony bring you out some warm water and you can wash up at the basin around the corner," as she pointed around the end of the log house. "There is soap and toweling. Take your time and when you are done, come in and have that coffee."

After the sheriff had cleaned up, he knocked on the kitchen door and went in to the warmth and smells of supper cooking. After having breakfasted and lunched on water and beef jerky, the smells of the frying steaks was mouth-watering.

"Sheriff, you said you were going to Rye Valley tomorrow?" asked Syrie.

"Yes, ma'am."

"Did you say you were going up there to transport a prisoner?" Syrie asked as she stirred the gravy. "Abigail, would you check those potatoes? I think they are done."

"Yes, ma'am," said the sheriff. "They had a shooting and one of the men was killed. The townspeople have the murderer in custody and I am going up to take him back for trial."

At the word 'murderer,' Abigail looked up from the pot of potatoes she had just placed on the table and focused on the sheriff and what he was saying.

"I'm glad they were able to find the guilty party so quickly," said Painted Pony with Syrie nodding agreement.

"Yes, apparently there were half a dozen witnesses," the sheriff informed them. "Fight over a dance, uh," the sheriff paused realizing that Abigail was watching him. "A fight over a woman and a rather large amount of gold."

"It's him, isn't it Ma? That's the same man who killed Pa! The sheriff said there was a lot of gold. It's the same man. It's Pa's killer!"

"Wait a minute," the sheriff held up his hands. "Just because this man killed another in a fight, doesn't mean he's the same man who killed your pa. There were no witnesses to your father's murder if I understand correctly?"

"No. No. There were no witnesses. Only Noah's horse and mule," said Syrie. "We have no idea who killed Noah."

"But it could be him!" insisted Abigail.

"I don't know, Miss Hickman," the sheriff said trying to placate her. "But, I will question him about where he got the gold and I will find out if he had anything to do with the killing of your pa. But I have to have enough evidence to present to a court before I can charge him with any more than the killing of this other fellow in Rye Valley. If he confesses, then that is one thing. But I have to have some proof before I can do anything else."

"But you said he had a lot of gold," pleaded Abigail.

"Miss Hickman, this is gold country. Lots of men make big strikes and have lots of gold. I said there was a lot of gold involved in the murder, but I don't know if the gold belonged to the man who was killed or to the man who did the shooting. Those are questions, I need to ask the witnesses when I get to Rye Valley.

"It is not an easy thing to find a murderer when there are no witnesses."

Syrie stepped over to Abigail where she stood by the table trembling with suppressed emotions.

"Abigail, we have to be patient. We have to let the sheriff do his job," Syrie soothed as she tried to put her arms around Abigail.

"No! No!" Abigail shook off her mother.

"Someone killed my Pa and I want to know who! And if you can't find out," she glared at the sheriff, "Then I will!" She ran through the parlor and into her room, slamming the door behind her.

"I am so sorry, Mrs. Hickman," said the sheriff. "I didn't mean to upset your daughter."

"It's not your fault. When you are 12, the world should be black and white. Good and bad, right and wrong should be clearly defined. Abigail is having a real problem believing her father is dead and no one is apparently, in her mind, going to pay for her loss," said Syrie on a sigh as she sat down. "I don't know how to help her."

"It will take time," Painted Pony said laying a hand on Syrie's shoulder. "She will come to terms with it in time."

Syrie reached up and patted the hand on her shoulder and looked up at Painted Pony. "But that time can seem like forever when you want answers."

A few days after the first hard frost of the fall, a lean man, dust heavy on his dark hair and beard, rode into the compound. He was riding a gruella horse and leading a pack mule. He stepped down in front of the log house. He took off his hat, dusted it by beating it against his chap-covered leg. His clothes were well worn and his animals were thin. He put his hat back on over his long hair, scratched at his beard and stepped onto the porch. He hesitated at the door to the parlor then went to the door to the kitchen. As he was standing there a young girl stepped out of the door to the parlor.

Daniel saw a girl approaching womanhood. She was nearly as tall as he, with blonde hair and blue eyes and she looked like his father.

"Abigail?" he asked.

"How do you know my name? Who are you?"

"It's Daniel. I'm your brother, Daniel."

"Daniel! Ma, come quick! Daniel's home!"

The kitchen door opened and Syrie stepped out followed by Painted Pony. Syrie only hesitated a moment before enveloping her son in her arms and crying tears of joy.

"You made it. You made it." she kept saying. "I'm so glad to see you."

She stepped back and said, "Let me look at you. You're all grown up."

She reached out and touched his face. "And you're a man now. I sent a boy away to Harvard and you've come home a man."

She hugged him again, before releasing him so Painted Pony and Abigail could hug him as well.

"Come in. You must be tired and hungry. We'll fix you a bite to eat and then we will warm water for a bath. Later you can tell us all about your time at Harvard.

"Abigail, would you run down to the barn and have Horace send one of the men to Lucreta's place and let her know Daniel has made it home?

"I can't wait to see all the family. I'm assuming you want to have a family conference about Pa's murder."

"Yes," Syrie agreed. "We have always been a family who worked and planned together. This isn't the time to change that."

"I guessed right about that. But right now, Ma, I would like to see where he is buried. Maybe it will make it seem real. Not being here when it happened, being so far away, it still doesn't seem real."

"I understand, Daniel. It's been hard on all of us.

"He's up on the bench by the cairns. There is a marker there. We will get a stone one someday, but for now it is made out of wood."

"Thanks, Ma and the food and a bath sound wonderful. Can you have one of the hands take care of my animals?

I'm just about done in. I've pushed hard ever since I left Cheyenne.

"That little gruella has been a great horse through it all. I can tell you I was amazed to find one of our horses in Cheyenne."

Syrie looked at the little horse and saw the Rafter S brand on its shoulder.

"You'll have to tell me about it later," she said. "Now go on up and see your Pa. Painted Pony and I will get you some food and then get the water going for your bath."

Daniel ate like a man who hadn't seen real food in a long time. After his bath Daniel shaved off his beard and Syrie nearly gasped when she saw how much he looked like her brother Jackson. It was almost like having her brother in her kitchen. Syrie cut his hair as she had been doing since he was a little boy. Since he was not wearing a shirt as she cut his hair, she was able to see there wasn't much flesh on him. His animals weren't the only ones who were thin. She wondered exactly how hard he had pushed himself and his animals. Daniel dressed in clean clothes from his pack, and he felt ready to talk to his family.

Theresa came in from working cattle and there were fresh tears of greeting again. It didn't take much prompting for her to agree to stay for supper and the family sat down at the big table in the parlor. Theresa couldn't believe how much Daniel had changed. He was a man now. For his part, Daniel had trouble grasping that his sister was sitting across from him dressed in buckskin breeches and boots. He had become so accustomed to the women in the east and their manner of dressing, that he took a moment to remember that the women in his family wore whatever they needed to get the job done.

First his mother wanted to know about her family in the east. Daniel had written to her about his visits, but having him here to talk to, made the visits and the family news somehow clearer for Syrie. She was excited to hear about the fine houses and the successful businesses they were now running. It also gladdened her heart to know none of her brothers were going to sea anymore. She knew how the sea had always worried her mother.

"What did you think of my mother?" Syrie asked him.

"She was wonderful. I cried when I got the letter informing me she had passed. She was so full of laughter and so proud of her family. She spoke of Grandfather Adams in such a way I could almost see him."

"Yes, she loved him very much. I don't think she ever stopped missing him. At least that was how it seemed from the letters I got from her. Did she seem very lonely?"

"No," Daniel considered before he fully answered his mother's question. "I don't think she was lonely. She missed Grandfather Adams, but she loved having her family around her. She seemed especially delighted with the great-grandchildren. She told me once she would never have believed she would live to be old enough to see great-grandchildren. She was very proud of all of her family."

"With my mother, family was always her greatest joy. I am so glad to know she was able to enjoy it for so long."

Daniel said, "It is obvious you have taken after your mother. I think all of us children have always known your family was your greatest joy."

"Yes, I guess you are right. My children, and now my grandchildren, are the only things I would give my life for now that your father is gone."

Then his brothers wanted to hear about Daniel's time at Harvard.

"It was harder than I could have imagined," Daniel told them. "The studying seemed endless and the breaks were never long enough.

"But I learned a lot. The law is more complex than just about any other field of study, except maybe medicine. The young man I roomed with my first year was a medical student and I think he actually spent more time reading than I did! The school encouraged us to do things outside of studying so I joined the rowing club, remember Ma, I wrote you about the races?"

Syrie nodded her head. "I read all your letters to the family right here around this table. We didn't always understand everything you did, but we all admired how you were putting everything you had into what you were doing."

"It was the way you raised me, raised all of us," Daniel said. "So, I mostly spent five years studying and rowing a little boat on weekends. The rowing helped to keep me fit and it helped to take my mind off the books. You wouldn't think rowing would do that, but you really have to concentrate on what you are doing when you are racing. The competition with Yale is especially fierce. We have the race once a year. Well nearly so, during the war, it wasn't held.

"I left before the end of the school year. My mentor and main professor, Dr. MacLeod - I wrote you about him - was gracious enough to go directly to the head of the university, President Hill, to plead my case. President Hill agreed if I could pass the final exam for Dr. MacLeod's class that he would sign my diploma and he would waive his customary fee due to Pa's passing. I took the test on a Monday and got on the train on Tuesday. I didn't wait for the results. Either I passed or I didn't. If I didn't, I'll see about continuing to read for the law until I can pass the test. I left all my books in Cambridge, but I can arrange to have them shipped to me here if I need.

"Now, can you tell me any more about what happened to Pa and what you have been able to do?" he asked his family.

"Not a lot really. We sent letters to Baker City, informing the sheriff of the murder and asking for help from the filing clerk." explained Syrie. "The sheriff rode out and talked to us. We told him what we thought had happened, what George Rogers found. He basically told us unless a witness comes forward, there's not a lot we can do.

"We also sent a letter to the assay office, but there are so many people making big strikes, we don't expect anything to come from them keeping an eye out for big amounts of gold. We don't even know how much your Pa had panned out, if any, when he was shot. We're just assuming, since he was gone about a week, he would have had more than was in his pan. We're hoping the clerk in the Lands Office, Mr. Brainard, might see something or someone might come in and try to file on our claim and let us know.

"All we know for certain is it was two white men. George tracked them until the tracks merged into the main road into Mormon Basin. One large man and one small. George said the small tracks were even small enough for a woman or a child, but he couldn't believe a woman or a child would be involved in something that brutal."

"Has anyone else been working his claim?" asked Daniel.

"I don't know. I have instructed everyone to stay away from there as I felt it was too risky. If the people who murdered your Pa did come back, they would not hesitate to kill again."

"No one has been working it," said Abigail.

Everyone stopped and stared at the girl.

"What do you mean?" asked Syrie. "How on earth would you know?"

"I've been up there." Abigail said defiantly. "Someone had to find out and I decided to go and have a look. I've been up there half a dozen times, and no one has done any work there. I did see a dark-haired woman there a couple of times. She looked like she was just out for a walk. I stayed well back in the brush so she didn't see me.

"What?" she said as her mother stared at her.

"Did you really think I was going to sit here doing school work while my father's killers are walking around free? I am Noah Hickman's daughter, and I will not let my father's killers go free!"

Abigail sat with her head held proudly staring back at her mother, defiance plainly written on her face. Syrie was reminded of the story Noah had told her about another Abigail and the day that Abigail's father had died.

'I should have seen this coming', she thought.

"You may be excused from the table," Syrie said calmly, her face betraying nothing of what she felt. "You and I will have a conversation before you go to sleep. Go to your room, change into your night clothes and wait for me there."

Abigail calmly arose from the table and with her back straight, went into her room. She closed the door softly.

Theresa looked from the closed door to her mother and back again.

"I can't believe she did that?! The little ninny took a terrible chance."

"It is my fault. I let her ride for as long and as far as she wanted. I felt the horses would be a good way for her work through her anger. I should have seen this coming. She is right. She is Noah's child and the woman she is named for was just as strong as your Pa. I should have seen this coming."

Daniel blew out the breath he had been holding. No one had ever disobeyed his mother and it was plainly going to be a huge war of wills between Abigail and Syrie.

"I can't condone her disobeying you, Ma," he said softly, "but she may have done us some good with her checking on the claim." He paused as he gathered his thoughts.

"I see this information two ways. One, the people who murdered Pa took what they wanted and moved on. Left the area entirely. Two, they are clever and are biding their time until they feel it is safe to make a move on Pa's claim.

"I tend to favor number two.

"If it was the former, they would have taken the stallion, the mule and the rest of Pa's outfit. Also, if it was the former, how would they know Pa had gold? Even a stupid thief doesn't plan a robbery on an armed man if they don't know what the rewards are going to be.

"With the second scenario, the killers may not have planned on robbery. They may be the kind of people who like to kill other people."

At the intake of shocked breath around the table, Daniel stopped for a moment and then continued.

"I'm sorry to say there are people like that. In my criminal law courses, we studied several men who had killed lots of people. They killed simply for the joy of seeing someone die. The worst ones made sure those they killed suffered greatly before they died. Most of these men are very clever and think through their crimes thoroughly. They also have a talent for deceiving people and making people see them as they want to be seen.

"If we assume the people killed Pa just for sport and then discovered his gold, we can assume they would have seen this as an opportunity. They will also be smart enough to know to watch the claim and make sure no one else comes around to work it or to claim it. I'm thinking they can't imagine a rich claim being left idle. They are, by nature, very greedy people and they will not be able to resist working the claim at some point.

"That is why you putting in a word with the lands clerk was such a brilliant idea, Ma, as well as not working the claim. As long as they think the claim has been abandoned, they will come forward at some point and file on it. Then it will be up to us to prove they killed Pa. Just filing on the claim isn't enough proof for a court of law, but I believe it will point us to his killers."

There was a long silence around the table. Finally, Michael spoke.

"So your advice is to sit and wait?"

"Yes, until we can get more information from another source, it is what I feel we should do. One of us needs to make regular trips into Baker City and keep the pressure on the sheriff and also touch base with the lands clerk. That is something I can do, since I'm not much help on the ranch anymore."

When Syrie started to protest, Daniel held up his hand.

"It's true, Ma. I will need to be retrained in the ranch's operations. So I am the logical one to make the trip to Baker City. Besides, my backside is tough as shoe leather now, so it won't be a hardship."

"I guess it makes sense," Syrie agreed. "I would like to go over this information with Lucreta and Young Noah when they arrive to see how they feel about it. We will decide what to do as a family, but I do value your counsel, Daniel. It is sound reasoning, and it may be our best bet."

Michael spoke up next, "But how is just finding someone who files on Pa's claim going to lead us to his killers?"

"The law says a man is innocent until he is proven guilty," Daniel said. "So you are right, Michael, somebody just filing on Pa's claim won't prove they killed him. They can claim they saw the claim was abandoned and they filed on it. They will claim they had no knowledge of his death. It is going to be up to us to prove they killed Pa and that is not going to be an easy thing to do. It is possible we may not be able to ever prove who killed him. More murders go unsolved than are solved right now."

Syrie felt her eyes fill with tears and she noticed everyone at the table was deep in thought for a moment.

"So," she said, "the white man's law is unlikely to help us in our quest for justice. Is that what you are telling us, Daniel?"

"I'm telling you it is a possibility. That's all. Not for a certainty, but a possibility."

"This is something that will require input from all the family," Syrie said. "We will speak no further about this until the rest of the family has gathered here.

"If you all will excuse me, I need to have a talk with my youngest daughter. I think you can all find your own beds. Daniel, you can get quilts from the trunk in my room. You will need to make up your bed. Good night."

Syrie arose from the table and went to the door of Abigail's room. The rest of the children could see her straighten her back and raise her head as she opened the door. "Abigail, I'm ready now and we need to have a conversation about what you did." Syrie closed the door firmly.

As Syrie entered the room, she could see Abigail still maintained a defiant attitude.

"I want you to understand the consequences of what you have done," Syrie began. "I gave the order that no one go to your Pa's claim as a way of protecting the members of this family. The safety of this family is my first priority. It was always your father's first priority. Having another one of us hurt or killed by the same people who killed your Pa is something I intend to try to prevent with every ounce of my being."

"But, Ma..."

"No 'buts'. When I give an order to do something, I expect to have it obeyed no matter how anyone feels about that order. If you didn't agree with an order or if you had another idea about how something should be done, you should have come to me and we could have discussed it privately. I might not have changed my mind, and in this case I certainly would not have changed my mind, but I would have listened to your reasoning.

"Abigail, you have shamed me in front of the rest of this family."

Abigail hung her head and Syrie could tell the girl was really listening to her for the first time.

"Abigail, you may not understand this, but I do understand what you are feeling. I know how hard it is to lose someone you love and how much you need to know the reason 'why'. A part of growing up is realizing the world is not always going to give you the answers you need. Sometimes there is no 'why.' You have to rely on your faith, on your family and on your inner strength to get you through the times when there are no answers.

"I never told you this because it is still painful for me. When I was a young woman making the trek west, my first husband, Jedidiah Boone, was drowned while crossing the Snake River at Three Island Crossing. I couldn't make peace within myself that he was gone so suddenly. I couldn't get past the 'why.' And because of that I nearly lost my mind and I nearly lost your sister Theresa.

"I want you to be able to learn to live without always knowing the why and the who. I want you to be able to continue to love in spite of this loss.

"Everyone in this family, everyone who ever loved your father wants to know 'why?' And all of us are looking for ways to answer that question. All of us are trying to find out the why and the who. But you have to be prepared for the fact we may never know the answer to either of those questions.

"I am going to ask you to trust me and trust the fact I have walked down this trail before. I want you to promise me you will not go back to the claim until I decide it is safe for any of us to do so."

Abigail sat in silence for a long time before she raised her head and looked at her mother.

"I don't know if I can promise that, Ma. I am so angry right now and I need to do something to find out who killed Pa. It just isn't right that he is lying in the ground and the men who did this are out there walking around. It just isn't right!"

Syrie went over to the bed, sat down beside her little girl and hugged her, drawing Abigail's head onto her own shoulder. Abigail began to weep tears of rage and grief, sobbing with great gulping breaths. Syrie held her until the episode subsided, then gently pushed her back and looked into her tear-stained face.

"Abigail, I promise you that I and everyone else will do everything we can to find out who did this. But, I need your promise you will do as I ask."

"I promise, Ma," Abigail sniffed.

"If you have an idea you think might help in the search, then I would value your ideas. You are a smart, brave young woman and I need you as much as I need any of your brothers and sisters."

"All right, Ma. I'm sorry I disobeyed you. I won't do it again."

"That's good enough for me. Now get into bed and I'll blow out the lamp."

"Ma, could you sit with me for a while until I fall asleep? Like you used to do when I was little?"

"Sure, honey, I would be glad to do that."

Syrie sat on the edge of Abigail's bed and stroked her hair until the girl fell into a deep slumber, then she sought her own bed and thought about how they were going to find Noah's killer.

CHAPTER NINE

During the days following the murder of the miner, Dottie monitored the healing bruises on her face. As she examined her face in the mirror, she watched the bruises and the cut lip slowly heal. She especially monitored her nose to make sure Billy hadn't broken it when he had hit her. As the swelling went down, she noticed with relief that it was returning to its former shape and size. Her black eye took the longest to heal, but she had normal vision in it and the redness was disappearing. When she was sure the evidence of the struggle had disappeared, she told Billy she wanted to go into Baker City.

Billy didn't argue with Dottie. He told his bartender they would be gone for a few days to a week and asked him to watch over the bar. He made arrangements with the cook at the boarding house to watch over that establishment. He told each of them to prepare a list of items they would need for the coming weeks. Billy told everyone his wife was so unwell, that she wasn't eating and wasn't sleeping properly and he was taking her to see a doctor. Dottie wore a heavy shawl and a hat with a veil. Dottie decided a veil would be beneficial as a look in the mirror that morning certainly did not reassure her she could pass for someone who wasn't eating or sleeping. Health shone from every plane of her face. She found both the shawl and the veil uncomfortable and confining, but resigned herself to accepting both at least until they were well away from the Basin. Neither was as uncomfortable as a rope around her neck would have been.

When they were well away from other travelers, Dottie began to complain. "I hate this buckboard. By the time we get to Baker City, my back and my ass will both be black and blue!"

True to his nature, Billy smiled and joked, "Yeah, but it is such a fine ass. It looks good no matter what color it is."

"I mean it! I'm sick of this thing! I want a carriage or at least a buggy. I can't be going back and forth in this bone breaker."

"It's not like we make this trip every week," Billy tried to soothe her. "Besides if we have a buggy how are we going to bring back supplies for the boarding house and the saloon?"

"You can pay someone to haul freight for our businesses. Hell, we'll start our own freight business. We don't have to travel like this."

"I thought you wanted to save money and not throw it around and call attention to ourselves."

"I think as owners of a successful boarding house and saloon, we could be expected to have a few of the finer things in life, like a buggy. Ouch! Are you trying to hit every rut in this cow path they call a road?"

Billy had thought an outing away from the gold fields would have meant Dottie would be in a good humor, but Dottie was in one of her moods and he didn't want to be the one to push her over the edge. People had died who had pushed Dottie too far. He decided agreeing with her was the best course. After all, they had been together more than five years and he had managed to avoid her worst temper, so far.

"Yes, you are right, of course. We will get a buggy while we are in Baker City and I will hire someone to drive the buckboard and the supplies back to the Basin."

"And I want a pair of fine horses to pull it."

"Okay. What color do you want, blacks or bays?

"Neither. Everyone has blacks or bays. I want something flashy, like palominos. Oh, I know. I want horses that look like the one that first miner had. You know, the stallion with all the spots! I really liked that horse."

"Okay, I'll ask around and see if anyone has any like him. I'll do whatever you want, Dottie, you know that."

Dottie sniffed at him as she unwound the shawl and took of the hat and the veil.

"God, that feels better. I thought I was going to suffocate. I don't know how women can wear this stuff all the time. I need to feel the sun and the breeze on me. If I could, I'd take off this blouse as well, but I couldn't get it back on in time if we met someone."

To Billy's relief, the worst of Dottie's mood seemed to have passed and she simply stared at the passing countryside. Dottie hated this scenery. Even with the autumn coat of reds and golds, mixed with the last of the green along the creek bottom, Dottie couldn't see the beauty. She longed for the verdant vistas of the South. She missed the moss hanging from the live oaks. The riot of color from the massed plantings and the topiaries in front of the fine houses in New Orleans. The country they were driving through was all browns and greys, especially along the trails where the fine dust covered everything with a grey powder. It was only in the spring that the hillsides were green and dotted with wildflowers. To her mind, this was nearly the ugliest country she had ever seen, maybe second only to the monotony of the flat plains country they had crossed to get here. She wanted to go home.

At midday they stopped to eat a picnic lunch the boarding house cook had packed for them. They didn't stop for long, eating a quick bite, stretching their legs, watering and resting the horses. They would have to make a camp for the night before continuing on into Baker City. Billy wanted to get in as many miles as they could in before nightfall. Dottie was never happy about sleeping anywhere except her own bed, and she hated sleeping on the ground. In order to make tomorrow at least tolerable, Billy had rolled up a feather bed with quilts and he would make her a bed in the box of the buckboard. He would sleep under the buckboard and he would cook all the meals while they were on the road. It was a pattern they had established since they were forced to flee New Orleans. It was another way to avoid Dottie's temper and black moods and to stay alive.

By the time they reached Baker City, Dottie's mood had improved greatly and she was looking forward to a few nights in a hotel, fine meals, new clothes and a new buggy. They drove to the livery stable first and had the team fed and bedded down. They told the livery boy they would probably be in town for a couple of days and they would be sending parcels to be stored in the buckboard. Next they checked into the Western Hotel on Front Street, where Dottie immediately called for a bath and for a ladies' maid to attend to her attire and her hair.

Upon being told there were no ladies maids in Baker City, Dottie nearly flew into a rage, but Billy gripped her arm hard and said, "That will be fine. Can you please just prepare a bath for my wife in our room and if you have any bath salts available it would be very nice. If you have none, could I trouble you to send someone to the nearest pharmacy or store and buy some for us? Thank you so much." He led Dottie firmly out of the lobby and down the street as he said between his teeth, "This isn't New Orleans! What the hell were you thinking? That is no way to behave if you don't want to get noticed."

"I don't care! I want a bath and I want someone to fix my hair! I want a new dress and I want to go dancing."

"Have you lost your mind completely? Dottie snap out of it. This isn't New Orleans!" He ducked into an alley with her where he shook her hard. "Dottie!"

"Oh hell! Can't I even have a good time after all I have put up with living in that God-forsaken gold camp? I just want to be at a ball and go dancing again. I want a fancy ball gown again. I want a maid to do my hair and attend to me. Why is that so much to ask?"

She laid her head against his chest and said plaintively, "Billy, why can't we just go back to New Orleans?" When she raised her head to look at him, he was surprised to see her eyes glistening with unshed tears.

"Honey, you know why. As long as that Creole planter is alive, our lives are worth nothing in New Orleans. He will hunt us down and shoot us both for what you did to his son. For what I helped you to hide. You know that. We just have to wait a little longer. You know your aunt will write to us as soon as it is safe to come back. You just have to be patient a little while longer. Soon we'll get the letter and we'll have enough to go back to New Orleans in style. Just like you want.

"Now, let's go see about getting you a new dress. You can have a bath, I'll help you change into a new dress and we'll go get ourselves a fine meal. Okay?"

"Okay. You take such good care of me Billy."

"I'll always take care of you."

They spent the next hour shopping for a new dress for Dottie, though for the life of him, Billy couldn't figure out why it took so long. There was only one store in town selling ladies' ready-to-wear clothing and they didn't have a very large selection, but Dottie was enjoying herself, so he waited patiently as she tried on every dress they had. She also wanted a hat to match the new dress, so more time was spent trying hats on. When Billy thought he might just be about free of the store, Dottie wanted a new dressing gown, so she had to try on every one of those. When they returned to the hotel, the clerk told them he hadn't been able to get away to go to the store and get the bath salts. Feeling Dottie tense up, Billy smiled and told him it was okay and to go ahead and take the water up and start filling the tub. Billy would find some bath salts. He sent Dottie on up to their room and he went to the general store to find bath salts.

When he got back to their room, he found Dottie already in the tub with a bottle of good Kentucky whiskey. Her mood was definitely sunnier and he decided whatever they had spent today, it had been worth it. He handed her the envelope of bath salts and poured himself some of the whiskey.

"Where did you get the whiskey?" he asked.

"Oh I just told the boy who brought u the water that you would be most appreciative if you could have a small glass and a bottle sent up before we came down for dinner. So he delivered it to the room. I tipped him for bringing it up since I can't be seen buying liquor. Now where are those bath salts? My backside is bruised.

"Don't forget you promised me a buggy."

"I haven't forgotten. We'll ask at the livery stable tomorrow to see if they might know of one that's for sale. By the way, I saw a shop that sells tinware and stoves while I was out. I was thinking about buying a new cook stove for the boarding house and maybe a little parlor stove for our quarters. What do you think?"

"I think it's a good idea. I've never liked fireplaces. They don't really keep a house warm and winter is coming. I think a parlor stove would be nice. And I'm sure cook would appreciate a real cook stove. I might also want to look at some of the tinware for the boarding house."

"All right. As soon as you finish your bath and get dressed, we'll go down to the dining room and have dinner. Then we'll get a good night's sleep and spend tomorrow shopping. How does that sound?"

"Sounds lovely. Any day out of that gold camp and being in what is close to a town is fine by me."

After a leisurely breakfast the next morning, Dottie and Billy walked to the tinware store. Dottie bought service for 20 of enamelware plates and cups, plus service for 30 of silverware for the boarding house, plus lantern holders for their quarters. They next looked at the stoves in stock. Dottie couldn't find any she liked for their quarters or the boarding house. The proprietor helped them pick out one they liked from his catalog and promised he would have it delivered. Hopefully before spring.

"Depends on how bad the snow is this year, both coming over the Cascades and getting into the Basin. That road can get pretty bad going into there and those stoves are going to be heavy."

"Well, we know you will do the best you can," Billy assured the man. "Whenever you can get them to us, we'd appreciate it."

They paid for their purchases and left the store walking along and window shopping in several of the stores. They went into a couple and bought a few small things and then went to the general store to do the bulk of their shopping for the bar and the boarding house. Rather than carry the parcels, they had them all delivered to the livery. Billy was pleasantly surprised Dottie didn't spend the morning complaining about how little variety there was in the stores. She had loved shopping in New Orleans and he was sure she missed it.

"Shall we go to the livery and see about getting you a buggy," Billy asked her.

"Let's get lunch first. I'm starving."

"That's my girl. Never late for a meal," Billy laughed and took her hand as they went to find a restaurant for lunch.

After lunch, which Dottie declared was "okay, but could have used a good red wine" they walked to the livery stable. They first checked on their team and then went in search of one of the owners. They found John Fuhrman in the livery office. He was able to show them two buggys, one of which was in need of repair and one which was smaller, but could be relied upon to get them back and forth to the Basin.

"Of course, it would be more serviceable if we had skis for it, but, unfortunately, I don't know of any rigs in the area available for sale with skis," lamented the livery owner.

After looking at Dottie and ascertaining that she would be satisfied with the smaller buggy, Billy said, "I think it will work fine. We'd like to buy it today if we could. My wife has a delicate constitution and I would like to make the trips to and from our home as comfortable for her as possible.

"We would also like to hire someone to drive our wagon back to the Basin so we can get our supplies there. Would you know of anyone who might be available?"

"There are a couple of young fellas around who are usually looking to pick up a few dollars. I am sure I can hook you nice folks up with one of them."

"What about a matched team to pull our buggy?" asked Dottie in her best, soft Southern voice. "I do admire a fine looking team with a buggy."

"Of course! A fine lady, needs a fine team to pull her buggy," agreed Mr. Fuhrman.

"I would prefer a team which would make an impression," Dottie slanted a sideways glance at the owner, "if you know what I mean."

"I do. Yes I do know exactly what you mean! I have as fine a pair of matched blacks as you will find anywhere in the area. They are right over there in those stalls," he said as walked down the row of box stalls along the edge of the livery and pointed out a pair of blacks with matching stars.

"I prefer something a bit brighter colored," said Dottie. "On our way from the East we saw a most unusual horse. It was dark brown or black on the front end and had spots on a white field on the haunches. A most unusual animal."

"Ah, yes. You were indeed fortunate to see one of the Nez Perce war horses. They are rarely seen outside of the Pacific Northwest. Mostly only the Nez Perce breed them. In fact, I only know of one rancher here abouts who raises them. They also raise Cayuse horses. The ranch is the Rafter S. The ranch is up along Dixie Creek on the way to Rye Valley. It is owned by the Hickmans. Lovely family the Hickmans."

"Do you know if they sell matched pairs for driving?" asked Billy.

"No, I don't think so. They sell mostly riding horses or cow ponies, that sort of thing and they are very well trained. I suppose a body could ask them to train a pair of driving horses, but I don't think that will get you what you want."

"Why not?" asked Billy.

"Because of the very nature of the Nez Perce horses, you really can't have a matched pair. Part of what makes them so special is each one is unique. And they will often change their color patterns somewhat over the course of their lives. Becoming whiter as they age.

"I can ask around and see if anyone has a pair of palominos. Or would a set of greys be more to your liking? Those are a more common color. Or perhaps dapples? I know a man on the west side who has quite a large group of driving horses. I can send word to him and find out if he has anything you might like," the livery owner said, not wanting a sale to slip away from him.

"Maybe we can do something like that later. I don't want to have to subject my wife to the return trip to Mormon Basin in the wagon, so we will take the blacks and the buggy," said Billy. "We'll pick it up tomorrow. Would you please contact some of those men who you said might be willing to drive the buckboard for us? They can ask for us at the Western Hotel.

"Thank you for your help. Good Bye." Billy took Dottie's arm and led her away from the livery.

When they were out of ear shot of the owner, Dottie jerked her arm free from Billy's grasp and stamped one small foot.

"I don't want a black team! I want a flashy team. I want something people will talk about when they see it."

Billy pushed back his hat and stared at Dottie.

"I don't understand you. One minute you are wanting to do everything you can to draw attention to us, throwing money around, buying flashy horses and the next you are telling me we need to be careful and not have people notice us. I can't do both at the same time, Dottie."

"I want it to be like it was in New Orleans. I want fine clothes, a fine house. I want fun again."

"Dottie, having 'fun' in New Orleans is what got us out here to begin with. And have you forgotten we have killed two men since we arrived? I don't think anyone knows enough to press charges, but if you want to go home with $50,000, we have to be careful, save our money, grow our businesses. You know, be solid citizens. Then when your aunt writes to us, we can sell out, leave and go back to New Orleans. The planter is the only one who knows we killed his son. If anyone else knew they would be looking for us no matter where we went."

"I don't like waiting," Dottie pouted.

Billy took her hand.

"I know you're not good at being patient, but we have to be patient for a little longer. How about we go back to the hotel, I'll get us a bottle of the best brandy they have, we'll rest a little while, then we will go out and have a fine dinner. How does that sound?"

"Okay, but I wish there was a dance or something we could go to," Dottie said as she continued to draw circles in the dust with the toe of her shoe.

"Next time there is a dance in Mormon Basin or Rye Valley or Baker City, I promise we will go. Okay?"

"Can I have a new dress?"

"We'll stop at the ladies shop on the way to the hotel and we will find out if there is a seamstress in this town. If there is, we'll get you fine material and have two of the best dresses made for you."

"Three. I want three dresses."

"Okay, three dresses. You can pick out the material at the store and if you don't find something you like, we'll order it."

Dottie clapped her hands.

"Oh, yes! I want a red one and a blue one and a green - no a yellow one!" Her eyes sparkled with excitement. "All made out of heavy shantung silk! No, I need one for summer. I'll have the yellow one made out of silk and organza."

She took Billy's arm again and continued to chatter happily about fabric and notions all the way back to the hotel. Billy understood little of what she was talking about, but she was happy and had stopped brooding, so he was happy as well.

The next morning after arranging for a driver for the wagon, Dottie and Billy went to find where they could file the paperwork on their "new" claim. When they entered the clerk's office, it was apparent he was a very busy man and they had to wait their turn. As they did so, they listened to the conversations around them making mental notes about where claims were being filed, who was selling claims and who were simply abandoning claims and moving on. When it was their turn, they approached the counter and Billy spoke to the clerk. .

"My name is William Lattimer and this is my wife Dorothea," he said as an introduction.

"Oh yes. Mr. Lattimer. I recognize your name from some transfers we have recently handled in this office. Nice to make your acquaintance. And yours, Mrs. Lattimer. My name is E. C. Brainard. How can I help you today?"

"We have recently become aware of a claim we think might be abandoned. It is a ways out from the diggings and we would be interested in knowing the status of ownership."

"Can you show me on this map, the location in question?" asked Mr. Brainard as he spread a hand-drawn map on the counter.

"I believe it is right here, from the information we have been given. We have not actually been out to the site ourselves. We are investors, not miners."

"I do believe there is an active claim in the general area. And you are right, it is a ways away from the main activity in the basin. Give me a few minutes to check my records will you? It may take me a bit. Would you believe we have processed over 1,000 claims through this office?," he paused. " Are you staying here in town? I can arrange to get word to you later on today rather than have you sit here and wait."

"Yes, we are staying at the Western Hotel on Front. You know the place?"

"Of course. I will send a runner over to you when I have the information you require. Good day to you both."

Billy and Dottie left the office and walked back to their hotel. They began to pack their belongings in preparation for the trip back into Mormon Basin. Billy requested a meal be prepared for their trip back. He walked to the livery to check again on their goods and make sure all was securely lashed down. Next he checked to see the bedroll was packed so it would be easily retrievable from the buckboard. He did everything he could for Dottie's convenience and comfort. Billy drove their new team and buggy back to the hotel, after instructing the driver they had hired to wait at the livery. He found Dottie waiting in the hotel's dining room, drinking tea with their bags stacked by the front door.

"I got tired of waiting in that stuffy little room," she complained. "I got the desk clerk to bring down the bags and I just decided I wanted some tea.

"Do you have your flask?" she asked looking around.

"Yes, in my inside jacket pocket where it always is."

"As soon as the waitress isn't looking, splash some into my cup. I am dying for a drink."

Billy did as she requested and settled down across from her to wait for the runner from the clerk's office.

"What is taking so long?" asked Dottie.

"You heard him say he has had over 1,000 claims filed through his office. It may just take some time to be sure he has the right one."

"I want to get on the road. I don't trust those girls without me watching over them. I need to get a house built and hire a madam. I am tired of dealing with those worthless slatterns."

"Dottie keep your voice down. People may hear." Billy tried to shush her, but he was afraid she was just going to get wound up. "Here drink some more of your 'tea.' It will make you feel better," he said as he splashed some more bourbon into her cup.

"Okay. But I really mean it. We need to build a house and hire a madam to watch over it."

"We'll talk more on the way back to the Basin, because I don't think this is the ideal place to discuss our prostitution business."

They continued drinking in silence until the runner from the clerk's office came into the dining room asking for Mr. Lattimer.

"Here, boy," said Billy. "I'm Mr. Lattimer."

"I have a note for you from Mr. Brainard," said the boy as he held out an envelope.

"Thank you, son," said Billy as he handed the boy two bits and took the envelope. The boy gaped at the money and disappeared before Billy could possibly change his mind.

"What does it say," demanded Dottie.

"Just a minute and I'll let you read it for yourself."

Before Billy could finish reading the letter, Dottie snatched the letter away and began to read:

Mr. and Mrs. Lattimer,

I have found the parcel you inquired about in our records. It does have a recorded owner attached to the property. I have also found the registered owner is a partnership.

As you have indicated that the claim appears to have been abandoned, I will make further inquiries about the partnership. If it can be determined that the claim has indeed been abandoned, then I will contact you in Mormon Basin and inform you of same. If the claim is still an active one, then I also will let you know that information.
Sincerely,
E. C. Bainard

"Now what the hell does that mean?" said Dottie as she handed the letter back to Billy. "Can we start working the claim or not?"

Billy re-read the letter and said, "I think it means we have to wait to be able to work the claim legally. We will just have to be patient. We don't want to get arrested for claim jumping. It could lead to all kinds of questions we don't want to answer."

"But if that claim is as rich as we think it is, what is going to happen to all that gold?"

"It will probably just lay there like it has for hundreds of years."

"I don't like it," fumed Dottie.

"I'm sorry. But I don't want to get the sheriff involved in our lives," soothed Billy. "We can be patient just a little longer. Besides, winter is going to be here soon and all the mining will slow down once snow flies, especially if the water freezes."

"I want that claim and I want it before spring comes," Dottie said as she shot a warning glance at Billy. "And you had better make it happen."

"Okay, Dottie. I will do whatever it takes. Now shall we load up our parcels into your new buggy? I would like to make some time today so we can get home early tomorrow. I am anxious about our businesses and want to get back."

Dottie seemed instantly mollified and helped Billy pack out their things and stow them in the buggy. As she settled herself on the padded seat, she said, "I want to go out to that ranch, the one the livery owner talked about. I want to get some of those Nez Perce horses to pull this buggy. You can sell or trade these nags once I get what I want."

"It may have to wait until spring," Billy warned. "We have a lot to do to get ready for winter. The Basin can get pretty cold and I want to make sure we have everything we need before snow flies."

"I guess that's okay," said Dottie and then she paused. "I wonder what snow is like?"

CHAPTER TEN

The rest of the family didn't come the next day, or the next, but Syrie wasn't worried. They had their own ranch to run and it wasn't always possible to drop everything and leave. Animals had to be tended and arrangements had to be made for that as well as the continuation of the rest of the chores like building fences, cutting and stacking hay, harvesting the garden, milking the cows and all the other things required on a ranch.

The buckboard pulled into the compound on the afternoon of the third day after Daniel's arrival. Young Noah held the baby while Lucreta stepped down, handed her the baby and started unloading kids from the back. Lucreta wrapped a sleeping young Albert in her shawl. All the girls made a beeline for Syrie for hugs. Lucreta hung back a moment helping Young Noah get something from the back of the wagon.

"My, it is so good to see all you girls!" Syrie said as she hugged each one in turn. "Now how many of you are hungry?"

After receiving four giggling affirmations that they were indeed hungry, Syrie ushered them into the kitchen with instructions to find Painted Pony and ask her for a cup of milk and one cookie each. "Don't be asking for more than one. You'll spoil your supper."

Syrie stepped off the porch and went to the wagon.

"What are you two doing?" she asked as Young Noah lifted a box out of the back of the wagon and one of their border collie bitches jumped down. Syrie squealed with delight.

"Puppies! You have puppies!"

"We promised you pick of the litter, Ma, so here they are. This is Molly and her six babies. The sire is Black Watch Captain."

"They are going to be great working dogs, and Molly has an excellent temperament for a companion dog, so I think they will be able to go either way," Young Noah said as he held out the box of squirming puppies for Syrie to look at. "Shall we take them in the house?"

"Oh my, yes! I want to get a closer look at all of them," Syrie exclaimed. "It will be so good to have a dog in the house again. I have really missed that."

"Ma, we have news from Mr. Brainard, the clerk in Baker City about Pa's claim," Lucreta said as she touched Syrie's arm. "We fed the boy who delivered the message and gave him a bed for the night. I sent a silver dollar back for the messenger and a $20 gold piece for the clerk. I'm hoping it will keep the news coming.

"And the boy brought out our mail and yours. I think there is a letter in there from that old friend of Pa's, Mr. Meek. The handwriting is awful, but I think the return address is Hillsboro, Oregon."

"You did right," Syrie said hugging her carefully so as to not jostle the sleeping little boy. "We'll talk after the little ones are in bed. You go on into the house and settle in. I'm going to go find one of the hands and have him go get Theresa. Then we'll start some supper."

After a pleasant supper with everyone getting caught up on family and ranch business and Daniel talking again about his years at Harvard, the children were put into their night clothes and readied for bed.

Syrie spent some time on the floor with the puppies as Lucreta and Theresa got the children ready for bed. Syrie took the puppies out of their box and set them on the floor, watching them carefully. All the pups immediately started to investigate this new place. Molly, their mother, watched them closely from across the room for a minute and then laid down to sleep. Syrie didn't call the puppies, didn't talk to them and none of the other family members did either. After a bit the pups started back towards their mother, except one. This one was more curious about everything and kept on exploring. When he came across Syrie's skirt, he stopped and looked up at her, tipping his head to one side as if saying, "What are you?" Syrie held out her hand. The pup sniffed it and crawled into Syrie's lap and licked her hand. Then he went sound asleep.

"Looks like you found your dog, Ma," said Daniel. "I remember you doing that when you chose Major all those years ago when Mr. Gregor brought the first litter of pups to us. I hope this one is as good as old Major."

Syrie stroked the sleeping pup who merely yawned and settled himself more comfortably on Syrie's lap.

"Mr. Gregor is the one who taught me to do this. He always believed, and I do too, that letting animals choose their humans is always the best way. Somewhat with horses, but especially with dogs because they spend so much time with us. This little boy will be a great dog and he will be a wonderful friend, hopefully for many years."

"What are you going to name him?" asked Abigail.

"I don't know. Do any of you have any ideas?"

"Probably should be something military since his daddy is Black Watch Captain," said Benjamin.

"What about Sarge? Short for Sergeant," put in Michael.

Syrie picked the pup up and held him so she could look into his sleepy face. "How do you feel about Sarge," she asked the pup. The pup yawned hugely and licked her nose. "I'll take that as a yes" Syrie laughed.

When Theresa and Lucreta came back from settling the children, the family once again gathered around the table. Syrie settled Sarge in her lap, took out the letter with the Hillsboro address, and began to read.

My dearest Mrs. Hickman,

It is with great sadness that I learned of the murder of my old friend, Noah. You have my deepest sympathy. Please pass this affection on to your children as well.

George tells me you are desirous of my help in finding and arresting those responsible for this reprehensible act. Unfortunately, my current circumstances do not allow me to come to your aid personally.

As you know, I am no longer a U.S. Marshal, but that does not mean that I have no friends or influence among the ranks of the august company. I am thinking in particular of a young man who is well skilled in apprehending evil people despite his young age. He is firm of conviction, upright in his character, brave of spirit and diligent in his duties. He has agreed to come to your aid in this time of great sadness. His name is Thomas Finley Hart. He will be leaving here as soon as he can attend to his current duties. He is prepared to stay in your locale until such time as the murderers are found and convicted or until it is clear there is no hope of solving this crime.

George has briefed Mr. Hart on the tracks and such he found, but any further information you have gathered would also be most helpful in his inquiries.

Again, my deepest sympathies on the loss of your husband. Please be assured that I am grieving along with you and your family.
Sincerely,
Joseph Meek

Syrie laid the letter on the table and looked around at the group. Benjamin was the first to speak.

"If he left right away he could be here any day."

"It may have taken him some time, several weeks perhaps, to wrap up his current work," Daniel pointed out. "We have no way of knowing unless we hear from Mr. Hart personally. Either way, it is good that we have someone coming who knows how to investigate a crime. I look forward to meeting him."

"I wish we had more information to give him," said Theresa. "We really don't know any more than George would have told Mr. Meek."

"I don't agree," said Syrie. "Thanks to Abigail, we know no one has worked the claim. That could be an important piece of information for him. None of us are trained investigators. Daniel comes closest with his law learning, but we don't know what is useful information and what isn't."

Lucreta reminded her mother about the letter from Mr. Brainard saying, "Maybe there is something more in his message."

"Oh, of course," Syrie said. "I forgot about it."

Mrs. Hickman,

Per your request, I am writing to you to let you know I have received an inquiry about filing on the claim belonging to you and your late husband.

A couple, fairly new to the area from my understanding, came into the office and requested to file a claim to your section of the stream. I was able to tell them the claim had not yet been officially declared abandoned because, of course, you still own it. I was able to delay them a bit in their inquiry, but I will have to give them an answer soon.

I took the liberty of making some quiet inquiries around town about this couple. As I said, they appear to be fairly new to the Mormon Basin and now own businesses there including a saloon and a boarding house. There have also been numerous claims transferred from the original owner to this couple over the last several months, though this is the first time I have ever met either in person.

The couple are named William and Dorothea Lattimer.

My best regards,
E. C. Brainard

"A man and a woman," exclaimed Theresa. "I don't know what to say. We were expecting a couple of men."

"Perhaps, they are acting for someone else," said Michael.

"Yeah, they could have been paid to act for someone, maybe from their boarding house," suggested Benjamin.

Young Noah shook his head and said, "I don't think this helps us at all. We will certainly show this letter to Mr. Finley, but this leads in a far different direction than the prints at the claim."

"We need to let Mr. Thomas Finley Hart form his own conclusions," said Syrie.

"Yes, Ma, I agree. But I think we need to talk about what happens if Mr. Hart can't make an arrest in this matter, or what happens if he does arrest someone and those people aren't convicted," said Daniel. "That is going to be a hard thing for this family to accept."

He turned to Lucreta and Young Noah. "I was telling Ma and the others, that just arresting someone doesn't mean they will hang for killing Pa. The charges have to go through the courts and it must be proven they are the ones who did it. It is possible Mr. Hart may arrest the murderers, but it is also possible they might never pay for killing Pa."

"Ma, is this true?" asked Abigail with fierce indignation on her face. "Those men might walk away free?"

"According to what Daniel knows about the law, yes, it is possible. I am trying not to let that influence my belief that whoever did this will pay, but it is something we need to be prepared to face."

"Ma, we can't let that happen!" Abigail burst into tears and ran to put her head in her mother's lap, awakening the sleeping Sarge. Syrie gently stroked her hair and murmured to her until she felt strong enough to take her place again at the table.

Young Noah cleared his throat and after a second started to speak very deliberately.

"There is not just the white man's justice in this," he said looking at Abigail. "There is also my people's justice. Do not forget Noah was one of us. Our ways do not depend on sheriffs and courts. Your father will be avenged, little sister."

"Yes he was one of your people and he was very proud of being a Cayuse," Syrie said.

Then she sighed before she continued. "I don't know if I should tell you all this or not. Ten Crows and I spoke of white justice and Cayuse justice before he left. He and I agreed if the white man's justice won't avenge Noah, then he would seek justice in his own way.

"I fear for him to do that, mostly for his own safety. Ten Crows deserves to have a chance to see our grandchildren grow up. I don't want him to sacrifice that chance to avenge Noah. I don't think Noah would have wanted it either.

"But, it isn't my decision. It is his."

"I always write to him," said Young Noah. "He is always anxious to know what progress we have made. I will write to him and let him know the young man from the Marshal's office will be coming soon. I think he will want to meet this young man. I will also let him know about the claim."

"You know your father is welcome here at any time, but he is well known on the reservation. If he leaves it will be noticed. If the Indian Agent's people come looking for him, this ranch and yours will be the first places they will search," noted Syrie.

"They don't know about my place," interjected Theresa. "It is off the main road to Rye Valley and even if they go past my place on the way to the Basin, they likely won't see it. Ten Crows could stay there and still be able to keep up with what is going on with the investigation."

"I will write to him, but I won't mention your place. I'm not sure how private his mail is. It could be read by others. If he decides to leave the reservation, we can talk to him about staying at your place. You don't mind moving back home?"

"No. I enjoy my little cabin, but my old bed is still serviceable," she laughed. "Though I don't know how Abigail feels about sharing a room with me again," she said as she reached over and pulled Abigail's long, blonde braid playfully.

"I guess I can get used to it again," Abigail said as she rolled her eyes.

The Crow family stayed at the Rafter S for two more days. Young Noah helped out with some of the fall chores and got re-acquainted with Daniel. As a family they made determinations about pairings for the coming breeding season for the cattle and horses. The stud books were updated and decisions about which animals to sell and which colts would be castrated were also made. Lucreta took the opportunity to visit with the other women in the household as her ranch was far from other women. She missed the simple pleasures of woman talk and sitting together while churning or quilting. Arrangements were made for Daniel and a couple of hands to go to the Rafter L, Young Noah and Lucreta's ranch, to help with building projects and fall chores there. The group would also deliver and bring back the animals they had decided to swap. It was a system which had worked well for both families since the marriage of Lucreta and Young Noah. Once Theresa had established her own bloodlines with her own stock, they would rotate the breeding around among the three ranches.

On the Crows' last day at the Rafter S, Theresa, Daniel, Syrie and Young Noah rode out to look over the animals as they made their final selections and double checked their decisions. Daniel rode the little gruella he had bought in Cheyenne, while Noah rode one of the horses from the ranch's remuda as did Theresa. Syrie rode the son of the filly Noah had given her so many years before. Both the women wore buckskin breeches and rode astride.

"It is so nice to see all the animals looking fit and fat from the summer," Syrie said she looked over the horse herd with a practiced gaze. "We are going to have a fine crop of yearlings next spring looks like.

"Oh, there is Noah's stallion. Daniel, I don't think you have seen him. Isn't he magnificent? He always throws such good color. Even on our solid-colored mares." She exclaimed as they rode closer to the stallion.

Daniel whistled and said, "Wow! He is even more impressive than Pa's old horse. He is incredible."

"Yes, he is. He has given us many fine colts and, hopefully, will do so for many more years" noted Theresa. "Noah do you want to take him back to your place this time?"

"No, I don't think so. I have a young painted stud I got this spring. I'd like to try him out and if I take this guy back to my place, he'll trounce the young stud."

"I sure wish he could talk," lamented Syrie. "He saw everything that happened that day and he knows who killed his friend."

"According to my father," Young Noah said, "that horse will never forget those men. He said a warrior's horse, a horse like this one, has abilities beyond the normal horse."

"Too bad we can't get him to testify in a courtroom," said Daniel. "But I doubt we could get a judge to accept the word of a horse."

"I, for one, would believe an animal before I would believe some people," avowed Syrie. "They are a lot more truthful and they have no allegiance to anything other than themselves and the people they love." She rode up beside the stallion, leaned over and scratched his ears.

"I believe there are more ways to the truth than the white man's laws and courts," said Young Noah. "I believe the spirits and the animals know a deeper and older truth."

"As an almost lawyer, I can't agree with that; but as Noah's son and as a friend of the Cayuse, I can believe it completely."

"Unfortunately, we will probably never have this horse and your Pa's murderers within a mile of each other," said Syrie, "let alone be in a position to have this horse testify and tell us what he saw.

"Daniel and Noah," Syrie said as they continue their ride, "Benjamin and I have been talking about breeding some pure bred drafts. We could keep some drafts-cross mares as well. We have been selling most of the draft crosses we have gotten in trade. What do you think about getting a stallion and some mares to breed for full-blood drafts? Benjamin and I think it is a good idea.

"Noah, have you heard about any good heavy horses in the area?"

"No, none of the heavy type for brood stock have been for sale. Just geldings already broke to pull. Those mostly get sold to folks going on to the West as their horses are spent. Some are going up to the diggings for dragging fresnos and also to the new sawmill for hauling logs and lumber."

"I'll write to Solomon and Vesta and see if they have any of the Shires they breed they might be willing to sell. They'll have some mighty fine stock by now, I'll wager. Their foundation stock was the best in New Hampshire. I'll get a letter done today and you can take it with you, if you would," she said to Young Noah. "I'd appreciate it. Maybe we could get some stock here by spring. I'm thinking it's too late this year to be crossing the Cascades with a bunch of stock."

"Ma, I was thinking of going on into Baker City before I come back here. I want to talk to Mr. Brainard in person. As long as I'm going to town, I could take Benjamin or one of the hands and we could drive any horses you might want to sell. I'd also like to talk to any lawyers who might be in Baker City."

"I think that's a good idea," put in Young Noah. "I have a few animals I could throw in to be sold as well."

"Okay, good idea. Might as well get the most out of a long trip," Syrie agreed.

"Well, we'd better be getting back. It's getting late and Theresa and I need to change before supper. At least I do," Syrie amended as she caught the dark look on her daughter's face.

Syrie waved good bye to Young Noah, Lucreta and the children the next morning. She knew they needed to get home and sort the horses they would be sending to Baker City. She dearly wished Lucreta could have stayed for another day or two, but Syrie understood that with the last of the garden to preserve and a home and business to run, Lucreta had a multitude of chores waiting for her. Syrie went inside to her desk in the parlor to write the letter to the Jensens about the horses they hoped to buy so the letter would be ready for mailing. Benjamin or Daniel could pick up a bank draft in Baker City and enclose it with the letter. She made a mental note to send enough gold with them to cover everything.

As Syrie prepared to send Daniel and Benjamin into Baker City on the following morning, she made a shopping list for the young men to take with them. This could be the last time any of them would be able to get into Baker City before spring, so she had to be thorough in her list making. After working with Painted Pony, Horace, and the others in her household, she had what she thought was an exhaustive list.

"Daniel, I'm afraid I am going to have to ask you and Benjamin to take a wagon with you. We need more supplies than you can bring home on pack horses."

"No problem, Ma. I'm sure one of us can handle a team," he teased as he gave her a quick hug. "Pretty big list?"

"Yes, I want to be prepared. You remember how bad the winters can get around here. I know we can get to Fort Boise easier in the winter than we can get to Baker City, but both are a good ways away, especially in bad weather. And I don't know how the situation with the Paiutes is right now. They have caused a good deal of problems for travelers in the past. So, as long as the weather is good and you have several riders going with you, I'd like to take advantage of that."

"You always were one for being prepared," Daniel grinned at his mom.

"You live two days away from the general store for 20 years and see how prepared you learn to be, young man," she teased back. "Maybe it is an attribute you should consider in your choice of a wife, someday."

"A wife and marriage is a long time away in my future, ma."

"Love doesn't have to follow a timetable young man. You remember that. I wasn't looking for love when I found your father. You may have the same thing happen to you."

"If it can get me a wife as good as you, I'll get married tomorrow!"

"Go on. Get out of here. Don't you have work to do?" said Painted Pony to Daniel as she watched the two of them tease each other. "It is good you are going to be a lawyer, because you sure have a way with flowery words."

"I'm on my way, ma'am! Always at your service," Daniel said in his best southern drawl as he did an elaborate bow to the two women and was out the door of the kitchen.

"I didn't realize how much I had missed that boy until he came home," sighed Syrie. "And he is all grown up and going to be gone again soon I'm afraid."

"He may settle close to here," offered Painted Pony.

"And he may go back to the East," said Syrie. "His choice and I won't stand in his way whichever he chooses.

Daniel found Benjamin down at the corrals and called out to him, "Change in plans."

"What now?"

"Ma's list got big and we have to take the buckboard."

"I figured as much. Already got a team picked out for the trip. How many hands do you think we'll need to drive 25 head to Baker City?"

"I didn't think we were taking 25 head."

"Well, we'll actually have more by the time we get the horses from the Rafter L."

"I would guess we will need at least two outriders, one to ride drag and one person to drive the wagon, so four total. Counting you and me, we'll need two additional riders. Who do you want to take?"

Benjamin thought a minute and said, "I'll go ask Horace who he needs the least to finish up the winter chores. We'll let him decide."

As Daniel continued to talk over the trip with Horace and Benjamin, he realized how much he had missed the simple life the ranch offered. Everything was laid out and easily quantified as to when it was done and what the next step would need to be. Unlike the law with its endless twists and turns, what ifs and random rulings by judges, life on the ranch offered few surprises. He found himself wondering how much he would miss the mental challenges of the life of an attorney. Then he wondered again if he would be an attorney. Had he passed the bar? Maybe a letter would be waiting in Baker City for him. He found he was suddenly anxious to know if he had passed. The events of the last few weeks had pushed the question far back into his mind. Now he wanted to know the answer.

"Good. That's settled," Benjamin said. Daniel started paying attention to the conversation again. "You sure those boys aren't going to get to town, get drunk and wind up in jail?"

"No," Horace said, "I didn't say that at all. They may very well get drunk and they may spend a night in jail, but they have enough wages due them to bail themselves out. I said they aren't in the habit of overdrinking, but they are both young and neither has been to town in a long time. They are good boys, but they are boys and will act like it."

Benjamin and Daniel both laughed.

"Well, if they do get thrown in jail, it will save us the price of a hotel room," Daniel said. "And they are paying for their own hookers."

"Shhh! Don't let Ma hear you talk about hookers. She'll have a fit if she finds out any of us have been with one of them," Benjamin warned. "You and I had better steer clear of the ladies. I don't know about you, but I could never get away with lying to Ma. Or Pa for that matter. I swear those two could see clean through me."

"I never could do it either. She would always catch me at it, even the littlest fib, so I just gave up when I was about 5 years old," admitted Daniel. "Some lawyer I'm going to make if I can't maintain some ability to at least stretch the truth."

Benjamin slapped him on the back as they started back across the compound to the house.

"Maybe the judges will be easier than Ma," he laughed.

CHAPTER ELEVEN

Syrie and Painted Pony were up well before dawn to prepare breakfast for the men who would be driving the horses into Baker City. Horace and the two additional hands accompanied the men in for breakfast as they would be bringing brood stock back from the Rafter L. They all believed in safety in numbers when traveling away from the home ranches.

The horses had been sorted and corralled the night before so the men would only have to throw their saddle bags or grips into the buckboard. After they had eaten they would be ready to start north. The women had also prepared a cold lunch for the men, knowing they would be spending the first night at the Rafter L and that Lucreta and Young Noah would feed them supper. In an area and a time when food was not always readily available, Syrie liked to make as sure as she could that her people were always well fed.

Syrie stepped out onto the porch to say good bye to her sons and the other riders.

"You have the list?" she asked.

Daniel patted his front ants pocket. "Right here."

"And you have the gold dust?"

"Yes, it is in the strong box in the buckboard," Benjamin assured her. "I put it there myself."

"The letter to the Jensen's?"

"Also in the strong box. And before you ask, the lunch hamper is also in the buckboard. Along with the canteens."

"Well, sounds like you are all packed up and I guess you had better get going. Promise me you'll be careful on the trail and in town?"

"Of course, Ma. I'll see to it everyone gets back safe and sound," Daniel assured her. "Try not to worry about us. We have a large enough group of men I don't think the Paiute will bother us. I'll check for mail at the post office as well. Maybe there will be something from Mr. Hart letting us know when he will be arriving and I will talk to the Lands Office clerk."

"I'm sorry, Daniel and Benjamin, for being such a mother hen," Syrie apologized. "I just can't help but worry."

"We know, Ma," Benjamin reassured her. "We understand we are still your children and you will always worry. But I promise we'll be as careful as we can."

With that, the two men joined the riders at the buckboard and set off down the road towards the Burnt River and Baker City beyond.

Painted Pony brought the wash water from the breakfast dishes out of the house and poured it out around the corner of the house.

"Are you ready to start cooking for the second batch of people?" she asked Syrie.

"Yes, I guess we had better make more biscuits at the very least. Do we have enough eggs or should I made gravy instead? Do you want to start preserving the cabbages after breakfast?"

The two women continued planning as they went into the kitchen to get the second breakfast ready as the buckboard rattled around the corner of the road.

Daniel and Benjamin both rode in the buckboard as they started out. It was really the first time since Daniel had been home that the two of them had a relatively quiet time to talk and get reacquainted. Daniel had been surprised when he had first seen Benjamin. When he had left, Benjamin had been 14 or so and he had just started into his growth spurt. He hadn't been able to find where to put both of his feet at the same time and he was constantly knocking something over. Now Benjamin was nearly as tall as their father had been and he had Noah's blonde coloring. He was also like his father in that he had an almost unnatural strength. But most of all Daniel was curious to see what Benjamin's plans were for the future.

"Have you thought any more about what you are going to do after we catch Pa's killer?" Daniel asked him.

Benjamin was driving and he concentrated on missing a rut where the road from the ranch merged with the trail along the Burnt River.

"Some," he said. "I am still leaning towards blacksmithing. I figure I could combine it with a business selling horse, buggies, wagons, that sort of thing. There is a new smithy in town and the owner is a good, honest man. I think I heard his name is McCord. I am thinking about talking to him about an apprenticeship."

"Good idea.

"I met an interesting blacksmith when I was in Cheyenne," said Daniel. "His name is Cletus Beauregard and he runs the only honest livery in Cheyenne according to the owner of the hotel I stayed at. He reminded me of Pa with his size and the strength of his hands. Real nice fellow. He knows his horses as well. If you can find a spot where a livery is needed, you could probably make a pretty decent living. You certainly know a lot about horses. It would be hard work though."

"I'm not afraid of hard work. Never have been. In fact, I rather enjoy it. I also like shaping things to the way I want them to be. Ma says I get that from Pa. She said he was always pitting himself against one thing or another and he was happiest when he was working and creating with his hands."

"Speaking of creating things. Did I ever show you this?" Daniel said as he removed his knife from the sheath at his belt. "Cletus made this for me and gave it to me as a gift before I left Cheyenne."

Benjamin handed the reins to Daniel and took the knife to examine it more closely.

"This is beautiful. This looks as good as the ones Ma has that came from England. It is sharp too! How does the edge hold up?"

"Fine. I mean I haven't hacked at bones or anything with it, but for normal use around the ranch, I think it has held up fine."

Benjamin continued to turn the knife over in his hands.

"You say this Cheyenne blacksmith, Cletus, made this himself?"

"Yep. I watched him hammer on it myself. He said he folded the metal to make it stronger. I had never heard of anyone doing that. Not that I have watched all that many blacksmiths. Just Pa mostly making stuff for the ranch. And I never saw anyone make a knife before, so it was really interesting."

"I wonder if he could teach me how to do this?"

"Why don't you write him a letter and ask him? I remember the name of the livery and the street it was on in Cheyenne. I'm sure with that and his name, he would get the letter."

"I can probably get paper and pen at the hotel. I'll write to him and post the letter before we leave Baker City. Can I tell him you showed me the knife?"

"Sure. I think he'll remember me."

They rode on talking about Cambridge, the east coast, the big cities and what had happened on the ranch while Daniel had been gone. They talked about their hopes for the future. But they didn't talk about their father or his murder. Until they had more information, they chose to avoid that subject. Every couple of miles they would swap out driving or one of them would untie their saddle horse from the back of the wagon. Then the rider would scout out the trail ahead or drop back to make sure there were no stragglers from the herd. They passed a peaceful trip to the Rafter L and got to the ranch well before sundown that evening.

After a pleasant night at their sister's ranch, the Hickmans gathered up the horses from the Rafter L and added them to the herd to be driven to Baker City. Two of the hands from the Rafter L joined them to manage the increased number of horses. It was a long day into Baker City from the Rafter L and they rode into town tired and dusty. They put the horses they had brought to sell into a large corral at the livery, boarded their saddle horses and the wagon team at the same livery. They made arrangements with the boy who was working to provide food and water for the animals until morning. Then the brothers went to the hotel to arrange for lodging for themselves while the drovers went to find a little fun. The Rafter S had an open account at the boarding house in town, so the hands would stay there, if they decided to sleep. The brothers next went to the general store to drop off their mother's list of supplies as well as the list their sister had given them. They told the store owner they would be back in a day or two to pick up the supplies.

The brothers decided to have a beer and discuss what their next steps would be over the coming days. They had just sat down at a table when the man who bought and sold horses walked into the saloon.

"Benjamin! Good to see you."

"Good to see you too, Richard," Benjamin stood to shake his hand. "Richard, I don't think you know my older brother, Daniel."

Daniel stood as well to shake Richard's hand.

"I remember hearing about Noah's oldest son," Richard noted. "Went away to college in the East didn't you? It's been, what five or six years, since you were here last?"

"Yes, I've been studying law in the East. Just got back a few days ago."

"Say, boys, I was really sorry to hear about your father," Richard said as he took a seat at their table. "Hard to believe he could be taken that suddenly. Any word on who might have done it?"

"Not yet," Daniel said, "but we are still hopeful someone will know something."

"Can we buy you a beer? We have some business to discuss if you have time," offered Benjamin.

"Sure you can buy me a beer and I always have time for business with the best horse breeders in the eastern end of the state. How many head did you bring me this time?"

The talk turned to business as Daniel signaled the bartender to bring another round and add one for Richard.

After they had their beer, the three men walked down to the corrals to look at the horses.

"As usual you have brought some fine mounts. All broke to ride, correct?" asked Richard.

"Yes. There is a matched pair of bays in there which are also trained to harness. We just couldn't pass up the opportunity when we saw how well they were matched, right down to their socks. We can show you which ones are trained to work cows. Daniel, how many did we have that can work stock?" asked Benjamin.

"I think there were 12 out of this bunch. An even dozen," said Daniel.

"Yeah, that's what I remember as well," said Benjamin.

"Good looking stock," noted Richard. "Sound and pretty. Just like always."

"We have a lot of color in the yearling crop and Young Noah just acquired a new paint stud, so we are hoping for good things from him for the future. Of course, we are still standing Pa's stallion so we'll have more color from him."

"Boys, the migration to the coast isn't slowing down any. I hear the railroad might actually get through to the coast one of these days. Hard to tell how long before it reaches us though. All in all, I think horsepower is going to be needed going across the mountains for quite some time.

"I can offer you $100 a head for the ones broke to ride, $125 for the cow ponies and $350 for the pair of matched bays. How does that sound to you?"

Benjamin stuck out his hand.

"You've got a deal," he said. "Can you deposit the money into our account at the bank, like you usually do?"

"Sure. No problem. I'll see the banker in the morning and get the transfer paperwork started.

"If you can get me more color next year, I can get you more money. People are looking for flash as well as good sound stock. Must be a sign of too much money and not enough need. At any rate, more color will bring more money.

"I'd best be getting home. I'm sure the missus will be waiting supper. Would you boys like to join us?"

"Thank you, but no," said Daniel. "We've had a hard couple of days and we have a lot of calls to make tomorrow. I sure appreciate the offer though."

"Maybe next time you're in town, you'll come out to the place."

"We'd like that," said Benjamin. "We'll be sure and look you up even if we don't have horses to bring in."

They shook hands and Richard walked down the street toward his house and his waiting supper. The brothers stood at the fence line for a little while longer. As they were standing there, one of the owners of the livery stable, John Fuhrman, walked up to them.

"Nice bunch of horses," he said after greetings were exchanged. "I sold a couple a buggy a few days ago and they were looking for a matched pair of Nez Perce horses to pull it with. I gave them the name of your ranch and told them a matched pair of those horses was rarer than hen's teeth. The little lady in question, seemed to have her mind set on it though.

"You don't have any matched pairs of Nez Perce trained to pull do you?"

"No," said Benjamin. "As you said, a perfectly matched pair just doesn't exist. We have full siblings who are blanketed completely different. Or one will have a blanket and the other will have all over spots. You just never know."

"Well, as I said, I gave this couple the name of your ranch. Maybe they'll be out to see you one of these days."

"We did bring in a matched pair of bays trained to pull this time, but we've already sold them to Richard. We expect a lot of color come spring and if we happen to have any matching, we could certainly train them to pull, but I doubt we will have such a pair," Benjamin agreed.

"No matter. I sold them a pair of blacks. Nice horses for sure, but that missus wasn't happy with them."

"Seems like a woman who knows her own mind," remarked Benjamin.

"I got the impression she knows hers and her husband's, if you get my drift. Pretty lady, maybe even beautiful, but I just got a feeling she wears the pants in that family.

"I was on my way home to supper when I saw you boys. Give my best to your ma. Sorry we couldn't make it out for the funeral. Word just doesn't travel fast enough, does it? At any rate, my best to you and your family. Good evening."

"Well, brother Benjamin," said Daniel. "My belly thinks my throat has been cut. How about we find ourselves some dinner. Shall we round up some of those hands and make sure they will be able to ride back to the ranches?"

"No. Let them have their fun. There is plenty of time tomorrow for getting them sober. Food and a bed sound pretty good to me as well," agreed Benjamin. "Have you got your day planned out for tomorrow?"

"I have some ideas. Let's talk about it over dinner. Are you staying in town after tonight as well?" Daniel asked as they walked back toward the center of the town.

"I don't think I'll stay much over another night. A lot depends on if I can see the blacksmith McCord and how long it takes the store to get our order ready. I know Michael and the hands are there to take care of Ma, but I hate being gone from the place for too long. Besides you never know in this country when the snow will come. If I can finish up tomorrow, I'll head back with the hands. How about you?"

"I asked at the hotel and there is an attorney in town. If I have word from Harvard about my test scores, I may want to stop and talk to him. Of course, I want to see Mr. Brainard, and I thought I would stop in and talk to Sheriff Virtue, just to let him know we are still looking and see if he has any news.

"The day actually kind of depends on what is in the mail. "

They had reached the hotel while they were talking.

"I'm going to stop by the desk and get paper and ink to write to Cletus, the Cheyenne blacksmith. I'll catch up with you in the dining room," said Benjamin. "Order me a beer will you?"

"Sure," said Daniel as he went to find them a table.

The next morning after breakfast, they got a bank draft then went to the post office, delivered Syrie's letters to be mailed and picked up the mail for both ranches. Since there was a fair amount to go through, they took it back to the hotel to sort through it. There was indeed a letter from Hart addressed to their mother and they set it aside without opening to take home along with the rest of the mail for the ranch. There was a letter addressed to Daniel from Dr. Angus MacLeod at Harvard.

"My future is in this envelope," said Daniel.

"Open it," Benjamin leaned closer. "Let's see what it says."

"Okay. Here goes," Daniel said as he opened the letter.

My dearest Daniel,

It gives me great pleasure to inform you that you have passed your final exam at Harvard. In fact, you did rather well.

I have received your diploma from the calligrapher and President Hill has signed it. He has also enclosed a note with your diploma. I took the liberty of crating your books so they are ready for shipment. I also had the few personal effects you left in your dorm room crated as well. Your diploma and the note from President Hill are safely crated among them. They are currently in storage at my home.

Congratulations on passing your exam. It has been a great pleasure knowing you and I am sure you will be a credit to the field of law. I look forward to hearing about the great things you will do in your career.
Sincerely,
Dr. Angus MacLeod

Benjamin reached across the table and slapped Daniel on the shoulder.

"You did it! Daniel, you did it! You're a lawyer," he shouted causing the people who were having a late breakfast to look up and smile at the large young man who had dragged the other man to his feet as he was shouting. Benjamin hugged Daniel hard. "You are a Harvard-trained lawyer. Yeehaw!"

"I can't believe it!" said Daniel shaking his head after disentangling himself from Benjamin's hug. "I can't believe I finally did it."

"We need to celebrate!" said Benjamin. "Let's have a drink."

"It isn't even 9:00 in the morning," said Daniel.

"Who the hell cares? How many times in your life are you going to get news like this? I'm going to get some brandy. Coffee and brandy coming up!" Benjamin practically ran to the bar to order the brandy and more coffee.

Daniel sat back down at the table and stared at the letter from Dr. MacLeod. His life as an adult had just started. He was no longer a student.

He was an honest-to-God lawyer! Now he needed to find a job and decide where he wanted to practice law. And what kind of law did he want to practice?

Benjamin came back with the brandy and a pot of coffee.

"Here we are," he said as he poured a generous amount of brandy in each of their cups and filled them up with coffee.

"Sure wish Pa was here to see this. I know he or Ma would do a lot better job with a toast, but," Benjamin stood and raised his voice so the whole room could hear him. "Here's to my big brother. Who had the sand at age 16 to travel across this whole continent to pursue his dream. To my brother, Daniel Noah Hickman, Harvard lawyer!"

The dining room erupted in applause and Daniel found himself blushing as cups of coffee were raised to toast him. "Thank you," was all he could say around the lump in his throat. "Yeah, I wish Pa was here to see this as well," he said to Benjamin. "We owe somebody for the fact that he isn't."

CHAPTER TWELVE

Daniel had been told that the lawyer, James A. McCroskey, had office space above the bank. When Daniel arrived at the second floor landing, he noted none of the doors had names on them and many of them seemed to be unoccupied. Not surprising he supposed as most of the commercial buildings in Baker City were new and, as yet, unoccupied. He started down the hall opening doors until he came to one where he saw a man who appeared to be about 40 sitting at a desk in the room by the window. The outer room was sparsely furnished with a small table and a couple of dining room chairs. The inner room had a desk made from local lumber and bookcases made of the same.

The man had long blonde hair, with liberal streaks of white and he sported the new fashion of facial hair trimmed away from his chin and neck, but full over the rest of his face. He was wearing glasses with wire rims and his suit coat was hanging over the back of his chair.

Daniel rapped on the door frame to get his attention.

"Mr. McCroskey?" he asked.

"Yes. I'm sorry. I didn't see you come in." McCroskey stood up and came toward Daniel to shake his hand. As he walked Daniel could see he had a definite limp and then he saw the lawyer had a wooden peg where his left leg should have been.

"I'm Daniel Hickman. I got your name from the hotel desk clerk."

"Yes. Of course. I have rooms there for the present time. Here let me get you a chair," he said as he retrieved one of the chairs from the outer office.

"Furniture seems to be in short supply here in Baker City. I do apologize for the sparseness of my office."

"No problem. I am used to doing with little myself."

"What can I do for you, Mr. Hickman? Do you have a legal matter you need help with?"

"Actually, no. I recently graduated from Harvard Law and I am thinking about staying here in Baker City and practicing as my family owns a ranch out toward Rye Valley. Although I am not 100 percent sure about that as of yet as I have ties to the east coast as well and could go back there and practice maritime law.

"I do have a prior obligation of sorts before I can commit to a choice between east and west. My father was murdered this spring and my family is still looking for the killer. I have promised my mother I will not leave Baker City until this matter is resolved."

"I thought I recognized the name Hickman. You have my condolences on the loss of your father. Is Sheriff Virtue hopeful of being able to resolve this matter?"

"Not that I have heard. My brother Benjamin and I will be meeting with him later on today to learn of any new developments."

"So, you are looking at opening a practice here. Are you looking to set up a single practice or are you interested in a partnership?"

"I only found out this morning that I had passed my exams, so I am trying to ascertain what would be available to me if I decide to stay in Oregon."

"I have only been here about a year. A little less. I came late last year. Just before the New Year. Business is really quite brisk. Most of the matters relate to family law; wills, transfers of property, that sort of thing. I have made the acquaintance of Sheriff Virtue and some other officers of the courts and I have been called upon to defend a couple of men who found themselves in jail. All in all, I would say that there is room for more than one attorney in this town. Especially in light of how fast this area is growing."

"I was pretty amazed at how much it has grown since I left five years ago. I didn't recognize the town at all. It was pretty much a few log cabins when I left and now there are streets and two-story buildings. And, as you say, it doesn't seem to be slowing down in its growth.

"May I ask what brought you here?" asked Daniel.

McCroskey stood up and looked out the window for a moment before he turned back and answered.

"That is a very personal and very painful story. Perhaps when we know each other better."

Mr. McCroskey hurried on when he saw the confusion on Daniel's face.

"Now don't get me wrong. I have done nothing nefarious and I am of strong moral character. It is just personal and painful. It is a story I rarely share."

"Tell you what, Mr. Hickman. I have a desk full of work I must get back to. I do really want to talk to you more about your studies and about the need for good lawyers in this area. How about we meet for supper tonight, say seven at the hotel? Will you still be in town?"

"Sounds good. My family is not expecting me back at the ranch for a few more days. I still have a couple of more stops to make today," said Daniel, "so I will let you get back to your business. It was a pleasure to meet you and I look forward to talking to you more tonight."

"Splendid. I'll see you there," said McCroskey as he showed Daniel to the door.

After leaving the lawyer's offices, Daniel stopped by the bank and asked the teller for paper and pen as he wanted to write a letter to Dr. MacLeod, instructing him to send on the crates of books and other effects. He also obtained a bank draft sufficient to cover the costs of delivery, plus a little extra to pay Dr. MacLeod for his efforts. Then he walked to the post office and posted the letter to Cambridge. Satisfied with his efforts thus far, he went in search of Benjamin.

As Daniel had expected, he found Benjamin at McCord's blacksmith shop. What he didn't expect to find was Benjamin stripped from the waist up and wearing a leather apron. Daniel could see he was already developing the heavy musculature of their father. He was wielding a hammer with studied precision as he shaped a horseshoe on the anvil. Mr. McCord stood off to one side watching him closely. Daniel stood and quietly observed his brother at work. It was almost like watching their father at the forge at the ranch, though Benjamin did not have the experienced hammer blows of Noah. Benjamin stopped hammering, picked up the horseshoe he was working on and turned to cool the iron in a bucket of water. As he did so, he saw Daniel.

"Mr. McCord wanted to see if I knew my way around a forge and an anvil, so I showed him," grinned Benjamin.

"Indeed you did show me," agreed Mr. McCord. "And you do fine work for one so young. I can't say I'm surprised. I always admired your father's work. It is obvious you paid close attention to him while he was working."

"Ma always knew where to find me," laughed Benjamin. "I loved to be in the forge with Pa."

"If you decide you want an apprenticeship with me, I would be happy to take you on. Any time you are ready."

"Thank you Mr. McCord. As I told you, we've promised Ma we would all stick close to home until Pa's murder has been solved. But I am very interested in this trade."

"I'll look forward to hearing from you," McCord said as he shook Benjamin's hand. "You must be Daniel," he said. "I see you have on your good clothes, so I won't shake your hand. It is nice you were able to come home and help your mother."

"Family always comes first. That was a lesson Pa and Ma taught us early in our lives," responded Daniel.

"Benjamin, if you are about done here, I thought we might go by the general store before lunch and see how our order is coming."

"Good idea. Let me get cleaned up a bit and I'll be right behind you."

Benjamin went through a doorway into the back of the forge and emerged a few minutes later, his hair wet and dressed again in his shirt and vest.

"Got most of the sweat and dirt off, but I could sure use a bath," he said. "Let's get to the store and then to lunch. Working at an anvil makes a man hungry and thirsty."

"I have to ask," said Daniel, "why did you take off your shirt and vest?"

"That is a brand new shirt Ma just finished making for me. If I had gotten holes burned into it, she would have had a piece of my hide. Better I get burned than a new shirt," Benjamin laughed and clapped his brother on the back. "Now let's get done at the store and then have a beer and some lunch."

When the brothers went into the general store, Daniel was surprised at how well it was stocked. They had only been in the store yesterday long enough to drop off the list when they first got to town. Now he had a chance to look around, he realized the store really did have most everything a rancher or homesteader would need. There were several catalogs on the counter from which customers could order items not in stock at the store. With transportation getting better all the time, goods would usually be delivered in under three months, depending on the time of year. The general store inventory was nothing compared to the shops in Massachusetts or New Hampshire, but Daniel was impressed by the inventory for a store that was basically on the frontier.

The owner was helping other customers, so Benjamin and Daniel looked around the store while they waited to talk to him about their order. He stood near the counter and was looking at some of the catalogs when a young woman emerged through a curtain from the back room of the store. Daniel's breath simply stopped. She was very tall. Nearly as tall as Daniel himself. She had milk white skin, red hair which hung in a braid to her waist and the greenest eyes Daniel had ever seen.

"Benjamin Hickman, how nice to see you again," the young woman said. "What takes you away from your ranch and into town?"

"Hello, Melanie. We brought horses to sell and we have a couple of meetings. Melanie, I would like you to meet my brother Daniel," he said.

"Miss Melanie Fletcher, this is my older brother Daniel, lately of Harvard in Cambridge, Massachusetts. Daniel, may I present Miss Melanie Fletcher, daughter of the proprietor of this establishment."

Daniel managed to get his breath back enough to speak saying, "Pleased to meet you, Miss Fletcher."

Melanie was tall enough to nearly look at Daniel on his level. She tipped her head to one side, smiled and said, "Harvard in Massachusetts? That is a long way from here. What were you doing at Harvard?"

Daniel found he had to exercise great concentration to keep from tripping over his tongue when he answered.

"I've been studying the law for the last five years. I only arrived back in Oregon a few weeks ago. I've been at our ranch since I arrived."

"You need to come to town more often Mr. Hickman," she said.

'Oh yes, indeed I do,' thought Daniel.

Mr. Fletcher, the store owner finished with his customer and came over to greet Benjamin and to get introduced to Daniel.

"So this is Noah's and Syrie's oldest boy. I have heard a lot about you. Your folks were real proud of you. You've been gone a spell haven't you?" he asked.

"I've been gone five years."

"I was sure sorry to hear about Noah. Does the sheriff have any idea who might have done it?" asked Mr. Fletcher.

"We don't think so. Sheriff Virtue came out to the house a while after it happened, and we haven't talked to him since. We are going to try to meet with him after we have lunch," explained Benjamin. "We just dropped by to see if you have had time to get our order together."

"Yes, I do have it done. In fact, I took the liberty of having it delivered and packed into your buckboard at the livery. Lucreta's packages are clearly marked, as are yours. It is all ready for you. Had my boy throw a canvas over the load, just in case. You can bring the canvas back next time you are in town, or I can add it to your bill."

"Go ahead and add it to the bill. We should probably have one in the buckboard just for times like this. If you would give us a copy of the ranch's account, I'll see to it you get paid before I leave town today," said Benjamin. "If you have Lucreta's account ready, I can deliver it to her as well."

"There is no hurry if money is tight with losing your father and everything. And Mrs. Crow's account is still in the black from the last money she brought in."

"We appreciate that, but we'll be fine. Just let me know how much we owe and I'll get the money withdrawn from the bank before we leave town. A copy for Ma would be appreciated. She likes to keep track of such things."

"Thank you for everything, Mr. Fletcher," Daniel said. "It was a pleasure meeting you Miss Fletcher. I'm sure I'll be seeing you again. I may have other business in town soon."

"I'll look forward to it," Melanie said with a smile.

Daniel and Benjamin left the store and walked across the street to the hotel to have lunch in the dining room.

"Why didn't you tell me about her?" asked Daniel.

"Tell you about who?" Benjamin said, puzzlement written clearly across his face.

"Miss Fletcher."

"Melanie?"

"Yes, Melanie. She is the most beautiful woman I have ever seen."

"Melanie?"

Daniel nearly signed in exasperation.

"Yes, Melanie. Why didn't you tell me about her?"

"I never thought about it. She's always just been there at the store."

"You must not have eyes in your head if you can't see how beautiful she is. I have been to balls at Harvard with some of the best dressed and wealthiest women in New England and not one of them can hold a candle to her."

148

"Okay," Benjamin said. It was clear he was genuinely puzzled by Daniel's reaction, then his face bloomed in a smile.

"You're smitten!" he exclaimed. "You are smitten with Melanie Fletcher!"

"So what if I am?" said Daniel. "She is a fine woman and she comes from a respectable family."

"Wait until I tell Ma and the others," Benjamin laughed. "Just you wait."

Daniel suddenly could see the reaction and the teasing he was going to endure from his family.

"How about if we just keep this between us for now?" he suggested. "I don't want to worry Ma about anything right now."

"Uh huh. I'm sure that is your main concern," snorted Benjamin. "But to keep peace at the dinner table I'll keep my thoughts to myself. Don't make me do it too long though, brother."

The brothers had a quick lunch and then went up to their room so Benjamin could wash off in preparation for their meeting with the sheriff.

"I forgot to tell you, I have a meeting with the local lawyer tonight at 7:00. Do you have anything else planned for the day after we see the sheriff."

"We could go see the clerk if we have enough time. Otherwise, no. I'll hang out with the boys. Try to keep them out of jail and reasonably sober. I'd like to get an early start so we can get to Lucreta's the same day."

They let the desk clerk know they would be staying another night and to please hold their room. Then they went to find Sheriff Virtue.

They found the Sheriff sitting outside his office talking to several men, most of whom looked like miners. They waited patiently until the conversation was finished before stepping up onto the porch. Benjamin introduced Daniel to Sheriff Virtue.

"So did you bring horses into town or are you in town on other business?" the sheriff asked.

"Both," said Daniel. "We brought horses to sell from both ranches, but we have a few calls to make as well while we are here. Do you have a few minutes for us?"

"Sure do. Come on inside. I think the coffee is hot."

"Thank you, no," said Benjamin. "We just finished lunch."

The sheriff led them into his office and sat down behind his desk. The brothers took chairs from against the wall and placed them in front of the desk.

"I expect you want to know if I have any more news about your Pa," said the sheriff as he settled behind his desk. "I'm sorry to say I don't. I asked around Rye Valley when I went to pick up a prisoner and no one had heard anything. I went up to Mormon Basin a couple of weeks ago on other business and the same story there. No one had been throwing a lot of money around. No one seemed unusually nervous and no one really fit the description that George gave us of the murderers. We seem to have come to the end of this trail on this one."

"I was afraid of that," said Daniel. "I've told my family we need good solid evidence in order to make an arrest and get a conviction."

"As have I," agreed Sheriff Virtue. "Your sister, Abigail, didn't want to hear it I'm sorry to say. But as an attorney, you understand what we are up against, don't you Daniel?"

"Yes, but as a son of a murdered father, I want justice. My lawyer side is being shoved under by the need for justice."

"I understand. I have seen it plenty of times. I can only tell you that as soon as I hear anything from anyone, I will act on that information. Until then, I can only keep my ear to the ground."

"Thank you, Sheriff, for all you are trying to do," said Benjamin. "We want justice, but we also don't want to accuse or convict an innocent man."

"Being the sons of Noah and Syrie Hickman, I can believe that. Your folks are some of the most honest people I have ever met. You do them proud."

"Thank you," said Benjamin, "that means a lot."

"If it is okay, I'd like to check in with you from time to time," said Daniel standing up. "I may be in town a bit more often and I'd like to just drop in and see what is going on."

"Certainly. I would enjoy seeing you. Drop into my office anytime you are in town."

They said their good byes to the sheriff and Daniel and Benjamin went to the bank to get a bank draft for the general store. Benjamin assured Daniel it was for more than enough to pay their bill. When they got to the general store, Daniel was dismayed to find Melanie wasn't there. He didn't dare ask after her as it would be too presumptuous as he hadn't yet asked her father if he could court her. Sometimes Daniel hated the fact he had been taught proper manners and respect for tradition. But only sometimes.

As they passed the various saloons, gaming houses and other establishments which catered to weary cowboys and miners, Daniel and Benjamin spoke to the hands and told them to be sober and ready to ride at sunup the next day. All of them said they would be ready to go on time and would meet the brothers at the livery at sunup.

Benjamin and Daniel then went to the Lands Office to meet with Mr. Brainard, the lands clerk. They found the Lands Office very busy. They took a place in line and waited their turn. When able to get up to the counter, they initially spoke with a young man who they learned was the junior clerk. When the young man heard the Hickman name, he immediately said, "just a moment" and went to the inner office to get Mr. Brainard.

E.C. came out of his office, spoke briefly to the clerk and motioned for them to come around the counter and into his office. He closed the door so they could speak in private. The brothers introduced themselves to the clerk.

"I am so glad to make your acquaintance. And you are the eldest son? Your mother wrote me and said you were coming home from Harvard and would likely be by to see me," he said addressing Daniel.

"Yes, I am Daniel. I just found out today that I have passed my exams and I am now a lawyer. Still seems rather strange to me."

"I am sure it does after all those years of studying. What can I do for you today?"

"First of all, we wanted to thank you on behalf of our family for the letter you sent. We really appreciate you taking an interest in our father's murder. It has been a great source of comfort to my mother. And frankly, this office may be one of the few leads we have to find his killer.

"We also wanted to find out a bit more about Mr. and Mrs. Lattimer, the couple who expressed an interest in Pa's claim. What more can you tell us about them. What do they look like physically?"

"No thanks are necessary. I liked and respected your father and your mother is a very gracious lady. It is my pleasure to help in any way I can.

"As to the Lattimers, I am afraid I can't tell you a great deal beyond what I said in the letter. I see a great many people in a day, Mr. Hickman, and if there isn't something very distinctive about someone, I just don't remember much about them."

"Do you remember if they both were tall, both were short, skin color, an accent maybe?" asked Daniel.

E. C. thought for a moment and then said, "Now that you mention accents, Mrs. Lattimer had quite a southern accent. Very deep south if I'm not mistaken. And she was a real beauty. Dark and rather exotic looking. Possibly of some foreign blood. I had forgotten about it until you mentioned accents."

"You said in the letter you believed they owned businesses in Mormon Basin. Do you have any further information about that?"

"Just what I have been told. You might find out more at the bank or maybe from one of the stores in town. They have to be getting their supplies somewhere."

"That is a good idea. I will do that. We're not leaving to go back to the ranch until tomorrow. If you hear or remember anything further, we are staying at the Western Hotel. You can leave a message for either of us at the desk."

"How long do you want me to stall them on the status of the claim?" asked E. C.

"As long as you can. You can tell them you have located the other owner and you can suggest your office pass along any offer they would be making. Not only to protect our mother, but I have a feeling it might be important that we know more about them than they know about us."

"You can count on my discretion," the clerk assured him. "I will wait another couple of weeks before I send them a letter. Draw this out as long as I can. Winter may close them in for a few weeks as well."

"Thank you again. We'll keep in touch when we are in town."

CHAPTER THIRTEEN

The two men shook hands with the clerk and walked outside. Benjamin almost instinctively checked the sun.

"I'd say you have just about enough time to take a bit of a rest and get cleaned up. I'm going to go find the drovers and make sure they remember to be ready at first light. I'll see you back in our room tonight."

"Yes, that's a good idea. We can see the banker and the other store owners first thing in the morning. I do want to clean up before my dinner meeting with Mr. McCroskey.

"I have my 'lawyer' clothes in my grip. But first I want a real bath, a shave and a haircut. Care to join me."

"Sounds like a fine idea," said Benjamin.

After Daniel felt himself to be presentable and after he had seen Benjamin off, he went to the dining room to await the appointed 7:00 hour. As he sat drinking his coffee, he watched the people around him. There were certainly a lot of people dressed as he was in the modern style. He had expected to see more rough clothes of the rancher or miner. Some of the women were wearing silk instead of homespun or calico. The hotel and the dining room were as nice as any in Cheyenne and weren't far below the scale of some of the ones he had stayed at in New Hampshire. Baker City was definitely trying to keep up with the rest of the country.

At quarter to the hour, Mr. McCroskey came into the dining room. He walked with a cane now and he went directly to the table Daniel had selected in one corner of the room. He waved to the hotel staff as he took his seat and another coffee cup was soon delivered to the table along with a fresh pot of coffee.

"Good evening, Mr. McCroskey," Daniel said in greeting.

"Please, call me James," he responded. "May I call you Daniel?"

"Of course. Would you prefer something stronger than coffee?" asked Daniel. "There is still a goodly portion of the bottle of brandy my brother bought this morning to celebrate my passing my exams."

"Thank you, but no. I still have some reading to do tonight and brandy makes me sleepy. Perhaps another time. Did you have a profitable afternoon?" James asked as he poured himself coffee.

"I think so. I made contact with the sheriff and with the Lands Office clerk. They are both aware of how much we want to solve our father's murder and they have agreed to keep looking and asking questions. I have a few more visits I want to make in the morning and then I will be heading back to our ranch. There is a lot to do there before winter gets here in earnest."

"I confess I was amazed when I got here last winter. I don't know what I expected, but the cold to this south Texas boy was brutal. I purchased two pairs of long underwear and I intend to use them again this year. I also am going to order some wool socks and some boots more suited to the snow than my Texas boots."

"I fully understand changing climates from what you are used to. I couldn't ever seem to get warm in Cambridge my first year there. It wasn't any colder, but the damp was unbelievable."

The two men passed a few minutes in polite conversation until the waiter came to take their order, pausing only to decide on what they wanted to eat and quickly making their wishes known to the waiter. They resumed their talk about the weather, the growth of the town and other items while waiting for their food. Once the food arrived, they got down to the business of the meeting.

"You mentioned today in my office that you were still deciding on what direction you wanted your career as a lawyer to go. Would you mind explaining what you are considering?" asked McCroskey.

"No. I don't mind at all. Let me give you an abbreviated bit of family history. My mother came west from New Hampshire in the 1840's. She met my father because he was the scout for the wagon train. He had already established a homestead of sorts here, so this is where they settled and started their ranch."

"Excuse me for interrupting, but I understood Baker City wasn't started until around 1863 or 1864."

"Yes, that is correct. When I left to go to Harvard, it wasn't here at all. Just a couple of log cabins. My parents were the first whites to settle themselves in this vicinity. There were no people here except for the local tribe, the Cayuse."

"Your parents must be very brave and resourceful people."

"Yes, I would describe them as that, along with hardworking and stubborn," Daniel smiled. "Someday maybe you will have a chance to meet my mother."

"I would be honored. Please continue. I interrupted your story."

"Yes, well. My mother came from New Hampshire and the rest of her family still resides there, her brothers and sisters. I knew about them, of course, but being so far distant I had never had a chance to meet them. My mother had told me her family were farmers and seafarers. When I was at Harvard I had a chance to meet my mother's family and I was very taken with the tales of the sea and the descriptions of the far-off lands. It piqued my interest in the sea and from that to the study of maritime law. It seems like a fascinating field and I have family there in the business so that will open doors for me.

"But my roots are here in Eastern Oregon. Being back home at the ranch made me realize how much I love the ranching life. Its hard physical work draws me, as does being in the outdoors and the simplicity of the life. However, the ranch is a far distance from Baker City, so I know I couldn't work our ranch and maintain a practice here in town.

"Just to complicate matters, I became very interested watching the people at the Lands office today. I can see a whole other set of possibilities in homesteading and mining claims.

"There are just such a lot of ways to go and I am unable, at the moment, to settle on any one area."

"That very thing is what drew me to the law initially," remarked James. "But it can also be a challenge when one is first starting out. My ranch was not far from Brownsville which is a major port for Texas. I dabbled a little in maritime law, but my focus has always been on the bread and butter of family law. Of course, in a town the size of Baker City, one takes work where one can find it. I find I don't really have the stomach for criminal law, but I do take a case now and again.

"Speaking of criminal law, would you mind telling me about your father's murder? I am afraid I have only heard gossip about it and I try not to put much stock in unfounded stories."

"There isn't a lot of hard information, I'm afraid," began Daniel. "But I will be happy to share as much as I know for sure.

"All we know is he was working his claim near Mormon Basin and he had been gone about a week. It just happened an old friend from his mountain man days, a man named George Rogers, came for a visit. When George learned my father was at his claim, he decided to go up there."

Daniel paused as he pushed back his plate and gathered himself. James could see this was very hard for him.

"When George got to the claim, he found my father dead. He had been shot. Just below the left eye. George said he was sure Pa was dead before he hit the ground. George scouted around the area. He determined there were two people riding shod horses. That means white men. One man was tall and the second one was very short and small. George said the prints were so small they could have been made by a woman or even a large child. He followed the tracks until he lost them when they merged onto the main road into Mormon Basin. The next morning, he brought my Pa, his horse and mule and his gear back to the ranch.

"Ma notified the Lands Office clerk and the sheriff. She also sent off a letter to Joe Meek, another mountain man friend of Pa's, who is a former U.S. Marshal, asking for his help. He responded and said he is unable to come, but that he has asked one of the Marshals - a Mr. Hart - to come in his stead.

"So, we have no witnesses. We suspect Pa had a fairly large amount of gold because it is a profitable claim and he had been gone a week. When George found him the only gold there was what was in the pan, which was still lying in the stream. But this is gold country so someone having a large amount of gold would not be unusual. We really have nothing to go on. Certainly not enough to bring charges or obtain a conviction."

"You said you met with the sheriff and the Land Office clerk today. Did they have any more news?"

"The sheriff has made inquiries that have not yielded any results. A man and a woman did request information about filing on Pa's claim because they said they heard it had been abandoned. They claimed to be investors only and were looking for a good money maker. The clerk was able to stall them about filing on it. It is not abandoned as my mother's name is on the claim paperwork as well. My mother doesn't want anyone to go up there because she is afraid the killers might come back.

"My youngest sister, Abigail, who is a strong-willed child, disobeyed our mother and has been to the claim a couple of times. She insists she has been careful and she was not noticed. The only activity she has seen has been a small, dark-haired woman. Abigail says it appeared the woman was just out for some walking exercise. There has been no mining activity."

James was quiet as he drank his after dinner coffee and sat pondering what Daniel had said. The waiter came over to inquire about dessert for the two men. They both ordered pie and more coffee.

"Do you want advice in this matter or have you already determined your own course?" asked James.

"I have some ideas. I thought about talking to the people at the bank and at a few of the local stores. But I would welcome hearing your advice," responded Daniel. James paused as the waiter delivered their dessert and brought more coffee.

"I would wait to make further inquiries until Mr. Hart arrives," James said and held up his hand as Daniel started to speak. "I understand you very anxious to find out who killed your father. I certainly understand that. I too have lost my father to an act of violence.

"You are a very bright young man and a trained lawyer, but you lack experience, especially in the field of criminality. That is a field of study unique to itself. You have the advantage of being offered the services of one who is specifically trained, and apparently experienced, in apprehending criminals. I suggest you take full advantage of that fact. My advice is to leave the ground untrampled so as not to throw off Mr. Hart's investigation."

Daniel quietly considered what James had said as he ate his pie. He soon realized he had been doing what Abigail had been doing in her determination to find their father's killers. In his zeal he was essentially taking the chance of getting in the way of ultimately finding those killers. He leaned back in his chair and looked at James.

"Thank you. You are absolutely right. There is no way to tell the harm I might cause by asking the wrong question of the wrong person. You are indeed a wise man."

"I don't know about wise, but I have been involved in a few criminal cases, especially when I practiced in Texas, so I just have more experience than you. I will say the U.S. Marshals are a fine and dedicated group of men. I have great faith in their abilities."

"That is welcome news indeed," said Daniel. "You said your own father was killed in an act of violence. Is that what you were referring to this morning when we met in your office?"

"That is part of the story. Someday when we have time, I will tell you about what drove me to leave Texas and settle in Oregon as I was looking for a place to escape the past."

James paused as the waiter cleared their table of all but the coffee cups. "Why I stopped in Baker City? I don't know. Maybe it was finally far enough away and enough time had passed."

"I am so sorry to learn you had a tragedy as well in your life. The loss of anyone we love is never inconsequential."

James nodded his head in agreement.

"We each handle grief in our way. Through this I have learned there is no right or wrong way to grieve. Some of us want to escape the places which remind us of what we have lost and some of us want to cling more closely to those places.

"James, I appreciate your time tonight and I will consider my future most carefully in the field of law based on what we have discussed tonight. Might I come by and see you again next time I am in town?"

"I would be honored. I think I will seek my room now. As I said earlier, I have reading left to do tonight. I think all the coffee I drank will be helpful in keeping me awake. Good night, Daniel. It was good talking to you. I look forward to see you again."

"Good night," Daniel said as he left the dining room to go upstairs to his room. As he left the dining room, he noted a dark-skinned man sitting at one of the tables apparently just finishing his dinner. The man had a broad, flat nose and full lips. His hat lay on the chair beside him and Daniel noted the stranger had very curly, dark hair. He was neatly dressed in a broadcloth suit, but it was obvious he was a traveling man from the dust on his clothes. Daniel nodded his head as he caught the stranger's glance and the stranger did the same. Daniel was surprised to see that the man's eyes were hazel in color. He got the feeling the man was committing his physical appearance to memory. Then he dismissed it from his mind and continued on to his room.

CHAPTER FOURTEEN

After a good night's sleep, the brothers packed up in preparation for the ride back to the ranch. They decided to get coffee before they joined the men at the livery as it wasn't yet dawn. As they came down the stairs and towards the desk, Daniel noticed the same dark-skinned man from the night before. The man was obviously also checking out and was speaking to the desk clerk.

"I wonder if you would know how to get to the Rafter S, the Hickman ranch?" asked the man.

"Of course, Mr. Hart. It is located off the Burnt River trail. You will catch the trail just to the south and east of town. It is well marked. It is the main trail to the Idaho territory. The Hickman place is on Dixie Creek. You shouldn't have any trouble finding it."

As the clerk raised his head from his account books, he saw Daniel standing on the stairs.

"Mr. Hart, you may be in luck. Mr. Daniel Hickman and Mr. Benjamin Hickman are just coming down the stairs."

Hart turned around and looked at the brothers and smiled.

"Well, this is indeed fortunate," he said as he walked over and extended his hand. "I am Thomas F. Hart, Deputy U. S. Marshal. I believe Mr. Meek wrote your family about me?"

"Yes he did," Daniel returned the greeting. "We just received your letter in yesterday's mail. Though we don't get into town often. It may have been at the post office for a while. We were just getting ready to check out and start back to the ranch. I have one stop to make and then we'll be riding out. We would be pleased to have your company on the ride."

"I also have a stop to make. I need to make my presence known to the local sheriff. Do you happen to know him?"

"Of course. Sheriff Virtue is a good man. Benjamin would you be able to make the introductions?"

"Yes, of course. Have you a horse or do we need to find one for you?"

"I came in on the stage. I have no horse, but I have my saddle and gear. I was thinking of renting one at the livery."

"We can throw your gear into the buckboard and my family will provide you with a mount for the duration of your stay, said Benjamin.

"That will be fine," said Hart. "If you are ready, we can leave now."

"Just let me settle our bill and we'll go," said Daniel.

The three men walked over to the Sheriff's Office. Daniel was conscious of the stares of the few townspeople who were out early. He wasn't sure if it was because Hart was a newcomer or because of the twin guns he wore low and tied down. If Hart noticed the stares, he didn't respond to them.

Benjamin introduced Hart to Sheriff Virtue, while Daniel excused himself and went to the general store. He told Benjamin he needed to order clothes, but he knew he wasn't fooling Benjamin who grinned broadly at his explanation. Still, he had to have a reason for going into the store. As soon as he walked into the store, he saw Melanie. She was standing on a short ladder dusting shelves. The act of reaching up caused her dress to raise up and Daniel could plainly see she had fine legs. Daniel blushed when he realized her father was watching him watch his daughter.

"I, ah, I need to order a couple of suits," he stammered to Mr. Fletcher.

"Oh Daniel," Melanie said as soon as she heard his voice. "I didn't think we would see you again before you left. We have a couple of small items that came in late yesterday which were on your mother's list. Let me get them for you."

She climbed down the ladder and went into the back room returning in a few minutes with two small parcels wrapped in brown paper.

"These are small enough they should fit in your saddle bags. Just some sewing notions and such. They don't weigh much."

"Thank you. I'm sure Ma and Painted Pony will be glad to have them."

"Now, son, what did you want to order?" asked Mr. Fletcher.

"A couple of suits. I will be starting to practice law soon and I only have one suit I can wear to court. So, I need a couple of suits and four shirts and some ties, please."

"Ok. This catalog here should be what you need," Fletcher said as he passed one of the catalogs over to Daniel. "Take a look and see if you find anything to meets your needs."

Daniel was sincerely sorry when Melanie went back to dusting the shelves and Mr. Fletcher stayed very close to him. He hurriedly picked out the items he needed even as he tried to think of some way to engage Melanie in further conversation.

"When do you think those will be in?" he asked Mr. Fletcher.

"Well, I would think in four to six weeks. They are coming from Portland, so it shouldn't take too long."

"That will work out real nice," Melanie said. "It will be just before the New Year's dance and your family will be coming to town for that won't they?"

"I don't know. I have no idea what the family does now for the New Year. I will be sure to mention it to Ma and see if maybe some of us can come to town for it.

"Thank you, Mr. Fletcher. Miss Fletcher. I had better be getting back to the ranch."

Daniel made a hurried exit from the store.

Idiot! He told himself. First you try to find something to say to her and then when she talks to you, you run like a scared rabbit!

Mr. Fletcher turned a stern eye on his daughter after Daniel left the store.

"Could you be any more obvious, Melanie?"

"Whatever do you mean, Father?" she laughed and went back to her dusting.

Daniel found Mr. Hart and the sheriff sitting on the porch in front of the sheriff's office, the sheriff smoking and both watching the citizens of Baker City. Mr. Hart stood up at Daniel's approach.

"You ready to go?" he asked Hart.

"Yes. I think everything is done that needs to be done this trip.

"Did Benjamin go on to the livery?" asked Daniel.

"Yes, he did," said Sheriff Virtue. "He said he wanted to make sure everything was ready when you got there.

"Daniel, I hope something opens up on your father's murder. Mr. Hart and I have been talking about ways to solve this case.

"Mr. Hart has told me he plans to spend some time in Mormon Basin. As he is not a miner by trade or experience, I have suggested he talk to Mr. Brainard about any abandoned claims that he might work. It might go a ways towards covering the fact that he is new to mining and make him more believable to the other miners in the area."

Daniel nodded his agreement. "Might not be a bad idea. I certainly wouldn't know how to fit into a mining camp. What do you think, Mr. Hart?"

"I think it is a good idea. Do you have time to stop by the Lands Office?"

"Yes. But we will have to hurry. I want to get to Lucreta's tonight. But, I'm sure Mr. Brainard would be happy to help. Let's go see him."

Sheriff Virtue stood up and said to Daniel, "I think Mr. Hart will have more luck than I have had. He is going to be able to devote himself strictly to your father's murder, so that will help. If I hear anything at all, I will let one of you know."

"If I am to be away from the ranch for any length of time," said Mr. Hart "I'll be sure and let the Hickmans know where I am and when I will return."

"That will be fine," said Sheriff Virtue. "Safe travels."

The two men went to the Lands Office and, as usual, they were doing a brisk business. Mr. Brainard saw them come in and ask his assistant to cover the counter and took the two men into his office immediately.

"Mr. Hickman, I did not expect to see you back again so soon," said the clerk. "Please take a seat."

"Thank you for seeing me again, Mr. Brainard," said Daniel. "I would like to introduce you to Mr. Thomas Hart, Deputy US Marshal. He is here to investigate my father's murder. He has a request for you."

"Pleased to meet you, Mr. Hart," said the clerk turning his attention to the newcomer. "How can I be of assistance in your investigation?"

"I plan on spending several days, possibly weeks, in Mormon Basin. I am an investigator and a lawman, but I have no experience in mining. Sheriff Virtue thought it might be a good idea if I had a claim sort of waiting for me in Mormon Basin. So he suggested we talk to you and see if there are any open claims or any abandoned ones that I might take over. I would, of course, be doing this on a strictly temporary basis and would return them back to you after I finish my work here."

"This is a most unusual request," said Brainard, "but I see the logic in it. For you to try to find and establish a claim would surely reveal you to be a non-miner." Brainard sat back in his chair and pondered a spot about midway on the front of his desk as he ran his hands back and forth across the front edge of the desk.

"Excuse me a moment," he said abruptly and left the office. When he returned, he had a map of Mormon Basin. "I think I have just the spot for you. It isn't too far from Mr. Hickman's claim, so you could keep an eye on that property as well. Here is Mr. Hickman's claim," he indicated a spot on the map, "and here is the parcel I had in mind. The gentleman who was mining this stretch of Dixie Creek had absolutely no luck and turned it back and left the area. It should suit your purposes very well."

"I think it will do just fine. And it being close to Mr. Hickman's claim will allow me to monitor any activity that might be happening there."

"Good," said Brainard. "Let me get the transfer paperwork together, so it all looks above board and legal. There is a $25 filing fee."

"I'll be paying that," said Daniel. "I'll just step out and go to the bank and withdraw the funds. I'll be right back if you want to start on the paperwork. Directions to the area and what to look for as far as markers would be helpful as well, as neither of us has a clue about mining claims."

"I'll make sure you can find the claim. Your brothers and your mother know where your father's claim is, don't they?" asked Brainard.

"I think most of the family knows where it is. I am the odd one out on that score," said Daniel as he left the office.

"I want to thank you for helping us like this, Mr. Brainard," said Hart.

"No need to thank me. Murder is a foul deed and whatever assistance I can provide, I will do so gladly."

Daniel returned with the filing fee and the papers were prepared and given to Mr. Hart. They shook hands all around and the two young men headed for the livery stable. Before they reached the livery, Hart asked Daniel to stop for a minute. Thomas untied and removed his guns, stowing them carefully in his saddle bags.

"Why are you doing that?" asked Daniel.

"I don't want any of your men knowing I am a lawman. If cowboys see guns like mine, they automatically think gunfighter. Say what you will about women gossiping, but it has been my experience that men over a few beers can out-gossip any woman."

The drovers had all made it to the livery and though their eyes were bloodshot from lack of sleep and too much booze, they were ready to go back to the ranch. All of them were mostly broke. But they all agreed it had been worth it and were in high spirits. Benjamin had the team hooked to the buckboard and his and Daniel's horses were saddled and ready to go. Daniel paid the bill and Hart loaded his few things in the back of the buckboard.

"How long will it take us to get to your ranch?" asked Hart.

"We'll make for the Rafter L tonight. We probably won't get there before dark though, as late as we are getting started," said Benjamin.

"I thought your ranch was the Rafter S," said Hart.

"The Rafter L belongs to our sister, Lucreta, and her husband," explained Daniel. "It is on the way to our ranch. The Rafter S belongs to our parents."

After they had left town, Daniel stepped down from the gruella, checked his rifle and withdrew his pistol and gunbelt from his grip. All the drovers checked their rifles as well and Benjamin retrieved his pistol from the back of the wagon and strapped it on.

"In case you are wondering, Mr. Hart," Benjamin said, "we have been having trouble with Paiute raiding parties in these parts. They probably won't bother us as we have a fairly large contingent of men, but I like to be prepared."

"Please call me Thomas," Hart said. "And I fully understand about being prepared. I did notice you didn't wear your pistols in town."

"I didn't figure I had need for it there," said Daniel. "I am not afraid of guns, they are a necessary tool out here, but Sheriff Virtue runs a peaceful town, and I am no gun-slinger."

"Understandable. Unfortunately, in my line of work, I never know when I will be called upon to use my weapons so they are more or less a part of me now. Since I'm riding in the wagon, can I borrow that rifle?"

Daniel remounted his gruella and they continued on to Lucreta's ranch. They encountered no other riders and they were able to make good time. As they had on the way into Baker City, Daniel and Benjamin took turns driving the buckboard and riding, though they didn't have any horses to worry about on this leg of the trip. Thomas asked questions about Noah's murder of whomever was driving the wagon. They gave him all the information they had, including the information Abigail had discovered as well as prior conversations with Mr. Brainard. Then Thomas asked about the local people, the gold strikes, Mormon Basin and Rye Valley. He asked about the landscape, the passes and access into Mormon Basin. He asked about weather patterns. Daniel told him one of the brothers, or their sister Theresa, would be able to help him answer his questions about topography and his ability to travel from place to place once they were actually at the ranch.

They made good time, but they missed supper. Being Syrie's daughter, Lucreta wouldn't let anyone under her roof go to bed hungry, so she brought out cold beef steak, made biscuits and fresh coffee. The men ate the cold meat gladly then made dessert of biscuits and homemade jam. After the children were in bed and the drovers had retired to the bunkhouse, Lucreta and Young Noah joined Thomas, Daniel and Benjamin at the table.

"My family would like to thank you for coming all this way, Mr. Hart. You can't know how much it means to us," Lucreta said.

As was his usual habit, Young Noah, didn't say much. He sat and watched and learned. If he spoke to a strange person, it was rare and he had to be sure it would be safe for him to do so.

"No problem, ma'am. Please call me Thomas. We are going to be seeing an awful lot of each other. This area is a part of our jurisdiction. It is only unusual in that this is not an investigation we are undertaking on behalf of the federal courts or the federal government. Murder is still murder and it is a crime no matter where or who.

"I need to learn about your father, about Noah. Would it be easier on your mother if you or some of the other children answered my questions or should I speak directly to her?"

"We would be happy to tell you all we can, but Ma knew him best. They were married 23 years, so I don't know of anyone who knew him better. Uncle George, George Rogers, should be coming here for the winter soon. He used to trap and scout with Pa, so he knows a great deal about him from his younger days. Then there is Ten Crows, who was my father's best friend for greater than 30 years. He will speak to you as well."

"Mr. Meek speaks very highly of both your father and Mr. Rogers. The stories he tells of their younger years! Must have been an exciting time.

"I would very much like to speak to Ten Crows and Mr. Rogers. Will Rogers be staying here or at the Rafter S?"

"Most likely the Rafter S. If we have a project or a problem that Uncle George can help with, he'll come here, but he makes his base at Ma's place.

"I'm sure he will make himself available to you. He wants to find Pa's killer as badly as the family does. He was the one who found him and it disturbed him down to his soul."

"Yes, Daniel told me Mr. Rogers had found him and that he did some tracking at the murder site.

"And where can I speak to Ten Crows?"

"That will have to be arranged," said Daniel.

"All right. What I need to know is what sort of man Noah was," said Thomas. "The more I learn about Noah, I feel the more I can figure out what kind of people killed him. To do that, I will be living with your family at least part of the time.

"I am tired after my travel today and the days prior. Do any of you have any questions before I find a place to stretch out?"

"I have a question," Young Noah spoke for the first time. "Were your people slaves before the war?"

Thomas stared at him with a level gaze for a moment. "How did you know?"

"I recognize the features. The mountain man, James Beckworth was also a friend of Noah's. His father was white and his mother was black. I saw him a couple of times when I was young. You resemble him. When you are marked, as I am, to the white man it pays to know your enemies. And your possible allies," replied Young Noah.

"To answer your question. No. My family is from Northern New York State. Not far from the Canadian border. Some of my ancestors were brought to this country as slaves, but they fought in the Revolutionary War and gained their freedom at that time. None of my family can ever remember being slaves. The majority of the white part of me is Irish. Who were also slaves, though in a different way. They came to this country as indentured servants. "

"Do you think slavery or false imprisonment are morally right, no matter what the law says?" asked Young Noah.

"No, I do not. Why do you ask?"

"Because I have to be sure you understand that there are different kinds of justice. Your people have experienced the differences of justice among white men and justice between white men and people of color, both brown and black.

"And do you understand some things are worth dying for. Doesn't matter whether they are against the law or not. And I also need to be sure you understand that in this family, family always comes first. No matter what."

Thomas Hart kept his hazel eyes on Young Noah for a time and studied him.

"I understand.

"Your name was not always Noah Crow, was it?" he asked.

"No. My true name is Spotted Buffalo. My father is Ten Crows. My mother was Spotted Fox. They are Cayuse. I am now a white man at the request of my father so he can see his grandchildren grow up free. My father is now a prisoner of the United States Government on a reservation in Umatilla. The rest of my family is dead. Killed by the white man's disease.

"Just as your people were once slaves, now my people are prisoners of the white man's government."

"I am aware of the slaughter and imprisonment of your people," said Thomas, "and I grieve for them.

"Even though I have jurisdiction over law breakers in this area as a Deputy U.S. Marshal, I have no stomach for imprisoning any innocent person. No matter the color of their skin. You should know one of my brothers died in the Civil War fighting to free the rest of our people. Had I been a little older I would have been there with him."

"I'll get a lantern and show you to the bunkhouse," Young Noah said and left the table.

"Good night, Sis," said Daniel as he too rose from the table. "I'll see you for breakfast, then we need to be heading on to Ma's place."

"Good night. Sleep well. I'll be up before sunup and have the coffee on so come on in when you wake up. I can make some food up tonight for you to take as well if you want to get an early start."

"No, you go on to bed. We have time for breakfast. I'll see you then."

CHAPTER FIFTEEN

The next day they awoke to a cold drizzle of rain. The fall rains had finally come and Daniel wouldn't begrudge the moisture, even though it meant a long, cold ride back to the ranch. As the first real rains of the season turned the grey dust into sticky, slick mud, there would be no cantering or probably even much trotting of the horses. Slow and steady would be their pace today.

"Hope you brought your slicker," Daniel said to Thomas as the latter yawned and sat up in bed.

"Sure do. Are we going to get rain today?"

"Already getting. Looks like it is going to set in good and give us a good soak. We need it if we are going to have any fall and winter pasture," said Benjamin.

"Being from the west side of Oregon, I never go anywhere without a slicker," laughed Thomas. "Getting caught one time out in those rains is enough for any man."

"We're going to the house. Lucreta will have the coffee on and a good fire going. I'll see you up there for breakfast."

"I'll be right along."

Daniel and Benjamin walked through the rain avoiding the worst of the mud, carefully kicked what mud they could off their boots, then stepped into the warmth of the kitchen. As expected, they found Lucreta already at the cook stove and smelled biscuits and ham cooking.

"I'd ask you if you were hungry, but you've been hungry since the day you were born, brothers," Lucreta said with a smile. "Pour yourself some coffee. Is everyone else up and stirring down at the bunkhouse?"

"Yes," said Benjamin. "They will be coming along any minute."

"What do you think of Thomas Hart?" asked Daniel.

"If he means what he says about not wanting to imprison innocent people, then I welcome him. Young Noah is not so sure, but I think talking to Mr. Hart last night eased his mind some about bringing Ten Crows home."

"It did relieve my mind," said Young Noah as he walked into the kitchen holding a sleepy-eyed Arthur. "Look who woke up wanting his Ma."

Lucreta chucked the baby under the chin and kissed his cheek, then went back to her cooking.

"Are the girls up yet?"

"I stirred them before I came in. They should be in here in a minute. Did you sleep well, Daniel, Benjamin?"

"Yes, fine," answered Benjamin.

"We hated to put guests in the bunkhouse, but the family is growing so fast, we haven't been able to get new rooms added on fast enough," said Lucreta.

"I believe Mr. Hart when he says he will not imprison an innocent man," said Young Noah, "but I will be careful about my father's safety. I don't know how he will cover his leaving the reservation, but he will find a way. He can travel fast when he travels alone, so we could see him any time after he gets my letter."

"Will you write him?" asked Daniel.

"I had planned to, but now that Mr. Hart is here, I will send a letter today with one of the hands to Baker City."

The talk turned to ranch business, the children, plans for next year's horse crop and family business as the girls, the drovers and Thomas entered the kitchen. Then the talk turned to the weather and how it would impact the rest of their trip.

Everyone saddled up after breakfast, the team was hitched and the load was checked. Then they started south for the home ranch. As Daniel had known, the pace today was considerably slower than it had been the day before. This gave the two brothers and Hart more time to talk and Daniel, especially found himself growing more and more comfortable with the dark, wiry man. He learned Thomas had come west after the Civil War was over. Thomas told him he had always been drawn to the law, but felt he was too much of a physical person to ever become a lawyer. Thomas felt he needed to be out doing things, so he had applied for a job with the U.S. Marshal's service and Joe Meek had hired him. He had high praise for the former mountain man and echoed what Rogers had said about Meek being a man you could depend on. Having Meek ask him to undertake finding Noah's murderer had been humbling for Thomas and he felt the heavy weight of expectation.

Theresa was leaving the barn and walking toward the house when she heard horses on the road behind her. She turned to look and saw her brothers and the drovers as well as another man. She stepped out onto the road to get a better look and saw a short, wiry, dark man riding on the wagon. She couldn't tell much about the way he was dressed because of the slicker, but she could see he wasn't wearing buckskins. She waved to the riders as they turned off the road toward the barn. She walked back to the barn to meet them and to see who this new person was.

Daniel stepped down from his horse and walked it into the barn. Everyone followed him with the buckboard coming in last. They started unsaddling and wiping down their mounts. Theresa entered the dimly lit barn and as she approached the men, Daniel stopped what he was doing.

"Theresa, where do you want these horses?"

"Those big stalls at the end should be fine for the saddle horses. They've been freshly cleaned and there is plenty of feed already. The team you can put into the covered run on the west side of the barn.

"You ride in from Lucreta's?"

"Yes, we left there after breakfast. She packed us a lunch but it was raining so hard, we didn't stop. We ate some of it in the saddle. These horses are pretty worn out."

"Well get them taken care of then. I'll go to the house and tell Ma you're here and that you brought a guest. I'm sure she will make something hot to eat."

"I'm sorry. I'm so tired my manners have left me.

"Theresa, this is Mr. Thomas Hart of the U.S. Marshal's Service. Thomas Hart, my sister Theresa."

"Pleased to meet you," Theresa said. "We're really glad you have come to help us." She reached out to shake his hand, hesitating an instant when she saw his hazel eyes, so bright in his dark face.

Thomas looked at Theresa and couldn't help noticing the grief and seriousness on a face that was clearly designed for laughter. Wisps of dark, wavy hair escaped from under her sodden, wide-brimmed hat. He noticed her hands were strong and covered with calluses. Unlike other women of her time and place, she was dressed in buckskins with a simple shirtwaist under her jacket. Two black and white dogs sat at her feet. What an uncommon way for a beautiful woman to dress, he thought.

He took her hand in his, but didn't shake it, rather covered it with his other hand in a kind of caress.

"I only hope I can help you and find your father's killers."

Theresa blinked away tears and nodded her head, called to her dogs, turned and went to the house.

When Thomas, Benjamin and Daniel entered the house they found fresh coffee and warm bread set out on the table with butter from the spring house. After Daniel had introduced Thomas to the rest of the family, the three men took out the remains of their lunch and sat down to eat. Painted Pony put on a shawl and took a pot of fresh coffee and tin cups down to the bunkhouse for the drovers.

Michael and Abigail started to pepper Thomas with questions, but Syrie shushed them and told them to let the men eat in peace and rest a bit. Reluctantly they complied and sat hovering as the men ate. Theresa drank her coffee and watched the newcomer, keeping her own counsel.

"You two are worse than a pack of hungry dogs," grumbled Daniel. "Don't you have something else to do?"

Michael smiled and said, "Nope. Not time yet for evening chores."

Daniel sighed, took his plate to the dishpan and freshened his coffee, then did so for everyone else. Painted Pony washed up the three plates and the silverware, as well as the cups she had taken to the bunkhouse. Sensing this was a family discussion, she put on her shawl and went out the back door of the kitchen.

"First of all, Mrs. Hickman," said Thomas, "I bring condolences from Mr. Meek. He was profoundly grieved when he got your letter. He told me some stories about the old days with your late husband. It was very obvious he held him in high regard. I consider it a great honor to have been sent in his stead and I will do my utmost to bring Mr. Hickman's killers to justice."

"We appreciate more than you know that you have left your regular duties and have come here to help us. We, of course, are at your disposal for any help we can give." The rest of the family nodded their agreement to Syrie's comments.

"As I told your eldest daughter and her husband yesterday, I will need to get to know all I can about Noah. It might help me build a picture of what kind of person killed him.

"I also plan on spending time in both Rye Valley and Mormon Basin. I understand his claim was roughly between those two camps? I will need a guide to help me find my way."

"I'll show you," said Theresa. "I run cattle up near there, so you can ride out with me whenever you are ready."

"Good. I will be gone several days or even several weeks during my stay in the two mining camps, depending on what I find. I will confess that I base a lot of my work on my instincts. If something seems off about a person or a situation, I will follow up on the feeling. This method has served me well in the past.

"I would prefer no one outside of your immediate family know about my time here. I have asked Sheriff Virtue to keep this confidence as well. I don't necessarily suspect anyone who works for you, but it does pay to be discreet in these instances.

"May I ask what part Painted Pony plays in your family?"

"She has been with us since the measles outbreak killed so many of her people. She was ill and was being run down by the cavalry. We hid her, nursed her and gave her shelter in our home. She has helped deliver my younger children and has taken care of all of them. She has become my right hand and a part of this family," explained Syrie.

"I gathered she is a discreet person by her exit just now, so I will not worry about her knowing my purpose here."

"She is a person who can be counted upon to protect this family," said Benjamin.

"I understand," said Thomas. Then he continued "I am nobody's cow hand, so I don't think I can pass as one of your hands. As folks tend to talk during long winter nights, it would be best if I don't sleep in the bunkhouse. If it is okay with you, I'll sleep in the parlor on the floor."

"Nonsense," said Syrie. "We'll fix you a pallet upstairs with the rest of the boys. But we have to have some way to explain your presence here. Did you have anything in mind?"

"He could be a friend of Daniel's from school," suggested Michael quickly. "They appear to be of a similar age."

"That's an excellent idea," said Thomas. "I can say I came west for my health and I am on an extended tour of the area. That would explain any long absences as well. Good thinking, Michael."

"Daniel, why don't you take Thomas around the compound and show him where everything is. Take your time and try to not track too much mud back into the house.

"Theresa are you staying for supper?"

"Thanks, but no, Ma. I have some stock I need to drive back up to my place. They busted through a fence and came down here. The hands have them in the corral. I think me and the dogs can get them back home.

"I'll see you tomorrow after breakfast," she kissed her mother on the cheek, grabbed her slicker from the peg and, calling the dogs, went out into the rain. Daniel and Thomas followed her out the door.

"Children, you might think about starting your evening chores early today. With this rain and clouds, it will get dark sooner than normal. I'll be in my room if anyone needs me."

After their soggy, muddy tour of the compound, Daniel and Thomas went back to the house to dry off and relax. Taking their coffee into the parlor, they each found comfortable chairs and enjoyed not being on the back of a horse or in a wagon for a while. As the younger Hickmans came in from doing their evening chores, the boys came into the parlor as well. Abigail went into her room and closed the door.

Thomas soon was up pacing around the room, looking at the family mementoes, the few tintype pictures, and the school books on the shelves. He recognized most of them immediately: McGuffy's Readers, Thompson, Ray and Colburn's Arithmetic, Smith's Grammar, Webster's Speller and Dictionary, Monteith's Geography, Cornell's Georgraphy, Cornell's Outline Maps, Sanders Primer, Davies' Arithmetic, Sanders Speller and Willard's History of the U.S. Additionally there were classics like Shakespeare, Thomas Aquinas, Chaucer and Milton. This family lived on the frontier, but their book collection was the equal of any he had seen in the East. He understood why the eldest son had been able to gain admittance to Harvard.

"Was your father a learned man?" asked Thomas.

"Pa could read, write and do sums, but Ma was the school teacher," replied Benjamin. "In fact, she taught several of the Cayuse when we were smaller, along with teaching us. According to her Young Noah was her best student."

"Indeed he was," said Syrie as she joined them. "I think I'll sit a spell with you all and enjoy the fire before we start supper.

"Young Noah was an excellent student. Noah and I offered to send him to college before Daniel left, but he'd had enough of the white man by then. Since there were no Indian schools we knew of, he stopped his formal education when I could no longer teach him. He and Lucreta have collected a fine library however, and I don't think he has ever stopped learning."

"He is an interesting man," said Thomas. "Caught between the two worlds isn't he?"

"Yes he is. He loves my daughter and his children, but a part of him will always long for the old ways. He is proud of being Cayuse and it half kills him to have to hide it from the outside world. Of coursem within the family we honor that portion of his life. Just as we honor his father. His mother, Spotted Fox, was my best friend. It nearly killed me when she, her mother, her daughter and her other son, Otter, all died within a week of each other. There was nothing we could do to save them.

"Her daughter, Little White Bird was Lucreta's best friend. The two of them were thick as thieves and they were both so good to help when Theresa was little.

"You will get to meet his father, Ten Crows. He has promised to come and help when we contact him."

"Young Noah sent a letter to him today. He is having one of the hands take the letter to Baker City for posting," said Daniel.

"It will be good to see him again. Remind me to tell Painted Pony that he is coming. And I need to tell Theresa so she can pack a bag to stay with us and to make sure her place is presentable. I love my daughter, but she will never make a housewife."

"From the looks of this room, your family spent a great deal of time in here. It isn't formal at all like a lot of parlors I have seen. More comfortable," noted Thomas.

"Yes, we spend a lot of time in here. In the evenings, especially in the winter, I would read aloud, Noah would work on some leather project and the children would help him or they would work on some project of their own. Painted Pony taught my two younger girls to do beading in the Cayuse fashion in this room. There are a lot of happy memories in this room," Syrie said and then grew quiet.

"I am almost dreading the coming deep winter when we will all be gathered in here again. It will be another reminder of what we have lost. But," she straightened her shoulders, "we will give thanks for what we still have, which is a great deal more than others have."

They heard the back door open and Syrie stood up.

"That will be Painted Pony. Must be time to start supper. Where is Abigail?"

"In her room," said Michael. "She went in there as soon as we got back in from chores."

"I'll check on her," Syrie said and knocked on the door to Abigail's room and went in. It was a long while until she came out again and went directly into the kitchen.

"My youngest sister is having a very hard time dealing with Pa's death," noted Daniel. "She has always been a passionate and head-strong child and none of us can get through to her. It is devastating for her that her father is dead and his killers walk free."

"Sometimes it is harder for children to understand death. Maybe it is because they are so full of life," said Thomas.

"If we don't find Pa's killer, I don't know how she will ever come to grips with the loss."

"Let's make sure we do find them."

CHAPTER SIXTEEN

When Ten Crows had returned from Young Noah's ranch, he began spending days in the sweat lodge trying to cleanse his body and his soul. Only then he knew could he hope for a vision. Day after day, he had gone to the sweat lodge. Finally the vision had come. In it he had seen a dark-haired woman with blood on her hands. With her was a tall man with red hair. They lived in a house that contained a lot of other people. Most of them men. They also had many bottles of whiskey and other spirits around them. In the vision he also saw a young dark-skinned man with light eyes who wore two guns. Ten Crows did not know exactly what it meant, but there had been no other visions save the one, no matter how many more times he had tried. From the time of the vision in the sweat lodge he had been planning his escape from the reservation.

The actions of the Indian Agent had made his task easier. According to the official representative of the U.S. Government, he was no longer the leader of his people. The Indian Agent had appointed a leader in his place. The leader he had appointed was a weak-willed man who would do whatever the agent wanted as long as the agent kept him supplied with liquor.

Because of this, he could no longer help his people and it broke his heart.

The old people of the camp still looked to Ten Crows for counsel, but their number was dwindling daily. His people were forbidden to travel off the reservation and they were forbidden to practice their religion and were instructed in Christianity. Instead of the spirit of cooperation and sharing to which they were accustomed, they were "encouraged" to practice self-sufficiency. They were no longer permitted to gather their native foods and instead grew gardens. They could still fish for salmon, but only in the rivers that ran through the reservation. They could no longer trade their salmon for buffalo. The game was scarce within the reservation boundaries because of all the white hunters, but they were forbidden to travel outside the reservation to hunt. So many changes from the old ways. None of them good in Ten Crows' eyes.

He had not heard from his son if the white law man had come. Ten Crows could no longer wait for a letter. He had to get away from the reservation to follow the vision and avenge his friend. At the same time he must arrange it so no one would come looking for him. The only way he could think to do this was to die. As the Cayuse buried their dead in mounds, he knew something had to be placed into the mound in his place. He would have to sneak off the reservation in the night, so he would wait for a time when there was no moon. He needed to have a good horse, one who was sure-footed and could travel quickly over the two week trip with little rest, water or food. His people's Cayuse ponies were famous for those traits and he would need one of the best of their kind.

Ten Crows had spoken to two of his closest friends from the old days, Red Deer and Broken Wing. Friends who had not been seduced by the white man's liquor or the false white man's promises. These friends he knew would keep a secret until they died. With their help, he had formed a plan. Ten Crows had carefully laid out his best ceremonial clothes then had one of the women construct a head-sized ball out of leather scraps. He had told her it was to be a present for his little grandson. This and the clothes, Ten Crows had stuffed with grasses. Having watched his mother and wife sew and do beadwork for years, Ten Crows knew how to sew and he attached the ball to resemble a head to the leather shirt. Then he topped the ball with his own felt hat. When he was ready to leave, he would cut off his braids and attach them to the ball under the hat. Until the time came, he kept the dummy he was constructing under a blanket in the corner. He was not worried about it being discovered because, as the failed leader of a failed people, no one paid any attention to him.

He would feign illness for a few days as the moon waned. He would let word of his impending death spread through the camp. He would pick out the site for his mound. Then one of his friends would report to the Indian Agent that Ten Crows had passed in his sleep. The Indian Agent would likely not respond to this news with any sort of investigation, he would simply tell the others to bury the body. His two trusted friends would arrange the dummy on a board and would carry it out to his burial mound. They would quickly cover the dummy before any questions could be asked. If the "new" leader attended, he would likely be drunk and not spot the ruse. Ten Crows didn't think any of the young people would attend his funeral and he could rely on the elders to keep his secret.

While his dummy was being buried, Ten Crows would sneak out of his home and hide until it was dark. Then he would take the supplies he had gathered, the horse he had chosen and paid for with gold and start for the south. The dummy was ready, and he settled in to wait.

But then Broken Wing, the oldest one of his friends, did die in his sleep. When Red Deer woke Ten Crows before dawn and told him what had happened, Ten Crows decided the time had to be now. The moon was waning and the fall rains were starting. Ten Crows decided there would be enough shadow to cover his escape. Red Deer cut his hair for him and they attached the braids to the dummy, letting them show on top of the blanket. Ten Crows pulled his shorn hair across his face and he and Red Deer carried the dummy to the mound site after they had carried the body of Broken Wing to his resting place. They accomplished this in the pre-dawn darkness before the camp was awake. Red Deer enlisted the help of other older members of the tribe and they began covering both with branches in preparation for the actual covering of the mound with soil. Ten Crows melted into the brush at the bottom of one of the canyons near the borders of the reservation. Later that night after dark, Red Deer would go to Ten Crows tent and bring the supplies he had cached for the trip. Ten Crows would get the horse he had bought and he would be gone long before the morning sun.

CHAPTER SEVENTEEN

The next morning Thomas started riding out with Theresa on her rounds to check the cattle of the Rafter S and her own stock from the Rafter T. It gave her an extra set of eyes in looking for cattle and it gave him a chance to get the lay of the land. He had been struck with the starkness of the Eastern Oregon countryside ever since he had entered the valley which contained Baker City. The lands around Pendleton and the valley of the Grande Ronde had at least seemed rich for the grazing of cattle with large pastures of tall grasses. This country, especially away from water, was rocky and stark. It was very alien to one who was accustomed to the green verdant landscape of northern New York State and western Oregon. There were few trees of any size here and then only along the creek bottoms. He was used to seeing great swaths of oak, maple, basswood and firs spread over rolling hills in his home state. The mountains around Baker City itself were spectacular, rising to immense heights from the valley floor with rocky, jagged points to their tops. New England had no such mountains. The Cascades of Oregon were magnificent, green and dense with conifers. But here in the canyons were the Hickmans made their home, he could see no mountains. Only the stark, brown hillsides rising up from the narrow creek bottom were visible, with their bunches of grass and mounds of rocks.

He had to admit the Hickman stock looked sleek and well-fed, so the dry bunch grass must be good feed. He wondered how far the cattle had to go to find enough to eat and he said as much to Theresa.

"Oh, we control a lot more ground than we own and the cattle range widely. If the government changes the laws so we can buy the range land, I'm sure we will do that. But in this country, if you control the water and the meadows in the bottoms for hay, you can range your cattle for several miles either side of the creek. That's what we do. We have some fencing, but it is mostly to keep cattle out of the hay fields, not keep them in anywhere.

"We do bring the stock into the fields in the harsh part of winter, but if the winter is open we let them range. We let them calve in the hillsides as it is cleaner than in a pen. We depend on the mama cows to protect their young from coyotes. Every mother cow we have has to come in at sorting time with a calf. If she doesn't, she is sold or butchered. Everyone has to pull their weight out here."

"That seems harsh. Surely it isn't the mother cow's fault if a coyote or wolf gets her calf?" Thomas said.

"Pa and the other ranchers along here have pretty much driven the wolves and the cougars back into the high country. Every mother cow we have had better be willing to fight to the death to protect her calf. A coyote isn't any bigger than my dogs. Any cow should be able to stomp something that size, even if there is a pack. Same goes for the horses. Every mare must come in with a foal in the spring."

She saw the doubt on his face.

189

"Listen," she explained. "This is a hard country. There is nothing easy about living out here. Nothing easy about bending nature to make a profit, whether you are farming, ranching or mining. We have no time for those who can't adapt and survive."

Now Thomas wondered if she was talking about animals or people. He decided it was both. He was finding out that this small, beautiful woman with the sensitive, elfin face had a core of iron and a will to match. He would remember that.

They followed this pattern for the first week riding sometimes in the creek bottom and sometimes high up on the hillsides. Thomas was frankly lost on several occasions, but Theresa seemed to always know where she was in relation to the home compound and her own little cabin. They stopped by her cabin one day so she could retrieve her tally book. Thomas wasn't invited inside and it gave him a chance to look at the neatly laid out area around him. The cabin was constructed of cottonwood logs and appeared to be one room with no loft. There was a tiny front yard where he could see the remains of hollyhocks from the summer. The barn was small as well, with a lean-to off one side and attached paddock. Theresa's spare horse was in the paddock. A small series of pens was attached to a larger corral, which Thomas assumed was for sorting stock and there was a patch of corn planted. He estimated the plot to be about 5 acres. The corn was still on the stocks and was drying in the chill wind. Obviously feed for something for the coming winter. Unlike the main compound, there were no chickens and he could see no evidence of hogs, a milk cow or a vegetable garden. He supposed Theresa got what she needed from the home place in those instances. It was a barebones homestead, but he had no doubt it would meet the definition of being "proved up" when the time came.

When Theresa was satisfied that the cows were more or less where they should be and that none of them needed to be doctored, they rode upstream and Thomas got his first look at the town of Rye Valley. Rye Valley was situated in a larger than usual clearing along the little stream. In fact the clearing covered a dozen acres. Calling Rye Valley a town might be stretching it a bit, he decided. Gold camp was a more accurate description in his estimation. There were a couple of log cabins and frame structures, but mostly it was a tent city at this point in its life. There were piles of stones and dirt everywhere where the miners had been at their work. Of course, there was a saloon, which also served as a de facto town hall, post office and community gathering place. If there was any kind of age limit on who could enter and drink, Thomas didn't see any evidence it was being enforced. He asked if they could step down so he could get a look at the town and its people.

"Great idea. I could use something warm. It is definitely not a day to be out any longer than necessary," said Theresa obligingly.

The day was brisk and the wind had a winter bite, so they ordered coffee with a whiskey chaser as they walked into the saloon. The bartender was used to seeing Theresa in his establishment and greeted her by name as they crossed the room to a table close to the stove. Theresa's dogs laid down under the table. They sat down, taking off their hats and gloves. Thomas found he was a bit shocked to see a woman so comfortable in a saloon and one who drank whiskey in her coffee. But he could find no fault with her decorum or manners. She was simply different than the women he had known before.

As the bartender delivered their drinks, he expressed his condolences on Noah's death.

"Sure is hard to believe he is gone. We got real used to seeing him when he would head up into the Basin. Always made sure to stop coming and going and spend a minute or two talking. Can't believe anyone would want him dead," the bartender said.

"Thank you, Johnny," said Theresa. "I'll be sure and pass on your condolences to Ma.

"Johnny, I'd like you to meet a friend of my brother Daniel. This is Thomas Hart. He was at school with Daniel back east and he has come west for his health. I'm showing him around the area. You'll probably see him getting out in the fresh air."

"Or he may want to do a little prospecting?" asked Johnny.

"Pleased to meet you, Mr. Johnny," Thomas said as he extended his hand. "Not sure about any prospecting."

"Just Johnny. No one calls anyone mister out here, less'n they're a law man or a preacher and heaven knows I ain't neither one of them." Johnny laughed and shook his hand. "We'll look forward to seeing you around some. You plan on staying long?"

"As Miss Hickman said, I'm here for my health. Fresh air and all out here. I'm not really sure. Maybe through the winter."

"Welcome then, however long you decide to stay. If you'll excuse me, I've got to get to my other customers."

When he had left them to go back to the bar, Theresa leaned over and said to Thomas, "Don't let that old buzzard fool you. He is smart as a tack and a savvy businessman. He knows everything that goes on around here. Where everyone goes, who got a strike and who's giving up. Make a friend of him and you'll have a steady supply of information on all of Rye Valley and half of the Basin."

"I'll keep that in mind," replied Thomas.

They spent the next half hour sipping their whiskey-laced coffee and watching the locals. It was a mix of the sort Thomas would expect in a gold camp. Mostly men dressed in workman's clothes and drinking to while away the cold winter day. There was a friendly faro game going at one of the tables. There were only two women in the bar besides Theresa and it was obvious they were "working" girls, likely getting a cut of the money on liquor sales. What else they did to earn money was none of his business as it wouldn't play into his search for Noah's killer. Thomas saw no one who aroused any suspicions in his mind. These were just hard working people hoping to strike it big one day. Most knew the odds were against them, but they were here to try anyway.

A couple of people stopped by their table to say a few words to Theresa about Noah, though it had been several months since his murder. The fact the murder was unsolved had kept it uppermost in people's minds. Theresa always thanked them and never failed to introduce Thomas to them, always with the cover story they had agreed upon. It would give him an opening with all the locals as it would spread far and wide through the gold camp. News was scarce up here and his unusual appearance would only add to the gossip mill fodder.

When the coffee and the whiskey had warmed them, they prepared to take their leave, Theresa calling the dogs to her as they walked out the door.

"Thanks for the coffee, Johnny," she said as they left. "I'll see you next time I'm up this way."

"Ride safe," he responded. "Paiutes are out there again."

She touched the brim of her hat in salute and they stepped back outside and into the teeth of the wind.

"Ugh! I had hoped it would slow down some while we were in there," Theresa said. "It seems like it is getting colder."

She turned her face into the wind and sniffed the air a couple of times.

"Snow's coming. Let's head back to the ranch house. We don't want to get caught out if it decides to dump 6 inches or a foot of snow. Not likely, but it can happen."

They mounted up and started back downstream towards the ranch house. They had only traveled about a quarter of a mile when Theresa's prediction turned out to be right. The snow was light at first. Tiny, dry flakes swirling on the wind. Thomas was reminded of a toy he had seen once that contained a tiny village inside a glass bubble. When the glass bubble was shaken, it would appear as if it were snowing on the little village inside the bubble.

"At least we won't have to worry about the Paiutes," Theresa said. "They have enough sense to be inside by a warm fire on a day like this."

"Maybe we can learn something from them," grumbled Thomas.

"We can get as far as my place with no problem. We may not make it back to the main ranch until tomorrow if this sets in like it means it."

"How is your mother going to feel about you being out all night with a man who isn't your husband?" asked Thomas.

"My ma knows me and she knows I can defend myself if I decide it is what I need to do. She will worry about my safety, but not about my being out with a man.

"Besides, she likes you and knows you to be an honorable man."

Obviously there was no issue here for her, thought Thomas. And she was right. He was an honorable man, but the woman was definitely beautiful and in different circumstances he would be courting her.

The snow fell harder and thicker, though the flakes were still dry. They were riding into the wind with their mufflers pulled up over their mouths and noses and their hats pulled down low. They had about an inch of their faces exposed to the wind and even that was too much. It was difficult to see much beyond their horses' ears and Thomas was hopelessly lost. It seemed like they had been riding for hours. He didn't know how they would find the turn off to Theresa's place and he thought they might have missed it. He remembered it was up a side canyon and was about a quarter mile off the main road to Rye Valley. He also knew Theresa had to have been out in weather like this before. He didn't like having to depend on someone else, but he had no choice in these circumstances.

Then he realized they were no longer facing into the wind. It was now hitting more to the left side of his face and he adjusted his muffler to protect his left ear more. He didn't remember any particular bend in the road to the west, but he was so hopelessly turned around now, he could have been halfway to Boston for all he knew. Then the wind lessened some, the snow cleared a little and he could see Theresa's cabin ahead of him before the curtain of snow closed in again.

The horses and dogs knew where they were going and all four made for the barn. They stepped off the horses and led them inside with the dogs running and barking to show them the way.

"Yes, boys, I know this is home," laughed Theresa. "I live here too, you know.

"You can hang your saddle over there," Theresa pointed to a row of logs jutting out from the wall of the barn. "I'll get some rags to wipe the horses down and them we can throw feed for them."

Theresa and Thomas dried and fed the horses and Theresa brought her spare mount in out of the paddock and fed her as well. The dogs had sat down in the hay and were busily picking the ice balls out of their feet.

She patted her leg and the dogs immediately joined her in the walk to the house. Thomas was glad the house was close, though the little canyon where Theresa's homestead stood, blocked a lot of the wind. They made the cabin door with no problem, stomping their feet on the stone step to knock most of the snow from their boots. The dogs bolted through the door as soon as it opened and stood by the hearth, tongues lolling out, heads cocked as if to say, "Mom, where's the fire?"

Theresa busied herself lighting the fire. She always laid the fire whenever she left the house as well as making sure the wood box was full. She had learned to do those things that were important in case of emergency long before she started living on her own and it only made good sense to her to have the ability to warm up the cabin quickly. The fire sprang to life and started licking at the logs. Soon it was burning cheerily, and the cabin began to warm. The dogs sank down gratefully on the hearth and were soon sound asleep. Theresa moved the kettle over the logs and got the water heating. Then she lit the two lamps that sat on the kitchen sideboard against the impending night.

Thomas had been watching her work with admiration. Not a wasted movement. Quick and sure with what she was doing, it was obvious she was an accomplished woman in her own home. He couldn't imagine any situation where Theresa wouldn't excel, either in the home or on the range.

Theresa finally removed her outer gear, hanging it on pegs by the door and signaled for Thomas to do the same. When he had done so, he saw her take down two tin cups from a cupboard in what obviously passed for her kitchen. A sideboard, a table with two chairs and a stand with a wash basin completed the kitchen. Thomas surveyed the rest of the cabin. There was an iron bedstead in one corner of the room and a small dresser with a mirror in one corner next to it. A shelf on the wall contained half a dozen books. There was one nightgown and one dress hanging on the wall, a couple of shirtwaists along with two pairs of pants.

He saw one pair of boots and one pair of regular shoes arranged neatly under them. There was a trunk in a corner of the living room with a buffalo robe folded on top. The house was well organized, but it was obviously in need of sweeping and dusting. If Theresa had any qualms about her housekeeping, it wasn't apparent to Thomas.

Theresa removed a cloth from a loaf of bread on the sideboard and cut off slabs, placing them on a tin plate. She got a pot of butter and another of preserves and placed them on the table.

"This and coffee or tea is going to have to be supper I'm afraid. All there is in the house, other than the little buttermilk and some meat scraps I have for the dogs. I wasn't planning on company. In fact I was planning on begging supper from Ma."

"That is fine," said Thomas as he stood next to the fire. "Right now, I think I want to stand next to the fire for a while."

They both looked out the front window of the cabin at the snow that continued to swirl and fall. Once in a while, the wind would shift and a dusting of snow would creep into the cabin either through the window or under the door. Theresa would sweep it into a pile and put it into the fire before it could puddle up and turn to ice overnight.

"Do you think it will let up by morning?" asked Thomas as he remembered the snowstorms of New England which could last for days on end.

Theresa shrugged her shoulders.

"Only fools and newcomers predict the weather around here," she said. "But probably. Most of our snowstorms don't last long. Sometimes we will have a chinook and it will melt overnight. Or it could set in and snow for a few days. Hard to say."

As she didn't seem too concerned, Thomas decided he wasn't either, or at least tried not to be. They both sat down at the table and ate the bread with butter and preserves. Thomas found it surprisingly good and he washed it down with hot, black coffee. Theresa ate lightly and then fed her dogs. They didn't talk. Felt no need to talk. He found he appreciated a woman who wasn't constantly needing to fill the air with sound.

"You can take the buffalo robe and stretch out in front of the fire," Theresa said. "The outhouse is out back of the cabin. The path is well marked, so you won't get lost in the snow. I'll get you a couple of quilts.

"This cabin gets chilly at night. If you wake up, I'd appreciate it if you would put more wood on the fire," she said as she placed the buffalo robe and two quilts on the floor in front of the fireplace.

"I'm going to go walk the dogs and check on the stock before I turn in," Theresa said as she lit a lantern, then put on her coat, muffler, hat and gloves. "I'll be back in a few minutes."

She quickly went out the door to keep the snow from swirling into the cabin. Thomas watched her through the window until her light disappeared into the gloom and snow. He decided to use the facilities out back, when he realized there was only one lantern in the cabin. She lived alone. What use would she have for two lanterns? So, he waited. And waited. Then he began to get anxious. How would he find her in the snow?

Then he heard her stamping her feet against the side of the cabin and opened the door for her.

"Damn dogs heard something and took off." She shook the snow from her coat and hat. "Not letting up any out there. Glad we decided not to try for the main ranch."

She looked at his face.

"What's wrong with you?"

"I was worried."

"About me? I'm in my own front yard. No need to be worried about me.

"We'd best turn in. If this lets up, I want to leave early for the main ranch house."

Thomas took the light and went around the house to the outhouse cursing himself as he went. She was right. This was her place. She knew her way around. She had lived out here alone for a time. She was in her element. She obviously didn't need him, or anyone, to take care of her. She was definitely different than the women he had known. Elfin face and iron will. What a combination!

When he got back inside, he found Theresa had changed into her nightgown and was already in her bed reading, both dogs asleep at the foot of her bed on an old quilt. She looked up when he came in and then went back to her book. He spread out the buffalo robe on the floor and then spread out the quilts on top of that. He removed his boots, his belt and put his pistol close to hand.

"Would you please pull in the latch string before you go to bed?" she asked.

"Sure. Don't you have something more substantial for a lock?"

"If it makes you feel any better, there is a board in the corner by the door. You can brace the door closed with that."

Thomas decided he did feel better with the brace in place and then went to bed.

Theresa just shook her head and went back to her book. She had her rifle and her dogs. That should be enough for anybody. She was about to decide Thomas Hart was a bit of a worrier. She wasn't entirely sure she liked a man, who wasn't her father, worrying about her.

CHAPTER EIGHTEEN

Ten Crows hadn't waited near the reservation to learn if his ruse had worked. By sunrise he was clear of the valley floor and well hidden in a dense grove of conifers in one of the draws along the base of the mountain. This close to the reservation he didn't dare light a fire, so he made a cold camp. He unsaddled his horse and picketed her where she could browse on cottonwood branches and dry bunch grass. He was close enough to the trail he could hear anyone coming along the trail yet he was far enough away to not be noticed by any but the most alert travelers. This late in the season he didn't expect any wagon trains, but there could still be freight wagons and stagecoaches coming through. Both of those made a lot of noise and he was a light sleeper, so he spread out his bedroll on the ground and soon was asleep.

He and his people had traveled this trail many times over the course of his lifetime. He knew where he could get off the trail and safely hide for as long as necessary. He also knew ways around the trail if there were people he didn't want to meet. He had chosen his outfit carefully, so it would appear that he was a worker for a rancher. He even rode a white man's saddle and carried a catch rope. His chopped off hair would further enforce the ruse. He would say he worked for the Hickmans as a ranch hand and that should allow him to not be questioned too closely. Noah and his family were well known in the area as friends of the Cayuse and they had employed many of his people over the years.

He slept for a few hours, then saddled his horse, watered her from his own canteen and began the long ascent to the top of the ridge. The hillside was very steep and he let his horse pick her way up the mountain, zigzagging back and forth across the face of the hill. He avoided the draws as much as possible, favoring sparing his horse over the chances of him being spotted. He thought his ruse had worked and he was relatively certain no one was looking for him and if they were they wouldn't be looking at the backside of the mountain, away from the main trail.

He stayed the next night at the place the white's called Emigrant Springs. He had watered his horse and filled his canteen at the spring before diving deep into the forest. He selected a spot where the tree branches covered over his space and lit a small fire to warm water to wash with before sleeping. He also took advantage of the small fire to make tea, a habit he had acquired while a student in Canada. Once again he spread his robe, and using his saddle for a pillow, went to sleep. It felt right to be out traveling freely once again. He missed his people, especially his family, but the thrill of traveling at his own pace in a manner chosen by him was exhilarating.

The next morning after a cold breakfast he traveled along the spine of the ridge for a ways before starting his gradual descent into the valley of the Grande Ronde. So far he had not seen any other lone travelers. He had heard a stage and several freight wagons, but he had slipped into the trees and had avoided contact. He wasn't pushing his horse and allowed her and himself to rest at least twice a day. He told himself he was saving the horse in case he had to take the much more difficult mountain route, but the truth was he was not as strong nor as young as he had been. He knew he was past 60 and his joints were beginning to tell him about the hours in the saddle. He got off and walked frequently to stop the protests from his knees. The truth was, the tough little Cayuse mare was handling the trip much better than he was.

He camped the second night at the base of the mountains in a spot that allowed him to look out over the Grande Ronde valley. He remembered a time when the vast horse herds of the native peoples had run free over those grasslands. His people, along with the Nez Perce and the Umatilla traveled to the valley every summer to harvest camas root and other plants. They also came to hunt, fish, and to trade. Later the mountain men had joined them in their summer gathering as the pelts of the beaver were not good in the summer. It wasn't until the white men who wanted to own the land and rip at it with their picks and plows had come that the trouble had begun. His cousins from the Umatilla tribe had fought with these white men until the soldiers had come to arrest their chiefs. Several people had died in the ensuing fighting before the Umatilla finally escaped. Now all the horses that grazed below him were owned by the whites who had taken possession of his lands. They continued to rip and tear at his mother with their implements of steel. He could never understand the logic of wanting to own land and to always be taking. It did him no good to think, "It is just their way. They do this wherever they go." He wanted to know why they couldn't see the beauty and the sacred nature of the land as it had been for all the generations of his forefathers. His friend

Noah and he had talked many times about this, but Ten Crows still didn't understand these whites.

This leg of the journey could be his most perilous. He had roughly 30 miles of open grassland to cover before he gained the relative safety of the next range of hills. He could keep to the edges of the forest along the fringes of the grasslands, but it would nearly double the number of miles he must travel and it would be much harder going on the horse. And himself, if he was honest about it. There were marshes he must avoid as well. If his ruse had been discovered, there would have been time to send an alert out on a fast horse and the rider could have easily been in the small settlement of LaGrande before now. There were many in the town who still harbored ill feelings toward any Indian.

He sat smoking in his little camp in the trees and thought about his options. He had deliberately not brought any weapons with him, save his hunting knife. He knew any show of force on his part would lead to instant death at the hands of most any white man. He would no longer be deemed a threat from his physical appearance as he had shrunk both in height and girth. His grey hair would likely lead most to think he was simply a helpless old man. Normally Ten Crows was a man who was meticulous in his personal grooming habits, but tonight he made the decision to change that. He would cover himself with dust in the morning so he would look ever more dejected and helpless. He would ride through the heart of the valley, only bypassing the settlements as a precaution. Anyone he met would likely pay him little mind. At least, that was his hope. He would take his dead friend's name, Broken Wing, if anyone asked who he was and he would say he was traveling back to the Hickman ranch after delivering horses to Pendleton. It should work.

CHAPTER NINETEEN

Theresa was up and dressed in a clean shirtwaist and pants before the sun had topped the nearest range of hills. The snow had stopped during the night. She wanted to put the coffee pot on the fire, but Thomas was sleeping squarely in the middle of the floor in front of the hearth. So she none too gently poked Thomas to wake him. To her astonishment, he had a gun aimed squarely at her mid-section when he rolled over.

"Touchy in the mornings are we?" she asked. "You'd best put that thing away and start stirring. I want to be saddling up in 30 minutes."

"Don't ever touch me when I'm asleep," was all he growled.

"Well, if you didn't sleep like the dead, you would have heard me and the dogs stirring around this morning. It is light enough for you to see your way to the outhouse without the lantern. There is still some bread and butter left for breakfast. If you will move, I'll put the coffee pot on the fire."

Thomas threw back the quilts and rose from the buffalo robe. He moved out of her way, grabbing his boots on the way to the kitchen to sit in one of the chairs.

"How long you been up, anyways?"

"About 45 minutes. I've already taken the dogs out and fed the horses."

"I'm sorry. I guess I was sleeping pretty hard. Must have been more tired than I realized. I'll be right back for that coffee."

He went outside and stretched and realized that for all the fury of the day before, there was not a lot of snow on the ground. He would have expected at least 8 or 10 inches from a storm like that one in New England, but here there was barely 4 inches. He noticed in places that it had drifted into deeper drifts, but there was not nearly the accumulation he had expected. They would have no trouble reaching the main ranch house in this, he thought.

When he re-entered the cabin, Theresa was pouring the coffee and had poured warm water into the wash basin on the kitchen table. There was clean toweling lying beside the bowl and a bar of soap.

"I don't have any shaving equipment here, but you are welcome to wash up if you want. I've already had my turn."

"Thank you," he said as he sampled the coffee. "I don't pack my shaving kit with me, so I'll settle for just a quick wash. I'll shave later at the main ranch."

He ran a hand through his hair saying, "Could I borrow a comb or a brush?"

Theresa went to the dresser and brought back a carved wooden comb.

"I think this might work on your hair. It looks like it is rather thick and heavy."

"Yes, it is sometimes a bit of a problem to get a comb through. I didn't inherit my mother's hair, only her eyes.

She was French-Canadian. She was a fine lady, a great cook and a wonderful dancer. She died when I was a little boy. I miss her still."

"I understand. I miss my Pa every day. I see him everywhere. Both here and at the main ranch. He made so many things. He was such a force of nature. It was almost like he was unconquerable and unstoppable. Like a storm. Maybe that is why it is so hard for me to believe he is gone."

Thomas wet his hair and washed his face, drying both with the toweling. Theresa watched him struggle to get the comb through his hair, until she said, "Here, let me do it," taking the comb from him and motioning him to sit in the chair.

Theresa had never touched hair like his. She had combed her sister's and brother's hair and her nieces and nephews, but none of them were like his. It was heavy and coarse like Young Noah's, but it was very curly. The fact it had grown long made it more difficult to comb, but she did get it all going in one direction, straight back from his face.

"You know, if you would keep your hair short, it would be easier to manage. You should have Ma cut it for you. She cuts hair for everyone in the family."

"I'll consider that. I hate to ask her for anything. She always seems to be going and doing."

"Yes, that's Ma. Even when she sits in the evening, she is reading or making clothes or mending. She doesn't seem to like to be still. The only time her hands are still is when she is rocking the babies.

"Ready to go?" she asked as she put the comb back on her dresser.

"Just need to get my outside clothes on. I'll take the bread and butter with me and eat it on the way."

They got on their winter gear, shut the cabin door behind them and headed to the barn where the dogs were waiting for them. Theresa took two pieces of bread from her coat pocket and gave one to each of the dogs.

"That will have to do until you can get Ma to feed you. I'm out of anything to feed any of us."

Theresa picked out the two horses they would ride that day using a criteria known only to her. Thomas thought he should offer to saddle her mount for her, but she already had the saddle pads in place and the saddle in her hands while he was still getting his horse groomed. The girl didn't waste any time. He again marveled how she seemed to excel at everything she touched.

When both horses were saddled, Theresa caught up her extra horse and put a halter on it. They mounted up and started the three horses down the trail to the main road and the home ranch. When they came back out to the main road, Thomas saw the drifts were higher in places here due to the direction of the storm, but still the horses navigated their way through them with little trouble. When he asked if this was normal, for the snow to be so driven and leave so little, Theresa merely shrugged and said, "Sometimes it does it. Sometimes it doesn't."

Again, Thomas wondered that Theresa didn't seem to have a need to fill the air with sound and they rode along in a companionable silence. Thomas noticed how the light snow had changed the landscape and somehow had taken the harshness out of it by softening the jagged edges of the rocks, covering the brown and the grey with soft whiteness which sparkled in the early morning light. The rising sun cast deep shadow in some places and shone brilliant white in others in an almost mercurial fashion. It almost made it seem magical somehow. He was beginning to see how this raw and harsh land could have a beauty all its own. They met or passed no other travelers and it appeared from the virgin carpet of snow they were the first ones out this morning.

"I love it when it is like this," Theresa finally said. "When everything is pure and white and untrampled. Even the deer and the rabbits haven't been out yet. Almost like we are the only things alive in the whole world."

He could see her point. It was completely unsullied by any creature, man or beast. Even the horses traveled differently with the snow muffling their hoof beats. The dogs trotted alongside the horses and didn't go chasing off through the brush after rabbits or birds. He was amazed at the silence and the beauty. He felt he could go on riding through this wonderland forever.

The sound carried far on the cold, winter air and they heard the main ranch compound before they saw it. The sound of voices, of harness jingling, of an axe on wood, of cattle and sheep. They walked the horses across the compound and into the barn where they turned them over to one of the hands, telling him to loosen the saddles and keep them handy in case they needed to ride out again. Then they walked back to the ranch house.

Syrie and Painted Pony were just starting the wash when they walked through the door.

"There you are! We half expected you last night until that storm blew in. You spend the night at your cabin?" asked Syrie.

"Yeah. We thought it was safer than trying for here. We weren't sure how deep the snow would get or how bad the wind might be."

"Smart thinking. I'm glad you took shelter there then."

"Have you eaten yet today?" asked Painted Pony.

"To tell you the truth, we really haven't eaten much since we left here yesterday. All I had left at the house was some bread, some butter and some preserves. If it wasn't for coffee, we'd probably never would have made it through."

Syrie tsk-tsk'd at Theresa and said, "I have told you numerous times, you need to pay more attention to the running of your household, even if it is just you. You should never let yourself get so low on supplies in this country."

"I know, Ma. I really will try to do better. I had more food for the dogs than I had for us," Theresa said as she reached down and patted both dogs. "And all they got was a piece of bread for their breakfast this morning."

Painted Pony had moved one of the pots of water on the stove to free up space and pulled down a cast iron skillet from its place on the cabin wall.

"Theresa, you go on down to the spring house and bring up some milk and butter, some eggs and some soft cheese. I'll fix you four something to eat. Thomas, there is fresh coffee in that pot on the fire. Help yourself."

Abigail came in through the parlor when she heard Theresa's voice and offered to help her carry items up from the spring house.

While the girls were down at the spring house, Painted Pony carved thick slices of bacon from a side which hung outside the back door and put them in the skillet. Then she sliced bread and set it out on the table along with preserves. When the girls returned, she instructed them to put the items on the table and reached up and got down four tin plates. While the bacon was draining, she broke eight eggs into the bacon grease and fried them up. She dished up two eggs into each plate, drizzled milk over two of them, added a small piece of bread and set them down for the dogs. The other two plates she put on the table for Theresa and Thomas.

She poured hot water into three tin cups and made tea for Syrie, Abigail and herself. Then she sat down at the table. Syrie and Abigail joined her and Abigail asked what they had learned in Rye Valley.

"Nothing much, but I don't feel it was a wasted trip," said Thomas between bites of breakfast. "I got to meet a lot of the locals and since I am associated with you now, thanks to Theresa's introductions, I feel they will be more likely to talk to me. Theresa tells me the local bartender is a fountain of potential information."

"How bad was the storm in Rye Valley?" asked Syrie.

"We didn't actually start getting snow until we had left Rye Valley and started back down the road," said Thomas. "I was amazed when I got up this morning. I figured after the wind and snow we had last night that we would wake up to at least twice the snow we did get. Back home in New York a storm like that would have easily dumped two, maybe three times, the amount of snow we found this morning."

Syrie nodded her head.

"I remember storms in New Hampshire like the ones you are talking about. I wondered about that when I came out here myself. The only way I can think to explain it is the difference in the snow. Back in New England, the snow is heavier. It is wetter. Out here the air is so dry and it seems the snow is drier as well. It is lighter. It drifts around more and it doesn't pack down like it does back East."

"I remember Mr. Meek said something about your being from New England," said Thomas. "Did you meet Mr. Hickman back there or out here?"

As they finished their breakfast, Syrie told Thomas about living in New Hampshire, about Noah guiding the wagon train, her journey over the Oregon Trail and about meeting the Cayuse. Theresa had heard this story numerous times, so she focused her attention on Thomas as he listened to Syrie's story. She saw an intelligent and educated man, who was gracious and polite to her mother.

He asked intelligent questions and seemed genuinely interested in what Syrie was saying. He wasn't just making polite conversation. She hadn't seen many people outside her family and the hired hands interact with her mother. She was impressed by Thomas' natural grace in his interactions with Syrie.

"I had better get back to this wash," Syrie said. "Ladies, we have a lot to do today, so let's get to it. These clothes aren't going to wash and dry themselves. Abigail will you get the drying rack? Thank you."

She stood up as did Painted Pony and Abigail.

"Thomas it has been nice visiting with you, but we have a ton of work to do."

"Yes, I need to write some letters myself. Seems like a good day to do that. Might I use your desk and supplies in the parlor? If you ladies will excuse me?"

"Ma, I need to borrow some supplies, then I'll head back to my cabin. I have some things that need doing there."

"Theresa you don't need to "borrow" anything. You take whatever you need. Did you bring an extra horse?"

"Yes, I did."

"The next time someone goes to Baker City or Fort Boise, I am going to make up a separate supply list for your cabin."

"I guess someone needs to. I never seem to get around to doing that. There always seems to be cows to doctor or some other thing."

Syrie hugged her daughter, then held her at arm's length.

"You know you don't have to do everything yourself. You could ask for a little help once in a while."

"I've never been real good at that, have I?"

"Not since you were a little, bitty girl. You came into this world, saying, 'lead, follow or get out of my way', I swear. Take a breath and ask for help once in a while."

"Okay, Ma. I'll try."

"We have got to get this wash done, so I'll let you get what you need. And take some supplies for baking. You know how to make bread and biscuits so start doing it."

"Yes, Ma."

Syrie plunged her hands into the wash tub and started scrubbing clothes on the washboard. Abigail and Painted Pony kept the tubs filled with hot water, rinsed the clean clothes, wrung them out and hung them on the drying rack. Soon the kitchen was filled with steam and the smell of lye soap.

Theresa took her mother's advice and packed up flour, sugar, lard, meat and other staples. Then she went to the spring house and gathered butter and soft cheese. She would have loved to have taken home milk, but she hadn't thought to bring any containers. She really needed to get her housekeeping skills in order she thought. Winter was here and she could get snowed in. Yesterday had just been a warning. Theresa sighed. Her mother had tried to teach her how to keep a house, but it just hadn't seemed to stick. She would simply have to make more of an effort or she and the dogs could be in real trouble over the winter.

After Thomas had finished writing his letters to his family and to Mr. Meek, he decided to go in search of Daniel. He found out that Daniel was in the lower horse pasture checking on stock along with Benjamin. He gathered his horse from the barn and set off in search of them. The warming sun was already melting the snow of the night before and the bunch grasses were showing their true form again.

He found the Hickman brothers riding slowly through the herd of horses, checking for condition and any horses which might be injured. They always kept the breeding stallions with their respective bands of mares in separate pastures. They kept the geldings, the mares with nursing foals and the dry mares in a large herd all together. There wasn't a lot of fighting among this group, but there were always some horses that got into it with the other horses and had nicks and cuts from bites or kicks. They didn't bother with the small stuff, but they would bring in any with large cuts or obvious lameness to the barn for doctoring.

This day they had a gelding who had a sizable gash to his off shoulder that they were haltering for the trip back to the barn. They already had a mare and her foal haltered and ready to go back. The foal had a noticeable limp in a hind leg. It would be a slow trip to the barn.

After they came out of the gate to the pasture, Thomas fell in with them for the ride back.

"Are you going to doctor those horses?" he asked.

"No, this is Michael's job. He really enjoys doing it and he seems to have a gift for it. The horses really seem to trust him and he gets good results. So we let him do all the doctoring. He does the cows, goats and the sheep as well. He has special pens he keeps them in until they are well and can join the herds again," explained Benjamin.

"He has always liked animals from the time he was little," said Daniel.

"Say, where did you spend the night last night? We noticed you weren't at breakfast this morning."

"We decided it was better to stay at Theresa's cabin rather than come back to the main ranch in the snow. I slept on a buffalo rug on the floor. Slept pretty good too. But your sister needs to learn to keep a bit more food in her pantry. All she had in the house to eat was bread, butter and preserves. I nearly starved before we got back here. Thank heavens she had coffee."

"Theresa never has been much of a housekeeper. Never had time for female things. Always out with the cows," said Benjamin.

"She is sure different than any other woman I ever knew," said Thomas. "They don't have women like her in New York or anywhere else in the East."

Daniel said, "That's for damn sure!"

Benjamin defended his sister saying, "She's just Theresa. That's just who she is. If they don't have women like her back East, then they are the ones who are missing out."

CHAPTER TWENTY

Ten Crows put out his breakfast fire, saddled his horse and set off down the mountain and into the valley of the Grande Ronde. He had decided to put his faith in his vision. His visions had never failed him in all his adult years. He knew he wouldn't have been shown Noah's killers, if he wasn't meant to be able to bring justice to his friend. He had his story all worked out and he was confident he would be able to cross through the little town in the valley, LaGrande. It was cool in the mornings now and he had found ice on the little creek where he had washed up and watered his horse. Ten Crows knew he had to make good time the rest of the journey or he would be caught in the winter snows. Though he knew he could get through the snow, he simply didn't want the discomfort it would bring.

He came to the outskirts of town late in the afternoon. People were starting to wrap up their business and go to their homes for their supper. After subsisting on jerky and tea for the last few days, the smells coming from the various houses and cabins were very inviting to Ten Crows. But the people inside wouldn't be. Even though he had gold, he didn't dare try to buy a meal at any of the businesses in town. He would have been lucky to have been able to even buy flour at the local general store. His "kind" were not welcome in this town.

As he came into town, he hung his head and didn't make eye contact with anyone. He deliberately made his posture even worse and pulled his hat down lower over his eyes. He was almost through town when he heard a voice behind him.

"Hey, Injun! Are you deaf? I'm talking to you."

Ten Crows stopped his pony and turned around. It took all his will to not straighten and face down this ignorant white man. He tried to mimic the slight lisp of his late friend, Broken Wing and keep the boarding school English out of his voice.

"Yes, sir," he said.

"What are you doing off the rez?"

Ten Crows could see the man wore a star. So this was the law of this town.

"I am not a reservation Indian. I work for the Rafter S. I work for the Hickmans."

"Hickmans. Shit!" the deputy spat tobacco juice. "No account Injun lovers anyway. How come you are out here by yourself?

"We delivered horses to the reservation. I stayed to visit with family. Now I am going back to the ranch."

"You got anything that says you got a right not to be on the rez? All you red niggas are lying bastards anyhows." The big-bellied deputy walked over and stood with his legs spread apart next to the pony. Ten Crows could smell the sour sweat and beer on the man from six feet. A short quirt hung from the man's wrist by a leather thong. The deputy slapped the quirt against his chaps. He pushed back his hat and greasy blonde hair spilled out. Apparently he didn't like looking up at Ten Crows, so he said, "Get down off'n that horse. I need to make sure you dinn't steal it."

Ten Crows stepped down and stood facing the deputy. Ten Crows was a good six inches taller than the deputy and that seemed to make the deputy even madder. His face flushed and his pale, blue eyes were nearly hidden by the fat on his face. He moved closer and squinted at Ten Crows. Then he grabbed the reins from Ten Crows and jerked on the pony to lead it away. The pony was not used to being jerked and sat back on the reins. The deputy raised his quirt to strike the pony and Ten Crows stepped in between the man and the horse.

"Why are you taking my horse?" Ten Crows asked.

"Because I'm bettin' you stole it. An' I'm confiscatin' it 'til I kin find out."

"I did not steal this horse. I have a bill of sale in my bags."

"I'll bet!"

"If you will give me back the reins, I will get it for you," Ten Crows held out his hand for the reins and the deputy reluctantly gave them back to him.

Ten Crows petted the pony and then went to his saddle bags to retrieve the bill of sale.

"Hold it. That's far enough!"

Ten Crows turned back to the deputy. The deputy had his gun drawn and pointed at him. By now there was a crowd gathering around the two men.

"I told you I had a bill of sale in my saddle bags. I was going to get it out and show it to you."

"Yeah. And you've also got a pistol in there," snorted the deputy.

"No, I don't. But you are welcome to get the paper for yourself," Ten Crows said calmly.

The deputy holstered his pistol, strode over to the pony and put his hands in the saddle bag feeling around for a paper. When he found a piece of paper, he pulled it out and unfolded it. It was the last letter to Ten Crows from his son. Ten Crows could tell from the way the man held it upside down, that the deputy was illiterate.

"Well, I guess it' okay. What other stolen stuff do you have in there?" the deputy demanded.

"I have nothing stolen. I have some supplies. Some pemmican and jerky. A change of clothes. That's all."

The deputy snorted again and started to pull things out of the saddle bags and throw them in the dusty street. When he got to the tin container of tea, he opened it, dumped the contents on the ground, then threw the tin into the dust. When he had emptied the saddle bags, he took Ten Crows' canteen, pulled the cork out of it, sniffed it and dumped the water on the ground. Then he started untying Ten Crows bedroll from the back of the saddle.

"Sir, I would appreciate it if you would let me gather my things," said Ten Crows struggling to maintain his accent and his false demeanor.

"You kin jest wait a goddamn minute 'til I'm through searchin' 'ur stuff," growled the deputy. Ten Crows could sense the man was getting angrier as he failed to find anything of value or something he could use as proof of theft. Ten Crows stepped to the head of the pony and rubbed her face, as much to calm himself as to calm the horse.

The deputy finally got the saddle strings loose and flung the bedroll and the slicker to the ground. Then he kicked everything around in the dust until all the blankets and hides were thoroughly filthy.

"You never did show me sometin' to prove you have a right to be off the rez," growled the deputy as he got within inches of Ten Crows face. Ten Crows had to swallow hard to keep from stepping back and holding his nose, the man's stench was so powerful. Knowing the deputy couldn't read, he searched through the pile of his baggage until he came to the bill of sale for the pony which he gave to the deputy.

"It says I am employed by the Rafter S and that I am on business for them," said Ten Crows.

"I know'd what it sez," said the deputy. "You think I caint read, red nigger?"

"No, sir. I never said that," Ten Crows said keeping his voice calm and inserting a little begging into it for good measure.

"You callin' me a liar? Are you sassin' me, boy?" shouted the deputy as he raised the quirt and brought it down across Ten Crows face, cutting his cheek.

Ten Crows stood perfectly still for a few seconds, maintaining the stooped posture and the dejected persona. But he couldn't keep the hatred from his eyes. Something the deputy saw in the depths of those black eyes finally got through the alcoholic haze and he stepped quickly away.

"Git your shit and git outa my town," shouted the deputy. "If'n I ever see you again in my town, I'll make you sorry!"

"Yes, sir. Thank you sir," said Ten Crows when he could trust his voice again.

The deputy strode off and most of the crowd followed him. Ten Crows wasn't surprised to see all of them go into the saloon. The man who stayed behind approached him holding out a handkerchief.

"Here, use this. You need to get the blood stopped. Is it deep?"

Ten Crows glanced at the man, placed the handkerchief to the cut and thanked him. The man was about Ten Crows age and he was short, but still powerfully built. His hands and face spoke of long years in the outdoors. He wore workman's clothes and Ten Crows could see a braided leather thong peeking out from the man's open collar.

"No, it is not deep," replied Ten Crows. "He has no strength."

"I can't abide that man," the Good Samaritan said. "Showed up here after the war. Says he's from Arkansas. I wish he'd go back. Don't know how he keeps his job as deputy. Drunk more than half the time. Let me help you get your stuff gathered back up," the man said as he bent down to help Ten Crows retrieve his goods from the street.

"He didn't ruin anything except my tea," Ten Crows said. "It will just take me some time to get it all packed back up."

"I heard you say you worked for the Rafter S. How long you known the Hickmans?"

Ten Crows stopped and looked at the man, trying to figure out if he was friend or foe. He let the silence drag on.

"I only asked because I heard a rumor that Noah was dead. Is it true?"

"Yes, it is true."

"My name is Walter Carter. I was on the last wagon train Noah guided west. I went to Oregon City, but I couldn't abide the rain. I remembered this valley, so after a few years, I came back here and started raising cattle. I never did make the trip to see Noah, even after I found out he had settled south of Baker City. Wish now I had.

"He married a woman, Jedidiah Boone's widow didn't he?"

"Yes, he did. They raised a family together."

"I tell you what, when that woman began to wail at the crossing of every river and stream, she liked to made all of us crazy. That was some kind of scary."

"She is a fine woman and a good mother. She was a good wife to Noah. And a good friend to my people," said Ten Crows.

"She was always real pleasant and helpful until Jedidiah died. Then she just kind of got lost, I guess. I'm pleased she found her way back.

"Well, at any rate, I'm sure sorry about Noah. He was a hell of a man. When you see his missus will you give her my condolences?"

"I will, yes," said Ten Crows as he shook out the last of his blankets and re-rolled his bedroll. "I am going to miss my tea in the mornings."

"The general store is still open. If you need some supplies to make up for what that idiot Elkins ruined, I'd be happy to pick some up for you. They won't serve you."

Ten Crows reached under his shirt and retrieved a leather pouch. He took out a silver dollar and gave it to the man.

"I would appreciate it if you would buy me some tea," he said.

"I'll be happy to do that," Carter said. "My late wife was Tillamook and I've never appreciated the way you folks get treated. She was as fine a woman as ever lived. I carry this in memory of her," he said as he took out what was obviously a woman's medicine bundle from under his shirt. "I don't necessarily believe all the magic stuff about this that she did, but it was hers and it is a way to remember.

"I'll be right back," Carter said as he went up the street to the store.

Ten Crows watched him for a second, then went to find some water to refill his canteen and to water his horse.

CHAPTER TWENTY-ONE

There was a trunk in the bunkhouse of the Rafter S that contained clothes of various sizes left behind by cowboys and hands who had moved on for whatever reason and clothes that her sons had outgrown. Syrie washed the clothes, mended what needed mending and packed the clothes carefully away for whoever might need them next. This was the trunk Thomas was digging through when Daniel found him one morning.

"Shopping today?" asked Daniel.

"Your mother said I should look in here before I went into Baker City to buy clothes. These will actually work better if I can find some to fit. These have been worn. Brand new clothes would look out of place on a miner."

"So you are getting ready to go into the Basin?"

"Yes, I will need to borrow a horse and a mule if you have one. I can put together an outfit from what you have around here. I just need a pan and a shovel."

"No, I think you will need more than that. Let me get Benjamin. He has been watching miners go past here for the last couple of years. Plus he would have helped Pa pack up for his excursions. He'll know what you need."

Daniel returned a few minutes later with Benjamin and the three of them went out to the tack room in the barn and started building Thomas' pack. Before they were through, Thomas was glad he had Benjamin's expertise because Thomas knew nothing about mining. Additionally, he planned to stay at a hotel or a boarding house until Benjamin said, "No. A down-on-his-luck miner would be sleeping rough. Might not even have a tent. But we can rig you up a couple of tarps and a bedroll so you don't freeze. You'll have to make a bit of a strike if you are going to have any credence in the camp. I'll get you a small sack of gold dust that you can salt a claim with to make your ability to stay in the boardinghouse more believable."

"Where are you going to get gold dust?" asked Thomas.

"Remember, our Pa was on his claim when he was murdered. We have the gold he panned out that day. Ma will let you have it for this."

When they had finished packing the panniers, they went to the house to talk to Syrie and to outfit Thomas with the supplies he would need.

"Are you sure you want to go to the Basin this time of year?" asked Syrie.

"Actually, I think it might be the perfect time of year," said Thomas. "The miners will be mostly shut down when the cold freezes up the creeks. That means more of them will be in the saloon and more of them will be gossiping. More chance for me to learn about them and what goes on up there. If there is a connection between Mr. and Mrs. Lattimer and someone else in the camp, it will be a good time for me to find that out."

"We will do whatever we can to assist you, but I fear for your safety to go in there alone," Syrie said.

"I appreciate that Mrs. Hickman, but this is my job. This is what I do. I feel I will have the best chance of finding Mr. Hickman's killers if I can learn more about the people there. I have met most of the people around Rye Valley in my travels up there and no one sticks out to me. That means if his killers are still in the area, they must be in the Basin."

"When are you going to leave?" Abigail asked.

"In the morning. Daniel and Benjamin helped me put my pack together and they have loaned me a horse and a mule to use. I just need to pack the food and then I'll be on my way tomorrow."

"Will you be coming back before spring?" Michael asked.

"Probably. If I can get back. If the winter closes in, I'll have to stay of course. I will try to get back whenever the chance presents itself. But I don't want any of you to worry. Sometimes things happen and I will need to stay in order to follow up on a trail of information, or if leaving would somehow compromise the investigation.

"I would like someone to go to Baker City the first chance they get and let Sheriff Virtue know where I am. There's nothing he can do if I get into trouble, but I want him to be aware of where I am."

"I'm sure one of us will be going to Baker City within the next couple of weeks. Is that soon enough?" asked Daniel.

"That will be fine," responded Thomas. "I just don't want him to be surprised if he comes up there and finds me."

"How much food do you think you'll need?" asked Painted Pony.

"I really don't know," said Thomas. "I would guess enough to last me a week or so. Surely there will be someplace I can buy supplies up there."

Benjamin snorted. "I doubt it. Mormon Basin is still kind of rough. I don't think they have a general store."

"Maybe I had better have enough for two weeks then."

"I'll pack you enough for two weeks," said Painted Pony. "Can you cook?"

"Some. Enough so I don't starve, but not much beyond that."

"I'll see to it you have some stuff made up then." Painted Pony started filling sacks with cooked food, biscuits, flour and other staples.

As they were talking about Thomas' plans for Mormon Basin, there was a knock on the door and George Rogers walked into the room.

"Uncle George!" screamed Abigail.

Immediately, there was laughter and talking and hugging as George tried to make his way into the room. When everyone had a chance to welcome George, he sat down at the table and said hello to Thomas and Daniel.

"Daniel, if you didn't look so much like your ma, I don't know if I would have recognized you," George said as he shook his hand.

"And who is this fella?" George asked as he extended his hand to Thomas.

"Thomas Hart, sir. Deputy U.S. Marshal. Pleased to meet you. I've heard a lot about you from Mr. Meek."

"Ah, the young man sent by Joe Meek. How is he?"

"Fine, sir. The last I saw him."

"I'm not 'sir'. I'm George."

"George. Yes, sir. Sorry. Long force of habit. I would welcome talking to you and having some of your time a bit later if I might."

"Of course. Of course. But first, I have to get caught up on what my other family has been up to over the summer."

"Did you stop by Lucreta's?" asked Syrie.

"Yes. Of course. I couldn't get over this way without stopping and saying 'Hi.' Those children of hers are growing faster than I can keep track of."

"Aren't they just!" said Syrie. "I can hardly believe how much they change from one time to the next."

The talk turned to the ranches and how the year had been. What the horse crop was shaping up to be like next year. George asked after Theresa and how her homestead application was doing. What the plans were for the three ranches for the coming year and whether or not Daniel was practicing law yet. All the little details of the family were discussed and shared with this "favorite uncle" over the course of the next couple hours.

Finally, Syrie said, "I hate to break this up, but we need to get our evening chores done and Painted Pony and I had better get supper going. Those hands are going to be hungry after working outside in the cold. Come on. Hop to it, children."

"George, you can go into the parlor and rest a bit. I'm sure you are tired after your ride in from Lucreta's. Maybe this would be a good time for you to talk to Thomas."

"Yes, I think that is a fine idea. Shall we young man?" he said as he refilled his coffee cup and went into the parlor.

"So what have you found out?" George asked as the two men took seats in the parlor.

Thomas briefed him on the information Daniel had gotten from the clerk, Mr. Brainard, about the disappointing lack of information from Sheriff Virtue and about Thomas' trips to Rye Valley.

"I'm glad you came when you did. I have hung around Rye Valley off and on over the past couple weeks and I think I have pretty well ruled out anyone from there as being involved. None of them feel right for the murder and none of them have come into any big gold strikes.

"I was going to leave for Mormon Basin in the morning. I've already got my pack together and Painted Pony has packed some grub for me. I was planning on spending most of the winter up there.

"Since you are here, would you mind taking me up to Mr. Hickman's claim and walking me through what you found? Syrie told me everything you said, but having you there and walking over the site might give me some more insight."

"Sure. But I would like to rest these old bones for a day before we start out. It's a far piece from my farm to here. I'd be happy to take you through what I found that day."

"The family told me you thought two people. Two white men. One large and one small. How did you come to that conclusion."

"Simply by the size of the tracks and the fact they were both wearing boots and riding shod horses," George said.

"Could it have been a man and a woman?" asked Thomas.

"What woman would be party to a murder and a robbery?" George was perplexed by the question.

"More women than you can imagine are capable of murder. There are cases in the criminal law which detail some horrific crimes committed by women."

George sat back in his chair and considered this. Finally, he leaned forward and said, "The smaller set of tracks could have been made by a woman. That just never entered my mind. I had never heard of a white woman who would commit, or be a part of, murder. Thievery I can see, but never murder. You really think it is possible?"

"Yes, I do. Especially in light of the fact the only people who have inquired about Mr. Hickman's claim were a husband and wife."

"I'll be switched," said George. "A woman committing murder. I never would have thought it possible."

"Not likely, but possible," rejoined Thomas.

Daniel, Benjamin, Michael, and Abigail came into the parlor after their chores were done. The talk turned to what George had been doing over the summer. How his crops had done the past year and general news from the west side of the state. Newspapers were still relatively scarce and any news the Hickmans might get was usually at least a month old. Soon they heard the dinner bell ring, then the tromp of boots on the porch. Usually the hands and the family ate together, but since they had company, the family ate in the parlor and the hands ate in the kitchen. Everyone formed a line at the cook stove and filled their plates then found their respective seats.

Conversation about the family continued and Benjamin was telling George about their last trip to Baker City to sell horses. That led to stories about memorable trades and deals gone wrong or spectacularly right. There were stories about people who got the best of them and stories about people who were especially lacking in knowledge about horses.

"Speaking about how dumb some people are about horses, when we were in town, John Fuhrman, told us about a couple who wanted to buy a matched pair of our Nez Perce horses to pull a buggy they had just purchased from him. He said the man seemed okay with the blacks he sold them, but the little lady was having none of it. The husband pulled her away before she could throw a fit, but she was demanding she have a matched pair of Nez Perce horses. Can you believe some people are that stupid?"

Thomas stopped eating and was listening intently to Benjamin's story.

"Benjamin, when was this?" Thomas asked.

"I don't recall the date, but it had to have been several weeks ago at least."

"Do you recall if the livery owner mentioned where these folks were from?"

Benjamin sat back and pondered for a minute, then turned to Daniel.

"Do you recall if he said where they were from? I don't think he did."

"No, I don't think he did either. He only said they had been there a few days prior when they bought the buggy. We heard it on the same trip when we met up with you, Thomas. In fact, it was the day prior to your arrival."

Thomas nodded his head and went back to eating, but he was filing away the information. With men outnumbering women three to one, a couple was a rare thing. Could they be the same couple which was in Mr. Brainard's office? The timing was about right. If they were the same couple, then the wife had a temper. Hot enough to kill? Maybe.

The next morning, Theresa rode into the compound and George went out to greet her.

"How you doing, short stuff?" he teased.

"Better than you, old man," she retorted as he gave her a bear hug. "It is so good to see you again. When did you get in?"

"Yesterday afternoon. Your ma said you'd likely be by today. How's the homestead coming?" he asked as they walked into the kitchen.

"I see you found my wayward child," Syrie teased. "Are you hungry, Theresa?"

"No, I actually ate this morning. Somebody sent me home with food the last time I was here," Theresa said as she kissed her mother on the cheek and hugged her. "Where are the boys?"

"I don't know. Around somewhere. They left in a pack right after breakfast."

Theresa wanted to ask specifically about Thomas, but she thought Syrie might ascribe more to the question than was warranted.

"I just came down to see if I could borrow Michael for a few hours tomorrow. I've got a cow that seems to have a bad joint on her forequarters. I wanted him to look at it and see if it can be fixed or if we need to make her into jerky. I'd hate to have to do that. She throws great calves."

"I'm sure he would be happy to help and I don't have any particular need for him beyond his regular chores. You'll have to ask him yourself, though. He may have something else going on I don't know about."

"All right. Painted Pony, you got any coffee in that pot?"

Theresa and George sat at the kitchen table talking with Syrie and Painted Pony until the boys came back to the house.

"Michael, my favorite brother," Theresa said.

Michael rolled his eyes and stared at her knowing she wanted him to do something.

"What are your plans for the rest of today?"

"I had nothing special in mind. We have some weanling colts we need to geld, but that doesn't have to be done today."

"If you will come back to my place with me and look at one of my cows, I'll give you a hand with the horses tomorrow. Deal?"

"Sure," he said and Theresa described what was wrong with her cow and Michael nodded.

"I'll make up a bundle of herbs in case we need to do a poultice on her. Then we can start out."

"How about you have lunch first," said Painted Pony. "Theresa is likely to forget to feed you because she often forgets to feed herself."

"Can we take it with us?" asked Theresa. "We don't have a lot of daylight this time of year."

"Sure. Let me make you something up," Painted Pony said as she started putting food into a handkerchief for them.

As soon as their impromptu lunch was packed, Theresa and Michael started out the door.

"Good to see you, Uncle George. I'll be back in the morning."

"Better make it early if you want to catch me. Me and young Thomas are going to your Pa's claim tomorrow and then we'll go on up to Mormon Basin."

Theresa paused at the door and looked at Thomas for a moment.

"Be careful," was all she said as she went out the door, leaving Thomas hoping she would have said more.

"I think it is time I went into Baker City again," said Daniel. "I want to see if an order I placed has arrived yet. I can pick up some supplies if needed. Would you like me to see Mr. Brainard again, Thomas?"

"Sure. It wouldn't hurt if you stopped by and talked to him and to Sheriff Virtue. Just to see if anything new has happened. If you think it is important enough, you can get word to me up there."

"I can do that. It isn't all that far. I can ride up and find you if it is important."

"Are you going to stay the night at Lucreta's?" asked Abigail.

"Yes, I had planned on it. Why?"

"I thought I might ride along and visit with her while you are in Baker City."

"I think that's a wonderful idea!" said Syrie. "I have some things for little Albert. Would you take them to Lucreta for me?"

"Sure, Ma. I'd be glad to do that."

"Daniel," said Benjamin, "if it isn't real important when you get to Baker City, we could use your help with those horses. We've got about 30 to do."

"Sure, I can put my trip off for a few days. Like I said I just wanted to check and see if my order was in."

Benjamin had to bite his lip to keep from laughing out loud. Oh, how he wanted to say something about Melanie Fletcher! Daniel glared at him and Benjamin nearly laughed in spite of himself.

Syrie watched the interaction between her sons and knew what was up. Daniel was sweet on someone in town. Sooner or later Benjamin would not be able to help himself and he would tell the family what he knew. She could wait to find out who it was.

CHAPTER TWENTY-TWO

George and Thomas arrived at Noah's claim mid-morning of the next day. Most of the trees and bushes were bare now and as there was no cover, they were forced to ride straight into the claim, without having the chance to scout for any trespassers.

George sat on his horse for a minute as he remembered what he had seen here so many months before.

"Are you going to be able to do this?" asked Thomas.

"Yes. Yes, I can. If it will help bring to justice those who took Noah's life, I can do anything."

The two dismounted and tied their animals to tree branches. George took his time surveying the place, then he pointed out what he had seen.

"Of course all the tracks are gone, but here is where Noah fell. I found his stallion standing guard over his body. The mule was still picketed over there by the cottonwoods, near the creek. His packs were there," he said pointing to a spot well removed from the creek. "I believe this is about where the horses they were riding would have been standing. I estimated the distance of the shot was about 20 yards. From the wound on his face, I would guess it was a smaller caliber weapon. Perhaps a pistol."

"Pretty fair shooting," remarked Thomas.

"Yes. I am amazed Noah let anyone threatening get that close to him. There must have been something about them that caused him to relax his guard. Noah was too long in the wilderness to become complacent about strangers."

"In my mind that just lends credence to the theory about one of them being a woman," said Thomas.

"Yes. It does at that, doesn't it?"

George continued telling Thomas what he had found that day, walking along the path until the path merged with the main road into Mormon Basin.

"That's where I lost the trail. Right where the path entered the roadway to the Basin. There were just too many other tracks. I couldn't sort one from the other."

"Understandable," Thomas said as he looked over the lay of the land. "This stream would have been running fairly high at the time of year Mr. Hickman was killed wouldn't it?"

"Yes, it would have been full of snow melt and running pretty good. Why?"

"I'm trying to recreate the murder in my mind with what I know about Mr. Hickman, the time of year, the probable distances for the shot and all the rest. I am thinking more and more that the smaller of the two killers was a woman.

"Could you tell if Noah had been carrying anything or doing anything when he was shot?"

"His Hawken was lying right beside his body, so he could have been carrying it when he was shot."

"Exactly where was it in relation to his body?"

George closed his eyes as he tried to remember exactly what he had seen that day.

"No, it wasn't next to him. It was under his body. He fell across the gun."

"That means he would have been carrying it. Had it cradled in his arms," said Thomas.

"Where was his gold pan?"

"Lying at the edge of the stream," George said as he walked over to the banks of the stream. "About here."

"So well out of the water. Could you tell if he had been panning?"

"Yes, he had. I remember seeing his prints in the mud next to the creek. So he had been panning that day. I can't tell you if he was panning when they rode up, but I don't think so. It is several steps from the side of the creek to where he fell."

"I can see that," said Thomas as he built the picture in his mind. "They rode into this clearing, saw Noah. Noah may not have heard them coming because of the noise of the water. I wonder what alerted him?"

"His stallion," said George.

"What?" said Thomas coming out of his reverie.

"Noah's horse. He would have alerted Noah to any strangers in camp. Noah always trained his horses that way. He built a bond with the horses he trained for himself. That horse would have protected Noah against anything. So I am betting money Noah's horse is the one who alerted Noah to the killers."

"That must be some horse," remarked Thomas. "How come I haven't seen it at the Rafter S?"

"I would imagine it is out with the mares. He is one of Rafter S's premier sires."

"Ok. I'll check on the horse when I get back to the home place.

"Noah is panning," Thomas said as he walked over to the stream to the point George had indicated earlier. "His stallion alerts him. He picks up his gun and turns to face the people who are riding into camp. They exchange a few words. We know Noah wouldn't have taken his eyes off them if he suspected danger. Why did he turn his head?"

"Why do you think he turned his head?" asked George.

"To my mind, that is the only way they could have lined up the shot. It had to be quick before Noah had a chance to raise his gun. I think they sighted on his head for a split second before they fired. They would have to have been sure before taking the shot. Noah was a large man and he was carrying a formidable weapon."

"Yes, that makes sense," George said. "Maybe they were asking for directions? Folks often times get turned around out here. There aren't any signs about where you are or what the direction you should go to get to your destination. If they weren't local, they could have been lost."

"That's a fine idea. Let's work with that. They ride into camp, they ask for directions to someplace, Noah turns his head to indicate the direction, they line up the shot and they kill him when he faces them again. He was shot in the face, isn't that right?"

"Yes, below the left eye."

"A shot from a pistol from a horse, so no dead rest, from 20 yards out. Shooting downhill. We are looking for an expert marksman here. Possibly even a professional. There aren't many men who could make that shot on the spur of the moment.

"Noah is down. They know it is a kill shot. They dismount, they go through Noah's pack, probably take out a sack or two of gold, remount and head on to Mormon Basin. How far is that?"

"The diggings and what passes for a town are a few miles to the north," said George. "I can take you there if you'd like."

"No, I don't think it would do for me to have a partner when I arrive. I would appreciate it though if you would help me locate the claim Mr. Brainard told me about. I'm not sure what to look for as far as the markers for the claim."

"Sure, I can get you to the claim. No problem. But aren't you going to need some help while you are up there?"

"I work better alone. No offense, but I don't want to have to worry about what someone else might do or say. I appreciate the offer though," said Daniel.

"If we are done here, I'll show you where the claim is and help you set up your camp. Then I'll get back to the ranch. They are going to need every pair of hands they can get with the gelding of those horses."

"Yes, I'm done here. I can come back if I feel the need. Mr. Brainard said the claim he found for me is fairly close to the Hickman claim. And I would appreciate any guidance you can give me on setting up a rough camp. I confess I have never had to do that and I don't want to freeze to death my first night."

"I'd be glad to teach you what I know," George said as he untied the horses and handed Thomas the reins to his mount. "I've camped rough a time or two in my life."

"Just a time or two?" laughed Thomas as they rode away from the Hickman claim.

After camp was set up, and Thomas had to admit it was a very efficient camp, he went towards the town in Mormon Basin and George turned toward the Rafter S. George promised to look in on Thomas in a couple weeks to see how he was getting on and to bring him supplies and any news.

Thomas got into Mormon Basin an hour or so before sunset and went directly to the saloon as it was the liveliest place in town. The town itself was nothing special, though it did boast more people than Rye Valley. As in other gold camps, there was the usual assortment of tents, log houses, some constructions which were half log and half tents or a mixture of other building materials, but no frame houses. There was a frame boardinghouse which looked pretty substantial having two floors.

The saloon was one of the structures which was a mixture of building materials. It had a plank floor, logs about four feet up on three sides and canvas for an additional three feet of wall and a canvas roof. The canvas for the roof and the sidewalls were held up by a timber frame skeleton. There was no proper door, just two pieces of canvas that overlapped and could be tied closed when the saloon wasn't open for business. Inside there were no proper tables and chairs, just planks nailed together to form rude tables and benches. The bar was more planks laid across empty barrels ever four feet or so. The back bar was the most substantial construction in the place having smoothed planks. It was well supplied with bottles of liquor, though the selection seemed to be limited to whiskey and rum. A red hot Franklin stove served to keep the winter chill off the place somewhat.

There was a dozen or so men in the saloon, two faro games were in progress and there were three females who were obviously working for the establishment. When one of the women would leave through the back flap with a man, another would come out to take her place among the patrons. The only other employee he could identify was the barkeep. He was a young fellow, heavy in the chest with black hair and a full beard. He was busy keeping glasses of whiskey and rum full. Thomas was sure he was the bouncer as well as the barkeep, just as he was sure there was a scatter gun behind the bar somewhere.

Thomas got a shot of whiskey from the barkeep and found a seat on a bench against one of the walls. He was almost immediately joined by one of the women. He wasn't surprised to find out her name was Jezzabel and she hadn't bathed in more than a month. He gently extricated himself from her insistent, wandering hands and firmly sent her on her way to profit from someone else. He slowly sipped his drink, watching all the patrons. He had been there for perhaps a half hour when a tall, red-headed man walked into the saloon from the back. He looked around the room, then went over to the bar and spoke in low tones to the barkeep. Thomas saw the barkeep nod in his direction. The red-headed man walked over to Thomas.

"Hi stranger. I'm Billy. I don't believe I know you," Billy said in a soft, cultured voice with just a hint of the South in it.

Thomas stood up and reached to shake Billy's outstretched hand.

"I'm Thomas," he said. "I just purchased Solomon Dailey's claim a little ways out of town."

"I thought it had been a while since I had seen Solomon around. I know most everyone in Mormon Basin," Billy said as he sat down next to Thomas. "So you just get into town?"

"Yes, I set up my camp then decided I'd come into town and see what was going on here. Nice place you got here."

"Oh, it will do for now. We are planning on putting up a real building come spring when it is a bit easier to get supplies in. I've been told the winters here can get pretty brutal."

"So you are new here as well?" asked Thomas.

"I guess we've been here coming on six or eight months. Don't rightly recall the exact date we got here. It was last spring. We've only owned the saloon for about five months though. The previous owner met with a bit of an accident. One of the patrons didn't like the fact he was watering the whiskey. Won't find that being done no more," Billy laughed as he said it. "Welcome to Mormon Basin. Can I buy you a drink to welcome you?"

"That would be very neighborly of you," replied Thomas. "Also, is there any place here where a man can buy a hot meal? I'm getting tired of jerky and beans."

"Don't take long to get tired of that," rejoined Billy. "We don't have a regular café in town, but my wife is supposed to bring me and Joseph there," he inclined his head toward the bar, "a bite of supper in a few minutes. I can ask if we have any extra over at the boardinghouse. If we do, I'm sure we can send it your way."

"That would be very gracious of you."

"Sure," Billy signaled Joseph to bring another shot for Thomas. "I'll talk to you later. I see a couple of boys I want to speak to."

Billy walked over to two men who were sharing a table and a bottle. He sat down and soon the three of them were deep in conversation, though Thomas was too far away to hear any details. It appeared the two men owed Billy money. Thomas got the feeling the repayment was late on that money. In only a few minutes, the men stalked out leaving half the bottle on the table. Billy picked up the half-full bottle and returned it to Joseph behind the bar. Thomas filed the incident away for later review.

Thomas continued watching the patrons, saw one of the men cash out of one of the faro games and another man take his place. Men left the bar and more came in. No hard feelings seemed to be evident among the patrons and no one was flashing an extraordinary amount of money. Everyone was just enjoying some company in a lonely place. Thus far, no one was getting drunk. It was all social and peaceful. Periodically one of the women would leave with a man and another would take her place. Thomas figured in his head at five dollars every time someone went out back, and they were averaging about four men an hour, the owner of the brothel was making a minimum of $20 per hour on those women in addition to the extra liquor. And it was early in the evening. Business was bound to pick up later in the night. Prostitution wasn't really illegal, because there were no laws out here, but in Thomas' experience, prostitution usually led to trouble in one form or another.

As he was watching the back of the tent, he became aware someone had entered through the front of the saloon. As he turned his head, he momentarily lost his train of thought as he found himself looking at one of the most beautiful women he had ever seen. Her hair was glossy black and was coiled around her head so it made it look like she was wearing a turban. Her eyes were black and slightly tilted up on the outer edges. Her lips were bare of color and her teeth were white and even. Her smooth skin was the color of coffee with lots of cream. She was tiny, Thomas guessed she would not even measure five feet tall and he doubted she weighed a hundred pounds. The dress she wore, while a simple grey wool, was cut and fitted to her perfectly. She had a heavy shawl on to protect her from the cold. If Thomas had to guess her heritage, he would have said Octoroon, as she was only a little lighter than he himself was.

She was bearing a tray with a towel over it and she went straight to the bar. Billy gave her a hug and a chaste kiss on the cheek as she took the towel off the food. She set a plate off the tray for Billy and took the other plate down to where Joseph was pouring drinks. As she passed back by Billy, he inclined his head toward Thomas and said something to her. She looked at Thomas and nodded her head. Taking the tray and the towel she went back out into the night.

In less than five minutes she was back again with the tray and plate for him along with a tinware mug of coffee.

"Billy said you were hungry and wanted a hot meal. I brought this from our boardinghouse," she said as she set the plate and cup down. "You needn't worry about paying for it. Consider it a welcome to the Basin." He could hear the slow, smooth roll of the Mississippi River in the cadence of her voice. "I wish you good fortune in your enterprise here in the Basin."

She walked back over to Billy at the bar and Thomas was mesmerized to find the view from the back was nearly as good as the view from the front. She walked very erect and seemed to glide over the floor. Her tiny feet were encased in boots to protect against the cold, but she could have been wearing ballroom slippers so smoothly did she move. Thomas knew the siren song of gold attracted all kinds of people to these camps, but he had never seen such a fine lady outside of the parlors of his home state. And Billy was obviously a cultured man from his voice and the manner of his dress. 'These two do not belong here', was his first thought. Then 'why are they here?'

Again, he filed the information away to review at a later time. Then he dug into his food and found it to be quite tasty. It was a simple meal of beef stew with biscuits and butter. He drank the coffee and found it to be quite good as well. The coffee was fresh and hadn't been sitting on a fire all day. He finished, then got up to take his plate and cup to the bar to put it back on the tray.

Billy asked if he had enjoyed the meal and Thomas assured him he had.

"Did your wife make it?" asked Thomas.

"No, we own the boardinghouse and we have a woman who cooks for us and the boarders. She is married to one of the miners. Isn't she a great cook, though? She's a real treasure."

"I don't know when I've had a better meal. You sure I can't pay you for the meal?"

"No. As Dottie said, consider it to be a welcome to the Basin."

"Do you have any vacancies at your boardinghouse?" Thomas asked.

"Not right now. Full up. I'm sorry."

Thomas waved it away.

"Don't worry about it. I really don't have the money to spend right now anyway. Just hoping for something better than a tent if my claim pays off."

"I understand. We're all hoping to have our claims pay off in one way or another around here. If you will excuse me, I need to take these dishes back over to the boardinghouse. Then I need to come back and relieve Joseph. It is time for him to go home."

"I had better be getting back to my camp. I don't want to be out too late. It's already dark and I have a fair piece to go."

"Travel safe," Billy said as he held open the door for Thomas.

CHAPTER TWENTY-THREE

When Carter came back with Ten Crows' tea and change, he asked "Where are you spending the night?"

"I am going to find a spot outside of town. I am not anxious to have Deputy Elkins kick me awake tomorrow."

"I have a cabin about a mile south of town. You are welcome to bunk there for the night. You'll be safe. It is outside Elkins' jurisdiction."

"That is very nice of you," said Ten Crows. "But won't it get you in trouble with the people around here?"

"I already have a reputation as an 'Indian lover' because of my late wife. To hell with them. I don't care. I mind my own business and do as I please."

"Well, it would be nice to not have to look over my shoulder for a while," Ten Crows smiled. "I'd be happy to take you up on your offer."

"Good, let me get my horse and you can come with me."

True to his word, Carter had a snug little cabin made out of cottonwood trees along a creek about a mile outside of town. There was a corral for the horses and plenty of meadow hay to feed them. Ten Crows unsaddled his horse and stowed most of his gear, except for his bedroll, in the barn. He followed Carter into the cabin. Ten Crows looked around and saw it was a cabin like most with minimal furniture and lots of skins and a few furs. It had a bed and a table, along with a few chairs and a couple of trunks. Ten Crows put his bedroll down by the fireplace.

"Sorry, it's not bigger, but it was only ever the wife and me, so we didn't need much. We never had any young'uns. Have a seat. I'll see what I can find to fix for some supper," he said as he went into what served as the kitchen. Ten Crows noted there was no cook stove, just the large fireplace that served for both cooking and warmth. "You have kids?" asked Carter.

"I have one son left," said Ten Crows.

"You Nez Perce or Cayuse?"

"Cayuse," Ten Crows affirmed.

"I thought so when I saw your mount. I sure do admire the animals you folks raise. Some of the best horses around here. I love them for gathering cows out of these mountains. Little devils can carry you all day long and half the night."

"Yes, they are good animals," Ten Crows agreed.

Carter continued making biscuits and placed them into a Dutch oven in the fireplace. Then he fried up some bacon and added it to beans which had been left to cook on the edges of the fire. As Carter cooked, Ten Crows took out his pipe and filled it. He sat on the hearth of the fireplace smoking and let his mind drift for a few minutes. Oddly enough he felt safe with this man and he allowed himself to relax.

"It ain't much, but it will keep body and soul together," Carter said as he dished up the beans and put a biscuit on Ten Crows plate.

"It is wonderful. I have been living on tea and jerky ever since I left the reservation," Ten Crows said. "A hot meal on a cold day is very welcome."

"You talk a mite different than you did when you were in town," noted Carter.

Ten Crows stopped with his spoon halfway to his mouth, then he slowly lowered it and looked at Carter. Ten Crows realized he had inadvertently dropped his false accent and was indeed speaking normally.

"Don't worry, none. I ain't gonna tell no one that you aren't what you say you are," reassured Carter. "I mean, I know you are Cayuse and I know you are from the reservation, but you aren't an ordinary man. I would guess you were educated in Canada when you were a boy. I would also guess that you had some stature in your younger days. Am I right?"

Ten Crows knew the man could turn him in at any time, so he decided his best bet was honesty.

"You are correct. My real name is Ten Crows and I am escaping from the reservation."

Carter slapped his thigh and laughed.

"Good for you!" he chortled. "The more of you who can live free, the better, is what I think. Damn reservations are nothing more than open air jails.

"Do you really know the Hickmans?" Carter asked.

Ten Crows went back to eating and said, "Yes. That is true. I knew Noah for more than 30 years. He was my best friend, white or red."

"Then that means you are traveling south to avenge his death," stated Carter.

"Yes, that is exactly what it means. I promised his wife, Syrie, I would wait until the white man's justice had a chance to work and I will keep that promise. If it fails, I won't."

"White man's justice. Bah!" said Carter. "You got a taste of what white man's justice is around here. Drunken white trash for deputies. That's no justice.

"You listen to me. Noah saved the lives of practically everyone on that wagon train. And he would have saved more if the damn fools had listened to him. I owe him my own life because of what he knew about the Oregon Trail. You find the bastards that killed him and you get revenge for all of us who knew him and owed him."

Ten Crows looked at him for a long moment and then said, "I will."

Ten Crows left the snug little cabin by the creek shortly after daybreak the next day. Carter had fed him breakfast and packed up some biscuits and cooked bacon for him to take on the trail. Ten Crows continued south and was over the next range of hills before nightfall of the next day. Again he camped at the base of the hills, keeping under cover as much as he could when he built his fire that night. He could see the Blue Mountains off to the west and he knew he had about three days travel to reach the Rafter L. He knew he couldn't stay at Young Noah's place for long in case someone came looking for him. The Rafter L and the Rafter S were the first places the authorities would look for him if they found out Ten Crows wasn't dead.

That day he knew he would be able to make good time as the ground was level and the fords across the Powder River were easy to navigate. He loaded up the little mare and started out across the valley. There was no cover here and he trusted that he was meant to complete this journey. He put the mare into a distance covering running walk and headed south. The mare had a remarkably smooth gait and, as Mr. Carter had said, the Cayuse horses could carry you all day and half the night. He stopped along the banks of the Powder River and had made a lunch of tea, biscuits, and bacon. As he ate his lunch he let the horse graze a little and he scanned the country ahead. There didn't seem to be any abnormal activity along the road. He saw only a few horses with riders and buckboards. He saw no military detachments or other large bodies of men. He had no choice but to go directly down the road with his cover story. If he tried to skirt the small settlement of North Powder, he would only draw more attention to himself.

He knew there was one man who could identify Ten Crows for who he really was in North Powder. Ruben Riggs had settled near the Powder River in 1851 and Ten Crows and his people had traded horses with him on numerous occasions. Ten Crows must avoid his ranch and get past the town without drawing attention to himself. He tightened the cinch on his saddle, checked to see the load was secure and mounted up again.

Again Ten Crows put his mount into the running walk and only slowed when he was within the little settlement of North Powder. He kept his eyes straight ahead and didn't engage with anyone in the town. Most people ignored him as just another traveler. He kicked the pony up out of the walk when he was past the town and headed for the foothills to the south. He didn't stop again until he had gained the foothills and found a ravine with a nice stand of junipers. He had light enough left to travel further, but he had pushed the little horse hard that day and he would push her harder still the next. He built a small fire and oiled water for tea and ate some jerky and the last of the biscuits. Then he rolled out his bedroll and went to sleep. One more dangerous spot passed. Tomorrow he would go on.

The next morning, he was again up before dawn. He kept his fire small and warmed water to wash with and to make tea. He would go down the south side of the low range of hills and drop down into the valley which held the town of Baker City. After he passed Baker City, he would leave the valley of the Powder River, cross another low range of hills and find the Burnt River and the valley where his son lived. It would be one of the longest days of his journey, more than 30 miles if he reached the Rafter L.

He saddled up, swung into the saddle, patted the little horse's neck and said, "Let's go home." Almost as if she understood, she took off at a lope and the ground flew beneath them. Ten Crows pulled the little horse up when he met anyone on the trail and walked her until he had passed them. Then he would kick her back up. Sometimes she went into a lope and sometimes she would pick a running walk as her preferred gait. Ten Crows let her have her head. She knew what she felt the most comfortable with and they were steadily getting closer to the Rafter L.

Ten Crows pulled the horse down to a walk when he reached the outskirts of Baker City. There might be some here who would remember him, but he doubted they would know him dressed as he was and not riding one of the Nez Perce horses he had always favored. Again, he kept to a walk through town and didn't make eye contact with anyone. No one hailed him and no one bothered him. He didn't stop even to water his horse. He knew she could drink her fill outside of town before he started up the next range of hills.

He breathed an audible sigh of relief after he had cleared town. He stopped at a ford of the river, just before it took off to the west and away from his line of travel. He loosened the cinch and let the horse drink her fill and graze for a few minutes. This time of year there wouldn't be a lot of feed in the Burnt River Canyon. He was just about to tighten the cinch and mount up when the first flakes of snow hit him. The day suddenly got very dark and the wind increased in volume. He knew he could be in real trouble if the snow set in for several days. He had to alter his plans. He thought about what lay ahead of him. The low range of hills didn't bother him in most kinds of weather. They weren't high enough or steep enough to present any problems in dry weather or even in a little snow. But with deep snow those hills could kill both man and beast if a horse slipped off the trail in the wrong place.

He decided to get away from the trail further up the Powder River and see if he could find a semi-sheltered place for the night. He mounted back up and started following the river as it meandered westward. After about half a mile he came to a little ravine which afforded some shelter from the wind and that had a good stand of cottonwood trees. There was browse for the horse there in addition to what she could pick off the trees. He unsaddled the horse and hobbled her. They might be there for longer than one night and he didn't want to limit her grazing by picketing her. He cleared an area under a large cottonwood, built a fire and set up camp. He didn't worry about hiding his smoke because in the storm no one could see it. He boiled water for his tea and pulled jerky and pemmican from his pack. The food supplies were nearly all gone now. If he was stuck here for several days he would be hungry. He had been hungry before he thought. And he would be hungry again. He would survive. He ate, drank his tea, smoked his pipe and spread out the ashes from the fire. Then he laid his bedroll down over the ashes and went to sleep with the snow howling around him.

When he awoke the next morning, he only found about four inches of dry, powdery snow on top of his bedroll. His mare was already brushing away the snow with her feet and eating the dry bunch grass beneath. He shook out his bedroll and hung it over the lower branches of the cottonwood. He gathered the twigs he had stacked against the bole of the cottonwood the night before and built a fire to warm his water. He ate the last of his jerky and drank his tea, then caught up his horse and prepared to continue his journey.

He traveled slower that day as even the small amount of snow could hide a hole or a loose rock which would plunge both horse and rider over the side of the trail. As the day progressed the warm sun and the continuing wind swept the snow aside and he was able to make better time. In areas where the trail flattened out, the horse stepped up her pace and Ten Crows again let her pick her own rate of speed. He stopped at mid-day when he found a place along the Burnt River that had a little dry bunch grass and loosened the cinch on the saddle. He didn't build a fire this time, just drank water from the river and rested from his time in the saddle. He didn't know exactly how far he was from the Rafter L, but he knew he had to be within 10 miles or so. When he re-mounted, he urged greater speed from the horse. It was impossible to know if it would snow again or not and he didn't want to spend another night in the cold if he didn't have to.

It was nearing dark when he saw the lights of the ranch house on Plano Creek. He rode up to the house, dismounted and tied his horse to the hitching rail. Then he knocked on the door. Young Noah was the one who opened the door.

"Father! How did you get here?" he exclaimed as he pulled his father inside.

"A horse," Ten Crows said.

Lucreta came out of the kitchen wiping her hands on her apron, followed by all of the children.

"Grandpa," they all yelled and mobbed Ten Crows. Lucreta could see the tears glisten in his eyes as he hugged each of them, then picked up little Albert.

"Father, have you eaten? Supper isn't ready yet. Can I get you something before we sit down?" asked Lucreta.

"Hot water for tea would be nice," said Ten Crows.

"Mae, run outside and take Grandfather's horse down to the barn and have one of the hands put it up for the night."

"Wait, Mae. Please don't do that," said Ten Crows. "Son, can I talk to you for a minute?"

"Sure. Let's go out on the porch."

"I'll make you some tea and bring it out to you," said Lucreta.

When the two men had taken seats on the porch, Ten Crows started to speak and he told Young Noah about his subterfuge, escape and journey south. Lucreta brought Ten Crows a mug of tea with sugar as he liked it and sat down with them.

"So you see, if one of your hands mentions I am here, all I have done will be for nothing. I know you have good men working for you, but I don't think I want to trust my life to them."

"Yes, of course. You are right. But you are worn out. You need to rest," said Young Noah.

"I agree a day's rest would be good for both my horse and myself," said Ten Crows. "I was going to ask if I could stay in the shack you built when you first came here. The one that is back up the canyon a ways."

"Sure," said Lucreta, "but no one has lived there in a very long time. I'm not sure what kind of shape it is in."

"If it keeps the weather off, I will be happy with it. If I could have a few supplies from you, I will go there tonight."

"That is no problem," Young Noah said, "but how long are you planning on staying there?"

"Just a day or two. Then I need to ride to the Rafter S and see Syrie. I saw a vision and I need to tell her about it."

"The family talked about what to do when you came back," said Young Noah. "Theresa volunteered the use of her cabin for as long as you need it."

"That is very kind of her. It might be a good place for me to hide for a while. I may have the same problem with the hired hands at Syrie's, though I don't think many of them realized who I was when I was there."

"Father, the investigator has arrived that was sent by Mr. Meek. He is at the Rafter S now," Lucreta told him.

"Is he a small, slender man, with skin darker than mine, light-colored eyes and does he wear two guns?" asked Ten Crows.

"Yes, he does," said Young Noah. "How did you know?"

"He was also in my vision," Ten Crows explained. "I couldn't figure out what part he played because George Rogers said there were only two killers. Now I understand. He is here to help us bring justice for Noah."

"What else did you see in your vision?" asked Lucreta.

"I saw a small woman with skin the color of coffee like you make it for the children, with lots of cream. A very beautiful woman and she had blood on her hands. There was also a man in the dream. A tall, white man with red-colored hair. They live in a house with lots of men and there were bottles of liquor all around them. Nothing else came after that."

"Are you confident they are the killers?" asked Young Noah.

"Yes, I am sure. I don't know where to find them though. The vision did not show me their location. But I will know them if I see them."

"Father, the men will be coming to the house soon for supper. Let me make you up something to take with you. Noah, will you fetch a lantern and walk your father back to the shack. I'll get some quilts."

"No, my daughter, no quilts. I have my bedroll. It is enough."

"Let me get a lantern, Father, and I will go with you," said Young Noah.

Lucreta stood up and walked over to where Ten Crows sat drinking his tea.

"Thank you daughter for the tea. You remembered the sweetness I like."

"It is good to have you home, Father. I will pray for your safety," she said as she kissed his cheek and went back into the house.

"Come on, Father. Let's get you settled for the night," said Young Noah when he came back out a few minutes later. "Here is some food Lucreta packed up for you. We'll bring you more food in the morning. When you decide what you are going to do, we'll get everything you need packed up for you."

CHAPTER TWENTY-FOUR

Young Noah rode into the compound at the Rafter S shortly before mid-day the following day. The snow had all gone by then and he had made good time from the Rafter L. Painted Pony was in the kitchen. Syrie had gone for her daily ride along with George. All of the children were doing chores or were out with the stock, so Painted Pony was the only one at the house. She came out onto the porch, followed by Sarge, when she heard the horse come up to the house.

"Young Noah, what brings you here? Is everything all right with Lucreta and the children?" she asked.

"Yes. Everyone is fine. But I bring news. Can we go inside?" said Young Noah.

"Of course. Come in. The coffee is hot," she said as she ushered both pup and young man inside. "Now tell me, what is this news which causes you to ride so far."

"Father came home last night," Young Noah said as he sat down and accepted a cup of coffee. "He rode in shortly after dark. He came alone. He has seen a vision and he wants to talk to Syrie about it. Is the young investigator here, Thomas?"

"No, George took him to Noah's claim and then on to the Basin. We don't expect him back for many days. George got home late last night. He is riding with Syrie this morning."

"I think I will wait and talk to them. Do you expect them to be gone long?"

"No, I was just getting ready to start lunch. They've been gone about an hour and Syrie always tries to be back before we cook lunch. I expect them any minute."

"Good. Then I'll just wait here and play with little Sarge. How's he doing anyway?"

They talked about the pup and how his training was progressing and other things to pass the time as Young Noah waited for Syrie and George. Painted Pony started the prep work for lunch for the family and the hands who had stayed on through the winter. She needed more wood for the cook stove, so Young Noah brought it in for her and split more kindling while he waited. He was just taking in a second armload when Syrie and George rode up to the house.

Syrie was flushed from her ride and for an instant she looked as she had when Young Noah had first seen her all those years ago. She was still a very handsome woman, he thought. He was glad she seemed to be in such good health and was happy from her ride. He loved her almost as much as he had loved his own mother and for many of the same reasons; generosity of spirit, courage, honesty, devotion to family and an inborn knowledge of how to help those who were hurting.

"Young Noah," Syrie exclaimed. "How nice to see you." Syrie got down off her horse and gave him a hug. "How are Lucreta and the children?"

"Young Noah, good to see you," said George as he got down from his horse. "It's been too long. Is everyone well?" he asked as he grasped Noah by the shoulders, then shook his hand.

"Yes. Yes. Everyone is fine, but I have news," Young Noah said. Syrie thought he almost sounded as he had when he was her student.

"Ok. Do we need to be sitting down?" asked Syrie.

"No. Nothing bad. Father came home last night. He came home for good," Young Noah said and told them about Ten Crows' straw-filled dummy being buried. "I'll let him tell you about his trip himself. Syrie, he has had a vision."

"A clear one?" Syrie asked.

"Very clear," Young Noah replied. "But it didn't give the location of the killers. Just their faces."

"Interesting," George said. "This could change the whole situation."

"Yes, it certainly could," agreed Syrie.

"I wanted to ask you if the offer still held for Father to stay at Teresa's cabin."

"Of course," said Syrie. "For as long as he needs. When is he going to come here?"

"He is staying at my old shack on the Rafter L right now. He is pretty tired. That is a long trip and he really pushed to get home. He may lay up there for a day or two. We are keeping him out of sight because we don't want any of our hired help to inadvertently let it slip he is there. Most of them know him pretty well because of the time he spent there last spring."

"Yes. That could cause problems. And it makes me think we need to come up with a story for him when he comes here. I'll bring it up to the family and see if we can come up with anything. George, after lunch can you ride up to Teresa's and let her know Ten Crows is here. She will need to pack her things and move back home. It may take her a day or two to get organized. I'll send someone from the family to bring Ten Crows here so there won't be any problems."

"He looks really different," Young Noah said. "He actually looks healthier. He has cut his braids and he is wearing white man's clothes, not buckskins. It is possible if we come up with a good story your hands won't even recognize him."

"I can cut his hair into a white man's haircut," volunteered Syrie. "That will help change his looks as well. You are about the same size as he is, Noah. Why don't you go through the trunk in the bunk house and get him some clothes. He will need a change or two from what he has on. If he needs more than that, we can order him some or Painted Pony and I can make some.

"Right now, I'm needed inside to help with lunch. We'll talk again after lunch. George, will you please take the horses to the barn? Thank you," Syrie said as she took Young Noah's arm and led him towards the house. "Tell me all about what your father said."

After lunch and a family meeting, Young Noah rode back to his ranch with a plan developed and approved by the Hickman family. They planned to have Ten Crows stay at the cabin on the Rafter L for two more nights, then he would travel on to the Rafter T. In the meantime, Painted Pony was going to pack up what supplies Ten Crows would need. Michael would take her in the buckboard to haul the supplies. Painted Pony would get Theresa's cabin prepared for Ten Crows and she would help Theresa pack up her stuff. They would use the wagon to haul whatever Theresa wanted to move back home. Michael grumbled because it would mean a delay in castrating the colts, but it couldn't be helped. Family came first and Ten Crows was family.

The rest of the men, including George, would ride along and move whatever stock Theresa wanted to move back to the main ranch. With winter setting in, she would want her stock close to her so she could monitor them and make sure they were well fed. It would put extra pressure on the pastures around the Rafter S, but they would manage.

They had decided Syrie would cut Ten Crows hair into a style more like white men wore, Ten Crows would put away his buckskins for the time being and dress as a white man. All this would be done so he would not resemble himself. He would be passed off as a man hired to train horses, which was a job he could do well. If any of the Rafter S hands recognized him, they would be told he was a brother to Ten Crows who had recently come back from living with the Nez Perce. If any pressed beyond that, Syrie would tell them it was none of their concern. Syrie was mostly concerned with making sure Ten Crows regained his former health. Young Noah had said he already looked better, but Syrie wanted him to gain back the weight as well as the strength he had lost. When he was rested up, he could start helping out around the ranch with small jobs and build himself back up gradually. Painted Pony could see to it that he had plenty to eat and he would eat with the family after everyone felt comfortable his ruse had worked.

Theresa joined the family for dinner that night and told everyone she had selected which stock she wanted to bring back to the Rafter S and which she would turn out into the hills for the winter. She and Painted Pony put a plan in place for the transfer of the cabin to Ten Crows. Theresa returned to her cabin immediately after supper that night to start sorting her things. Abigail went to her room and started making room for Theresa to move back. Painted Pony excused herself and went to her cabin. The rest of the family and George went into the parlor after supper.

"Ma, what are your plans for when Ten Crows moves here?" asked Michael.

"I don't know I that have any 'plans' other than making sure he is comfortable and safe and he get his strength back. I was so dismayed when I saw him last. He was so thin and weak. Not at all the man I knew."

"I agree," said George. "It is really sad to see such fine man, and a great warrior, in that kind of shape. It is one thing to get old – it happens to all of us – but to see him so thin, was really disheartening to me as well."

"I think we can help return him to his old self," said Daniel. "Just being around the horses, having something productive to do and being outside may be what he needs. I know the horses aren't his anymore, but couldn't we arrange for him to have the ability to start his own herd?"

"I think that is an excellent idea," said Benjamin.

"As do I," said Syrie. "What do you think about letting him use, say 20 mares, of his choosing and your Pa's stallion. He can keep all the foals out of that mating. We'll provide the pasture. After a few years, he could have quite a sizable herd. It would never number in the thousands like he had before, but it would be something that was his."

"Do you think he would accept such a gift?" asked George.

"I don't know. We'll need to think of a way to phrase it so he will take it," said Syrie.

"Perhaps, we could say Pa 'left' them to him, like in a will," suggested Daniel.

"Already thinking like a lawyer," teased Benjamin. "But it might work. As a gift from Pa, it might work."

When Abigail came out of her room, they were still talking about Ten Crows.

"Young Noah told me Ten Crows had a vision," said Syrie. "It was a clear vision and he could see their faces. He couldn't see the location where they were, so we still have that problem."

"Speaking as a lawyer again," Daniel began and Benjamin groaned and rolled his eyes. Daniel shot him a look and continued. "I know we are all willing to accept any vision Ten Crows has. We have all been witness to how accurate his visions can be. But," he looked around at his family, "we can't have Sheriff Virtue swear out an arrest warrant and we can't admit it into a court of law. So we are still left with the same problem as before. We don't have any evidence."

"If Ten Crows can identify the killers, then why can't we just kill them ourselves? The Bible says "an eye for an eye", doesn't it?" said Abigail.

Syrie paused before she answered her. "Abigail, that law was written for another time. And it wasn't written so anyone could exact retribution for anyone else just because they thought the other party was guilty. It was written as a guide for the judges of the ancient Israelites as well as the people.

"If we kill the people we think killed your Pa, then we are guilty of murder in the eyes of the law today. I will not put anyone in this family in the position of going to jail for life or, more likely hanging, for such a thing. The taking of the lives of those men are not worth losing the life of anyone in my family.

"Do you understand?"

"No," said Abigail. "I do not. If we know who killed Pa, then why can't we expect justice for Pa?"

"Because," said Daniel, "that isn't justice. That is revenge. They are two different concepts or things."

"What is wrong with revenge?" asked Abigail. "My Pa is dead and they aren't. How is that justice? If they were dead, it would be even."

'O Lord, give me the words,' thought Syrie.

"Abigail, there comes a time in everyone's life when they have to stand by and see a wrong committed and not

261

be able to right that wrong. In fact, there will probably be many such instances in a person's life. I myself have had more than a few.

"These wrongs can be anything from a puppy dying for no reason, to losing a friend to an accident, or to losing someone you love to murder.

"We pay a price for living in a civilized society with laws and protections and government. Part of that price is choosing justice over revenge. If we exact revenge, then the family of those men would also have the right to exact revenge on a member of our family. It might be the person who killed those men or it might be any one of the rest of us. And the cycle would go on. I cannot lose, I will not lose, another member of this family. What you are suggesting is sure to cause the death of another member of this family."

"Abigail," Daniel said, "I have been studying the law for a long time and I will agree with you that what happens isn't always justice no matter how hard we try. But as Ma said, that is part of the price we pay to live in a civilized society.

"If say, Michael were to kill those two men, what do you think would happen?" asked Daniel.

"Then they would be dead just like Pa," said Abigail. "That's what they deserve."

"Yes, the people who killed Pa, if we have justice, would be put to death for that crime. But that isn't what I asked you. I asked, 'if Michael were to kill those two men, what do you think would happen?'"

"I don't know," Abigail admitted.

"What would happen is Sheriff Virtue would come and he would arrest Michael. There would be a trial and Michael would hang for murder. Or, if Michael got away before Sheriff Virtue got here, Michael would be running and hiding for the rest of his life. We would never see Michael again.

"Are the lives of two men worth that for Michael, or for any of us who might kill those two men?" asked Daniel.

Abigail looked down at the floor and took a long moment before she spoke. She raised her head and tears were staining her cheeks. "No. Nothing is worth losing one of my brothers. Or anyone else in the family."

Syrie rose from her rocker and went to her daughter and gathered her in.

"Oh honey, I know this is so very hard for you. I wish I could give you the comfort and the answers you want. But sometimes we just can't have what we want. We can't always have justice.

"Thomas Hart is in Mormon Basin right now and he is looking hard for the killers. If you want to help find out who killed your Pa, then I suggest you start praying for guidance for that young man. Pray he will find what he needs to convict them."

"Yes, Ma. I will do that," said Abigail softly. "I am just so angry about all this."

"I know dear. I pray every night you will find a way to set aside that anger. It is important you learn to do that."

"I will try, Ma. I promise."

"That is all I ask," Syrie said as she kissed her daughter's tear-stained cheek. "Now, it is late, and we have a big day tomorrow. I would like you, Abigail, to give Painted Pony and Theresa a hand with the changeover at Theresa's cabin. Would you do that for me?"

"Sure, Ma, I'll help," said Abigail.

"Good. Off to bed everyone," said Syrie as she released Abigail. "George I'd like to talk with you if you have a minute in the kitchen."

Syrie waited until everyone had trooped off to bed. Then she opened a door to the breakfront in the parlor and pulled out a bottle of whiskey. "Shall we?" she asked.

"Of course," said George.

Syrie led the way into the kitchen and sat down at the old, scarred table Noah had built.

"So many memories around this table," she mused. "Holidays, birthdays, just everyday things. I would give anything if I could return it to the way it was a year ago."

"I know how you feel," said George. "So would I."

Syrie mentally shook herself and looked at George.

"George, I need a favor."

"Anything, Syrie. Just name it."

"I want you to talk Ten Crows out of taking revenge on those killers."

"You don't ask for much, do you? You want me to talk him out of what his culture tells him is his duty?"

"I know what I am asking. I feel like we are getting a member of our family back with Ten Crows leaving the reservation. The thought of him having to hide the rest of his life or, worse yet, swinging at the end of a rope, breaks my heart."

George contemplated her request as he swirled the whiskey in his glass.

"Syrie, all I can promise you is I will broach the subject with him. But you also must realize he is showing a great deal of patience in letting the white man's justice have time to work. Remember that his people have believed in revenge for generations. He took that in along with his mother's milk. It is a part of him, blood and bone.

I know Ten Crows to be a very resourceful individual. He is aware of what he is risking by killing those men. He has already lost a great deal of time with his family, and I am sure he will do whatever he has to do to make sure he will not lose any more. I know he loves those grandbabies of his, yours, as much as anything in this world.

"When we were bringing him here last spring, we had a lot of time to talk. He was telling me about all the things his grandfather and his uncles taught him when he was a boy. All the things his father taught Spotted Buffalo and Otter. I know he really wants to teach those things to little Albert. He doesn't want his culture to die, and I respect that. There is much about the Cayuse way of life that is admirable, and it shouldn't be lost.

"So, I will bring up the subject, but don't be surprised if I don't make any progress with him."

"I was afraid you'd say that," said Syrie. "I would just be so heart-broken if we lost him as well."

"I know," said George. "We've all lost too much."

He reached over and placed his hand over hers.

"Please try not to worry. Don't borrow trouble, Syrie. It does no good for anyone."

CHAPTER TWENTY-FIVE

Thomas woke up and was momentarily confused when the first thing he saw was canvas over his head. He felt the ground beneath him instead of ropes in a bedframe. Then he remembered he was in a tent in Mormon Basin. And he was cold. Very cold.

His hands were shaking as he threw off the blankets and the canvas of the bedroll. He rolled over and sat up as he rubbed his hands together to get the circulation back into them. He reached into the bottom of the bedroll and retrieved his boots and put them on. He stood up outside the tent and began slapping his arms against his chest and his sides to bring some blood back into his arms and his chest. He was glad he had put his boots at the foot of his bedroll under the covers, otherwise it would have been like putting chunks of ice on his feet. He took his coat from the bedroll where he had used it for another layer of protection against the frigid night and slipped it on.

His hands were still shaking slightly when he reached down and stirred the remains of his campfire. Dead. No sparks at all. He reached back inside the tent and gathered kindling and tender from under the shelter of the tent. He was thankful to George for suggesting he store the fire starter there, otherwise the thick layer of frost would likely have made starting a fire nearly impossible. He carefully laid the fire and reached into his coat pocket for matches. No matches. Where had he put them? He started going through his supplies and found them in with the flour and coffee. Kind of made sense because he needed fire to make coffee and bannock bread. But he really had to get this rough life figured out because he had already been told by the locals at the saloon last night, it hadn't really started to get cold yet. That would come in February.

Thomas sincerely hoped he was a long way from a tent in Mormon Basin before February rolled around.

Thomas broke through a thin layer of ice over a man-made depression in the stream and filled his coffee pot, then he dumped in a handful of coffee grounds. He hoped that was the way Painted Pony had told him to do it. He didn't have any egg shells to put into it. Since he didn't have any eggs, it was unlikely he would have any to put into it anytime soon. He would just have to let the grounds settle and try not to drink too many of them.

He took out some raw bacon and some bannock bread dough Painted Pony had prepared for him. Following her directions, he pulled off a couple of lumps of the dough and flattened and smoothed them around the end of sticks. Then he wound the bacon around the bannock bread and tucked in the ends to hold it in place. He placed the two sticks over the fire. He had no way to anchor them because the ground was frozen, so he had to hold them and keep turning them. He tried to keep the bacon from dripping into the fire and flaring up, but he was only minimally successful. As he was watching the bannock bread to keep it from burning, the coffee pot boiled over into the fire, nearly putting it out. Transferring the bannock bread sticks to one hand, he reached out and grabbed for the handle of the pot, burning his fingers. He swore and pulled his hand inside the sleeve of his coat and managed to drag the pot out of the fire before it went completely out. He had no salve for his burns, so he rubbed his fingers over some raw bacon, hoping the grease from the bacon would soothe the burns a little bit. This day was not starting off well. He was getting a new appreciation for the "civilized" life he had led up to now.

After scalding his mouth on the coffee and eating the well-done bannock bread and burned bacon, Thomas decided he needed to make an effort to seem like he was panning for gold. His horse whinnied at him and he realized he hadn't let the animals down to the stream for any water since last night. He untied the horse and the mule and led them to the creek so they could drink. As they drank, he realized he needed to find something for them to graze on. He didn't see any grass around his campsite so he would have to walk somewhere and find some. He strapped on his pistols and grabbed his rifle.

He couldn't see very far because his camp had been set up in a pocket of brush to give him some protection from the wind. He walked out to the road and looked around. All along the road he saw land which had been dug up and raked over by previous miners, so he started up the nearest hill to get away from the water. He walked about half a mile and looked around again. He had gained a little altitude and he was able to see a bit further now. He saw a small meadow nearby which appeared to have some bunch grass still standing, so he led his animals there. He traded the lead ropes for hobbles and turned them loose. They were well trained and he had no doubt he would be able to catch them again.

He decided to climb higher still and get a better perspective on the basin. Leaving the animals to graze, he set his rifle on his shoulder and climbed further up the hill. He saw mostly bunch grass and some low-growing shrubs for vegetation. Further up there were thick stands of conifers. And of course there were rocks. He had never seen such country for rocks. In truth there were just as many rocks where he came from, but over the years there they had been used to construct structures and fences. Here they seemed to have been placed strategically to trip a man, turn his ankle or break bones. He climbed higher still and turned around to look below him and back towards what passed for a town.

Mormon Basin had been aptly named as it was a large bowl with mountains rising steeply on nearly every side, though he didn't know where the "Mormon" part came from. He could plainly see the water courses in the bottom of the valley delineated mostly by the piles of rocks and gravel that had been dug out of the creek bottoms. The brush and cottonwoods that remained along the water courses were all nude now and it gave the area a harsh face. The little settlement was dwarfed by the immensity of the bowl and the mountains. It was alien to this wild place and had no beauty unlike the settlements of his home or even the new towns on the west side of the state. The structures were scattered higgledy-piggledy across a flat stretch of the bottom of the bowl. Some of them were already falling down having been hastily constructed and just as hastily abandoned by those who had constructed them. Smoke drifted from a few chimneys. He could plainly see the boarding house which rose above everything else. The human mind seemed to need symmetry in order to find beauty in something. The towns of his home were carefully laid out and maintained so he found them beautiful. There was none of that here.

He had sat down on a large rock which had been warmed by the sun and he found himself dozing in the morning sunshine. He heard a rock roll and he came immediately awake with his rifle ready in his hands. He found himself face to face with the largest elk he had ever seen. It was much larger than the elk he had seen near Hillsboro. The animal seemed as surprised to see a human as he was surprised to see an elk. The two of them stared at each other for a full second before the elk stamped his forefoot and walked regally away. Thomas belatedly realized he had just let a large quantity of meat walk away. Then he realized he had no idea how to dress the animal and prepare it for eating, so he was thankful he hadn't shot the animal. He was gaining a new respect for those people, both white and red, who had lived out here for so many years and made a life and thrived in that life.

He started down the hill and checked on his animals which were still contentedly grazing. He left them there and continued on down to his camp. He would let them graze until mid-day and then he would picket them close to his camp. He continued back to his camp and dug out the gold pan and shovel from the panniers. He began to dig between the markers George had shown him and carry the gravel to the stream to wash it. As he expected, he found no gold. Had there ever been gold? Who knew, but the man who had turned it back at the Lands Office had apparently never found much. He worked at 'finding gold' for a couple of hours, doing it mainly in case anyone was watching him. He stood up and stretched his back, put away his tools and went to get his animals. He would heat up his coffee and try his hand again at the bannock bread, bacon and maybe some beans, then he would go back into town and see if anyone new was at the saloon. He expected to find that any information that came his way would come from the saloon.

After he had picketed his animals and eaten, he walked the mile or so into the settlement. It felt good to walk and stretch out the muscles which had been cramped up from the digging earlier in the day. It was relatively warm and he made a mental note to get back to his camp before the dark and the cold set back in. George had told him to pile dirt around the base of his tent to help with the drafts and he thought he would try to do that tomorrow. He was also going to try putting some branches under his bedroll to elevate it from the frozen ground. He couldn't do much about the lack of a feather bed though.

Thomas pushed his way through the flaps of the saloon and again found Joseph behind the bar. Thomas waved to him and Joseph nodded an acknowledgement. Thomas again ordered a single shot of whiskey and sat at his place on the bench with his back against the wall. There were a couple of new people, but again, no one seemed out of place or suspicious in any way. There were three faro games today and the players seemed to be evenly winning and losing, exactly what one would expect in an honest game among experienced players.

Thomas sipped his drink slowly for a few minutes and decided he would sit in on one of the games when someone left. It would be a way for him to get acquainted with the locals. He had some seed money and he had the gold dust for salting the claim. He could afford to lose five or ten bucks if it led him to some information.

Thomas had just ordered his second drink when one of the miners, stood up and said, "My wife will be coming to look for me, so I'd better get home. I think she has some projects for me and I've avoided them about as long as I can." Everyone at the table laughed and wished him well. Thomas walked over to the table.

"Mind if I sit in?" he asked.

"Help yourself, stranger," said one of the men. "I can take money from you as well as I can take it from anyone."

"Thank you. I'm Thomas Hart."

"New to the Basin?" asked another.

"Yes, I bought Solomon Dailey's claim. I just got here yesterday."

"So you're the sucker that bought Solomon's claim," chortled the third player.

"I don't know that I'm a sucker. Seems to me it is as likely a place as any," returned Thomas. "He never said it was a bonanza and I am just looking to make wages."

"Well, you'll be lucky if you make wages on that hole," said the first player.

"I'll work it a while and then see what happens," said Thomas.

"It'll be your back you're breaking," retorted the third miner.

"Can we just play cards," said the second miner. "Deal."

"Okay. Keep your shirt on," said the first miner who held the deck and was acting as the banker.

Thomas played cards for about an hour with the three miners, but they were serious players and weren't given to gossip. Thomas lost five dollars and won seven, so he figured it was time to head back to his camp.

"Thanks for the game boys," Thomas said. "I walked into town, so I think I'll be going before it gets dark. Maybe another time for another game?"

"Sure, anytime," said the third miner. "I didn't mean nothing personal about saying you were a sucker. Good luck with your digging."

"No offense taken," said Thomas as he donned his coat and hat and headed out the door.

As he lay in his bedroll that night, Thomas reviewed his first full day in the Basin. Pretty dismal as far as investigating went. He certainly hoped his luck turned around some in the next few days. He fell asleep trying to figure out if he should tough it out in the tent until George came back, but he felt he needed to be closer to the action in town if he was going to make any progress in finding Noah's killers. He really felt the killers were here. He didn't think they had left. They were too greedy to walk away from a rich claim. He just had to smoke them out somehow.

The next morning Thomas awoke to a light dusting of snow. Again he was thankful for George's advice about keeping dry fire starter. His cooking skills hadn't improved overnight however. He burned the bacon and bannock bread again but he didn't burn his fingers making coffee, so that was better. He untied his animals and led them to the stream to drink then walked them up to the meadow to graze again for the day. Then he started 'working' his claim again. Later in the day he secured his animals at the camp site and walked into town again, intending to go to the saloon. On the way there he passed a small, rough cabin that had curtains in the window. The miner whose place he had taken in the card game the night before was sitting on the front step, carving a toy gun.

"Howdy," said Thomas. "I saw you in the saloon last night. I'm Thomas Hart."

"Oh yes," said the man, "I remember. I'm James Swanson. Pleased to meet you."

"What are you carving?" asked Thomas.

"Oh, I'm making a toy gun for my boy. He'll be two in about a week so I'm sitting out here so he doesn't see it. I'm making it for a birthday present for him."

"Doing a right fine job, I'd say."

"I've always liked working with wood. Seems to calm me some. Keeps my hands limber after digging all day."

"So you're married? Not many women folk up here," observed Thomas.

"Me and the missus, we was married before we came here. Got married back in Kansas. Her family's from there.

Our little boy, J.J., was born in Colorado. We've moved around a bit. Seems to be a miner's lot. Always following the strikes."

"Yes, indeed. I've done a fair amount of moving myself," lied Thomas.

The door to the cabin opened and a full-figured woman with mousy brown hair stood in the doorway. She had an air about her that made Thomas believe he wouldn't want to tell her 'no' about anything.

"Thomas, I'd like to introduce you to my wife, Katie. Katie this is Thomas Hart."

"Pleased to meet you, Mr. Hart."

"Please, call me Thomas."

"All right then, Thomas. James, I need to go over to Millicent's house. I have some red thread and she said she needs some to finish a dress. I should be back in a few minutes. Can you come inside and watch J.J.? He's sleeping, but I'd feel better if you'd keep an eye on him."

"Sure. I can do that. Thomas, how about a cup of coffee. You can keep me company while I watch J.J."

"Coffee sounds mighty good," said Thomas.

Katie grabbed her shawl from the inside the door and kissed her husband on the cheek as she walked out of the cabin.

The two men walked inside the tiny space. Thomas noted it had a bed in one corner with a trundle pulled out for the sleeping baby. There was a table with two chairs, a small chest of drawers, a trunk and a very small wood stove. Despite the size, it was clean and there were curtains at the two windows and colorful quilts on the bed. It was very homey.

"I would say you are a lucky man, James. Your wife has made quite a comfortable home for you."

"Yes, I am blessed beyond anything that I deserve," he said as he looked over at his sleeping son. "My wife and son are what make my life worth living. I just wish I could find the riches that Katie deserves. I want to give her a grand house and beautiful dresses and all the best things in life."

"A worthy goal," said Thomas.

James invited Thomas to sit at the little table while he took two tin cups from pegs on the wall. He poured coffee into them and joined Thomas at the table.

"So, tell me about Mormon Basin," began Thomas. "I've only just arrived."

"Oh, it's just like every other mining camp. Some good and some bad. Not too many murders all things considered. In fact, we've only had one and I don't guess you could call it a murder really."

"Why, what happened?"

"Have you met Miss Dottie?"

"Dottie? Billy's wife? Yeah, she gave me supper from her boarding house last night. Seems like a real lady."

"Yeah, she's real quiet. Doesn't socialize with anyone really. Not even the other ladies. Now Billy, he's a different story. Billy has never met a stranger. Friendliest guy you ever want to meet. Always ready to help someone."

"Sometimes opposites attract, don't they."

"Yeah, they do."

"Anyway, Dottie walked this miner home one night. She said he told her he wasn't feeling well and asked her if she would help him home. So, being the lady she is, she agreed. Well, when she got him inside his cabin, he attacked her. Tried to ah, take advantage of her. You've seen her. She's tiny. This guy was about 200 pounds and was a good eight or ten inches taller than her. Anyway, Billy had closed up the bar and followed her to make sure she could help get this guy into his cabin. Good thing he did because when he got there, Billy said the top of

Dottie's dress was ripped nearly plumb off her and the guy had hit her and liked to broke her nose. There was blood all over her. The guy had his pants off and had his union suit fly open. Billy said the guy was completely crazy. Well, Billy had no choice. He had to shoot him.

"The shot woke a bunch of us up, so we went up there. It's the cabin at the end of the street. My missus went flying up there, grabbed Dottie and wrapped her in her own shawl. Didn't care nothing about the blood, my missus. The other ladies in town took Dottie home and got her cleaned up and into bed. The missus said she was just as pale as she could be. Shaking something fierce. Had no expression on her face. The ladies stayed there with her in their rooms at the boarding house until they were sure she was asleep, then they all went home.

"We took Billy to the saloon to get him a drink. Poor fella sure looked like he could use it. When we finally got him back to his place, the house was dark, so we knew the little lady was still sleeping, so we went away real quiet like.

"But poor Miss Dottie, she was so shook up, she didn't come out of her house for the longest time. The cook up at the boardinghouse told my missus that she wouldn't even come out to have her meals. Billy took every meal to her on a tray for a long time. Finally, he took her into Baker City to the doctor there. Said her nerves were just shot. She came out wearing a big, heavy shawl and a hat with a veil. My missus thought maybe that scoundrel had broke her nose and she was ashamed of it. But she came back from Baker City without the veil and her nose is fine. She seems to be feeling better as well. She seems back to her old self. Thank heavens for that."

"What happened to the man who attacked her?"

"Billy blew a hole nearly clean through his chest. I saw him as he was laying there in his cabin. His eyes were fixed and staring at the ceiling. Blood everywhere. He was dead for sure. We buried him the next day. Didn't have no service, because of what he did. Just dug a hole and dumped him in."

"That is a terrible thing to have happen," said Thomas. "So that's the only killing?"

"Yes. Though we've had a couple of shootings over card games and dance hall girls. You know, the usual for a mining camp. Nothing too serious. Men around here are miners, not sharpshooters, so they were mostly flesh wounds."

"Yes, I've seen plenty of those in other mining camps.

"Say, is anybody living in that miner's cabin? The one Billy shot?"

"No. No one who was around here and knew him wanted to live there after what happened. I don't even know if anyone cleaned up the blood. I don't think anyone has been in there since we took his body out."

"Does it belong to anyone?" asked Thomas.

"I don't think so. He had no kin that anyone knew of. Why?"

"Well, I'm finding my tent is none too comfortable at night," admitted Thomas. "I was wondering if I might hang my hat there, at least until spring."

"When the missus comes back to watch J.J., I can take you over there. We might ask Billy about it. Seems he would have a claim to it if anybody did. You know, for what that guy did to Miss Dottie."

"Okay. If you could show it to me, I'd be obliged."

The talk turned to other camp gossip; which dance hall girl had the most 'gentlemen callers,' who to avoid playing faro with, who was an honest merchant in Baker City. They were on their third cup of coffee and it was growing late in the afternoon when Katie Swanson came back to the cabin.

"I'm so sorry. Millicent is so lonely, I just had to stay and visit for a spell. She has no one since her man died to talk to and she just wouldn't hush. Is J.J. still asleep?"

"Yes, not a peep out of him," said James.

"Well, I'd best wake him or he won't sleep tonight," said Katie.

She went over to the trundle and picked up the little boy. He let out one muffled whimper as his mom picked him up. She brought him over and set him in James' lap.

"Hello, my little man," said James as he brushed J.J.'s hair out of his eyes.

J.J. opened his eyes and looked around. When he saw Thomas, he pointed and said, "man". James laughed and said, "Yes, that's a man. J.J. this is Mr. Hart. Can you say Hart?"

J.J. shook his head and buried his face in his father's chest.

"He's a little shy until he gets to know you, then he'll talk your leg off," Katie said. "Mr. Hart would you like to stay to supper? All we've got is some elk stew and biscuits, but there's plenty if you'd like to stay."

"That sounds wonderful. I was going to have to go home to bannock bread and beans, again," said Thomas. "I'd love to have some elk stew. Speaking of elk, let me tell you about what I saw yesterday," and Thomas told them about encountering the elk. That led to James telling about bringing down the cow they were about to have for supper.

The stew and the biscuits were excellent and Thomas had a full belly when he left for his camp. He had arranged to ride into town in the morning and meet James at the cabin where the killing had taken place. He didn't understand why a cabin would set vacant for so long with winter already upon them. Maybe people didn't fancy living where someone had died. Thomas was not a believer in ghosts.

Thomas had seen more than his share of dead bodies and they didn't bother him. In fact, he had a fascination with understanding what people actually died from. Was it from loss of blood or an organ that quit working? He was also interested in finding out about angles of bullets and stab wounds, wondering if that could tell him anything about the height of the murderer or what hand they used to hold the murder weapon. It wasn't a subject he brought up in polite company. Too many people thought he was some kind of ghoul. He rarely shared the fascination with anyone other than the doctors and undertakers who he worked with as they were the only ones who understood it as a scientific fascination.

The snow was gone by the time he left the Swanson cabin. The day had warmed up considerably and the evening was almost pleasant. He had a nearly full moon to guide him on his way home. When he got back to his camp, he took the horse and mule down to the creek and watered them before he secured them close to the tent for the night. He checked his rifle and laid it beside his bed. He stirred the fire and put a fairly large chunk of wood on it, hoping it would still have a little life left in the morning. He warmed water and washed up as best he could. He would love to have a bath, but that wasn't happening any time soon so he did the best he could with warm water and toweling. When he crawled into bed, he thought about Theresa and wondered if she was comfortable in her little cabin tonight. Probably more comfortable than he was going to be, he thought as he drifted off thinking about her.

CHAPTER TWENTY-SIX

It took nearly all of the short winter day to get Theresa moved back into her old room and get the supplies and everything Ten Crows would need taken to her cabin. Painted Pony insisted on cleaning every surface of Theresa's cabin, beating the feather bed and the hides, shaking out all the quilts they were going to leave and generally going over everything in the cabin. She had even brought extra wicks and oil for the lantern and the lamps.

"Ten Crows is used to sleeping in a tent on the ground. Why are you doing all this?" asked Theresa.

"He is a guest and this is an extension of our hospitality. I want everything to be ready for our guest."

"Ten Crows isn't a guest," said Theresa. "He's family."

"Just the same, I want to make him feel welcome."

Theresa could never remember winning an argument with Painted Pony who had been a surrogate mother to her since she was a girl. It was almost like arguing with Syrie. So Theresa just gave up and did what Painted Pony asked.

Painted Pony had brought basic supplies of flour, sugar, salt, tea and jerky in addition to the food she had precooked for Ten Crows for the first few days he was there. He would be staying at the cabin and wouldn't be taking meals with the family until they were sure he wasn't being hunted. She had made stews and roasts, as well as baking bread and biscuits. She had made pies and cookies. She brought preserves and soft cheese in crocks as well as butter.

"There's enough food here to feed him for a month," said Benjamin as he brought in another box of supplies.

"Just hush and get the rest of the stuff from the wagon," said Painted Pony. "Grab some of your sister's things and take them out as long as you are going."

"Yes, ma'am," Benjamin said.

"I don't remember her being this bossy," said Daniel.

"She is like a general on a campaign," said Benjamin. "She is determined she is going to get this conquered."

"Who knew she had those kind of skills?" said Michael. "She is really cracking the whip."

"I think we had just better duck our heads and do as she says," said Daniel. "Be safer all around."

His brothers agreed and they all grabbed another box or bundle to take inside.

Abigail and Theresa concentrated on getting Theresa's personal items packed up while the boys were carting the heavy items in and out of the cabin. Painted Pony kept everyone moving like a well-oiled machine. When Painted Pony was satisfied everything was up to snuff, she climbed into the wagon along with Abigail and started back down to the main ranch house. Theresa saddled up her horse and, with the help of her brothers, started moving the cattle she wanted to keep closer that winter on the road behind the wagon. It was an easy trip back as the cattle were used to following a wagon as that was what they were fed out of if the winter got heavy.

Once they got back to the ranch, it was quick work to get Theresa's things unloaded. As Abigail had already consolidated her few belongings, there was no trouble finding room for Theresa's things in their room. Theresa put her books back on the shelves in the parlor and she was finished moving back home. Abigail and Theresa went into the kitchen to join Syrie and Painted Pony in preparing supper.

"What time did George take off this morning?" asked Theresa.

"He left right after you all did. He should be to Lucreta's place before nightfall. I'm sure he will leave early tomorrow morning to bring Ten Crows here. No one wants to be traveling at night right now. The Paiute raids have slowed, but there is still danger from them."

"Is he going to take Ten Crows directly to Theresa's?" asked Abigail.

"No, I think he will stay here with us the first night. He and I need to talk. We will just need to keep him out of sight of the hands until I can get his hair cut and we can agree on a cover story," said Syrie.

"He can sleep in my cabin like he did before," said Painted Pony. "He can stay there during meal times as well. No one ever goes to my cabin. He'll be safe there."

"That's a good idea," Syrie remarked. "We'll plan on doing that. He and George can leave for Theresa's after breakfast."

Supper and the evening passed as they usually did, with everyone gathering in the parlor after supper, some reading, some sewing, some working with leather or wood. The Hickmans were not a family to be idle. Everyone was waiting now to see how Ten Crows' vision was going to change their lives. They all expected it would.

George and Ten Crows arrived shortly after mid-day the following day. They immediately went into the house and Theresa took their horses down to the barn to unsaddle and feed them. She was admiring the mare that Ten Crows rode in on and asked him about her when she went back to the ranch house.

"I bought her on the reservation," Ten Crows explained. "I think she is as fine an animal as I have ever ridden. Has a wonderful running walk and she has great endurance. I have seen two of her colts and they are excellent as well. She would be a great foundation dam."

"I can see she's got excellent bone structure," Theresa said. "I'm not surprised to hear she throws good colts."

"Speaking of horses," Syrie said, "I wanted to talk to you about raising horses. Noah would want me, us, to help you regain your herds. I know we can't give you back the thousand head you had when you went to the reservation, but we would like to get you started again on raising your own herd."

"I don't have any money to pay for seed stock," said Ten Crows.'

"I'm not talking about selling you seed stock, I'm talking about giving you seed stock."

"You know I can't accept such a gift," said Ten Crows.

"Could you accept such a gift from Noah?" asked Syrie.

"That would be different. Noah and I were brothers. What one had, both had," said Ten Crows.

"Ok, then I am going to tell you Noah would want this. He would want us to do whatever we can to keep you safe and help you prosper. We can, of course, offer you employment and we can offer you land, either here or at Lucreta's if that is what you wish. But mostly, I feel you need to have your own herd of horses again."

"Let me talk to Young Noah about this. He and Lucreta will be here later today. It would be good to have my own horses again."

"Good. We'll talk more later.

"Painted Pony has offered her cabin for you to stay in until we can get you to Theresa's place tomorrow. If you are tired, you can go there now or I can cut your hair and you can stay here and rest in the parlor."

"I think I would like to go to Painted Pony's cabin. I am tired and lying down would be nice. At least until the children get here."

"I'll take you out and get you settled," Painted Pony said.

Lucreta, Young Noah and the children pulled into the compound a while later. The women were already preparing supper and stepped outside to greet them and pass out hugs. Abigail came out and took young Albert and the girls into the parlor to keep them out from under foot of the women and the cooking. Young Noah went to Painted Pony's cabin to talk to his father. Lucreta went into the kitchen and sat down at the table to talk to her mom.

"Supper smells wonderful," Lucreta remarked.

"Pretty hard to mess up a Rafter S beef," said Painted Pony.

"I know. I really prefer beef to venison or elk. Anything I can do to help?"

"No, we have it under control. It should be ready in about an hour, maybe a little less. You can wash up the children and get them ready. I think Abigail has already set the table, but you could check."

"I will in just a minute. I need to rest. I'm extra tired this last little while," said Lucreta.

Syrie stopped what she was doing and looked at her eldest daughter.

"Why?"

"Oh, the usual, I expect. Albert is about two, so I would guess it is time for another grandchild. I've missed my last two times of the moon, so I'm pretty sure."

Syrie and Painted Pony both rushed over to Lucreta to hug her.

"That's wonderful news!" said Painted Pony. "Does Young Noah know?"

"I think he suspects. After all this is a road we've been down before. We had just planned an expansion to the house. Looks like he's going to have to expand it a bit more," Lucreta laughed. "He and I do seem to be able to make babies on a pretty regular basis."

"And you make such excellent babies," said Syrie. "I couldn't be happier for you. When are you going to tell the rest of the family?"

"I'd like to wait a couple more weeks, just to make sure."

"Your secret is safe with us," said Painted Pony. "But I will look forward to rocking another one of your babies. They have all been such sweet babies."

When supper was done, Painted Pony made up two plates and took them to her cabin for herself and Ten Crows. The rest of the family settled in the dining room with the hands gathering in the kitchen. The family kept the conversation focused on ranch business until the hands had finished and had gone back out to their last chores for the night. The family knew the hands would gather in the bunkhouse and wouldn't be back to the house until breakfast the next morning.

After the dishes were cleared, George went out to Painted Pony's cabin to fetch them back in for coffee and a planning session. Syrie and Abigail boiled water and put the supper dishes on to soak, then made fresh coffee and carried it into the parlor. While they were doing that, Benjamin and Theresa made one final check of the livestock. Ten Crows and Painted Pony came back in the house and everyone settled in the parlor. Painted Pony and Abigail sat the children down and gave them toys and books. Sarge was anxious to play with the children, but Syrie made him lie down with Theresa's two dogs. Normally they would have taken the children, and possibly even the dogs, into Abigail's room or the kitchen, but these decisions involved the whole family.

"First of all," Syrie started the conversation, "I think we would all like to hear about your vision."

Ten Crows set aside his tea and said, "It is one of the clearest visions I have ever had. I saw a dark-haired woman. She had blood on her hands. A tall man with red hair was with her. They lived in a house that had lots of other men living in it also. They had another building which had many bottles of whiskey. These were two separate places. I also saw a young dark-skinned man. He was a little darker than me. But not one of us. He had light eyes and he wore two guns. That was the end of the vision."

Abigail was the first to speak saying, "The young man with the two guns. That sounds like Thomas."

"Yes, it does," agreed Daniel. "It sounds exactly like him."

"Young Noah told me about him," said Ten Crows.

"He is Thomas Hart, Deputy U.S. Marshal," said Syrie. "He is the man who was sent by Noah's friend, George Meek, to find the killers. He is in Mormon Basin right now. George took him up there a few days ago."

"It would make sense he would be part of the vision. Not as part of the murder, but as part of the solution to the murder," said Benjamin.

"As Syrie said, I took Thomas to Mormon Basin," said George. "On the way there he wanted to stop off and see the area where Noah's claim is, where he was shot. He walked around and asked me a lot of questions. The result of it is, Thomas thinks there was a woman involved in the killing."

"Why didn't you mention this before?" asked Michael.

"I was going to tell your Ma, but things just didn't work out that way with everything being so busy. Also I wanted to see what Ten Crows had to say.

"At any rate, Thomas thinks the reason they were able to get close enough to shoot Noah with a small caliber weapon, and Thomas thinks it was a pistol, was the fact that one of them was a woman. Noah wouldn't have been afraid of a couple. He wouldn't have suspected a woman of being involved in a crime, especially a murder."

"That makes sense," said Syrie. "Noah was no fool, but a woman would not likely have raised an alarm in him. A woman being in the party would have caused him to relax his guard a little. Maybe just enough to get him killed."

"Thomas also thinks they are the kind of people who are going to be very greedy. He is counting on that to capture them," George finished.

"So, he is hoping to get a confession," noted Daniel.

"That would be my guess," replied George.

"That could be a tricky thing," said Daniel, "unless he can work them one against the other. That is usually harder with a married couple. They will want to protect each other. It is more likely, from what I have read, the man will take the blame to spare the woman."

"Do you really think the woman pulled the trigger?" asked Lucreta.

"It is rare for a woman to be a murderer, especially with a gun, but it does happen," explained Daniel.

"Yes, that is what Thomas told me as well," said George.

"So, where does this leave us?" asked Syrie.

"I think one of us needs to go to Mormon Basin and tell Thomas about Ten Crows' vision." Said Daniel. "George should probably be the one to go since no one is likely to know he is connected to us. I don't think we know anyone in Mormon Basin, but someone may have seen some of us in town and could put two and two together. It might endanger the investigation."

"I'll be glad to ride up there in the morning," said George. "If I get an early start I can be back before sundown."

"Good. That's taken care of," said Syrie. "Now, Ten Crows can you tell us about your escape from the reservation and what we can do to help you stay safe."

Ten Crows recounted his original plan about faking his death and about how his timetable had gotten moved up with the death of Broken Wing. He told them about his journey south and about his run-in with the deputy in LaGrande and the kindness of Walter Carter.

When he had finished, Daniel asked him, "Since you were a leader of your people and the Indian Agent knows you have friends on the outside, do you think he will write and let us know about your 'death'?"

"I hadn't considered that. It is possible," said Ten Crows. "If he does that, then we will know for sure my death has been declared official."

"Let's hope that happens," said Syrie. "It would allow all of us to breathe a bit easier.

"Speaking of which, how about I cut your hair while these children get bundled off to bed?"

Lucreta stood and said, "Yes, bedtime is an excellent idea," to a chorus of moans from the older girls. "Where would you like us to bed down tonight?"

"You and Young Noah take my room and you can make pallets for the children in there. Theresa and Abigail can double up and I'll take the second bed in their room. Ten Crows are you going to sleep at Painted Pony's again?"

"Yes, the buffalo robe on the floor of the cabin suits me fine," he said.

"Good. Okay everyone, you know what you need to do. Ten Crows if you will come with me into the kitchen, I'll cut your hair and see if I can turn you into someone else," Syrie said as she retrieved her scissors from her sewing basket.

CHAPTER TWENTY-SEVEN

Thomas managed to get the fire going and cook his breakfast with a minimum of fuss and no burns. He congratulated himself on getting this roughing business down pat. After a breakfast of bannock bread and bacon, he saddled his horse and was on his way to town when his mule set up a terrible racket, pulling at the lead, rearing up and braying. Sighing, Thomas went back, dismounted, untied the mule and holding the lead, remounted and started for town again.

"No account animals. More trouble than you are worth," he said out loud. He thought back to being able to rent a horse from the livery or take a stagecoach to get where he wanted to go. Certainly was much easier living in civilization. The mule trotted along happily behind the horse and rider and he was in town quickly. He went immediately to the Swanson cabin and tied his animals to a nearby tree as the only hitching posts were in front of the saloon. He knocked on the door and Katie answered holding little J.J. This time J.J. said "hi" before burying his face in his mother's bosom.

"He's a character, isn't he?" said Thomas.

"Oh, he keeps us real busy," Katie laughed. "James is at the diggings for a couple of hours. He said you were coming and asked me to keep you company until he got back. I hope you don't mind."

"No. Of course not. That would be real nice. Give me a chance to get this little J.J. guy to warm up to me some."

Upon hearing his name, J.J. turned his head enough to gaze up at Thomas and flash him a smile before he buried his head again.

Thomas laughed and stepped inside the cabin. Again he was struck with what a comfortable home Katie had made with what was obviously limited funds. Nothing was new and everything had a purpose, but it was arranged in such a cheerful and comfortable manner, one ceased to see the scarcity of it. She sat J.J. down long enough to take a cup off its peg on the wall and pour a cup of coffee for Thomas.

"Are you joining me?" he asked.

"No, thank you. I've already had enough coffee and I simply have to get some mending done."

"I imagine James is hard on clothes being a miner. I know my clothes always seem to fall apart too fast," Thomas said as he found himself lying again to conform to his assumed lifestyle.

"It isn't just James' clothes. To bring in a little extra money, I do mending for the other miners who don't have wives. I even do some mending for the women who work at the saloon. I enjoy the work and it allows me to watch J.J. and keep the house so it is a good thing all around."

She rocked J.J. until he demanded to be set down. Then he toddled off on his fat little legs. Katie picked up her sewing basket.

"You are a very industrious woman," Thomas noted.

"James works so hard and I just have to help him somehow. He is so determined to make a go of this mining thing. I just wish he wouldn't work so hard," she lamented.

"Sometimes finding gold gets in a man's blood."

"Oh, I don't think it's that. James says he wants to give me everything, a fine house, expensive clothes, you know all that stuff. I can't seem to convince him I just want him, a home and his children. That's the greatest wealth to me.

"He was a farmer when I met him. We had a nice little farm in Kansas. Then someone came through our little town and started talking about the gold strikes in the west and how rich people were getting. Next thing I know, he has rented out the farm to a neighbor, cleared out our soddy and packed everything into our farm wagon and we are off for Colorado. We've been chasing the next big strike ever since."

"And what would you like to do?" Thomas asked.

"I don't want you to think I don't love and respect my husband. I mean no disrespect to him."

"I know you don't," Thomas reassured her. "I think you are a loyal, loving wife who is doing the best she can with what she has. In fact, I think you are doing a remarkable job in a very bad, inhospitable place."

Katie sighed and set her mending aside.

"I would really like to go home. I really miss my soddy and my friends in Kansas. This cabin is always cold. I can't plug up all the drafts. I tried to chink it this summer, but I must have missed spots. My little soddy was always so cozy.

"And I don't want to end up like Millicent, the lady I went to see last night. Her husband died last summer when a tree fell on him when some of the men were cutting firewood. She's all alone now and doesn't even have enough money to get to Baker City and get a stage back to her family. She's waiting right now for money to come through so she can go home. Outside of James, I have no one here.

"And some of the people here are strange."

"How do you mean?" asked Thomas.

"I don't want to gossip and carry tales," said Katie.

"No, I would really like to know," said Thomas. "Is there someone here I should be concerned about? Remember, I am brand new here and I haven't had the time to get to know these people."

Katie picked up her mending again and began to work on it. J.J. toddled over to her to show her a bug he had found on the wall and Katie calmly told him to put it back where he had found it and watched him to make sure he didn't put it in his mouth. Most women Thomas had known back east would have screamed and squashed the bug.

"Some of the folks are real nice. Millicent for one. And Susanna, the lady who cooks for the boarding house. Her husband is a miner.

"But others of the women kind of make the hairs on the back of my neck stand up."

"Like who?" asked Thomas.

"Like the lady from the saloon."

"The 'working girls'?" Thomas asked.

"Oh no. Those are the nicest gals. They are just trying to keep body and soul together. They don't have families. Most of them are orphans or widows. A couple of them like to drink too much. No, not them."

She paused again and paid attention to her sewing. Thomas wondered if she was going to say anymore and drank his coffee. One thing he had learned from Joe Meek was to let people find their own time and own way to tell their story. He waited. Katie finished the piece she was working on and folded it neatly, then picked up another piece from a basket on the floor.

"I'm talking about Dottie," she said at last.

"Billy's wife?" Thomas asked.

"Yes, Billy's wife."

"Why her? What makes you uncomfortable about her?"

"I don't really know. I just get the feeling something is off about her. She really doesn't belong here. She has nothing to do with the other women of the town. There being so few of us, we tend to cling to each other pretty tightly. Other women are the only support we have out here. She wants no part of that. And the night the big miner was killed was the strangest of all.

"James and I were some of the first ones through the door. Her face was all bloody and her nose was already starting to swell. There were tear marks down her cheeks, but her eyes were what caught my attention. There wasn't fear in them. There was, I don't know, triumph? Elation? Some kind of pride? Like she had done a good thing? Something was just off.

"And then when we walked her home, I put my shawl around her shoulders to cover her," Katie made a circle over her own breasts, "because her dress was all torn and bloody. She kept wanting to draw away from me. I held on tight to her. I have seen women who have survived attacks before and every one of them wanted to be held. Wanted comfort. Wanted to cling to someone. Not Dottie.

"She finally kind of gave up and we got her home, but by the time we got to her rooms at the boarding house she was shaking like a leaf. I don't think it was a reaction to the killing, I think it was anger. She tried to keep her head down where we couldn't see her face, but she was so rigid, like a child having a tantrum. I really think she was furious. I don't know at what, but she was really angry.

"Susanna went into the kitchen and made her tea and brought it out to her. Dottie thanked her, but was kind of talking down to Susanna. You know what I mean? Like Dottie was doing Susanna a favor by taking the tea from her. And one of the women had made up some water for Dottie to wash the blood off herself with, and another woman asked her where her nightgown was. So she could change out of the bloody clothes. Most of us keep our nightgowns hanging on a hook in the bedroom. Not many of us have any furniture. Dottie said her nightgown was in a trunk in her room. That made no sense at all to me. Why would it be in a trunk? And the woman who got the nightgown said there was only one. And it was brand new. Never been worn.

"And strangest of all, Dottie didn't want to talk about the attack. Every woman I've known who was attacked, and it didn't matter who attacked her, wanted to talk about it. Seems like talking about it kind of takes away the sting of it. The women want to make sure there was nothing they could have done different. Not Dottie. She answered questions about where things were and she thanked people, but not one word about the attack itself.

"Like I said, something just isn't right about that woman.

"I've talked entirely too much," Katie said. "If you'll excuse me, J.J. is being entirely too quiet. I need to check on him." Katie got up and started searching the cabin. After a minute she pulled J.J. out from under the bed. He had fallen asleep on the trundle clutching a rag doll. "Isn't he the sweetest little boy? I want a dozen just like him. I just don't want to raise them in a mining camp," she said as she cradled her son and sat down to rock him.

Thomas helped himself to another cup of coffee and went outside to check on his animals. He saw James coming down the street with a big smile on his face.

"Must have been a good day at the claim," said Thomas.

"Yes, I think I actually made more than wages today," James said. "How are you?" he asked Thomas.

"I am well. I have been enjoying talking to your wife and son. You are a very blessed man."

"Yes, I am. I truly am.

"Let me put this pan and shovel around back and I'll walk with you down to look at that cabin."

When the men stepped up on to the porch of the abandoned cabin, it was evident no one had been inside for a very long time because of the amount of cobwebs all over the door.

"Should have brought a broom," said James. "I hate touching those things." He looked around and stepped off the porch and grabbed a branch which was lying nearby. He used it to clear a path through the cobwebs so he could pull the leather thong attached to the door. He pushed his way in, using the stick to clear a bigger hole in the cobwebs. Dust lay thick over everything in the cabin and the two men left prints wherever they stepped. James had been right, there had been no one in the cabin since the night of the murder.

Thomas saw it was a typical cabin, very small with a bed in one corner, a table and a stove and a couple of chairs. There were no covers over the windows beyond some bits of tent canvas which had been nailed in place. Thomas didn't know how it was possible, but it seemed colder in the cabin than it was outside. Thomas' attention was drawn immediately to the bed and to the dark stain on the floor near it. He crossed to the bed and looked at it closely. What he saw really didn't surprise him. There was an outline of a woman's torso on the quilt. It was outlined in the miner's dried blood. There was a trail of that same blood which extended off the bed and onto the floor.

"You can see where we found him," said James as he pointed to the stain on the floor. "He was lying right there beside the bed. Dottie said he threw her onto the bed just before Billy came in."

Thomas shook his head and said, "Terrible that a woman would have to be subjected to something like that, isn't it?"

"Yes, we all felt really sorry for Miss Dottie," James agreed. James shivered in spite of himself. "Why is it so cold in here?"

"I was wondering the same thing myself," said Thomas.

"If you think this will work for you, we can go over to the saloon and have a talk with Billy. See if he has any problem with you living here for a spell."

"Yes, I would like that. It'll take some cleaning, but it is a great sight better than a tent."

"Most of the miners who had only tents left the Basin last fall. I think you are the only one here who doesn't have some kind of house. Of course, some of them houses are wall to wall beds, but it beats sleeping rough."

"Let's get out of here and go talk to Billy," said Thomas. "I'm anxious to get out of that tent before it sets in and starts snowing hard."

"Sure," James said as he pulled the door closed.

James and Thomas were standing at the bar talking to Billy when George walked in. Thomas caught his eye and shook his head so George ordered a whiskey and took a seat at a table.

"I don't have any claim on that cabin. None of his kin have come forward to lay a claim to it. He kept to himself mostly and I never heard anyone say he even had a family. If you want to clean it up and move in, I don't have a problem with it," Billy told Thomas.

"It'll take a bit of work to clean it up, but I'm concerned I am going to freeze to death in that tent when winter really sets in," said Thomas.

"Don't blame you a bit. Never did like sleeping in a tent. Had to do a fair amount of it coming out here and Dottie positively despises it. Got a roof over her head as soon as we could. Makes living with her a mite easier," Billy said jovially.

"Do you want me to talk to the woman who cleans for us at the boarding house? See if she wants to help you clean it up? She charges a real reasonable rate. Hard worker. You'll get your money's worth from her."

"Yes, if you wouldn't mind speaking to her, I'd be obliged. Or you can let me know where I can find her and I'll go talk to her myself," said Thomas.

"I can show you where she lives," said James. "She and my missus they are friendly. I'll take you by her cabin on the way back to my place."

"Good. That's settled. You'll be safer in town anyway," said Billy. "Those Paiutes have been getting more and more bold. They haven't come into town, but they have been attacking people on the road."

"Thanks again, Billy. I'll be seeing you around," said James.

"Safe travels, you two," said Billy and waved at them as they went out the door.

George didn't get up right away, but leisurely finished his drink. Then he buttoned up his coat, put on his hat and went out into the cold.

Billy leaned over and said to Joseph, "You recognize the old fella who was just in here?"

"Never saw him before," said Joseph. "Don't know who he is."

"You know, no one ever 'passes through' Mormon Basin. Wonder why he's here?"

Joseph shrugged and went back to cleaning tin cups.

Billy decided he would keep an eye out for the stranger if he came in again.

George went back out of town towards the camp he had set up for Thomas. He had waited at the claim for a time before he decided to come into town and look for Thomas.

The slight shake of the head from Thomas in the saloon had been enough to warn George off and had told him that Thomas didn't want the people in town to know they were acquainted. So George waited beside the road until Thomas rode back out of town. When Thomas was nearly abreast of where he was, George entered the roadway so Thomas could see him.

"Hi, George. What brings you to Mormon Basin?" asked Thomas.

"Ten Crows came home last night and the family asked me to come and find you and let you know what he said."

"I don't want people in town to see us together. You have been around the Rafter S enough that someone might recognize you. Let's go back to my camp. We can talk there."

The two rode on back to Thomas' camp where they built up the fire and warmed up some bacon and beans to have for their evening meal.

"I'm sorry I didn't bring any food. I was expecting to ride in, talk to you and ride straight back to the ranch. Hadn't planned on staying in the Basin this long."

"No worries. I have plenty of food for the next few days. Sorry I wasn't in camp when you got here, but I got a lead on a cabin in town that I can stay in, at least for a while. I've been cultivating a friendship with a married couple and I have developed some pretty good leads, I think."

"That's good news. Syrie and the family will be excited to hear that. Can you tell me what you've learned?"

"It is looking more and more like it was a man and a woman. And I think the woman may be the shooter."

George was very surprised and said so. "Are you sure?"

"Short of an actual eyewitness, I'm as sure as I can be. I am also making the assumption she killed another man here in the Basin. Probably after she killed Noah."

"So what are we dealing with here?" asked George.

"Someone who has no rein on her temper. Someone who is a deadly shot and someone who places no value whatsoever on human life, except her own and maybe her husband's."

"Why do you think she murdered the miner?"

Thomas stirred the beans and added more fuel to the fire before he sat down on a log that passed for a chair in his camp. George likewise got comfortable on another log.

"I think it was a con game that went sideways. There is an old con game usually run by a couple. If the woman is beautiful, and this woman is, it is more likely to return big dividends. The way the con works is they pick a victim with something of value - money, land, influence - and they have the woman start flirting with the man. She lets the victim know she is interested in him, sexually. She arranges to be alone with the victim and allows nature to take its course, usually removing at least some of her clothes in the process. At an agreed upon time or signal, the outraged husband bursts in on the victim and his wife in a compromising situation. In order to keep the 'scandal' from going public or to keep the wife of the victim from finding out, 'payment' is extracted from the victim.

"I think in this case the miner wasn't willing to play the game, he didn't care if word got out, and was going to sexually assault the woman, whether her husband was there or not. At some point the woman wound up on the bed of the miner's cabin. I think she is the one who shot the miner."

"Why do you think it was her and not her husband?"

"The blood pattern on the bed."

"I don't understand," said George.

"The couple I told you about, the ones I am making friends with? They were some of the first ones on the scene. The shooting took place late at night and apparently the shot woke just about the whole camp. They both told me that when they got into the miner's cabin, the miner was lying on the floor. The husband said the miner was face up and that he had a hole in his chest. That would indicate to me the miner turned around when the husband entered the cabin and the husband shot him where he stood. If that is what happened, all the blood should be on the floor, except for what might have gotten sprayed by the shot. There should not have been blood on the bed. There was a nearly perfect outline on the quilt on the bed of a woman's torso."

"I'm sorry, Thomas, I still don't understand," said George.

"One of the things we are trained to do is to look at a crime scene very carefully. One of the things we study is how blood is sprayed or pools from a shot or a stab wound.

"You have seen men killed?"

George nodded in the affirmative.

"And you have doubtless killed hundreds of animals."

Again, George nodded.

"What have you noticed about the difference between shooting someone or something and a stabbing?" Thomas went on before George could answer. "Blood is spattered in a shooting. In a knifing the blood is pooled, unless you hit an artery.

"So, in this case, I would expect blood spray to be going away from the body and for tiny droplets of blood to be scattered all along the walls and furniture. Being shot in the chest, there should have been at least one artery severed by the bullet.

"But that isn't what I found. I didn't find blood spray on the bed. I found an outline, a void if you will. The blood on the quilt was not in a spray pattern, it was in a..." Thomas searched for the right word, "a soaking pattern. Like whatever was bleeding was on top of the woman whose outline is on the bed. In this case, it was a very small woman's outline.

"And there wasn't enough blood on the floor to have come from a large man. There was only a blood stain about six inches or so wide. Blood from a man the size that was described to me should have been two to three times larger.

"The crime scene doesn't add up to the story."

George was clearly impressed. "I had no idea you could tell so much from looking at where someone died."

"You can't always. Where Noah was killed it was outdoors, the elements had been at work and animals and other things had been walking over it. In the case of the miner, the people took out his body and shut the door. The only things that have been in there since were mice and spiders. So the crime scene was essentially untouched since just after the shooting. I got very, very lucky," said Thomas.

"So you have suspicions of not one murder committed by this woman, but two. Daniel is always talking about proof and warrants and arrests and trials. Do you have enough proof to get a warrant? To go to trial?" asked George.

Thomas tested the temperature of the beans, found them to be warm and ducked into his tent to get dishes for himself and George.

"No, I don't. That is the problem. I have a lot of conjecture, some educated guesses and people telling me things about the people involved. But, no, I don't have any proof. And, at the moment, I haven't yet figured out how to get proof."

George and Thomas ate in silence for a minute.

"You said Ten Crows was home and that the family asked you to bring me news," said Thomas. "What news?"

"The Cayuse have a long tradition of visions," George started.

"I have heard of mystic visions," said Thomas.

"Ten Crows had a vision while he was still on the reservation. He came home to tell Syrie and the family about it."

"What was the vision?" asked Thomas.

"Ten Crows said he saw three people in this vision. A dark-haired woman with bloodied hands, a tall red-headed man and a young, dark man with light eyes. The woman and the red-haired man live in a house with many other men and they have a lot of whiskey bottles. The young man wears two guns, strapped down to his legs."

Thomas sat at a loss for words, finally saying, "You know I can't use any of that in a court of law. I can't get a warrant on that information."

"Yes, Daniel has explained all that to everyone in the family. But you should know Ten Crows has a history of having very accurate visions. He has been right many, many times in the past."

"I can respect that, but as a man of science and someone who reports to a federal judge, I can't allow myself to be swayed by a mystical vision," explained Thomas.

"I can understand that," said George. "My thought, and Syrie's, was you take this information and see if it helps you narrow down your group of suspects. Maybe give you another road to investigate."

Thomas ate in silence for a long time. He was trying to decide if he should tell George the physical description of the man and the woman in the vision exactly matched Dottie and Billy, his two prime suspects. He decided to hold on to the information a little while longer. He was also more than a little disconcerted Ten Crows had described him so accurately. It was uncanny as he had never even met this man. And he couldn't un-hear what George had just said. No matter that he was a man of science and logic, he was impressed and it would influence his thinking.

"Please tell Ten Crows," Thomas said at last, "I thank him for the information and I will put it to good use. I doubt he would understand anything beyond that."

George put down his spoon and stopped eating while he looked at the young man.

"I will excuse that remark because you are young and you have never met Ten Crows and you likely have not met a great many native peoples.

"But let me tell you a thing or two, Mr. Hart. Ten Crows has a formal education greater than most white people you will meet in this part of the country. He was educated at a very fine boarding school in Canada. He has continued to learn and study all through his life. He not only speaks English and his native tongue, he also speaks French and some Spanish. Painted Pony and my late wife, though not formally educated are, or were, some of the most intelligent women I have ever known.

"I am really surprised someone of your heritage would cast scorn on any other people."

With that George sat his plate down and went to take care of his horse for the night.

Thomas was aghast at what he had just done. George was right. He had no call to be dismissive of someone he had never met and he certainly had no right to be scornful of any other people, no matter their background. When George came back to the fire, Thomas apologized.

"I will accept your apology on behalf of Ten Crows and others. But you would do well to remember Ten Crows was a fearful warrior in his youth and his pride still burns strong. You will be taking your life in your hands if you ever say anything like that around him or Painted Pony.

"I will sleep next to the fire tonight," said George. "I will wish you good night." George placed his saddle against the log, leaned against it, covered himself with the saddle blanket and pulled his hat down over his eyes.

CHAPTER TWENTY-EIGHT

Daniel and the rest of the men on the Rafter S gathered the young colts to be gelded. It would be a long day and they needed to get an early start in the morning, so they penned the colts and their mothers in one of the small pastures near the house. They would keep them there after the gelding so they could be monitored for bleeding or infection. They tried to geld the colts before they were a year old if the animal was physically ready. With them being so young, the horses weren't as strong as they would be at two or three and they seemed to heal up faster when they could go back and be with their mothers.

The last time Daniel had helped geld colts, they had thrown the colts to the ground and used ropes to hold them. It had been a hazardous task. Even with the strength of his father and Young Noah, sometimes one of the cowboys or family members had received some pretty sharp kicks. No broken bones had occurred, but some of the bruises had been deep and painful. Daniel knew they would miss the strength of his father this year, though Benjamin was filling out fast and would be more help every year.

In talking with Benjamin and Michael, they had told him they had devised a different method of holding the colts that protected the people working on them as well as keeping the animal still so a knife didn't slip during the process. After the colts selected for gelding had been penned up with their dams, the three of them had walked down to the new set up by the barn. A special alley and gate set up had been installed. Benjamin and Michael demonstrated how it would work. The colts would be brought into the small holding pen after being separated from their dams. Once the surgery was complete, the colt would be freed and let back into the grassy paddock to rejoin his dam. With 50 or so of them to do, it was going to be an all day job as they wanted to keep the animals as calm as possible. They would be moving slowly and quietly in the handling of the colts to reduce, or at least lessen, any harm to man or beast.

The Hickmans always tried to castrate the colts in winter to lessen the chances of infection as horses weren't as resistant to infection as cows. Unfortunately, that also meant there were less hands employed by the three ranches. When the calves were castrated in the spring, they usually had a full crew. Not so in the middle of winter. Young Noah came for the day from the Rafter L to help. Because they were working with a skeleton staff, everyone was pressed into service, even the women. Usually Syrie and Painted Pony were in charge of making sure the knives and pliers were clean and the knives razor sharp. To do this, they kept them in a basin of cheap whiskey. As Theresa had grown older she had started taking a more active role in the actual castration. Today, she and Horace would be teaching Michael how to do the surgery. It had always been her dad's job to do the actual surgery with Horace and Theresa assisting.

The whole family went to the working facility as soon as breakfast was over. Syrie took the first shift sterilizing the knives while Painted Pony cleaned up after breakfast and prepared lunch. After lunch, they would switch places. This was Abigail's first year helping with the castration and she was assigned to work with her mother keeping the knives and pliers ready. Benjamin went to the blacksmith shop and retrieved two sets of pliers to be placed into the basin of whiskey. Syrie brought the sharpened knives from the house. Everyone was anxious to see the new chute at work and Benjamin and Michael ran through it again so everyone would be familiar with it.

They brought the first colt in and Daniel dropped a loop over his head while Benjamin closed the gates. Young Noah snaked a rope out and caught one hind foot and passed the lariat to Daniel to run through the neck loop. Daniel snugged the lariat up tight to the neck loop while Benjamin secured the swinging gates behind the colt. Syrie passed one of the knives to Theresa who make the initial incision into the scrotum. Horace reached in and retrieved the testes and used the pliers to crush the cords. After the cords were completely crushed, Theresa removed the testes and Horace washed the incision with whiskey. Daniel loosened the lariat which had held up the hind foot and let the colt set the foot back down and regain his balance. They let the colt stand for a few minutes to allow the clotting to start while they were setting up for the next colt. Then they turned the colt into a small enclosure where the clotting could continue. After they had done half a dozen colts, they would turn the first out to join his dam if the bleeding had stopped.

Syrie had just turned from accepting the knife and pliers from Theresa and Horace when she noticed a strange horse and rider along with half a dozen head of Shires approaching. The newcomer stopped and stepped down off his horse. Syrie saw a tall young man with broad shoulders, long blonde hair so light it was almost white, hanging from beneath his hat. He had large blue eyes, his nose was straight and sharp. He smiled a broad smile. He removed his hat as he approached the fence.

"Good morning," he said, "I'm looking for Mrs. Hickman."

Syrie straightened and looked at him closely. "I'm Mrs. Hickman and I know you," she said.

"I've never been here before," the stranger said.

"Nevertheless, I know who you are. You look exactly like your father, who looks exactly like his father. You are named for that grandfather. You are Swen Solomon Jensen. I remember very well the day you were born."

"Yes, ma'am. I am Swen," he said smiling. "My folks send their best. They sent me out the day after they got your letter. They wanted to make sure you had the Shires to start breeding with right away. I've brought a letter from them for you," he said as he patted his coat pocket.

"I can't wait to read it, but Swen, as you can see, you have caught us in the midst of working these colts. As soon as we break for lunch I'll take you to the house and we can catch up on family news."

"I understand. If you let me know where I can put these horses, I'll be glad to give you a hand. Quite the set up you have here. I'd like to take a closer look at it later. The design might prove useful in our operation."

"Of course. Michael and Benjamin will be happy to show you how they designed and built it.

"Theresa, would you show Swen the barn and corrals? Put the stallion in the stud stall in the barn and put the mares in one of the paddocks. Swen, Theresa will show you where to put your gear in the bunkhouse and she will show you where you can put your saddle horse for the night. I really have to get back to this.

"Michael, step up and take Theresa's place please. Horace will show you want to do. Daniel, please take your spot at the head of the colt. Let's get back to this. I'd like to have at least 20 head done before lunch."

Everyone followed Syrie's directions and the process was soon well underway again.

Theresa took the reins for Swen's saddle horse and led the way, while Swen took the lead line for the massive Shires. She was surprised at how quiet the stallion's behavior was. He was one of the most docile horses she had ever seen and definitely the calmest stallion she had ever encountered.

"Is he always this easy going?" she asked.

"Yes. He's naturally a sweet, calm horse and we work with the studs from an early age to ensure they are extremely well behaved. They are too big for us to allow them to be otherwise," explained Swen.

"I'd be interested to talk to you about your training methods," Theresa said. "And I'm sure my brothers would be as well."

"I'd be happy to share any information you need. Or your brothers," he added.

Theresa tied the saddle horse to the hitching rail in front of the barn and led Swen to the stud stall in the barn.

"You can put him in here. All of our studs are out on pasture right now. I'll show you where you can put the mares after you get him put away."

Theresa watched Swen unhook the stud from the string and walk him into the stall.

'Quite a pair of fine young animals,' she thought as she watched them.

Swen patted the huge animal like he was a dog and fastened the stall door firmly. The stud poked his head over the top of the gate and gently pushed Swen as he tried walked away. Swen laughed, turned around and scratched the horse's ears for another moment then walked away again.

"That's a game we play," Swen explained. "I always have to scratch his ears before I can get away from him."

He took the line from Theresa and followed her on through the barn and down past a couple of paddocks until they can to two empty ones.

"We'll put them in here for now," Theresa said. "After we talk to Ma, she'll decide where she wants to keep them."

Swen nodded as he loosed the five mares into the two paddocks.

"If you'll show me what hay to feed them, I'll do that before I come up and help you."

"Let's get your stuff into the bunkhouse and get your saddle horse taken care of first. They'll be fine at the castrating for a few more minutes," Theresa said as they walked back through the barn to where Swen's horse was tied.

"Put him in this stall here and hang your gear on one of these logs. The bunkhouse is over there," she said pointing to the long, low building. "Most of the bunks are empty this time of year. Pick whichever one suits you. You'll be able to tell which one belongs to Horace. It has the Mexican blanket on it.

"As to the feed, you can toss some down from the loft for the stud and your horse. If the mares need to be fed before the regular evening feeding, you can fork some down from the loft and into the handcart there in the alleyway. I'd better be getting back," she said and turned and walked away.

"I'll be there as soon as I see to the animals," Swen said.

Swen watched Theresa stride away as he was unsaddling his horse. He decided she was a fine woman to watch in her buckskin breeches and short leather jacket.

His grandmother had told him what a sweet and beautiful baby Theresa had been. His mother had told him what a handsome woman Syrie was and that Theresa's father had been a small, wiry man with a face like one of the mythical elves. Theresa certainly seemed to have that type of face and she was a lot of woman in a small package. So very different from his sisters who were all tall, strong women. Not that he thought Theresa was a weak woman. She could obviously hold her own. He finished unsaddling his horse and carried his gear to the bunkhouse thinking about the beautiful, uncommon young woman.

CHAPTER TWENTY-NINE

Ten Crows was settled into Theresa's cabin. He borrowed books from Syrie's library, and he was enjoying having the time and the luxury of just reading again. He had the time on the reservation, but he didn't have access to quality reading material most of the time and if he did, he had no place safe for the books. So this respite was welcome. Painted Pony had left him plenty of pre-made food and he had tea and sugar, his pipe and tobacco, so he had everything he could need or want.

He felt like he was home. Not that the cabin necessarily felt like it was home, it was more the canyon and the people. When Noah had been alive and before the treaty had been signed removing his people from their land, he had spent a lot of time at the Rafter S. He had helped train horses and he had even worked cattle some. He had still traveled the seasonal circuit with his people, but he was comfortable here along this creek.

Syrie stopped by to see him on her daily rides and sometimes he saddled up his mare and rode with her and George. Three old friends riding through familiar country.

Syrie would bring him more books in her saddle bags and Ten Crows would send back the ones he had read. The winter had been remarkably warm and open. There had been some snow flurries, but they hadn't lasted long and had melted quickly. Ten Crows wasn't fool enough to think the weather would stay that way all winter, January and February could be very cold and wet, but for now he was enjoying the weather. He often sat outside in the evening to smoke his pipe. He didn't know if Theresa would mind the smell of his pipe in her house, but he had always preferred to smoke out of doors in any case.

The days passed and Ten Crows noticed he was putting on a little weight. The pants Syrie had given him no longer had to be held up by a belt and the shirts no longer hung off his shoulders. Besides reading he kept himself busy by doing minor repairs around the homestead. He had never understood why white people wanted to be tied to a place, but that hadn't kept him from learning how to maintain and build while he worked alongside Noah.

He missed his friend every day. It was good to see Syrie and to see how tall and strong Noah's sons were becoming, but he missed Noah. None of the sons could ever take the place of the father. His own son came to visit as often as he could get away from his own place and occasionally he would bring one of the girls. Lucreta said little Albert was too young yet to make the trip, especially in the winter. If they all came in the buckboard, then Ten Crows got to see his only grandson. Those times were precious to him.

Ten Crows had asked George when he had returned from Mormon Basin if what he had seen in his vision had helped the young investigator. George hadn't given him a yes or no answer but had said Thomas couldn't take a vision to the sheriff. Ten Crows had understood that and, indeed, he valued the vision more for his own uses than for the use of the white man's justice. It made little difference to him who meted out justice for Noah's murder. The vision had validated what Ten Crows needed to know in his own mind and that was enough. If he ever saw those two people, he would act. It was a very simple matter for him.

He did give a lot of thought to how he would dispense justice. He wasn't fool enough to forget the white man didn't forgive an Indian for killing another white man, no matter the justification. He had told Syrie no one would know who had killed the people, only that it would happen. He would have preferred to confront them head on and kill the man in battle, but he couldn't have that honor. He did want to be able to see his grandchildren grow up. And he knew Noah would not have wanted him to suffer hanging just to avenge his death. That meant he had to kill them from a distance, something he really didn't like, or he had to catch them away from anyone else and kill them there. George had told him Thomas was sure they were still in the area. There was a lot of lonely trail around Baker City and Mormon Basin.

One sunny morning while Ten Crows was smoking his pipe and reading after breakfast, a young man with dark skin and light eyes, rode up to Theresa's cabin. Ten Crows immediately recognized him from his vision.

"Is Theresa here?" Thomas inquired.

"No, she is staying down at the Rafter S, Thomas," Ten Crow said.

"How do you know my name?" asked Thomas.

"I saw you in my vision. Syrie and her family supplied the name."

Thomas dismounted and tied his horse to a tree.

"You must be Ten Crows," he said and extended his hand to Ten Crows. "Syrie and her family speak highly of you. I met your son. He is a fine man."

"Thank you. Will you come in?" said Ten Crows as he tapped the ash from his pipe, put the pipe in his pocket turned to go inside the house. "The water is hot if you want some tea. Or I can make coffee if you would prefer?"

Thomas had to admit he was a little taken aback to hear the Queen's English being spoken by a Native. He was glad George had told him Ten Crows had been educated in Canada.

"Tea will be fine," Thomas said as he followed Ten Crows into the cabin. Thomas could see Theresa had taken her personal belongings with her when she moved to the Rafter S and that Ten Crows had moved in very little other than a few books, a few clothes and a bedroll on the frame of the bed. The man must travel very light if this is all he brought from the reservation. Thomas hung his hat on the pegs inside the door of the cabin and sat down at the kitchen table.

Ten Crows made tea for the two of them and gave one cup to Thomas, then joined him at the small kitchen table. Thomas saw Syrie and Painted Pony were keeping Ten Crows well supplied with food as the small sideboard was fairly groaning with cookies and pies. There was a pot of something simmering on the hearth.

"Would you care for some cookies, or biscuits as I was taught to call them, to go with your tea?" asked Ten Crows. "The ladies are wonderful bakers. I think they are trying to fatten me up," he winked at Thomas.

"Yes, I would love some cookies. They look delicious."

"Tea and these cookies, and other desserts, are things I am glad the white man brought to this country," said Ten Crows as he set the plate on the table and helped himself to a cookie.

"Tell me how your investigation is proceeding."

Thomas sipped gingerly at his tea and took a bite of cookie. "It is going as well as I could expect. It is infinitely more difficult because there were no witnesses and a great deal of time has elapsed since the murder. I cannot find any physical evidence after this long a time, if there ever was any. All I can hope for right now is that I can stumble upon a confession from one of the murderers."

"So you agree with George and I that there were two murderers?" asked Ten Crows.

"It is the most likely scenario. And your idea about one of them being a woman makes sense."

"It is not an idea," said Ten Crows softly. "She is the murderer. The red-haired man was a bystander. An accomplice. Of course he is also a thief. They both are."

"I'm not disagreeing with you. I have heard stories in Mormon Basin from reliable people that make me believe she has killed again in the Basin. There was a miner who was killed after Noah's death. Supposedly Billy killed him as he was attacking Dottie and trying to rape her."

"Those are their names? Billy and Dottie?"

"Yes. They own a boardinghouse and a saloon in Mormon Basin. Seem to be very well off financially."

Ten Crows sipped his tea thoughtfully then said, "That follows my vision as well. In my vision I saw them in a large house that was also home to many men. And there were lots of bottles of whiskey around them. A boardinghouse and a saloon connected to the two murderers would explain that part of the vision."

"Ten Crows, how much do you know about what I do? What my job is?" asked Thomas.

"Really, nothing," said Ten Crows as he shrugged his shoulders. "I understand you investigate crimes and you take people to court and you take guilty people to prison. Other than that, I know nothing about your work. The law didn't come to this valley, this canyon, until after I had moved to the reservation. Before that, there was the military and they have their own laws and ways of doing things. Why do you ask?"

"I want you to know that I respect your culture and I respect your belief in what you saw in the vision. George tells me your visions have been remarkably accurate in the past. I will confess I am somewhat shaken by how closely your vision matches what I am discovering in my investigation.

"However, no matter how much I believe, or want to believe, in what you saw in your vision, I cannot let it influence what I do. I have to have hard, science-based evidence or eye-witness evidence before I can arrest Dottie and Billy. Right now I have neither. Until I find an eye witness or until one of them confesses to the murder, I cannot arrest them and take them in for trial. If I were to arrest Dottie and Billy, take them to Baker City for trial and the judge refused to hear the case for lack of evidence, they would sell out, leave this country and we would never be able to bring them to justice. I have to do this according to the rules of the law. I have to do this in my own time and in my own way."

"White man's justice is strange," said Ten Crows. "I know those two people killed Noah. I know it as surely as I am sitting here. I do not understand your need to get evidence, go before a judge or any of the other things you are talking about.

"However, I have promised Syrie I will not do anything until the white man's justice has a chance to work. I will keep that promise."

"Thank you, Ten Crows. I have no desire to hunt you down and take you in for murder. You know what would happen to you if you were found guilty in a court, don't you?"

"Of course," Ten Crows shrugged his shoulders again. "I would hang. Just like my brothers hung for killing the Whitmans who poisoned our people.

"I have no desire to hang."

Thomas finished his tea and cookies, then stood to leave.

"Can I wrap up some of these desserts for you? There is more here than I can eat."

"That would be very nice. It is a real treat to have sweets like this," Thomas said as he took the towel-wrapped cookies. "Please tell Theresa I stopped by when you see her next," he said to Ten Crows.

"No other message?"

"No, just let her know I tried to see her. I will come down from the Basin again. Please let George know I have a cabin now in town. So I have moved off the claim. He can find me there if any of the Hickmans need to get a message to me.

"I will have to make a trip to Baker City before the deep snow comes to lay in more supplies, so maybe I can see her on that trip," Thomas said. "Thank you for the refreshments. I appreciate your time and being able to meet you." Thomas extended his hand after he took his hat from the peg by the door.

"I am also glad to have had this chance to talk to you. I am interested in the progress of your investigation," said Ten Crows shaking Thomas' hand.

Ten Crows walked with Thomas outside and watched as he mounted his horse and turned toward Mormon Basin. 'Interesting,' he thought. 'Thomas knew there were pegs inside Theresa's cabin for hats and coats. I wonder when he was in the cabin. I wonder how he and Theresa are connected?'

Thomas was disappointed Theresa had not been at her cabin. The ride to see her had been a spur of the moment decision and he really couldn't say what had prompted it. Maybe he just wanted to see a familiar face and be with someone who knew the real him, not the made up character he was in Mormon Basin. As he rode back to the Basin, he started daydreaming about Theresa and what it would be like to be married to her. It was a very pleasant daydream. Coming back from a day at court and having her there in his little house just outside of Portland. Talking about his cases with her as she sewed or cooked his dinner. He wondered what their children would look like. He wondered what she would look like out of the buckskins. He was so deep in thought he was nearly to the Hickman claim before he realized where he was. He nearly missed the team and the buggy that were pulled off to the side of the road a few hundred yards ahead of him.

He recognized the team as belonging to Billy and Dottie. What were they doing away from town? He reined his horse over to the side of the road and put a small copse of trees and brush between himself and the buggy. He sat and waited to see who was driving the buggy, praying that his horse or the mule wouldn't alert them to his presence. He was thinking about giving up and riding on when Dottie came out of the brush and got into the buggy. He could see she was wearing men's trousers and had on a coat that was several sizes too big-likely one belonging to Billy. She had a small sack in her hands which seemed to be heavy as she was using both hands to support it. He watched as she set the sack on the floor of the buggy, took off the trousers and coat and put on a skirt and a heavy shawl. Thomas expected to see her look around and he rehearsed what he was going to say if he was spotted. To his surprise, she settled herself in the seat of the buggy and slapped the reins on the horses' backs to start them back towards the Basin.

Thomas stayed where he was for a few minutes to give her time to get ahead of him so hopefully she wouldn't know he had been on the road behind her. Dottie drove the team straight back to the boarding house and got down and went inside. Thomas turned around and went back to the Hickman claim. As he had suspected, Dottie had been working the claim as he could clearly see shovel marks where she had been digging in the stream and the prints of her small feet at the edge of the creek.

'Now why would she take a chance on working the claim?' he thought as he hurried back to the Basin. 'Were they in some sort of trouble financially? That didn't make sense. They had two profitable legitimate businesses he knew of, in addition to the loan sharking and prostitution. Was she simply that greedy? That arrogant?'

Thomas rode back into the Basin and went to his cabin. Mrs. O'Leary had done an excellent job of cleaning the place. He unsaddled his horse and put the horse with the mule in the little enclosure he had made behind his cabin. The blood stains would never come completely out of the raw, unpainted pine planking, but he didn't really care. The same with the bedding. He had simply laid his bedroll over the bed and used the cleaned quilts as extra padding. He built a fire in the little stove and put water on to heat and started slicing the last of the bacon and put beans on to cook. He had just moved the pot to the back of the stove when he heard a knock on his door.

Katie Swanson stood on his porch with J.J. on her hip.

"James got a buck and he wondered if you would like a haunch?" she said.

"Fresh meat would be very welcome," Thomas replied. "Let me get my hat and coat and I'll come help him."

"He's nearly done cutting it up, but I'm sure he'd enjoy seeing you. How's the digging going?"

"Fine. Got a little color today," he lied. "Always tomorrow, right?"

"That's one thing miners and farmers have in common," she commented as they stepped off the porch and started up the road to the Swanson cabin. "There's always the next strike, the next day, the next crop. Always hoping for a better tomorrow and forgetting to be thankful for what they have right in front of them."

When they got to the Swanson cabin, Thomas could see that James was nearly finished with the deer. It was a nice-sized buck and Thomas congratulated James on his success.

"Yeah, he was a big one. I think we'll get the better part of 100 pounds of good useable meat from the carcass. A lot more than we can use. I'll probably sell a side of it to Billy for use in his boarding house. Wouldn't want it to go to waste. Plus, it gives us a little cash money."

"Cash is always good," Thomas commented. "Can I give you a hand carting it over to the boarding house?"

"Sure. I'd appreciate it. I'll just hang up this front quarter for you to take home later."

James had cut the deer skin into pieces and he and Thomas each draped a piece over their shoulder with the hair side down, then hoisted a quarter of the animal to their shoulder and set off down the road to the boardinghouse. When they got to the boardinghouse, James led the way around to the back where the kitchen door was. He set his quarter on the porch and Thomas did the same. Thomas looked around for the buggy and noticed it had been put away and the horses were in an enclosure behind the boardinghouse. Susanna answered the door to their knock.

"James, what have you brought me?" she said in greeting.

"Got a nice buck this morning, Susanna. Thought you might be able to use it here at the boardinghouse."

"Sure I can. Let me get the missus to pay you," she said as she turned around and turned right back. "Oh, I forgot, she's been poorly this morning and kept to her room. I'm afraid I'll have to ask you to go to the saloon and ask Billy for your money."

"No problem," said James. "Have a good day."

"Thank you again. Good bye," she said as she shut the door.

"Give us a chance to have a quick nip," James elbowed Thomas and winked.

"Yes, it will," he replied.

Arriving at the saloon, they stood at the bar and ordered a whiskey each from Joseph and told him their business with Billy.

"He'll be right in. He had to run out back for a bit," Joseph informed them.

James and Thomas took their time sipping their whiskeys and waiting quietly until Billy pushed through the tent flaps at the back of the saloon. He straightened his tie and adjusted his vest and coat and put a smile on his face. Thomas could have sworn he saw rage on his face when he had opened the tent flap. Was one of the working girls causing problems?

"Well, hello, James. And Thomas. Can I do something for you?"

"I just delivered a side of venison to your boardinghouse. Susanna said she could use it and that we needed to come down here and get the money from you as your missus is feeling poorly today and has kept to her room," explained James.

"Dottie is sick?" The puzzlement on Billy's face was quite evident to Thomas before Billy re-arranged his features into placidity again. "Oh, right, I forgot. I get so busy here that things like a woman's minor complaints slip my mind.

"Of course, I can pay you for the venison and I thank you for thinking of us," Billy said as he turned to the till and opened it. "We always appreciate being able to serve fresh meat to our guests."

"I hope Miss Dottie is not too unwell," Thomas said.

"Oh you know how women are," Billy said as he counted coins into James' hand. "Always one thing and another with their little aches and pains," Billy laughed.

"Well, I hope she gets to feeling better," James said. "I'd better be getting back to the rest of that deer. Thanks and we'll be seeing you later."

James and Thomas left the saloon and walked back to James' cabin where Thomas hoisted his front quarter to his shoulder with the hide padding, thanked James and Katie and went back to his cabin to think about what he had seen that day. Things were not adding up in his mind and he hated when he couldn't get events to line up in an orderly fashion.

Obviously, Billy was not aware of Dottie's supposed "illness" and Thomas didn't believe for one minute there was anything physically wrong with the woman. That meant that her subterfuge was meant for Billy as well as for Susanna. With few miners in the area this time of year, she probably had thought her little trip to the Hickman claim would go unnoticed by any save her immediate circle. And she had covered for that by the change in attire. 'The woman was clever,' he thought.

Now the question became why was she there? Obviously, she was panning for gold. Now the question was why? Did they need money? Thomas didn't think that was the case. Greedy? Yes, definitely fit the type of criminal. Was she hiding it from Billy? Maybe, but why? Was she building a nest egg in preparation for severing the relationship and striking out on her own? Possibly. If so, that might be the wedge he needed to get a confession. Now, how could he exploit that? Thomas kept turning all these things over in his mind. He needed a way to get closer to Dottie. A way to become her confidant. Could their shared heritage help him? More questions and few answers.

Thomas paced and thought. He turned over different scenarios in his mind of a way to get closer to Dottie. There were several pitfalls to pursuing this path including the fact that Dottie, and probably Billy as well, were stone cold killers. Neither would hesitate to put a bullet between his eyes. She was undoubtedly one of the ablest criminals with whom he had been forced to match wits. And Billy wasn't very far behind her in his mental abilities. One of the few things Thomas had going for him was the fact that he believed both Billy and Dottie were exceptionally greedy and arrogant. Dottie especially. Thomas believed that her being forced to live in a mining camp would be grating on her nerves. If he was right, it might be the one sore spot he could poke and prod until she exploded. He just hoped he would be able to be far enough away from the blast to survive.

CHAPTER THIRTY

The rest of the morning working the colts passed quickly and Swen Jensen proved to be a valuable addition to the work crew with his knowledge of horses and his size and strength. They reached Syrie's goal of 20 head and broke for lunch, leaving Horace and Benjamin at the working corrals to watch over the colts. Two of the boys would eat and then come and relieve them so they could eat lunch and have a bit of a rest.

Everyone stopped at the outside washing station and cleaned up before they entered Syrie's house as well as knocking off as much of the mud as they could from their boots. Syrie's temper regarding her floors was legendary on the ranch and no one wanted to experience it today. Painted Pony had prepared a lunch fit for the hard physical labor they had all been doing and had spread a cloth over the table in the kitchen. Abigail had rallied from her fainting spell and had set out plates for everyone. When Syrie came in with a stranger, Abigail immediately started moving around plates, bowls and platters until they could squeeze in one more. Syrie got Swen seated and took her place at the head of the table. Painted Pony and Abigail finished filling the serving bowls and everyone dug into the meal.

First the talk was centered on the news Swen had brought from Oregon City, how large the herd of Shires had become, how his folks and siblings were doing, how many grandchildren Solomon and Vesta had now and other items of Jensen family news.

"I was so sad when your mother wrote me about Mattie's passing," Syrie said. "Mattie was a great influence on my life. Her volunteering to stay here with me when I was pregnant with Theresa likely saved both our lives."

"Grandma always talked with great fondness about you and your daughters," Swen said. "And she always had a great nostalgia for your ranch. Do you know, she sought out native women near Oregon City and learned all she could about the native plants? She spoke often about a Cayuse woman she said had taught her about the local plants here. I've forgotten the woman's name."

"Snow Goose," Syrie said softly. "A wise woman and so very kind."

"Yes, that's it," Swen said. "Did Ma tell you how she died?"

"No, I think Vesta was hard pressed to just get the words on paper when she wrote to me. I think your grandmother's death was very hard for her."

"Yes, it was," Swen agreed, then went on. "We found her out in the woods with her gathering bag. It was a painted, parfleche bag."

"Yes, I remember it. It was a gift from Snow Goose," said Syrie.

"She had apparently been gathering plants," Swen went on. "We found her sitting on a log, leaning against a tree with her face tilted toward the sky. She sat down and went to sleep."

"I am so thankful her ending was as gracious as her life," Syrie said. "I will not mourn for a life well-lived and such a peaceful ending.

"But on to happier things," Syrie said. "Tell me about the horses you brought."

"The stallion is a direct descendant of the horse you sent over the mountains with Pa and Ma in 1844. As you know, he became the foundation sire for all of our horses today. That reminds me, Pa sent all your money back. He said he owes you more than he can ever repay. Said you gave them the start they needed in their new home.

"The mares are all from bloodlines different from the stud, but they are all good mares. They have all had at least one foal and they are all excellent mothers except for one. The last one is a filly that Ma took a special liking to. She said the filly has something extra about her. Ma seems to have a sense about these things. The filly is out of our new stallion who came directly from England. So that is the entire package. I have all their pedigrees, ages and such written down. The papers are in my bags at the bunkhouse."

"I'll be anxious to see them," said Syrie.

"As will I," said Michael.

"Michael is training to take over the horse herd. I really think Michael is going to be our best person with the horses, though all of my children are very capable in all areas of management of the ranch."

"Now let's talk about where everyone is going to work this afternoon. I'll be staying here and splitting the domestic chores with Painted Pony so she can get some time outdoors. Does anyone have any problems with how things went this morning?"

The talk swirled around the table as everyone gave their opinion on what had gone right and what might be improved. When Michael and Daniel left for the working corrals and Benjamin and Horace joined the group, they added their insights in how everything had gone. There would be a more detailed critique held about the facility and the process over the coming days, but the general consensus was that everything was working smoothly. Horace neatly summed it up when he commented, "Sure beats getting the stuffing kicked out of you by those colts all day long."

After everyone had gone to finish working the colts, Syrie put a roast on the spit on the fireplace and placed a dutch oven beneath it to catch any drippings. She washed potatoes, turnips and carrots to roast later, made pie dough and set it to cool on the porch. She warmed water and started the washing up of the lunch dishes, pots and pans. Syrie had never really minded the washing up. If she did it with Painted Pony or one of her children it gave her a chance for some one-on-one time with whomever was helping. If she did it by herself, as she was doing today, it gave her time for uninterrupted reflection. Today those reflections turned to the Jensens and the trek west. Such hard times and such wonderful friends. And to Mattie, her second mother. The woman to whom she owed her life and the lives, not only of Theresa, but of all of her other children. She had been gratified to learn that Mattie's passing had been so peaceful. She had never dared to ask Vesta for any details about Mattie's death as Syrie had known how close Vesta and Mattie were.

Young Swen would have made Mattie so proud. The fact he was a carbon copy of her Swen had undoubtedly gladdened her heart. Syrie was also sure that Vesta and Solomon were proud of him. He was a fine young man. No doubt he was an excellent horseman and probably good with other livestock as well. She hoped he would be able to stay for several days or even weeks. He would be a good match for Theresa, though she would never mention it to her daughter. Though very different physically, as she and Noah had been she reminded herself, their paths seemed likely to converge around ranching, horses and livestock.

Thinking about matches for Theresa brought to her mind another fine young man, Thomas Hart. He was definitely interested in her daughter. His eyes followed Theresa when they were in the same room together, though Theresa was oblivious. She doubted that the match would be a happy one, however. She would be very surprised if Theresa could live in Thomas' world and if he stayed in Theresa's world, he would have to abandon his work. That might be a tough decision for him.

And what of Daniel? By the ribbing Benjamin was giving to him, there was someone special in Baker City. Though Syrie didn't know all the young women and girls in town, as she only went there a few times a year, she thought there might only be a half a dozen young women in his age bracket. Although it was likely several others had moved in over the last several months. She wondered which one it was. She would just have to wait and see. Perhaps she would accompany her sons on the next trip to town.

Thinking about her babies getting married made her feel old. One married and two more of an age to do so. She really wasn't old, she told herself. She was healthy. She stayed active and busy. She could easily live another 20 years she thought. Twenty years alone. 'Stop that!' she admonished herself. She needed to turn her thoughts away from this path. She needed to be thankful for all the things she did have: a warm home, plenty of food, beautiful children, good friends, loving grandchildren, being able to live in such a beautiful place. She would not go to that dark, soft, peaceful place again. She would not.

Syrie finished the dishes, carried the wash and rinse water basins outside and dumped them into the dry well at the end of the cabin by the washing-up area. She built up the fire in the cookstove to increase the heat in the oven. She checked the roast on the spit, then placed the vegetables into the Dutch oven which had been catching the juices from the roast. She put a lid on the Dutch oven, cleared a space closer to the heart of the fire and put the Dutch oven on the cleared area. Then she shoveled a few coals onto the lid of the Dutch oven. She retrieved the pie dough from the porch and started rolling out dough for pies, then carefully placing it into the pie pans. She had set dried fruit to rehydrate the night before and now she added sugar, spices and flour to the fruit. She carefully ladled the fruit into the pie plates and covered it with more dough to form the top crust. She crimped the edges and cut designs in the top to allow the steam to escape. She then held a piece of paper in the oven box, carefully counting the seconds until the paper began to brown around the edges. She slipped three pies into the oven and decided that it was time she took a break.

She poured hot water into her tea pot, added mint she had grown and dried, along with honey and set it to steep. She took down her one fancy china cup and saucer from the shelf and waited for her tea. When it was ready, she poured herself a cup and went into the parlor to her rocking chair. She pulled over a little stool that the children had used when they were small for her feet, leaned her head back and closed her eyes. That is how Young Noah found her when he arrived an hour later.

"Mother Syrie," he said softly. "Mother Syrie."

Syrie stirred, lifted her head and said, "Oh my. I must have fallen asleep. My tea is cold. What time is it?"

Young Noah handed her the cold cup of tea and said, "It is about 3:00."

"My pies!" Syrie put down her cup and started to get up.

"Already out of the oven. They aren't burned but they are a little brown," Young Noah said. "I smelled them when I came in through the kitchen, so I took them out of the oven and set them on the table. I wasn't sure where you were."

"I must be getting old. I never nap in the middle of the day."

"Maybe it's time you started," Young Noah said gently.

"Oh, shush! I'm not ready for that. I'm just not used to being out and working stock, I guess. Did you stop off and see how they are doing?" Syrie asked.

"No, they were obviously busy, so I just waved and came on up here. I stopped by on my way to see Father."

"Is everything all right?" Syrie was instantly on her guard. "Are they coming for him?"

"No. Everything is fine. But I have a letter and I want you both to be there when I read it," Young Noah said. "Drink your tea and wake up. I'm going to go get Father and we'll try to be back in time for supper. Actually, probably the whole family should be here when I read the letter.

"I'll be back as soon as I can," he said and patted her hand. "I promise, it's good news."

Syrie drank her tea after Young Noah left, then got up and went to the window to check on the amount of daylight left so she could time the rest of dinner. She saw that it was lightly raining. That would only make the work harder, she knew. She turned away from the window to tend to the rest of dinner. She ran through her mental to do list; make coffee, get milk from the spring house and skim it, get butter and soft cheese from there as well, make biscuits and get the table set. After being out in the cold all day, her people would be very hungry. She did not intend to disappoint.

331

The crew started returning to the house shortly before dark. Syrie had already set the coffee pot on the table and people began pouring coffee and moving to the hearth to warm up as soon as they had hung up their hats and coats. Abigail and Theresa went into their bedroom to change out of their damp clothes. Syrie's boys and the rest of the men stood by the hearth and the steam rolled off them as their clothes dried in the fire's heat. Painted Pony had gone to her own cabin to change out of her damp clothes. She came in the back door a few minutes later and asked Syrie what there was left to do. Finding nothing left to do, she went into the parlor and sat in front of the small stove there. As Syrie had done, she used the children's stool to prop up her feet. Swen had came in later with the papers he had brought regarding the horses. He, Michael and Benjamin stood a little ways away from the others in the kitchen looking over the pedigrees and talking.

As soon as the biscuits were out of the oven, Syrie called everyone to dinner. Syrie had set extra places for Young Noah and Ten Crows, but they hadn't yet arrived. It was possible they wouldn't be there until the morning. She wouldn't hold food from her hungry crew on a chance they would arrive in time. She wouldn't worry if they didn't show up until breakfast.

After everyone had filled their plates, they gathered around the old, scarred table in the kitchen and started talking about the work that day. Everyone had finished eating dinner and Syrie and Painted Pony were clearing the table and getting ready to serve pie, when Ten Crows and Young Noah came in the kitchen door.

"Let me get you two a plate," Syrie said. "Pie can wait a bit. Do you need to wash up?"

"Yes, please," said Ten Crows. "Supper smells wonderful. Is that peach pie I smell?"

"Yes, of course it is," laughed Painted Pony. "You can smell a peach pie from a quarter mile, I think."

Ten Crows grinned sheepishly and said, "Guilty. Especially one of Syrie's with the cinnamon."

When the two men returned from washing up, they sat at the places Syrie had assigned for them. There was little conversation as they hurried through the dinner of roast beef and vegetables. Painted Pony cleared their plates away and Syrie put all three pies on the table along with a fresh pot of coffee, the milk pitcher and plates and forks. Everyone served themselves pie and refilled their drinks. After everyone had their pie, Syrie introduced Swen to Young Noah and Ten Crows.

"Jensen," Ten Crows said. "Are you related to Mattie Jensen who was with Syrie her first winter here? And Solomon Jensen who came the spring after Theresa was born?"

"Yes, Solomon is my father. Mattie was my grandmother."

"Good people," Ten Crows said nodding his head. "My mother, Snow Goose, had a great fondness for your grandmother. Kindred spirits I guess you would say. My mother gave her, your grandmother, her favorite gathering bag."

"Yes, we still have it. It hangs in a place of honor in our house beside a picture of my grandmother," Swen said.

Ten Crows nodded his head again and said, "It is good."

"Young Noah, you said you had a letter to read to us?" Syrie said. "You can speak freely in front of Horace and Swen."

"I know Horace. I was just unsure about your guest. I don't remember the Jensens but father obviously does. So I will trust you both.

"I received this letter late yesterday. Too late to ride here. This is what it says:

Mr. and Mrs. Crow:

I found your name and address in the personal effects of Ten Crows. It is with great sadness that I regret to inform you of the death of your friend, a leader of the Cayuse people, Ten Crows.

I do not have a lot of information about his passing, other than he apparently died in his sleep. Oddly enough it was on the same night that his good friend, Broken Wing, also died. According to the customs of his people, he was buried immediately.

I have gathered his few effects together. If you would like me to send them to you, please let me know.

Again, you have my condolences.

Sincerely,

Rex Moorhouse
Clerk Umatilla Reservation

Everyone sat in silence, until Theresa jumped up and started to shout. "You're free, Ten Crows! You're free. They'll never hunt you again!"

She ran over to Ten Crows and surprised herself by throwing her arms around him and giving him a hug. Then everyone was congratulating Ten Crows on the fact he was dead and free. Young Swen was confused and sat still in the middle of all the tumult. The most emotional one was Painted Pony, who had tears of joy running down her face. Syrie couldn't stop smiling and she kept blinking away her own tears. After a year of ups and downs, this was definitely the most joyous news they had received since Daniel had ridden up.

When the tumult had died down, Young Noah asked his father, "What are you going to do now?"

"Since Ten Crows is officially dead, I guess I need a new name. Would you be upset if I called myself Otter, to keep your brother's memory alive?"

"Of course not. Since I cannot name my own son after my brother, it is right that you should honor his memory in this way."

"From here on, I will be called Otter," said Ten Crows.

"We'll all have to help each other remember," said Syrie. "Perhaps me most of all."

"I will need to move out of Theresa's cabin," said Ten Crows.

"There's no need to hurry," Theresa said. "You have time to decide if you want to live on the Rafter S or the Rafter L or if you want to have your own place."

"It will not be possible for me to homestead. So I will have to have a place on one of the two ranches."

"Why not a place at both ranches?" asked Daniel. "Young Noah and Lucreta would be happy to have you live with them and I know Ma would be delighted if you would live with us. Why don't you let us build you a cabin or at least your own room at each place?"

"I hadn't considered splitting my time, but that may be a good idea. Let me think about it for a little while will you? I will decide in the spring. No one can build until then anyway," said Ten Crows/Otter. "Can you let me use your place a little longer, Theresa?"

"Sure. That is not a problem. We've already got all my stock here and we're pretty well settled in for the winter. I can easily wait until spring to move back to my place."

"That sounds like a wonderful idea," said Young Noah. "You can have a quiet retreat when our kids get to be too rambunctious for you."

"Perhaps they will become trying. I do not know. It has been too long since I have had five children around me."

"Six," said Young Noah.

"I thought there were five; Mae, Edna, Hazel, Pearl and Albert," Ten Crows counted them off on his fingers.

"Number six doesn't have a name yet because we don't know if it is a boy or a girl," Young Noah said smiling.

"Six?" said Ten Crows as his face lit up. "I will be able to hold my sixth grandchild?"

"Yes, Father, you will," Young Noah said as he grasped his father's shoulder. "From the very first minute."

"This calls for a toast," said Daniel as he raised his coffee cup. "To number six. Welcome to the family."

A chorus of "here-here's" rang out in the warm, snug house as the moon rose outside. Syrie looked around and said to herself, 'I am so very blessed. I know you are hearing all this, Noah, but I still want you here. …Most of all I want your killer found and punished.'

LIFE AND THE HUNT CONTINUES IN
BOOK THREE – *SYRIE'S REVENGE*

ABOUT THE AUTHOR

Dena Smallwood is a retired civil servant and life-long country gal. Dena was raised within 100 miles of where her heroine, Syrie, settled in the book. Dena has always been fascinated by the Oregon Trail and the first women who made the trip to the West.

Husband Michael Photo

Dena is mother to one biological daughter and two adopted daughters, who have blessed her and her husband, Michael, with nine grandchildren. She currently lives on a small acreage in northwestern New Mexico with six horses (including Hammer, pictured), two dogs and two cats.

"Writing the Syrie stories has given me a chance for the first time to really explore the lives of these brave women and examine the hardships and joys they experienced," she says. She is now at work on her third novel about the Hickman family.

www.ingramcontent.com/pod-product-compliance
Lightning Source LLC
Chambersburg PA
CBHW071919130726
47909CB00014B/2084